An Urban Fantasy

A BITE of the PAST

Undying Love - Book One

L. Nightingale

BROWN
DOG
BOOKS

Published under licence by Brown Dog Books and
The Self-Publishing Partnership, 7 Green Park Station, Bath BA1 1JB

www.selfpublishingpartnership.co.uk

ISBN printed book: 978-1-83952-009-9

ISBN e-book: 978-1-83952-010-5

Cover design by Andrew Prescott
Internal design by Andrew Easton

This book is printed on FSC certified paper

MIX
Paper from
responsible sources
FSC
www.fsc.org
FSC® C013604

Printed and bound by CPI Group (UK) Ltd, Croydon, CR0 4YY

CHAPTER ONE

'Whoa, Hossy-Stink, that ain't one of your hosses!'

Cleve, the flank rider, was right. The biggest and meanest bull of the eighty or so in the two and a half thousand-strong Longhorn herd had bellowed his disagreement at being rounded up and made a bid for freedom. He'd made a pretty good job of it too, ploughing up the No Man's Land prairie as he went. Cleve's shout, though, was all too late.

Teddy, the young wrangler yearned for the thrill of the chase. His headstrong Quarter, Blue Scrub reared, whinnying a warning to the bull that she intended to hightail it after him. Or perhaps the warning was for her rider. Teddy couldn't be sure. Maybe he should stop her. He swapped Blue's reins into his left hand.

Chirking his tongue and reaching for his rope, he heel-kicked her into action. Blue snorted, she didn't need his encouragement. She took off so fast that Teddy had seriously expected gravity to suck his head clean off his shoulders. Now he knew why it was called 'breakneck speed'. He raised his coiled rope high and signalled that the bull was his.

'You cain't rope him all by yourself,' the nearest tail rider hollered. 'Dent, what's your call?'

The bull was too strong for the boy to handle alone: he knew that. He slowed his horse. The teamwork code that was tantamount to their safety got the better of his need for speed. Blue Scrub snuffed her disapproval.

'Now don't get all snuffy with me,' he said, hunkering down close to her ear.

'Quit spooning that horse!' the caporal yelled. 'Git that bull. Moon and Charlie are on their way.'

'Gee up, Blue,' the boy said.

Blue didn't need to be asked twice. This was what she lived for. This was what her breed did – speed. The wrangler pressed his feet down so hard on the soles of his borrowed boots they might've burst right through, breaking the stirrups in two. He drafted his upper body to Blue's fluid lines and let her take the lead. Dust clouds clotted with dried husks and dead grass billowed as high as the top of his boots' shaft.

The bull was surprisingly fast. It was little more than a mirage on the flat landscape, as angry and black as the sky. And, as though in total agreement with it, the sky grumbled.

Darn No Man's Land weather, the wrangler thought.

Blue closed the gap between them and the bull on the horizon in minutes. The wind slapped away her rider's second-hand hat, nearly garrotting him with the stampede strings. He choked and caught the hat, placing it firmly on his head. Anchoring himself to the speeding Blue with his knees, he lengthened out the rope. Gripping one end with the reins' hand, he raised his right arm.

Lazily, unassuming and casual-like, Teddy curled and flipped his wrist, drawing out the loop high above his head. He wasn't fooling anyone, though, except perhaps the bull. He was the best at his job that the Midwest had to offer: Ranchers from one side of Texas to the other side of Kansas wondered at his uncle's luck in payrolling him; roping runaways was just one small part of it. Teddy knew the truth, though: he was little more than a slave on Silas Truss' ranch. If it wasn't for his horses he'd have died of despair a long time ago.

He twirled the loop faster and faster, gaining momentum until he could hear it whipping and slicing the hot, cloying No Man's Land air.

'All in the follow-through!' Dent hollered.

I know. It was difficult for the wrangler to hear himself think, let alone Dent's barked orders: the hooves of the Flanks' Appaloosas racing to catch up thundered so hard they made the ground sound hollow.

The long, strap-like muscles of the Wrangler's forearm were so taut as he worked the loop that he could almost feel the tendons plucking on his wrist bones. Just as Blue came almost level with the bull, he threw the loop.

He let out a joyous holler that rivalled the thudding of the sky when the rope clattered about the bull's long, upturned horns. The cowpokes bellered and heckled in return.

The bull, though, was less than pleased. Instantly it veered off course. Blue was having none of it: her strong hindquarters hardened and almost sitting, she ground to a halt. Teddy yanked on the rope. The hondo closed tight round the long horns. All he had to do now was hang on till the others arrived.

The bull's escape plan scuppered, it, too, stopped running. But it seemed to have neglected to tell its own back legs. Their velocity tossed them crooked and dusty over its head. The bull was over on its back. Teddy congratulated himself once more and began to dally as fast as he could. He wound his end of the rope around the short saddle horn: each time his hand passed, it cut his knuckles open. Darn it, if he didn't need his own saddle. Smudges, maddeningly itchy and the colour of love-apples, pock-marked the back of his hands. Still he wound frantically.

Blue began to back up slowly. The bull had no intention of coming in quietly. It twisted its whole body and looked for all of No Man's Land like an unthreading rawhide braid, all hooves and horns flailing against the ominous backdrop. Back on its feet, bellowing its rage, it shook its head violently.

The formidable bank of black clouds in the sky swallowed up the sun, shrouding the prairie in cold shadow. The wrangler's hard work was undone and the rope flicked away from the saddle horn. He held firm, though: with the reins and the rope in his left hand, he grabbed the fleeing end with his right.

'No, you don't,' he muttered and tugged it back in, his biceps almost ripping with the exertion.

A tearing sound of cataclysmic proportions hammered across the sky. Sonic booms bounced between the clouds and the earth. Instinctively, Teddy ducked. The thunderbolt was so loud he'd felt it in his chest and, even though he'd stopped being afraid of storms years ago, his stomach tensed with fear. The bull jumped and panicked. Blue whinnied and reared up. The rope was yanked away from him once more.

Massive splats of rain, sporadic at first and then so dense it was hard to see, muffled the cries of the cowpokes behind him.

'Charlie's down.'

'Hold on, son. A little help, Virg.'

Teddy's help was curtailed before it got to him. The might of the rain bent the brim of his hat out of shape and water jammed into his face and neck. In seconds he was soaked. The rawhide rope was slippery, forcing him to hold on tighter. Blinking the rain from his eyes, snivelling as it tumbled over his nose, he hauled hand over hand, dragging the fearsome bull closer. In a few minutes he'd gained enough slack to start dallying again.

His arms and torso strained with each wrench on the rope, the reprieve in between not long enough for them to revitalise themselves. His biceps, chest, elbows, wrists and even his stomach were fit to seize up, insubordinate at his ignorant refusal to stop overusing them.

Blood from his knuckles was now a constant dripping, streaking Blue's flanks and reddening the mud below. Who knew that there was so much blood in a little knuckle nick? Blue took one more expert step backward.

As instantly as it had started, the rain stopped. The clouds moved on, taking their deluges elsewhere, and the sun returned. It baked the prairie and toasted everything on it, human, flora, fauna: it wasn't proud. The herd lowed and complained. The bull, being black, attracted its full force. Steam rose from the scalding of its skin. The wrangler could almost hear its sizzling; worse than any branding they'd ever put the cattle through. The all too familiar stench of charred rawhide wedged at the back of his throat. This burning was prolonged. The bull screamed in pain. It was sent spiralling into a suicidal madness, tangling itself in the rope. It pulled with such ferocity that the wrangler swore he heard the tendons at its neck snap.

At his end of the rope, all hope was lost. It flicked and whizzed. Rising up in arcs around the saddle horn it looked like a rattlesnake, arching its body to make itself scarier to predators. It whipped and sliced too close to the vulnerable and yet most important part of the wrangler. He sucked in his body and sat up straight.

He grabbed and fumbled to catch the rope, his hands still slick, the rope a white-hot line of tinder, entwining around his fingers and stinging each time he touched it.

The sun still broiled all around him as he stared at the rope. The realisation of his fate deafening him, he could no longer hear the calling of the cowpokes, the herd or the senseless screams of the bull. Even Blue's grunting was silent. He stared at the rawhide, watching it as though he were part of a demonstration of its professional braiding, a testament to its abrasiveness. It smouldered. It was tied around his middle finger like a noose.

With the super-strength of insanity, the bull gave one last pull on the rope. It was all that it had left and it was all that was needed. The wrangler's pain was as intense as it was instant. The smouldering rope snapped shut. His finger was sliced clean off.

The cut was so quick his body couldn't keep up. The gap where his finger had been sitting there, an obscene window showing his sheared-off bone framed by lead-coloured skin and one or two diehard hairs, golden against the purpling rim. He even had enough time to consider how his future hand might look. *Not so bad after all.*

Thoughts are fleeting at the best of times and this one was whisked away from him along with the tranquillity of that slow-motion moment of numbness that comes before debilitating pain and chaos. The newly missing finger's hole bubbled red.

'Dent?' the wrangler said.

But it came out weak and slurred. He had to do something to help himself. Blood was tumbling from his hand now. He plucked, one-handed, at his kerchief: it would serve as a makeshift tourniquet; that was what he'd been told anyway. He'd just hoped he'd never have to use it. Without it covering his nose, he'd have no dust mask, but that was too bad: the dust clouds had plummeted along with rain anyway. The useless hat had hardly protected him at all, and his neck, back and the knot in the kerchief were sodden.

'Dent!' he shouted.

He was fast going into shock. One-handed, he worked at the impossibly solid knot, his fingers seemed sympathetic to the injured hand and refused to grip. His consciousness began to blister. The space around him heated up into one impenetrable mist which settled about his shoulders like a hot, thick cloak.

'Dent!' he shouted.

Sweat soaked his already slimy body, it prickled on the ridges of his scalp, turned his eyebrows to oily slicks and coursed down his face before pooling on his lips. The sun instantly dried it and added salty discomfort to pain. The sudden disappearance of traction tipped his hat forward over his eyes, shielding him from the blood-curdling wound. Then it slid down his nose and tumbled to the muddy ground, streaking itself in blood on the way. So much blood. He lost all coordination in his hands and kept missing the injury with the bandage.

'Dent,' he garbled, 'I'm gonna die. I don't want to die.'

He was briefly aware of how immature he sounded. And then nausea hit him. With it came a loss of memory and control over his limbs, his insides, his mind. Evidence of last night's mysteries and music roots erupted deep inside him, travelling upwards, retching at the back of his throat. Its arrival on his lips was a nasty surprise. Blue whinnied and danced sideways as though to avoid the smell of her rider's stomach contents.

'Sorry, Bluey,' he breathed, but couldn't be sure he'd actually said anything at all.

The No Man's Land prairie swirled and writhed around him in a wash of dead bull black, husky ochre and vibrant blue. All too soon the silver bits and brown leather of his mount loomed in front of him and he swooped to the ground, sliding out of the stirrups and dowsing himself with his own innards on the way.

The intense rainfall had softened the ground, so the wrangler's fall cost him no more than bruising. He groaned and held his now abnormal hand aloft for a moment. Then the closeness of the weather sapped the last remnants of his strength and he drifted into his faint.

Chapter Two

Daytime! Teddy knew the signs; if he didn't then it stood to reason that he'd be cowchips in the bone orchard by now. The first time he'd noticed it, he'd thought it was some sort of gas escaping his shabby body, which had been quite nice really, as he hadn't thought he had any such gases left inside him at all. Up until then, he reckoned he'd just fallen down dead where he stood. He'd asked László, eccentric old vampire, his only friend and mentor, about it. László knew everything. Especially about their kind. László had protected Teddy ever since he could remember, always been there, always answered his questions, always laughed at his mischievous ways, however murderous they may be, and he always had a huge smile for him as he gorged on the blood of their victims. Always, ever since he could remember.

László, in his smooth, bee-sweeting, melodious voice, had told him not to stay out so late; then he wouldn't have to suffer it again. So that was that. Teddy recognised the slight and yet significant drain on his energy. It was so small it was barely obvious at all and stunted his already short attention span. The clock in town clanged. It was time to head home.

Behind their house the sky began to turn a pale shade of whatever colour the weather had chosen for the day: gunmetal grey as opposed to starless black. The standard vexation of his kind began to brow-beat the optimism that was his own unique personality into submission for another day. That personality, that optimistic cynicism, had over the past few nights started to take hold of him. He'd been careful to keep it hidden, he just didn't know why. He looked at his feet for help; the chocolate-coloured nubuck of his boots, the ones he'd found outside his door good as new when he awoke; cleaned by the housemaid, László told him was blackened heavily by precipitation in the atmosphere. Morning time!

Teddy set off at a resigned trudge. Although he had no idea what he was resigned to, it just seemed to fit his sullen character. The house, thanks to the height of its ceilings, old stone of its walls and elaborateness of its tall windows, looked nothing like the small homes of the little town just down the road or even the larger city a long way further up. Teddy only cared for those houses night by night in terms of hungry and fed. By sundown the next day the memory would be gone again replaced by the all-encompassing need to replenish his energy levels.

That old house with László was the only home he needed. Lately, though, he'd noticed a deep, enticing desire to look over the grounds, gaze into the distant countryside, hear the call of the stag and the answer from his subordinates and wives in the herd, climb high into the sturdy branches of the gnarled, old trees spread sporadically over the estate or clumped together in its woodland borders, and occasionally, if he dared get close enough to the town without the bravado of László beside him, the inexplicable and yet unquenchable rush of heat from his belly to his hat when a car sped past too fast. It kept him outside and apart from László after the hunt. Every night that desire seemed to hold a strange, unfamiliar pleasure, one that didn't come from bloodshed and feeding, and he knew he'd end up doing the same the next night. And the next. Perhaps this was what he was resigning to: an unwelcome necessity to leave the outside and go in? Whatever this was, what was even streakier was that he didn't want to tell László about it. He told László everything. He frowned. He didn't know why he was frowning. Or what at.

The dim flicker of a candle appeared in one of the dormer windows over the kitchen, a long, low building sitting opposite the stable and set at an angle to the house so that the whole thing formed a horseshoe shape around a brick-paved courtyard. The maid was rising dutifully to look after her two masters, although their night-time business habits kept them firmly behind 'DO NOT DISTURB' notices all day and they rarely met. Did she not wonder why when there were light switches and cars in the town, she still used a candle? Silly old slummy. Any liaisons with her were dealt with by László; Teddy knew very little about it. He didn't care to even remember what she looked like. Come to think of it, he couldn't if he wanted to. He wasn't sure how to. Memories weren't something he had many of at all. He didn't need them either; László had told him that. They'd only bring him sadness.

Since he'd been loitering in the woods on the opposite side of the unkempt field at the house's back, or its front, depending on which way you looked at it, he was still a little way off yet. The grass here grew long and waved up in unruly tufts. It was also trodden down in places by the constant wind that had no care for the prettiness of a meadow or the ease of a stroll across it.

The house's other side, where he could not go, faced the sea: there were only a narrow lawn and low wall between it and the cliff. He took up a nonchalant jog, slowing to climb over fallen trees and savouring the slight crunch of his booted feet on the twiggy woodland floor. He might be able to delay the exhaustion of daytime a little once he was out of the fresh air, but not for long. In any case, why bother?

Gradually, the woods grew more cultured and he broke into a run, taking strong masculine strides; if he wasn't careful he'd be at full speed and miss the house completely, ending up in the sea. Then he'd be for it. He'd got too close to the sea once, he remembered that: it had drained his energy until he'd wanted to die. László had consoled him and told him not to go near running water. An allergy, he'd said: the sea might look inviting with its delicious, black depth and its high, enigmatic waves, but it could take him away, far away and he'd be lost. And alone. Probably dead. Inland was best.

Teddy ran faster, the wind hardly having time to catch up with him and in its defiance threatened to steal his precious Stetson from his head. *Never, he thought, no one but me wears my hat.* He grinned.

'Haulloa, stranger!' he shouted.

Darn it, I sound good.

Heading for the courtyard, running straight as the crow flies, he jumped low, sweeping boughs, pushed off trunks and swung from handholds high in the branches. Then, when he was clear of the woods, just for fun, just because he could, he dove high into the clean air ahead. He stretched out his lean, cowpoke body. His T-shirt flicked free of his belt buckle, exposing his pale, ranch-hardened middle. Carried on the momentum of his dive, the velocity of his speed, he flew freely across the field. The wind buzzed about the features of his face, gravity kept his hat firmly in place.

As though blades, clean and new, sliced into him, the chill of the early hour slashed his belly above his jeans. Startled by this ambush he lost concentration, his landing went out of control and he crashed head over shoulders, legs in the air, into the massive stone urn in the centre of the courtyard.

'Sakes alive!' he muttered. 'What the dickens was that?'

Stumbling and scraping, he scrambled to his feet. His boots' heels got hooked into the dull iron grille set into the ground at the base of the urn and he performed a half-cocked fandango to free himself.

Once again the anger so inherent in his kind threatened to turn him pessimistic. He didn't intend his existence to be over tonight. He bared his teeth, balled his fists and biceps, and whirled around, snarling. Pointless: he was barking at a knot. Anyone who knew what they were dealing with would know that to stay hidden was their best bet.

No one ever came up here. The three of them were always alone. The courtyard was empty. The grounds were still, the only light being the maid's which, although it had moved to a different upstairs window, was still as dim. Teddy focussed on his ears and listened for the clues from his surroundings. Nothing. No difference to the usual early morning chirruping of the insects dashing for darkness between the flagstones, the breeze in the budding branches of the woods and the mysterious booming of the sea.

He dispensed with attack mode, returning to the Old West cowpoke that he was – well, by now more of a kid in someone else's jeans, T-shirt and boots. He wondered if he'd ever had new clothes or had always just worn someone else's. He couldn't remember. It wasn't important, László said. But the hat was. He knew that. Somehow. He just couldn't place how he knew. The Stetson had always been his.

He grabbed it up and teased out the dents, tapping it on his knuckles, gently smoothing and scrubbing at a smudge made by some unknown substance, probably some careless victim's innards. Teddy himself had no bodily fluids and so he couldn't lick and he had no breath to buff it with, *take more care,* he thought and a voice somewhere in his mind, a woman with a smile and a wave of a utensil of some kind, scolded him for not thinking before he acted. He didn't recognise her and he never "thought". He always just 'did'. Anyway, as László often told him; in over one hundred years he'd neither sustained any injury nor been destroyed.

He ran a hand through his hair and with only three of the four fingers needed fitted his hat back on his head. Slowly, cautiously, he pulled up his T-shirt fully expecting to see a gash across his stomach, the width of his body almost cutting him in half; such had been the ferocity of the slicing he'd felt. But there was nothing. It was odd, he'd never felt anything so stunning before. Come to think of it, he'd never felt anything at all before. Ever. Had his body healed itself from such an immense impact already? He thought it only did that when he was dead.

Still, he was standing and moving about okay, wasn't he? He twisted and flailed, hunting for the source of the weird impaling sensation. He even peered under his jeans. Still he found nothing; nothing unexpected and with nothing of the experience lingering on him, he let his clothes alone. Gingerly now, he took a step towards the stables. Nothing ailed him. There appeared to be no after-effects of the strange stabbing at all so he carried on step after step until he stood just in front of the huge, heavy stable door. It wasn't until he reached out to push it open that he realised he was in the wrong place.

He didn't reside in the stable! And they didn't own any horses! They hadn't owned horses for a long time. He couldn't place exactly the time of their last having owned a horse. But he knew it had been a whole heap of towns ago. Sam 'ill he'd named her. Sam Hill was her proper name, after the Devil. He didn't know why but naming her such had given him an almost overwhelming sense of empowerment. After her loss, though, he'd been filled with rage, he'd gone on a murderous spree, smashed artefacts, furniture, walls, anything he'd laid his hands on. Since then, he'd found himself steered in the opposite direction every time he came into contact with horses. He'd loved Sam 'ill, something they'd only really noticed when she'd died.

László had consoled him. The decrepit-ness and disintegration of those around him while he remained young and growing in fitness was something he'd end up facing again and again. The initial blast of losing them and the eternal ache of missing them, the sadness of no longer being able to talk with them, the guilt of laughing without them, and the slow degeneration of their memory was his penance for immortality. 'Best not to get too close to anyone or anything again,' László had advised him. 'Don't forget the horse and the horrible way it has made you feel,' László had said. 'It'll help you shun any sort of love for the rest of your days. Ya?' And, as ever, László was right.

The only thing Teddy cared about now was his hat. Still, he didn't know why. But he didn't need anybody. He had László. After that, it hadn't taken him too long to recover and the two of them had once again run the town that had been their home at the time with fear, inflicting the very pain Teddy sought to avoid on their peers, the ordinary people and especially the peasants. Peasants always had a special type of taste, like a spicy addition: indulgent, wicked, satisfying. Teddy knew to look forward to it, but he never hung onto it.

How come, then, an instinct to head into the stables had taken advantage of his predicament, possessed and programmed him? Curiosity that he reckoned came with ignorance, except that he wasn't stupid, joined forces with a rebelliousness that László had told him all cowhands had and he was spurred on. He pressed a hand flat on the patched and peeling wooden door. The building was unused and the door's hinges stiff, even for him. He growled at the door and tried a little harder. Finally, it juddered open.

The zigzag brick floor was orange-coloured and covered in a damp mix of dust and grit. The scuff of his boots when he stepped inside echoed off the plain walls. He looked into the first of the three spacious, cobwebbed stalls which the building housed. Ancient, dirty brown straw packed itself into the corner, reddening iron baskets hung from the walls with the remnants of feed clinging to cracks and under flakes in the eroded spokes. Teddy walked into the stall and pulled at one of the metal loops set into the wall. The groomed horse's reins would've been secured in that loop. It held fast.

He steadily, dreamily massaged its dull, grey surface.

'Hmmm,' he said, 'must be cast and finished. Bespoke.'

He turned and tenderly stroked the open door of the stall, pondering over its smoothness under the constant hands pushing it open and then closed. There was a whinnying as if a ghost of the life that breathed in there shifted its stance and clip-clopped its hooves on the floor. Teddy wasn't afraid of ghosts. There was nothing in here or for that matter anywhere that was worse than him. But he couldn't resist closing his eyes and looking inside his mind which was a place that he usually kept shut down. He'd expected it to chuck him back out in disgust, but it didn't. His own mind welcomed him in and it showed him the horse that he'd heard. It had a fine, caramel-coloured mane that wafted free as it shook its head; its wide molasses eyes twinkled and blinked away some annoying flies. Languidly lowering its beautifully long, black lashes, it swished its unbraided tail. Its cocoa-coloured coat was healthy and shining from its grooming, its socks were white, and its dusty hooves were too close to the floor.

The horse snuffed and shifted again. It nickered and grunted. Teddy cast an eye over the rest of the horse; it looked fairly happy and, judging by the state of its stall, well cared for. So why the moaning?

The horse snorted, blew down its nose and shifted again. Teddy glanced to its feet. It was going easy on one. He looked to the window and then back out of the door. The ground around here was strewn with flint and bits of rock which nestled in the earth, telling tales of farmers and agriculture; the horses would need shoes. This one needed a check-up. *When's the farrier coming?* Immediately he moved to check the charter, standard in stables to find out.

As soon as Teddy stepped forward, the horse, its tack, the whole dream vanished. He stood alone in the stall once again. The musty air of the uninhabited stables had been so disturbed by Teddy's opening the door that it had become visible in the oblong of dawn light ominously creeping in the one high, narrow window. Fatigue clutched his insides, however crumbling and smutty they were, and he doubled up.

Teddy dashed from the stable leaving the door wide open; the maid could shut it if she cared to. He couldn't linger in the courtyard anymore, he'd collapse where he stood. And he didn't want to think about what might happen to him when the sun or at least the dawn tumbled over the stable's roof, bathing the courtyard in daylight. His heels clicking on the stones, he skittered down the steps just outside the door into the old tunnel that ran under the courtyard and up into the house.

Halfway along under the iron grille at the ornamental courtyard urn, the tunnel was joined by the one that led to the kitchen, the fresh dawn-time air shortly followed by the daylight would filter in. He needed to get a wiggle on. He grinned, he had the gift of speed and he loved to use it. He darted into the tunnel and bounced off the sides where bioluminous algae turned the floor bright and slimy. He vaulted over miniature limescale fjords edging sluggishly down the cracks that lined the old walls.

Seconds later he was under the house and he slumped against the wall at the bottom of the stairs. He took off his hat and checked that nothing had disfigured it. Then he ran a hand through his hair and replaced it. Something was tickling inside him. No, it wasn't that all dragged-out sensation, he knew tiredness; tiredness was more of a restraint. This was a fizzing behind his eyes and it seemed to be inside his top lip, too. He noticed a smile on his lips. He hadn't done that, he knew it. He hadn't put that smile there, he was sure of it. The smile and the tickling seemed to be enticing him, beckoning him back to picturing again the horse in the stable stall.

The stub which was all that remained of the middle finger on his right hand tingled. So that's what had happened to it? Something to do with his horse. The tingling stopped. Or any horse? Curious! He couldn't remember any sensation there before. He focussed on it and wiggled it. It tried. All the rest of his fingers waved okay. Somewhere way back in his past, some or other way to do with the handling of horses, he'd lost that finger. *Dang! That must've hurt.* He made a mental note to ask László about it. As far as he could remember, which wasn't that far, his finger had always been like that.

Teddy lingered there indulging in the elation of this newfound and proper satisfaction. He was fulfilled. He'd known something about the horse. About the stable. He didn't think he knew anything other than hunger, hunting, feeding and gratifying his abhorrent need for the enjoyment of suffering in others. What in tarnation, though, was a farrier? And how had he known that the horse needed reshoeing just from standing there watching it, listening to it? Or what the ring in the stable wall was made of or that there would've been a chart and a diary? Grooming? What was grooming?

Deep inside his mind, he'd known something. He actually knew something. A strangeness came over him. He didn't want this sensation to be suppressed. He liked it. It felt good, like when he read in his victims' eyes the realisation that he was going to kill them horribly and that their trust in him and his accomplice had been in vain, that they had failed and that this was their end. *You mudsill,* he thought, *not good like that.* Something else. A pleasure. A reward even. He closed his eyes again and let his smile spread. He liked himself. He actually liked himself. And he liked that he was likeable.

He hadn't thought about it before, but now he had a mind of his own, a knowledge of his own and he liked that. He just had to find it again. It must come from somewhere in his past. What was it? A trade of some description? Something that society needed him for? Something someone would call on him for? He might be valued. He might actually be wanted for something. Or by someone.

Tuneful humming accompanied by pretty words reached his ears. Then a scraping and clunking sound. An outside door opening and a sharp intake of breath, no doubt at the freshness of the morning air, followed up those sounds. The day was beginning. The maid was up and about preparing her lonely world for the day ahead, lighting up the old log-burner; she needed warmth, hot food and drink inside her, air to breathe about her.

Teddy felt the smile disappear. The anger ignited in him once again. He wasn't human, was he? He didn't need any of those things necessary to keep a human life going anymore. So why was he angry about her needing them? He didn't know. Nary one did he have time to figure it out. And that just made him even angrier until he wanted her blood for his supper. He snarled. Nobody wanted him. Nobody wanted an old, life-vaporising vampire.

CHAPTER THREE

'Schatzi!' László was calling him.

László, eccentric, old, life-vaporising vampire upstairs, needed him. A tiny prod pricked at the back of Teddy's head. He took off his hat once again and inspected it. There was the pulpy little lump at the back of the sweatband as usual, but there was nothing else on it anywhere. So he pushed himself off the wall and turned to snatch at whatever had poked him. The wall was flat. There was no gnat or spider that needed squashing between his fingers. Although pasting their entrails on the pale wall would leave a pleasing black-red smear.

'Schatzibar,' László called again, 'Is getting late. Where are you?'

'Here,' he answered, replacing his hat.

Teddy grinned to himself and started singing: loud, baritone and completely out of tune, rhythm and anything else needed to sing pleasingly for others. For some reason, he wanted to annoy the maid.

He took the short flight of steps two-by-two, noticing that the walls changed from plain, pock-marked concrete to insipid green-coloured concrete. At the top he pushed through the door and stood for a moment in the hall. On this side the door to the tunnel was completely camouflaged. It was the same colour and décor as the hall walls, and once closed it would vanish. The rest of the room was ornate to say the least, with gold-coloured statues of some or other god, wearing only ineffective swathes of clothing, and holding some or other demigod or beast. Copper and black-coloured marble-effect pillars or columns, or whatever you wanted to call them, pretended to hold up the ceiling. Darkened by age, oil on canvases hung in every available space in any available size. Teddy sauntered up to one and peered at it. He leaned in so close that their Butler would've twitched lest the Master's breath dampened it. When he'd realised that the Master had no breath, that Butler had soon resigned and departed. The painting was of the estate on which this house stood. It viewed the house from the sea side. The sky above a swirling, white and pale blue, the house grand, square and flanked by woodland that back then was cultured and cared for like a collector arranges the pieces he's amassed. Smudged in the sky, almost little more than a suggestion, was the semicircle of the moon. Teddy had never seen the estate in the daytime and the picture amused him.

'Schatzibar, there you are.' László's sing-song, syrupy voice alighted, smiling, on his shoulder and began tugging on his ear. 'Don't sing, ya? You never could sing.'

'You in a brown study again, László?' he said.

'Is Blue Room, Schatzi.'

Teddy frowned. That wasn't what he'd meant. But he couldn't be sure what he did mean. He just didn't think a brown study was actually a room at all. And he knew that this was the 'Blue Room'. Blue, he reckoned, because of the wallpaper, patterned with the velvety silhouettes of fancy blue birds. Or the heavy dark blue drapes trailing from the picture-painted ceiling to puddle on the white and, you guessed it, blue chequerboard floor. He pulled at his earlobe and sauntered through the doors, throwing himself into an expensively carved chair. The house, its furniture, the painting and all the luxury didn't suit him. He slouched low and spread his knees wide and then he sat up and shunted sideways, swinging a long leg over the arm of the chair, pivoting his booted foot this way and that.

'Fledermaus,' László cooed. 'You are, what is it, played out?'

'A bit.' Teddy stared at him. 'And in over five hundred years you haven't lost your accent.'

László glared at him. Five hundred was obviously wrong. Still, he'd thought it sounded pretty good. László was old. He just couldn't remember how old.

'Is more like seven hundred,' László said, his voice and his body turning languid again. 'And neither have you. Of course, you are just babi.'

Babi? Annoyance growled inside him. It didn't feel like the usual kind of gratuitous and baseless inherent anger that Teddy was used to — this was a different inherent. He just didn't think he liked being called a "babi", which was strange because László must've called him it before.

László looked the exact copy of one or other of the many deities in the many paintings around his house. Perhaps he shouldn't mock. It wasn't as though either of them could check themselves out in a mirror. Copying the paintings was probably the next best thing. Teddy watched him through half-closed eyes. Nope, he was definitely posing on that chaise longue. Although to Teddy's mind it was more of a half settee: the deadbeat in the shop hadn't bothered to nail on the other arm. Teddy could see plainly the reflection of the fringe with its posh tassels that looked more like fine ladies dancing in the highly polished toe of László's knee-length boots. He looked to the floor. Nope, he couldn't see himself.

'Lala,' László said.

Was László singing now?

'Lala ahin Pasha,' he continued.

Teddy had no idea what he was talking about and drifted off into his own world, fighting to keep his eyes open and maintaining his smile as László talked and gesticulated. They'd been here too long. Much longer than any of the other little towns where they'd pilfered large houses from the owners. The place suited László. He seemed at home here. Teddy was restless, though. Or was it just angry? Again.

'Ottoman Empire….' László's melodic accent pierced his thoughts, '…stole my crown…'

His long, magenta hair was swamped over the one arm of the settee and it bucked and bowed like a blanket beaten in the wind as he spoke. His body convulsed and lurched with enthusiasm for the saga he obviously thought he was regaling Teddy with.

'Forcing me to flee my regal palace…'

There was a speck of red on László's pristine white shirt. Probably a dribble of his dinner. Teddy made a note to point it out. If László ever stopped talking.

'…..run to the mountains, live in caves.'

Teddy thought of László living in a cave. A swelling gripped his belly and he thought his chest would burst open. In one action he swung his leg back over the arm of the chair and hurled himself forwards, falling onto his knees on the busily decorated blue and gold rug, his mouth wide and his teeth bared. He clutched his belly as laughter guffawed from him.

'Stop, László,' he said. 'You lived in a cave?'

Teddy rolled onto his back. He was grinning, his eyes narrowed towards László.

'You never told me that.'

'Yes, I did,' László said, 'lots of times. One good thing about not remembering anything: it makes you laugh anew every time, ya?'

'László, this estate is massive.' Teddy stopped laughing and lay there regarding László, waiting for his reaction, 'You really should go take a gander yonder, you know.'

'Don't sit on the floor, Schatzi, you look out of place.'

'Doesn't matter where I sit, I look out of place here.'

'Hmmm, perhaps it's your boots. Take them off.'

Teddy sat up, reached down to adjust his jeans and pulled off his boots. He flattened out his knees, lengthening his legs along the rug and wriggled his toes.

'No,' László said, 'not the boots. The hat, perhaps?'

Teddy removed his hat. László was watching him: he'd moved ever so slightly, and Teddy felt his gaze heavy on him, like it was a super-leech, draining his defiance. He ran a hand through his hair and replaced his hat.

'The land, László,' he reminded László.

It was a game they'd played the evening before and again after the hunt before they'd separated. He had a morbid feeling that they'd played it before that, too. László would never get his hands on his hat, though.

'Mighty fine collection of trees over yonder.'

He turned to smile at László.

'Is much bigger than anywhere else we've lived.' László relaxed, his thin lips pulled back in one of his self-congratulatory grins.

His front teeth looked square this morning. It might be the late hour, though, and the exaggerated canines either side of them. Teddy ran his own tongue over his teeth: he hoped his own canines were as sharp and piercing. So far, all evidence pointed that way.

'And the pieces in it. I mean statues an' urns and stuff all over the place. And guess what I found in the woods?'

Interlocking his own long canines and trying to copy László's smile, he gave him a moment to answer. Which of course he couldn't. László shook his head: his healthy, tanned face had paled just a little with the dawn, and his dark, almost black eyes were turning grey. His smile waned, leaving his jaw a tad donkey-like.

'A swimming pool!' Teddy gushed. 'Empty of course, it looks like some old stone summer house or awngery from the outside.'

After all these years, all the different places that they'd stayed, he still couldn't say "orange". Some uncomfortable link to humanity made him twitch. László smiled. Teddy sensed it.

'Why, for God's sake, do you need a pool when you're this close to the sea?' he said and looked sidelong at László to see if he'd got a rise out of him.

It was a funny little niggle of László's: he would chastise Teddy and remind him that he was reminding him again of the divinity of God. Which Teddy didn't understand, considering that they were vampires, undead, spawn of the Devil. There was a word for it, a name like some sort of creature, as if László wasn't creature enough. It was on the tip of his tongue, he was sure he knew it. As usual, though, he couldn't remember what it was, and in the early hours he couldn't be bothered to try. So he opted to forget about it. Again.

László hadn't bitten at his bait. It seemed more important to him to keep up his lethargic appearance on his satin-covered unfinished settee. Teddy watched him raise a floppy arm to the ceiling and make an L shape with his thumb and forefinger, framing the semi-naked, voluptuous angel and sad-faced sinner depicted there.

'Flittermouse,' László said, 'God forsook you a long time ago.'

How do you know? He wanted to ask. Instead he shook himself. The smile of intimidation in László's voice was more than apparent. Teddy's inherent anger loomed large again; its target, the ridicule in his friend's voice.

'I'm just sayin', is all, László,' he said.

He planted his feet squarely on the rug and pushed himself up. He crossed to the window and leaned with one hand on the frame, the other on his hip. Now he was the poser. He knew he was. He also knew he wasn't anywhere near as good at it as László. He slouched and pushed his hat back on his forehead to get a better look outside. On this side of the house, the moon looked high in the sky. Teddy wondered if the picture in the hall was right. Did the moon stay up all day? It, that imperfect, ever-changing circle, was one of only two constants of his life. It and László. For a moment he longed to see the moon in the daylight. That impromptu smile appeared on his lips again. And there was that security, that cosy pillow of pleasure inside him.

'This place is gonna need maintaining, looking after, and we don't got any dinero.'

'Money, Schatzi, this country deals in pounds.'

Teddy hadn't meant it to be correct. He knew that they weren't in Spain. 'Sides, hadn't he always said, "dinero"? László just liked the sound of his own voice. There had been a graze of harshness in it, though.

'You care about the place. I knew you would. Is beautiful, ya?'

Nope. It was gone. He must've imagined it. He screwed up his face. Couldn't happen – he had no imagination.

'Ya, László,' he said, 'is beautiful.'

He wanted to move on, leave this place. He turned to László on his chaise longue to stress his point. Their noses collided. With no sound or warning, László had risen and closed the gap between them. His ghostly sneaking about didn't faze Teddy. Somehow dealing with it had become second nature. Perfecting its use had been a different matter. He'd tried. For a while, probably just to make his hunting more productive, László had encouraged him. But he could never sneak up on him. Teddy couldn't work it out. Likely as not, it was down to his own inability to flit about silently like the pet name László had for him. He was certainly no flittermouse. He was just too heavy on his feet, and no matter how snug he wore them: his jeans swished.

It wasn't like László could smell him, he had no breath, neither of them did, and without it, they couldn't sniff. Right now, though, he probably did smell rank, eau de early morning death, with the tag line: should have decayed a long time ago!

Actual physical closeness to László wasn't something that Teddy was fond of. Nary one was trying to fool him having the desired effect. Even the hat thing hadn't worked. He wasn't having fun.

Perhaps he was tired, but there was definitely something unsavoury about it all; he sensed an odd detachment and it was twisting about itself in his insides. Twisting insides was something he normally did to others. Or László did. The usual effect was that it made them both laugh. Teddy wasn't laughing now, though. He didn't like it being done to him. In any case, he'd never actually thought of himself as having insides. He sidestepped around László, taking care not to touch him.

'Perhaps we should move on. Leave the place to the deer and the townsfolk.'

'Schatzibar,' László cooed.

It meant treasure. Or bear or something like that. László had once told him its meaning, but he couldn't remember it properly. The Old High German was the most endearing part of László's charm. This morning, though, it felt slick and cloying. He kept his back to László and closed his eyes against it.

'I thought you liked it here. Okay, so the food isn't great, but it will do. Especially when we have all this sumptuous glory all around us to make up for it. Perhaps we can make some friends, ya?'

Make friends? Who'd be their friend? Sadistic old vampires didn't make friends. Unless they were tonight's dinner. Even then, the friendliness was feigned. Any friends they made would have to be exact, carbon copies of the two of them. What was László on about? Literally making friends? He opened his eyes and went to stomp his boots. But he had taken them off when László had told him to. Suddenly, he didn't like himself anymore. None of this had the mood of a game anymore. He took his hat off, ran a hand through his hair and put it back on again.

Lilting notes drifted into the room. László had seated himself at the grand piano and began to play. László played beautifully. *When had he learned?* Teddy wondered. If ever he had learned anything, besides murdering and feeding, he couldn't remember it. But really, he didn't care. Listening to László play calmed him like a remedy.

'Schatzi,' László said, 'you like the outside, don't you?'

Teddy said nothing. He dropped down onto László's chaise longue. Languidly, he raised his feet and placed them on its open end, curling his toes and letting his knees flop open. Closing his eyes again, he settled his middle into the seat's satin cushion. *Ahhh, that's what this shez lonj is for.* He relaxed.

'Tell you what…'

What?

'Why don't you take on the upkeep of the grounds?'

What? "Tell you what…" He knew that phrase; he'd heard it before. He opened his eyes wide. He studied László. He knew that smile as well. He'd seen that somewhere before, too, but where? An unfamiliar image began to blur his mind. He flinched. Taking the place of László's supercilious face was a cruel and ambitious rancher. It was the face of his uncle. It was as clear as though he was standing right there in front of him. He wore the same smile. Teddy felt small and insignificant. The eyes of the man in front of him were brimming, seething with an almost physical hate. Why? What had he done to his uncle? The last time he'd seen him had been in 1884. 1884? It was no longer 1884. He was sure of that. His uncle should be long dead.

He winced suddenly and pressed a hand to his stomach. Something had just jabbed at him. And then at his jaw. He rubbed his cheek. His cousin's face was leering at him, too, now and somewhere deep inside, Teddy knew they were about to deal out pain. But he couldn't feel pain. He couldn't feel anything. Except for a strange vulnerability. He jumped up and shook away the memory.

'I cain't deal with the grounds, László,' he snapped.

Anger and defiance were easier, more regular, plus they made him forget the helplessness.

'I only get into them in the middle of the night.'

Teddy moved away to the next tall window and admired the view again as László continued to play. Damp, gauzy edges to the clouds touched the lawn; the trees and hedges that lined it were gangrenous with lichen, but they broke free of the fog and poked up through. The place looked as haunted as it actually was.

'Let's throw a party,' he suggested, changing the subject.

Whatever way he looked at it, though, the discussion wasn't going his way.

'Have us a real hog killin' time.'

He noticed that László was watching him closely. He tried his best smile.

'C'mon, László, we haven't done that for ages.'

Okay, so he couldn't remember when they had ever had a party. In fact, he wasn't too sure what a party was. But it sounded good.

'We could get the local lords and ladies around, show them the paintings and the statues.'

László continued to study him. He'd stopped playing.

'Well, you can. And Peggy...'

'Margot,' László interrupted.

Darn that slummy.

'...can cook them something.'

He laughed and licked his lips.

'And we can eat any that linger too long?'

László rubbed his chin. He seemed to be mulling the idea over.

'What do you think?' Teddy tried again, 'You wanted to make friends.'

It was taking a little too long. Teddy's smile faded.

'Calm down, my fine Fledermaus.'

The mesmerising piano playing started up again, and it seemed to Teddy that László was no longer talking to him, but instead to the monster inside, using his voice to caress and tease and coax it back into its subservience. Teddy shifted his balance and looked to the floor. Then back at the window. Anywhere that wasn't at László.

'Let's start slow,' László said. 'We don't want to give the house a reputation before we've even settled in properly.'

Settle in? They'd been there for what seemed like forever. Teddy looked out over the seascape. His neck felt stiff and the curve of his spine rusted. But he couldn't look at László. If he did, he might agree with him and he really didn't want to agree.

'We need staff for a party,' László told him.

'We have staff.'

'So quiet down, Schatzi. You'll wake her.'

'Then stop playing the piano.' he rounded on László. ''Sides, she's already awake. Because she's a maid. So, who cares if I wake her? And why do you keep her anyway?'

László turned to him. He'd stopped playing. Teddy had his attention now.

'You'll scare her. She doesn't know you,' László said.

He hadn't answered the question.

'For a dinner party in a house this size, we need more than one housekeeper.'

He stood and in one movement stepped into Teddy's space. Teddy took a step away, stumbling into the window. László laughed as though Teddy's fall was little more than clowning around. He reached out a strong arm and an open hand to steady him.

'If you want to invite people into this house, you will need staff. The Lord of the Manor needs servants; butlers, footmen.'

László waved his hands high in the air as he listed out his knowledge of the running of stately homes. He advanced on Teddy. There really wasn't much space left to fill between them: Teddy shrank further away.

'Stewards will be needed. Valets, a groom and stable boys. We'll need cooks and a chef, parlour maids, bellboys. The list goes on and on.'

'I don't think they'll come on horseback and I wasn't thinking of having a sleepover.' Teddy raised his hands in front of himself in an effort to stop László, he was aware that he was squeaking. 'And Lord of the Manor? Who's Lord of the Manor? I ain't no Lord of the Manor. Nor flittermouse or bear or treasure or whatever that was you called me.'

He didn't really know his own name. He'd only ever answered to László, and László called him strange German names.

'This is your house, Teddy,' László said, his voice soft and warm, his dark brown eyes searching deep in Teddy's for something, his healthy, honey-coloured face so close Teddy could see flecks of white in his red black hair, 'Remember?'

Teddy dropped his hands and looked at the floor again. László's boots were so shiny.

'Yes, László,' he conceded, 'I won it, didn't I?'

László nodded.

'It was a card game. You set it up with slobberin' Lord Stupidname.'

He wrapped his arms around his stomach, bending slightly as though trying to forge an infinity with the ground, as though that was where his memories were held, rather than with László. He frowned deeply. There was more to this card game.

'You set it up. You must've known I'd chisel...'

'...hustle.'

'...him out of his house.'

'Schatzibar, you are the weirdest, most perfect delusional twenty-year-old boy I have ever had the honour of playing Faro with.'

'Yeah, László, I never wanted to actually live in this house, though. Not for this long anyhow.'

Teddy straightened and stared at his friend. Hang fire! How would he have known how to play in the first place?, let alone hustle the other players. Perhaps it was just the coming of daytime, but something was tinkering around with his mind, trying to reveal itself to him. He didn't know what it was. He didn't like not knowing. He drooped against the window. He was so tired.

'László, I ain't never gonna be no Lord.'

'Please, Schatzi,' László said, supporting Teddy's chin on his fingers, 'Let's stay here for a while.'

'László,' Teddy said, 'you're touching me. Don't touch me. And we are not Lords. We never will be. We're killers, László, c'mon you told me this. We're murderers. We can't help ourselves. I see Lady Highfalutin' or Lord Bully-Blowhard and I gotta kill them. Not spend time with them.'

'Killers.'

László closed his eyes. A look of pure serenity brought an extra peachy spark to his forever wholesome features. He raised the other hand and placed it on Teddy's shoulder. Teddy followed it with his eyes wide, returning to watch intently as László appeared to be pondering over his words. The unease in his mind swirled and expanded, gripping his chest, tightening his jaw.

'We're not just killers, we're sociopaths. Psychopaths, Pseudological,

Pathological. Don't you remember what that good doctor said the other night?'

'No.'

Despite his negative declaration, the babbling and very vivid accusations of the doctor crammed their way into his mind. With a voice gurgling full of superfluous spittle, the man's eyes had stared in incredulity as he'd spat out all manner of practised descriptions for the same thing: a sadistic serial killer. The memory pounced at Teddy, punched him in the stomach, slapped at his face, stung in his eyes and bit his lips until he thought he actually knew the doctor's pain when he'd ripped into him. He slapped a hand flat on the base of his neck where the taut muscles should meet those of his shoulder; there'd been a tiny pinprick there. Something had landed on him. When he drew his hand back and looked at it, there was nothing there. He had no blood pumping. His veins, arteries, sinews and muscles, all the tasty stuff was all long gone, nothing would ever bite him. He clutched his neck with both hands, folding his arms over his collarbone as though to shield himself. He slid down the window frame and scrunched himself into the corner.

'I don't remember.'

His voice dropped to a whisper as though he didn't want anyone to hear.

'I don't want to remember. I just feed, kill and move on.'

This was ridiculous. First the horse, then his uncle and cousin and now this? It was too early and he was exhausted. Murderous memories were more like nightmares. He didn't want those kinds of memories. He wouldn't be able to cope with them.

'The sun will be up soon, Fledermaus.' László crouched in front of him, he clutched Teddy's biceps, 'Go to bed.'

'Sakes alive,' he ignored László, 'you remember the old pill?'

László's hold on him was tight. His fingers crushed into his arms. Teddy had no sensation of it, he could see it, though, and the lasciviousness in László's smile.

'An' before him? You remember it? Every time?'

László didn't move.

'Are you telling me that you've remembered everyone that you've ever killed? That's over, hang fire, how many years did you say?'

'Schatzi. You never have remembered? Can't you hear their screams? Their pleas for mercy?'

László was smiling a proper full smile this time. It pushed its way over his whole face; his spotless, fearsome teeth gleamed, his brow, lined in pleasure, animated his preened and well-controlled, long hair which sort of flourished as he spoke. Teddy shook his head although it was more of a tremble.

'No? You can't smell their fear? You can't feel their quivering? Doesn't it make you feel good?'

Teddy leaned his weight on László's hold.

'Smell their fear? Feel their trembling? We can't smell and I never thought we felt anything – trembles or otherwise.'

The blue room was long, open-plan; and it was cold. Teddy secretly flattened a hand on the blue and white tiles; they were hard. The drapes so close to him were stiff where they looked soft and he wondered if they'd ever been closed. The birds embossed in the heavy material were sticky.

'Do we feel things? Do we have emotions? I mean, remember things, too?'

A sort of rattling began in Teddy's belly: it juddered its way upwards through his body and he knew it was evident in his fingers. His thighs, legs, knees even, began to shiver and he curled his toes up. Was this fear? It was alarming, intimidating, terrible. It was inconceivable. László was scaring the flinders out of him.

László, though, was calm as though this was completely normal. Dull, foreboding little probes prodded at Teddy's arms. László was watching him. Teddy couldn't release himself from his gaze. And the more he looked at László, the more he quivered.

'Tell me.' László inched his hands to Teddy's shoulders and squeezed at his neck.

Teddy flinched. He should move them. Or move himself away. He didn't like László touching him. Until now, as far as he knew anyway, László never had. Did he know what was going on inside him now? He'd just said he knew how his victims were feeling just before he killed them. More like talons, László's fingers were long, and they pressed into his shoulders, almost meeting under his collarbone. László was feeling, no, grabbing for something. László was the ultimate killer. The only one, or so Teddy had always believed, strong enough to hurt him.

'Teddy, if you can't feel touch, how is it that you have kissed so passionately, hmmm?'

A question. Answer the question. Focus on the question.

'I don't know,' Teddy said.

His voice shook, a mixture of the fear he was sensing and something else, something that reminded him of watery, cold and thin, belly-wash coffee. That had been on the ranch. Back in the 1800s.

'It wasn't passion.'

The truth, the truth was giving him strength: cling to it.

'I can tell you that much. I don't know what passion feels like, László. Do you?'

Slamming into him like falling from his horse, his self-control returned.

'And don't touch me.'

Surprise? László actually looked surprised. But then he would, wouldn't he? He had senses, moods, feelings. Teddy scrambled to his feet. He had to get away. The great listlessness that came with the sunrise was inching its way into the room. He wouldn't be able to stop László a second time. Physically or not. His resolve to do anything at all wasn't strong at the best of times, and with dawn literally around the corner, he'd be weak.

His bare soles slapped on the stone floor as he pushed László aside and strode to the door, scooping up his boots on the way. Every step he took seemed to bounce off the Blue Room walls, echoing as though the house laughed and tittered at him the way whores did at a tenderfoot.

'Teddy.'

László was in front of him before he could get to the door. Of course he was.

'Who?' Teddy said.

'Don't go,' László whimpered.

'I need sleep,' Teddy cut him off: he couldn't listen to him anymore, he didn't want to, 'Darn it, László, I don't even know my own name.'

'Teddy, stay,' László said.

Teddy's stomach wrenched and his limbs softened, the sleep was coming. He yanked open the door and stumbled out.

The night was almost over. Teddy's emotions, however, were just getting started. Feelings were rushing and sprinting through him, jabbing at him, breaking him apart inside. If he could make it to the tunnel, he might survive until he could get to the stables.

Chapter Four

NO MAN'S LAND – 1883

Under the No Man's Land wind, the prairie had gotten chilly. Winter was done, the spring had arrived and on occasion the weather was balmily airish. Every now and then the yip-howl of the coyotes sang out, a cowpoke hollered and the cattle lowed. Grasshoppers climbed and tumbled, rustling their way over the rough terrain, chirruping loud and quick as they went. Some folk found their constant ruckus annoying, but to the young wrangler, tracker by nature, it was a sure sign that the night had fallen. The nocturnal creatures had woken up. The cowpokes weren't the only ones out here.

'He's out cold,' one of the outfit said.

An odd voice, like it was trying too hard to fit in. It was out of place, foreign and he didn't know it. The vowels squashed and harsh, and yet in a growling, rolling sort of way it was melodious. The voice wasn't old, but it wasn't young either. And it wasn't the usual Western or Spanish or even Irish. German, that was it. They didn't have any Germans in the outfit at the moment, did they? Must be a new guy. Or perhaps it was next door's round-up rep. Something like that.

'That's the way I like them.'

He knew that voice. Couldn't place which one it was, but he knew it.

I ain't out cold, the young wrangler said.

No. No, he didn't. He hadn't actually made a sound. For a second, although it could've been longer, he'd drifted off into sleep. Until the pain of his injury woke him up. Again.

The middle finger of his right hand was throbbing mercilessly, an overblown pulse, it spread along his arm, took in his torso and continued until his entire body was one sweltering mass of internal bubbling. He winced and tensed, trying to quiet the raging torrents that barrelled up and down his bloodstream.

It was touch and go for a moment, but eventually he won out and got all sensation back. The frayed edges of whatever had been used to bandage his hand pinched his remaining fingers together and brushed against his thumb.

'It's his first time off the corral. It won't look good if I lose him.'

Dent. He definitely knew that voice.

''Sides, he's a good worker.'

'Quit worrying. You cain't die from losing a finger. He'll be right as a trivet with a stump and scar. And don't get your dander up, he'll still be as pretty.'

At that the young wrangler tried to open his eyes. He was rewarded with stabbing pains as though the sockets were splitting. He kept them closed.

A sort of blackness closed in on him then. Something disturbing, evil, foreboding, worse than yesterday's skyline. Or whenever it was. This eerie, silent phenomenon was terrifying. It really did feel as though death was standing right next to him. It was threatening to suffocate him. He sucked in a breath so deep it tore at his lungs, his chest rose high and he coughed. He was cold – no, freezing. He began to shake.

'I think he's waking up.'

Nope, didn't know that voice at all. The code of the West, that unwritten list of laws by which they all lived, told him to give the new guy a chance. He had no real reason not to and consideration of others was tantamount to their survival. Dent swore by the code, it made cattle trailing up and down and all around the country easier, he said. And he should know. He was the boss.

This new guy, though, he was strange. There was nothing to him, he was sort of 'empty'. More of a presence than a person. He was grinning, the wrangler could feel his grin. The sensation that grew in his heart was one of fear. It was like when the cowpokes told their ghost stories. It didn't matter if they told them in the dead of night in the dice house or the middle of the day at the dinner table, his body and soul quivered: there'd be a spontaneous twinging at the top of his nose and his eyes would water, his skin prickled and his jaw twitched. He felt just like that right now.

Perfect, the word echoed in the wrangler's ears, *He's perfect, like treasure. What's his name? Say his name.*

It was that accent again. It was in his head.

'Help me,' he tried to say, but it wasn't coming out right.

'Don't tell him,' he tried again, but it was a mumble.

'You're gonna be just fine, Ted,' Dent told him.

Ted. Treasure Teddy.

Dent couldn't hear the voice? Teddy felt pressure on his hand as the bandage was shifted a little. Instantly, there was a popping feeling and the wound glooped blood. Pent-up goo was released and he felt it ooze out of him. The stranger smiled. Wooziness engulfed Teddy, his stomach turned, he rolled over and retched. His throat was sore and his chest smarted, he had nothing left to throw up. All he could manage was a dry gagging.

'Hold still, son. It's really not that bad.'

Mort. The voice was Mort, the Barber. Today's, or was it yesterday's, left flank swing rider. 'The Wagon Surgeon', the cowpokes called him.

A hand pressed his shoulder down hard to the ground. With no inner strength left, he let it and lay still, breathing heavy and fast: murky, sickly sweat coated his body and beaded on his face.

'Beeves bedded down, Dent.'

And that was Charlie.

'Can you pokes stoke up the fire?' Mort said.

The stranger grinned. Teddy could feel it. How could the cowpokes let him get this close? It was like he was enjoying this whole showdown, Teddy's desperation, his injury and his bleeding. Especially his bleeding.

The foreigner seemed to be looming over him, he could almost smell him drooling from every pore. It was revolting. He felt like the sacrifice to a tyrant at some sort of powwow the cowpokes had been brainwashed into agreeing to. He was coated in blood and dirt, exhausted by the onslaught and subsequent management of pain, trussed and dressed and awaiting a putrefying demise. This guy was so ravenous for the feasting, he was having difficulty hiding it. Teddy could feel the man's jitters vibrate through the ground, he was so anxious for the party to get going.

Horrified, Teddy tried to reach out, to grasp one of the cowpokes, force his attention on the newcomer. His fingers touched a face. It was a smooth face, it felt young, there were no pockmarks, no wrinkles, the only lines were those at the edge of its smile. The face had no stubble, not even a hint of it. It made him think of a fine gentleman and he snatched his hand back. The man was not one of their outfit. Not even cowpoke. No cowman would ever send out a rep with no range experience. The face disappeared as his body was moved again.

Teddy opened his eyes. They stung him. He ignored it. He'd dealt with two black eyes before, he could do it again. They gushed salty water which coursed down his cheeks as though he were crying, and his lips twitched in embarrassment: he probably looked like he was crying, too.

Slowly, his surroundings merged into focus. There was no moon in his blurred and blinkered view. He could see the stars, though, and they were out in their millions spreading across the sky, almost obliterating its blackness. Teddy tried to find the face that he'd felt. He even tried to move his head to see further: he had a yearning to at least catch a glimpse of it, a morose curiosity to see what had sounded and felt like the Devil. He'd know its splendour anywhere. But he couldn't find it.

The cowpokes' fire was white-hot. It roasted the side of his face nearest to it. The branding irons poked out of its centre. Perhaps the hour was later than he'd thought. Maybe it was daybreak and the sky was indigo blue with the dawn. The cowpokes must be getting ready early for branding. Odd, though, as they hadn't got the heard back to the corral yet. Branding was normally done there.

'Haahlloa, strangers.'

Thundering hooves reverberated through the ground, tenderising Teddy's head. Or perhaps that was just his insides rattling. Moon had returned from wherever Mort had sent him. Teddy rolled his eyes over to where Mort squatted in the dust. He was the oldest member of the crew. He had a kindly if somewhat worried-looking face. Other than his skills with a razor, they knew precious little about him. Come to think of it, they knew precious little about any of them. Other than himself of course, often sporting the evidence of his ancestry's disapproval of his existence in the form of abrasions from abuse suffered at the hands of his cousins. Everyone knew his family didn't want him around and they tried in vain to get him to accept it. But what good would accepting it do him? He had nowhere else to go, did he?

'Okay, let's do this thing,' Mort muttered, 'darn finger's started bleeding again. I wanna cauterise it before it makes too much mess.'

'What?' Teddy became animated then.

Suddenly, he had a voice. He started to scream, he wriggled and tried to get to his feet looking for all of No Man's Land like one of the prairie's scorpions, only his tail had been put on the side and it weighed him down. He fell over again. Now there was pain, burning pain, everywhere.

'What in the tarnation?' Mort exclaimed. 'Put him out, will ya? Darn it, Ted, at least try to stay calm.'

Calm? He was shaking violently now.

'Don't be such a tenderfoot.' Cleve joined in and then added, 'Addleheaded kid,' for good measure.

Code or not, Cleve was not known for his sympathy towards fellow cowpokes. Or anyone for that matter.

'Brand....' Teddy mumbled.

'Sake's alive, Mary, you'll be lucky. Moon, what you got for him?'

'I don't want ....'

'Help me hold him down, you fellers, would yer?'

Gnarled and calloused cowpoke hands cupped Teddy's jaw from behind and his head rested on someone's knees. The rough and chunky top of an open bottle was offered to his mouth. Teddy had never had whisky. He hadn't ever had any kind of alcohol for that matter. Alcohol was something that the cowpokes did in town, mostly at the end of the drive. So, for Teddy, the 'town' was a long way away. He readily took a gulp.

'Rotgut.' he spat as much as he could back out.

The smell of damp stable stalls, charred cornfields and sun-blackened, decomposed prairie dogs hovered like low clouds. Having tasted whisky, he would never need to imagine how damp stable stalls, charred cornfields and sun-blackened, decomposed prairie dogs tasted. He knew. And people got silly over this stuff? He recoiled and tried to turn his face away.

'Murderers,' he croaked.

If the shock of being branded didn't kill him, then the whisky would.

Dent planted himself at Teddy's side. He turned to face the fire, grasped Teddy's arm, secured it under his own and held Teddy's hand out to Mort. The whisky was offered to Teddy's lips again: its stench tore the delicate fibres inside his nostrils. Teddy kicked and bucked.

That's right, Schatzibar, don't let them do this to you.

That voice, patronising in its crookedness seized any rationality he may have had left.

'Devil,' Teddy cried, 'he's right here.'

He wrenched his arm so savagely it should've come right out of his shoulder. Little good that would do him. He strained and glared about wildly, trying to seek out the face in the clutch of cowpokes gathered around him. The heels of his hand-me-down boots scored lines in the earth, shredding the grass as he struggled to get a better view.

'Mort, get on with it, he's getting crazy.'

Cleve sat on his knees. He cried out again. He was terrified. Cleve was twenty-one, heavy-set and only bony where it counted. Which, for a cowpoke, was nowhere. Teddy's knees bent and buckled between Cleve's weight and the dirty prairie. Charlie grasped his other arm and Moon perched on his chest brandishing the whisky bottle. It – or was it Moon himself? – stank of sweat on a burned bull's underbelly. The loss of the use of his limbs seemed to make his heart stronger; his breathing became exaggerated, his stomach swelled, and he opened his mouth to exhale long, and hopefully, some of his pain. Moon seized the opportunity and he was fed more of the home-made whisky.

'Darn it, Moon,' he slurred, 'get off. Let me up.'

'Aw, cowboy up, Teddy.' Moon laughed; he didn't move.

Teddy lay still for a moment. He was petrified, his arm still throbbed, his knees were spraining the wrong way and at any moment his chest might collapse. In short, he was totally sewn up. He was pinned to the prairie and about to be branded by the cowpokes. Wait, wasn't this what they did for a living? Well, the others did; he didn't actually get paid. Right now, he felt like a corralled acorn calf. Somewhere in the mists of the whisky, the taste of which was growing on him, he wondered if he looked like one. He smiled then. Deep in his chest, his heart gave a sudden sympathetic lurch: it seemed to want to relieve his soul from the desperation he was feeling.

The unwinding of the makeshift bandage tugged and peeled away at his wound as it was removed. His stomach turned again: fear and nausea retched along his spine, knotting in his chest. He groaned: a film of sweat so thick it must've been tangible soaked every inch of his skin. The cowpokes leapt up. Teddy's throat closed down, nothing came up and the cowpokes came back. His newfound ability to make them jump made him grin.

'You got a freeloader gummed up in here,' Mort mumbled.

The nerve ends in Teddy's hand twitched involuntarily as Mort picked at a stray cotton thread that had become embroiled in the ravaged, blackened flesh. Congealed blood and gelatinised tallow had formed a glue-type substance and stuck his undamaged fingers together.

'I'm gonna need to pull these apart,' Mort said, 'if I'm gonna get to that there hole.'

The copious amounts of tarantula juice or coffin varnish or whatever the cowpokes wanted to call the whisky they'd fed him helped to convince him he was going to be flayed. However accidental it might be.

He'd never had any serious injury. The ranch owner's sons frequently gave him bruises, violently purple eyes and swollen lips, not to mention a stiff abdomen and smarting thighs. These grievances, though, were self-healing and took little more than time to mend.

The first time it had happened was almost four years ago to the day. That was the day he'd been unceremoniously disowned and dumped, totally chawed up, in the bunk house. Greenhorn and trembling, he'd been so afraid that night that his family would forget about him. Now some nights, he hoped they would. Only some, though.

They were meant to be his family, the ranch's owners. His birthday present, they'd said. It's outside, they'd said. Thirteen, his uncle had told him, is big enough to work on the Cross Truss ranch. That had been right before he'd made him swear to stay away from the main house at all costs. Even if he was bleeding slowly to death, he was to do it alone. And the present they'd talked about? A proper trouncing and a new home: the bunk house.

The second time had made him bawl broken-hearted like a sweetheart given the mitten. Thinking back on it made him wince. He shrank away from the memory of how he'd whimpered and grovelled on the floor. In his defence, he was only just fourteen and had in all honesty thought they'd come to take him home, that his stint with the cowpokes had been some sort of punishment although what in tarnation for, only Dickens knew. Just being in the way, he guessed now.

The third time would have been shocking had it not become an expectation. Still, knowing what was coming didn't make it any easier to take. Now the beatings were a way of life. He didn't cry about it anymore. Hadn't cried about it for a long time. He'd learned not to cry about anything at all. It still hurt, though. He guessed it would never stop hurting. The sad fact was, that to his family, he had been no more than an unwanted appendage. If only he knew what had happened to his parents. But he couldn't even remember them.

At age thirteen, his aunt and uncle had cut him off and cauterised the wound. Just like Mort was about to do to his finger. Except he wanted his finger. His family didn't want him. His cousins, Erastus and Kenny, wanted him. When they were drunk or bored or had had a bad day and needed to take out their frustrations on someone. Or, as was often the case, just for no real reason at all.

When the old wrangler hadn't returned from the trail, the job had become his. So, now his cousins knew exactly where to find him. His horses had made a fuss the first time they'd showed up and beaten him to a pulp. That had brought the cowpokes to the scene. He'd been down but not quite out when the threats of job losses on account of any interference had been bandied about. His cousins, the Cross Truss heirs, weren't well liked. To be fair to them, though, they hadn't been before he'd arrived in the bunk house that night.

The cowpokes had taken it upon themselves to teach him how to defend himself. Embarrassingly compassionate of his predicament, they'd reasoned that at least now he could fight back. But when it came down to it, he'd lost his sand. Getting the better of the big boss's sons wasn't a good idea. Especially when the big boss hated you in the first place. And after all that, they were still his family; or so he kept telling himself. For some inexplicable reason, he clung to the hope that one day they'd behave like it. Until then, he'd just keep on doing as they told him to, which was usually: stand-up, fight back, even stay down.

Tonight, though, the testosterone or the cowpoke stubbornness that had been ingrained in him since, scarpered into the shadows. He continuously flinched and squeaked in terror. A terror not solely caused by anticipation of the sadistic operation about to be performed on him. The demonic presence had become overbearing. It was so close, so stifling and lying prostrate under the cowpokes as he was, he was humiliatingly vulnerable. For a moment, the cloying entity threatened to overpower everything, usurping even the deadly wildlife of the prairie.

Schatzibar, please, don't let them do this to you.

'Schatzibar!' Teddy yelled.

'Whoa, boy, where in the Sam Hill did you learn that?'

'Never mind where, what in the Sam Hill is a See-chat-zee-barr?'

A cussing contest followed. The whisky put in frequent appearances. Teddy fought its repugnance as much as he could, but in the end the alcohol got the better of him. His mind and fears were fragmenting fast until he wasn't too sure which was foremost. And then he found himself smiling at the ingenuity of the cowpokes' wordsmithing. Perhaps he just didn't care anymore.

The snap of a sudden movement in the fire brought Teddy back to his senses.

Blaznit, Teddy.

A crack reverberated across the prairie; the sound seemed to carry for miles as though hungering for something to bounce off.

'You all awoke the Devil!' he screamed.

His panic was ignored. His three good fingers were folded into what would've been a fist and Dent tightened his hold.

'Whatever you do, Mort,' he said, 'don't miss.'

Hoping for the element of surprise, Teddy yanked his arm. It worked and Dent lost his hold.

'Thunderation, Ted, you wanna keep on bleeding?'

Yes, the voice in Teddy's head said.

'No!' Teddy shouted.

He began frantically waving his free arm. He twisted and tried to unseat Moon.

'I cain't do this now,' Mort said.

Yes, the voice said again.

'No,' Teddy cried, 'Moon, get off.'

'Help me out here!' Dent yelled.

'Help me!' Teddy cried! 'Get the Devil away.'

Teddy stared up at whoever it was that was holding his head. He craned his neck and gazed into Virgil's uncompassionate, grey eyes. He tried to clutch at his shirt, but he hadn't got the full use of his fingers yet.

Schatzibar, throw these men off and let me help you.

Virgil's deadpan face disappeared. The weight of the cowpokes sitting on his body was lifted. His arms were no longer in human traction. He could move.

The ever-present wind had dropped and the prairie felt almost balmy. There were thousands of stars fuzzed against the pitch black of space. He watched them, incredulous at their intricate beauty. The lowing of the Longhorns was now unhampered by the coyote, the scuttling of the creatures in the grass was intriguing and there was the unmistakeable chirp of a mountain lion. The mountains were miles away on the horizon, though. Still, the cowpokes did not holler; instead they slept. Only one was awake. He sat in the starlight absent-mindedly humming and murmuring Beautiful Dreamer. The boy wore a new Stetson, white-gold hair flicked out from behind his ears, his boots stood to attention beside him and he wiggled his toes in the night air. He must've only been about seventeen. And he had a pure, innocent voice.

'What in tarnation,' Teddy spat out. 'Is that me? I punish the air with my voice. It's the Devil, the Devil is here. He's showing me visions.'

Sweating and almost suffocated by the horror of the very real apparition, he blinked long and stared hard. The corners of his eyes stung as though grated. He blinked again. He'd been mesmerised by it. And that scared him more than the prospect of cauterisation pains. He blinked again and again. His eyes finally watered.

A shivering that he just couldn't stop wracked his chest, his stomach was jittering and even his spine was shuddering. Inside his head his skull seemed to be leaking, damp ran in torrents from surfaces that had never before had an outlet. The sides of his nose seemed to transform into a sieve. He glared hard and far into the distance; searching for something to concentrate on. In the past, this desperate feat had halted his feelings from oozing through his eyes. But there was nothing tonight, tonight the prairie was boundless, flat and formless.

'Darn it, Mary,' Virgil said, shifting Teddy's head. 'Don't let the prairie get your sand.'

Teddy's nose ran, he snivelled and gurgled.

'Mort, Dent, he's gone sappy as a purley purdy little shaver.'

'No, no I ain't,' Teddy tried to tell them, 'It's the Devil. He's here.'

'Quit panicking,' Moon said.

Taking the obvious course of action, Moon raised his fist and slogged Teddy directly in the nose. Pain massive as the prairie sky spread upwards from Teddy's top row of teeth, blood vessels exploded as his lips swelled, and his nose was numbed beyond breathing. Moon's punch felt like the hammer to the gong that was Teddy's face. The thudding was dull, the ache shimmered. Teddy gulped his intake of air.

'Sakes alive, Moon, you wanna keep your muck forks off mine?' Virgil's surprise matched Teddy's.

'Shut your cock-holster, Virgil, my muck forks are dripping wet with the tranklements of Ted's face.'

Instinctively, Teddy's hand flew to cup his nose. Surely, Moon had splattered it across the entire circumference of his face. As soon as he did, Dent grabbed it and forced it back to Mort, holding it in traction.

Blood ran from Teddy's nose. It settled in the crevice between his lips. It seeped over the sensitive gums and lined his teeth. Impulsively, he licked his lips the way he'd done when they'd been thickly sugar-coated from Coosie's Bear Signs. But this time they were messed up with his own blood. Faintly metallic, treacherously rare, it at least tasted better than the whisky. His own blood? He was savouring the taste of his own blood. He swallowed and the infinitesimal tasty twang was lost.

Drink.

'Drink,' he said.

Moon poured a copious amount of alcohol down his throat. It was vile. He was vile for enjoying the taste of blood. He coughed and floundered through the murk of his own mind striving to remember just who he was: human, cowpoke, God-fearing.

'Drink,' he said again and chugged down more of the foul belly whip.

It ripped at the top of his mouth and grated his tongue as it passed. He screwed up his face as it burned its way over his tonsils. Then he relaxed in a homely hearthside glow when it warmed the inside of his chest. He tried to ignore the nausea it generated when it settled in the pit of his stomach.

He couldn't fight anymore. Submission to the upper hand when your own movements are totally restrained usually translated into comfort; of sorts anyway. He resigned his survival to the cowpokes and let his limbs go limp.

Mort's cauterising was an agony of out-of-body proportions, the numbing of which was not at all stimulated by the whisky. In fact, the alcohol did little more than make him nauseous. As soon as only so much as a whisper of the branding iron touched his wound, a sickening, singing hiss steamed over the prairie. Pain beyond screaming pitch shot along his arm as he twisted and arched, centre stage in an arena of torture.

The bone marrow boiled and Teddy convulsed. He swore. Wailing and crying was added to the spitting of scalding blood and sinew just like a flame-grilled steak might whine. The brand scoured up all the leech-like parasites that had set to colonising, pus spreading and tallow curdling the mouldering hole.

Teased out like splinters, bright new cells in red and white were instantaneously extracted from the tributaries of Teddy's blood system. He winced and writhed and shivered as each harnessed blue flame soldered itself to the next. They knitted and linked again and again, a billion times over until his skin, the tough, leathered skin of a cowpoke, melded and stretched inhumanly before shrinking to fit and sealing the cavity. It was quick, almost forgettably so, but the torment it left behind was immense.

Teddy's soul sought to escape the brutality. It soared high above him and seemed to linger there, uncertain of whether to resume life or accept defeat. He stared up at it pleading with it not to give up yet.

The cowpokes scrambled, cussing and coughing away from the fetid stink that oozed from Teddy's scorching skin. In reaction to any poisonous vapour, his own windpipe closed; he choked and was forced to drive and heave breaths through the gunked-up cavities of his nose.

The rifle sight leaf straps of the knee-high grass rasped and swayed with the swimming of Teddy's consciousness. He felt rather than saw the cowpokes get up stumbling on high-heeled boots never intended for running.

You took him.

He clearly heard that voice. The foreigner's voice. No longer in his head. It was in the wind, wild and booming off the landscape. It slapped at the snugly fitted Stetsons, buckling the wide brims and knocking the crowns sideways. It laid the blue-green grass flat, switching and tossing anything that moved. And then, pokerish silence. A menacing, straining stillness pressed across the entire prairie.

Teddy curled into Dent's back. Dent shifted. They weren't in the habit of closeness, none of the cowpokes were. Dent hadn't heard the voice.

The fire gutted and spat. It shot coals as bright and deadly as bullets in Dent's direction. Dent cussed. He dropped Teddy's arm, jumped up and began to cut a caper on the spot, flicking at the straying fiery pebbles with the pointed toes of his boots.

'Stop,' Teddy cried. 'Dent, you'll annoy him.'

The Devil was in that fire, Teddy was sure of it. It was the Devil that had thrown it like exploding shrapnel at Dent. It was the Devil trying to set Dent alight. The fire jumped again. A rippling, yellow and red line of fire blazened a trail towards the cowpokes. Dent set off after it in a crazed, high-legged gallop.

'Don't,' Teddy said.

It came out as incoherently as anyone who'd drunk as much as he had.

'I ain't absquatulating,' Dent grumbled, 'but nary one am I gonna get burned to cowchips by that fire.'

'No.'

Frustration seized Teddy's insides, making them grind and tense. That wasn't what he'd meant. Dent's hightailing it out of there and leaving him alone hadn't been his first thought at all. All too often he was ridiculed for a deep-set sensitivity that the other cowpokes just didn't seem to have, but he considered Dent to be his only good friend. Dent was cowpoke to the core; proud, angular and fearless. Not always the best way to be. Dent might like to think he could take the Devil on, but he'd soon go up in smoke.

'Please, Dent,' Teddy begged.

He couldn't see straight, he couldn't speak properly and thanks to Moon, he had no nose. He was Devil fodder for the taking. So now Dent came to mention it, he didn't want to be left alone at all. The Devil was here. He was in the air, the ground and he wanted to be inside them. Teddy knew it.

To his relief, Dent was feeling protective. He stopped dancing, straightened his hat and shuffled his boots ready to sit back down again.

You stole him from me.

The prairie juddered beneath them. It moved physically and in its entirety. Everything on it was yanked sideways at once. Nothing was prepared, everything jolted, all too late. A good few of the cows tipped over in a collective thud. They immediately started lowing their fears. The remuda of horses began to cry out for the reassurance of their wrangler. Anxiety for them tightened Teddy's chest: he wanted to call out to them, but he couldn't place which way the sound had come from. The fire collapsed, leaving behind it a smudged trail of ash and charcoal. The cowpokes whooped and yelled and cussed each other's spurs.

'Quake!' Moon yelled.

Teddy.

The voice echoed around him again. Couldn't Moon hear it either? Teddy had a bad hunch that the unsuspecting cowpoke would be heading back towards them. He rolled onto his back, straining his eyes upwards, backwards, anywhere to find Moon. He stopped moving, though, when he noticed the stars. They'd ceased the enchantment of their twinkling. They glowered down on the cowpokes.

'Moon!' he screeched, unsure of what way to aim it. 'Drop.'

The prairie shifted back the other way, stopping short where it had started that day. Anything and everything that had righted itself fell the other way. It would've been funny, if it hadn't been so real. If this continued, the fire would be shaken out and finished up, the herd would be good for nothing and the horses were likely to start breaking legs.

Sssss......schatzibar.

'Go away,' Teddy said.

He didn't want this, any of it. He hadn't asked for it. Something, his blood, his fear, his pain had brought forth the Devil. Teddy's nose was running and bubbling so badly that once again he was forced to breathe through his mouth. Each intake of the foul and fetid air quaked as bad as the prairie had: each exhale was like a tornado.

'Come home, Teddy, my schatzibar.'

Teddy's rancid, sweaty body turned icy, his heart trembled, his spine shuddered, the pressure in his head burst through the corners of his eyes, and salt water soaked his face.

'Leave me, Satan,' Teddy whispered.

Then he fell quiet. It was better that he stayed quiet. It was sacrilege: what he was about to do. If the cowpokes knew, if even one tiny inkling of a thought raised their suspicions that he was somehow in cahoots with the Devil, they'd kill him, shoot him dead where he lay. And they'd be right to.

He couldn't clasp his hands together, so he tried to focus his soul, align it with the wind or the ground or wherever the force of the Devil had seated itself. And he began to pray. He prayed to the Devil.

Leave me, Satan, he thought with as much passion as he could add without hollering out, No one keeps me!

It was a lie. He just hoped the Devil would get his drift.

No one. Especially not you. I'm stayin' right here. The cowpokes here have saved me. They stopped my bleeding and with it, ended your fun. You ain't never gonna take me and you sure as darn it ain't gonna take them.

Teddy had no idea if the Devil had heard him or not. For all his praying, he felt no different. He lay still, his face screwed up, his teeth gritted. At the end of his arm which felt like it was a long way away, his hand hammered out a relentless, agonising, unpredictable tune.

In the calamity of the quakes, the wind had dropped back down to normal No Man's Land night speed. At the time, it hadn't seemed as important. Now, though, it whipped skywards creating dust and ash devils, making a tiny, tittering noise. Its erratic rushing around in the long grass calmed to that of a sleepy infant's breath. It guffawed one resounding last gust and loped away towards the county line. The prairie was silent and still. Teddy waited.

'You wanna try callin' me Satan again, boy!'

Moon had not been swallowed whole. He had arrived and wasn't pleased at apparently being called Satan.

'Hesh up, Moon,' Mort rumbled, 'he's jest seein' snakes. A bit leaky mouthed an' all, mebe fixin' to go into a fever.'

Moon grunted and began shuffling around in his yannigan bag. Teddy's unique sensitivity tore a slit in his soul and this time real tears flowed. 'It ain't you, Moon,' he thought. A groan was all that he said.

'Darn No Man's Land weather.' Moon retorted, rattling a tinderbox.

Teddy winced at the sound. Mort growled.

'Reckon it's hell-bent on harassing the good folks of Kansas now.'

Teddy's arm was taken up again, bent at the elbow and his hand held aloft. Instantly the hammering raged war on his senses. Teddy curled over again, gritted his teeth and pushed his screams to the back of his head. Somehow that made his nose throb. He rolled back over and glared at the sky.

'Quit moving about,' Mort berated him.

The No Man's Land night sky was once again a sparkling fuzz of tranquillity. Teddy's nose pounded against his skull which felt as though it were fixin' to crush right through his face. He twisted back over and his stomach rolled around. Once or twice he thought he'd retch but it came to nothing. Feeling oddly melancholy, he curled up and gazed at his knees. The ache in his nose slid along the side of his face and rested around one eye.

The night herder's hooves galloped around the cattle, checking for injury, soothing them with his hollering. The night wrangler cooed at the horses, complimenting them on their coats, their manes and their shoes. *'They like a compliment,'* Teddy remembered telling the cowpokes, *'just like anybody does.'* He'd thought they'd ignored him, humoured him as just jawin' horse feathers again. But no, it seemed they'd taken him seriously. His spirits lifted. So, he tried to find another good memory. It wasn't easy. He finally settled on the sound of his sister reading to him. The memory was dim and worn by age, dating back to when they'd first come to live on the Cross Truss, but the sound of love in her voice made him smile.

Slowly the fear that resonated inside him, causing the occasional tremble, began to dwindle. He was left with an odd niggling humiliation, as though he'd somehow been duped or should've known better about something. But he couldn't place it and so blamed the whisky. The thought of the whisky made him smile. The smile made him brave. He searched all his feelings. The stranger, the Devil, whatever it had been, was nowhere to be felt. So Teddy sent his fear with it.

The grass next to Dent crunched. Presumably Moon had just sat down. Teddy's arm was passed to him.

'Keep his hand up,' Mort said.

Teddy closed his eyes hoping to ease the dull pain that glooped through his body each time he moved. Orange blobs, keeping time with the throbs of pain, danced about on the back of the lids as the latest fire took hold. And then, just as he'd mastered the beat of his own pulse, his arm was passed back again and his serenity was dislodged.

The fire cracked and puffed the scent of the countryside into the crisp night air. Moon spat weed into the grass, no doubt aiming at, and most likely missing, one of the prairie's gargantuan grasshoppers, and then he began to play his guitar. Moon could sing the Spirit Guides to Christianity. They'd never tell him that of course. The wind, now nullified, joined him in lamenting the fate of the Longhorns.

'Thunderation, Moon,' Mort said, 'you strum women like that?'

Moon kept on singing.

'Dang good job those doggies cain't understand a word you're saying or they be pulling a stampede.'

'All in the melody,' Moon explained, spat weed again and returned to humming the country to sleep.

Teddy's pain relented, too. Finally. Perhaps his system was conforming to its original owner's control once again. Carefully, so as not to alert the rest of his body, he unfolded his grimace and looked up. From the other side of

Dent, a delicate, mystical loop of smoke coiled into the air. Was his finger actually smoking? Whatever it was, he didn't care. He actually, pleasantly, didn't care.

Lying motionless, he studied the grass; it was a sort of aquamarine colour. It swayed and rippled and turned dark blue before waving back the other way and changing colour again. He wondered if that was what the sea looked like. Fixing his eyes to its listing and bowing he concentrated on it, consciously letting the whisky in his head and stomach drift along with it. He rocked his body back and forth. Then he started to sing.

Dent turned, stuffed a quirley between his lips and turned away. Teddy smiled, sucked and puffed, mostly in the wrong order, and eventually passed out.

CHAPTER FIVE

SOMEWHERE ON THE SOUTH COAST OF ENGLAND – NOW

'Schatzibar?' László said. 'What have you done?'

Teddy, figuring he must be badly barrel-fevered, didn't move. He didn't dare. Just a few more moments, then he'd come to his senses.

'My little Fledermaus,' László continued to disturb him, 'have you been here all day?'

Teddy raised his eyelids enough to look over the bottom rims. It was like peeking over the sill of a window covered by moth-besieged blinds. Blinds, dang they were ding aggravating. Allers sticking, dangling or ticking.

Teddy still didn't move, though; didn't want to. Not just yet. There was something safe and secure about his bunk. 'Sides, his mind was all fizzed up, like a soda some beef-headed addle-pot had shaken hard. It needed time to settle. So, he feigned sleep.

'What a mess you are in now. Thank goodness for miserable, overcast British weather, ya?'

This wasn't his normal bunk, then. There was a note of concern in László's voice. Or perhaps it was chastisement. The disorientation and sluggishness that was pinning him down was becoming unsettling; he should be up and about, full of energy, irritable, jumpy and ravenous for breakfast. Or rather, dinner, as the case may be.

From under the cover of his half-closed eyes, Teddy stretched his vision from side to side, covertly hunting for clues to his whereabouts. He spied trees. All of different types. Some with white, papery bark, tarnished with silver stripes where the moon shone on them. One or two with black, silken bark, magnificent golden bands circling their slim trunks. Most, though, were the standard chocolate colour. On his other side, he saw more trees. These were fantastically gnarled, their huge and solid branches swooping low to the ground before curving upwards again. One was completely hollow and yet still living; strong and surly. Just like him. He curbed an involuntary smile that threatened to give away his consciousness. He didn't want László to know he was awake. He should've hidden in that tree before succumbing to death.

'Come, let's get you inside.' László smiled at him.

He knew. He always knew what Teddy was up to.

'You need clean clothes, ya.'

Here and there, all over Teddy's body, dull probes prodded at him. If blood had pumped around his being, which it didn't, he'd have bruised. As it was, his body remained unchanged, restored, refurbished and reanimated. Fingers pressed his flesh and traced the shapes of his bones. One facetious little jab took a minute or two to fade away. He twitched and smiled. His arms were lifted high and he was hauled to his feet.

Instantly, anxiety sluiced through him, leaving him nauseous. He creased up his face and tried to pull his arms back in. 'Quit it,' he said. Or he thought he did. In his head, his voice had been so vivid, a little choked perhaps, but loud enough. Only, he couldn't be sure anything had actually come out of his mouth.

'I cain't take any more,' he tried concentrating this time: any more of this brutal lacing and he'd be lynched good and proper, 'Quit it now. Please.'

The punches that he could've sworn had spun him around on his axis, the stinging slaps to his face and the hate-filled blows to his ribs, his kidneys, his stomach, never came. He clung to László and whimpered his gratitude.

'Is just a dream,' László said. 'Don't dream, ya?'

No, it wasn't just a dream. It'd been like this since this morning. Every time he'd flopped down to die there'd been faces, thousands of them flashing before his eyes. They were loved ones he recognised. He'd cried out to them in a voice hoarse and sore from a hundred years of suppressed grief. Barely conscious, he'd wailed that he was afraid, pleading: 'Don't leave me.'

There'd been others, too. Distaste and cruelty in their faces swamping him in such a fear that he'd thrashed about. Most, he didn't know at all and the desperation, humility and pain in their eyes blasted him with a need so frantic he'd vowed he'd turn himself inside out and scrape away the revolting symbiont skulking inside him.

Hundreds of places and times, too. Balmy evenings, summer mornings, springtime flowers, autumn frosts. The homely scent of freshly ground caffeine, the baking of biscuits and bear signs, sweet harmonica sounds, pianoforte, lullabies and moonlight guitar lulling him further into sleep.

Then came the shake of a rattlesnake rousing him. That was followed by the howl of a hungry coyote, the slice of freezing wind and the debilitating burn of a red-hot branding iron. A harsh, treeless and uninhabited grassland stretched far in front of him, as far as he could see. He'd be tethered, kept at bay from the land or he was trapped and crying. But he had no tears. Then the land rose in front of him in waves and peaks higher than ever the wildest ocean could muster. But he couldn't go near the ocean, could he? Then those waves solidified around him, over him, corralling him only to slide then into a quagmire of yellow mud and dust, packing itself onto his face, gritting his teeth, gunking up his eyes and suffocating him. But he had no breath. So, it whipped and slashed at his body, dismantling bits of him, cutting off his fingers one by one.

'....worn gloves,' he mumbled.

'Mein Schatzi,' László said, grasping Teddy's hand in his, 'I have you now and no one is going to hurt you.'

'László.'

Teddy flinched at the sound of the name, especially to hear it coming through his own lips. His voice sounded so normal, heavily accented, but so human. Not that of the creature in his nightmares. Somewhere deep inside was the notion that László was duping him. Somehow. He was so confused. And his head ached. But László was holding him close.

'Teddy, is no, as you say, "shakes", mien schatz, I'm here,' László was saying.

Again Teddy closed his eyes and leaned on László. A watery-coloured movie projected itself onto the back of his eyelids, making him smile. He'd never been to the movies. A young boy, only twenty or so, was seated ever so lightly in the superstructure of the Clear Creek Bridge. The boy should hold on: if he didn't he'd topple into the thundering water below. He slumped, obviously exhausted. He wore a Stetson, it was dark and new. His snug, chapless jeans and ripped collarless shirt were both brown with muck and stiff with blood. His jaw, neck, forearms and what was visible of his body shone slick and blood-red, too. And his hands were coated, so much blood, they would've been unrecognisable as human, had it not been for the stub of a missing finger on his right hand. And then he was joined by László. Pristine, polished László.

That filthy boy was himself; Schatzi? Schatzibar? Teddy? Whatever his name was. What was it László had said to him that night? It must've been important. It'd stopped him from jumping at any rate. What was it? And what was it he'd told László to do? Or not to do? He couldn't remember.

'Who....' he said but couldn't complete what he'd thought he wanted to say.

He was scared. Again. But there was no one and nothing around to be scared of. And László, of course, was there. A trembling took up in his belly. It was becoming familiar. Yet it was completely uncontrollable. He needed to tell László about it.

No. No, he didn't. He didn't want to tell László anything which was odd because he told László everything. He did need to tell him something, though. Something about not wanting him so close. He couldn't quite remember what that was either.

'Look at you,' László said, his melodious voice soft and soothing. 'What a mess you've made of yourself.'

László shifted him until he had an arm around his waist. Teddy, so boogered up, couldn't move his arms, so they hung useless. László hooked one over his shoulders and grasped the dangling hand. He was grinning. His grin was too close. It made Teddy shudder.

'László,' he murmured again.

Darn it, what was it he needed to say?

They made to move forward. Teddy tripped over something. Something large and malleable. He shrieked and fell into László, clinging on stupidly.

'Oopsy,' László said, 'I've got you.'

Teddy searched the ground for the thing that was the cause of his stumbling fright. Right at his feet on the twig-strewn floor was a body. It must've been what he'd tripped over. Next to it, lay another. And another. There must've been at least one hundred carcasses there. He was standing in the middle of the estate's herd of fallow deer. And they were all dead.

The whole herd was dead. The fallow deer were the most beautiful thing about this place. They were wild, ornery and skittery. They roamed where they wanted to, they rutted when they needed and then roared and bellowed for effect. Teddy loved them.

Puncture wounds, resplendent with drips of blood as bright and red as the ruby on László's finger, festered at the throat of each deer. All had been ruthlessly slaughtered. Had the herd not fought back? Stampeded? Obviously not. Obviously, who or whatever had done this was fast, systematic, desiring nothing but death. Disgustingly so, it had dribbled as it passed from one neck to the next. Who could've done this? What could they possibly hope to gain from it?

Teddy froze. Distress and incredulity at bloody desecrated life isn't something that should irk a vampire, but the barbarity that surrounded him, dumbfounded him. Searing, stabbing, painful deaths, together with so much blood created a low, heinous maze. And as mazes are prone to do, the path led to a spectacle at its centre: Teddy and László. Teddy and László stood at the centre.

László tried to hustle him away. Teddy refused to be moved. László's arm circling Teddy's waist jerked upwards, crushing into his ribs. Remorse so powerful, so insufferable, doubled Teddy up. But the dead don't vomit. Too miserable to rebel, he let László steer him through the massacred deer towards the edge of the wood.

'László,' Teddy whispered.

'Don't fret, ya,' László said, adding a good deal of shushing and stroking the back of Teddy's hand. 'Let's get you home. We'll have you cleaned up in no time.'

László's touch made him grimace. Limply, he raised his other hand to grasp the wide lapel of the old vampire's coat. The gold brocade was patched and antique, but it dazzled him. Even in the dark. Teddy's hand was stiff and the fingers glued together as though secured in some sort of traction. Along his forearm, up and beyond his elbow, an odd, reddish-brown second skin tugged on the downy, blond hairs, pricking his skin. As he moved his hand, it ruptured, ballooned and ripped. Strange: people didn't shed their skin. Not until they were properly dead. And then it sort of fell off, sank between the bones like the decrepit skin on burned gravy.

'László…'

Teddy became aware of the same thing at his jaw when he tried to speak, only whatever it was had dried on so tight, he could barely move his mouth. He turned his head. A curious stretching pulled on his skin as the parched covering was prized away from his throat and lifted across his collarbone. Scores of tiny lumps rose over his skin. He shivered and noticed now that his T-shirt was torn at the neck and drooped loose. In fact the front was ripped open and hung, heavily misshapen, caked in something thick and damp.

Teddy never left his shirt open or showed his chest. It just wasn't done. Not even on the ranch; too risky in the summer, too cold in the winter.

'Why do I need to get cleaned up?' His words came out slurred as he avoided further bubbling discomfort at his jaw and chin, 'What's this stuff?'

'Come, Fledermaus,' László said, 'let's get you home.'

László didn't answer the question. They emerged onto the wide back field. Without hesitation or mercy, the wind attacked. László's perfect hair was whipped high into the air. Immediately, as though recognising the master of the estate, it abandoned its assault and László's hair fell again knotted and tangled about his young, handsome face. Stampede strings. Teddy's hat had lost its stampede strings. Now the wind might take his hat.

The sodden brown clouds of evening had been blown away, silhouetting the estate against a sky that shimmered with an enchanting array of stars. So bright, it singed Teddy's eyes; the moon was aloof in a black ring of space. It was the Thunder Moon and it was huge; it belittled the house. The cowpokes in the doghouse had had a name for what it did tonight. What was it? An illusion?

The house, an eerie deception itself, may as well have been derelict as it was of course in darkness. László tossed his hair and set off towards it.

He muttered incomprehensible Old High German chunters as he picked his way across the grass, trying to avoid any molehills. Teddy couldn't stop his smile at László's fastidiousness. At this time of night, the ground would be recovering from the weather and the footfall he reckoned went with the day time, although no one ever came up here. The grass looked to Teddy to be as sumptuous as the Blue Room and he longed to lounge in it under the sun. László, on the other hand, would see only the inconvenience that the grass was set to cause. A bit like Teddy had with the chaise longue the night before.

Time, as usual, was moving forward and the field was moulting. László wouldn't like that so early on in the night, with no slummy to clean them, his polished boots would be wet and stuck with insipid, dead grass. László didn't do nature; he couldn't control it and he didn't seem to like anything that he couldn't control. Teddy's skin bristled and he came over uneasy.

They veered off course a little, avoiding one more large carcass. Its eyes still staring, its mouth still open as though screaming, its terror halted by its death. Whatever had attacked this one had really gone to work on it. Its antlers, the animal's inbuilt weapons, much like Teddy's own teeth, had been useless against its hellish attacker. This deer was the stag, the herds' guardian. Its neck had been all but torn away; chunky blood-encrusted cubes, the edges of which flapped in the wind like rejected suede swatch pads, were dispersed about the leech-infested carcass. The head remained attached to the body, but only by its stringy, sinewy spine. Fur, innards, flesh, lumps of unrecognisable hard stuff, hoof and antler were scattered about in dark, blood-coloured patches. The stag's attacker had pretty much destroyed the rest of it in the same way as it had the neck.

Teddy tried to get closer. He'd been transfixed by an obscene realisation. An insurmountably painful void lodged itself in his chest. It expanded then throughout his whole body, threatening to swallow him whole. Then it began to throb; harder and harder until it was all that he could hear, somewhere in the middle of his head.

László tried to tug him away, but he wouldn't go. He looked to the ground. Immediately, his eyes darted back up to his own body again. He stared at the remains of the stag and the stains in the grass, most of which wore the shape of cowboy boots. And they led his gaze on a damning trail the way that he and László had come — and back again. Fate, it seemed, had waited once again in the back of his subconscious, now it would emerge triumphant; somehow it had led him to stand in the exact same spot that the ripper had also stood. A ripper that wore boots with soles identical to his.

'No one ever comes here,' he said.

He followed the path of repulsive, bloody clues one more time and his eyes led his gaze up and along his own body. Horrifically, he pieced together the crime and the perpetrator.

'No how,' he cried, 'no ding how.'

He pushed himself away from László. The disgusting second skin, the fatigue and the nausea slipped into insignificance and he stumbled back towards the stag.

'Schatzi…' László started to say something.

'I did this,' Teddy interrupted.

Any strength he had deserted him, and he fell to his knees in the grass and the muck.

'László, I did this.'

He burned inside, he yearned to cry, but he had no tears.

'I butchered this stag. And I killed the herd.'

He began to howl and wail and moan, railing against the excruciating guilt that was tearing at his insides.

'Schatzibar,' László started again, 'you went on a bit of a, how you say, 'bender' this evening, that's all.'

Teddy reached out a shuddering, blood-coated hand and laid it reverently on the lifeless creature's muzzle.

'I'm sorry,' he whispered, 'I'm so sorry. I'm so, so sorry.'

Surely, if he kept saying it, the stag would hear, regenerate and jump back to life. And then he'd feel better. Maybe even let things get back to the wondrous way that they had been.

But it didn't happen. Nary one, did he feel any better. And he couldn't go back. Inside himself, right in the core of his being, he sensed badness, he'd do anything to turn back the clock, undo his sick, sadistic deeds. He was embarrassed, too, vulnerable and scared. He was ashamed. Truly ashamed. He'd never done anything so sickeningly contemptible before to be as ashamed as he was right now. Hang fire! Yes, he had. Deep inside, deep, deep down, he knew he had. It was just that, until now, he'd never consciously been faced with what he'd done. It was truly disgusting. He was truly disgusting.

Do something. He had to do something for this creature. It should be more than just a meal for these leeches. He grasped his hat by the crown, removed it slowly and set it brim-up on the ground beside him. Now he wasn't quite sure what to do.

'Sorry. I'm so sorry,' he said again.

He ran his dirty hand through his clean, fine hair.

'Come on now,' László said, 'let's go home.'

'No,' Teddy said.

He ran his hand through his hair a second time and stopped mid-scalp. He closed his fist, taking in a good clump and pulled as hard as he could. He pulled so hard that his head jerked, knocking him to the ground. Any sensation that he'd enjoyed earlier on had gone again.

'My herd!' he screamed. 'I killed my beautiful deer.'

He pushed himself back up and grabbed a fistful of hair with the other hand, the good hand, the four-fingered hand.

'I feel so terrible,' he said, yanking hard.

Outside, he sensed nothing. Only inside, it seemed, did he feel pain.

'Stop now,' László said.

'No!' he shouted.

He knelt and began thumping his thighs. He reached as far as he could down his back and dug his too long, grimy nails into himself, scraping them back up to his shoulders. He picked and prodded at his face and jabbed his fingers into his ears. But his body would not submit.

'How?' he raked at his neck. 'How can I deal out so much pain and terror and yet not feel anything? This ain't right.'

László crouched beside him. He grasped Teddy's face and forced him to look into his eyes.

'Stop this, Schatzibar,' he said. 'you can't hurt yourself.'

Teddy glared back at him. László's eyes were dead.

'It's what you are. This will happen again and again. It is inside you always.'

'It?' Teddy was incredulous. 'You mean like a beasty or something?'

László said nothing. He shifted and held Teddy close.

'Sakes alive, László, how did it get there?'

'Schatzibar,' László said slowly, 'you know all this. You know what you are. And what you have been.'

'No.' Teddy's voice was a strained growl. 'Get it, the deuce out.'

'I can't, Schatzi, you know that.'

Teddy stared at László.

'It was you, wasn't it? You put it there. And you made me do this. You made me into this thing, this monster, this murderer. I don't even know words vile enough to describe what you made me.'

Teddy scored his jeans with his nails, gathering shavings of dried blood and smearing them to a paste between his thumb and forefinger. What little he'd collected he daubed on László's face. But it was meaningless, hopeless; László loved it. He revelled in it. Hadn't he told him so last night? Hadn't he? He slapped László's hands away from his jaw.

'You made me do it.' He shook his head. 'Somehow. And then I wanted to do it again. And again. All because of you.'

'Teddy, mein Fledermaus,' László said.

'No!' Teddy shouted in his face, 'You told me, and you keep on telling me to go have me a hog killin' time. Only I wasn't killin' hogs. I was killin' people.'

He pressed his hands to his temples.

'It was what the people wanted me to do, you said. What they expected me to do. I shouldn't let them down.'

Now he knew what grooming was.

'You told me that if they found me they'd smash out my teeth, rip out my tongue, tear off my head, shear off my legs and arms and burn the rest. And then when you'd scared me almost irretrievably, you taught me to be just like you.'

László stood. The pleats of his second-hand frock coat wafted as though the ghost of its owner was trapped there, writhing in everlasting pain.

'You stroked and coaxed and complimented me to do as I was told. By you. Always by you.'

László folded his arms. He looked down at Teddy. His black eyes were blank; there was nothing in there. They weren't deep like the hypnotic voices in Teddy's head told him they were. And they weren't mystifying. They were empty, cold and flat. They held no feelings at all. Surely, though, Teddy was used to that. He must be. He'd been looking into those eyes for the past century or so. Now he came to think of it, László's emotions were only ever really apparent in his gesticulating. Teddy shook his head.

'Well, we gotta stop this now.' he frowned. 'It just ain't right. Not for me, not for no one and I cain't do it. I ain't no murderer.'

'Schatzibar, we can't stop.'

In one big picture show, the Clear Creek Bridge vampires came back to him. He hadn't wanted this back then either. It'd been his first time and he hadn't wanted to do it. He'd just murdered someone.

'Forget it. That's what you said. Forget everything. Everything. Never remember anything. Give up everything.'

'Is for your own good, Schatzi.'

'Why? You don't forget everything. In fact, I reckon you remember everything.'

He glared up at László.

'For over five hundred years?'

Disappointment flickered in László's eyes.

'At least that I know of,' Teddy snarled.

László was still patronising him. The anger boiled inside him. He was still falling for it. Teddy jumped up, although he wasn't too sure what his intentions were. To challenge László? That was just plumb loco, beef-headed. László was older, faster, stronger. He'd slog Teddy into next Sunday's cocked hat. If only Teddy knew when, where and what that was.

'And I'm still jawin' like it was 1887!' Teddy shouted. 'How come?'

His mind was at sixes and sevens.

''Sides the fact that you never let me go out, I cain't jaw normal. I ain't never learned to jaw normal. Why is that?'

'Schatzi, I don't keep you here,' László said, 'you can leave whenever you want to.'

'Quit yer yammering, László, you know, I cain't go anywhere without you.'

Teddy's stiff hands had begun to tremble. He looked down at them: the dried blood covering them was beginning to peel, adding horror to the anger. He tried to keep them still.

'I take you out, Teddy,' László said. 'I took you out just the other night.'

László smiled. Teddy could sense his superciliousness and he couldn't resist staring at him. László was gazing at him from under half-closed eyelids then he placed his hands on his hips.

'Mein Teddy. So that is what all this is about,' László said, 'You want to go out? Why didn't you just say so?'

This was László's attempt at friendly and open.

'What? No.' Teddy rubbed his forehead, a sandstorm of confusion was seeping in, 'You're twisting my words. I cain't go anywhere becase, I don't know anything. Becase, I only know what you say and that's killing and feeding and surviving and more killing.'

He raised one trembling, bloodied hand in front of László's face as if to show him that he intended to use it. László gave him an overacted withered look. Teddy overacted his defiance. He placed his hand flat on László's chest.

'You've been controlling me all along,' he said. 'Since 1887 when you took my memories, you've been filling me with anger and unleashing me when you need some murdering done.'

He shoved László. László didn't move, didn't even stumble. But his smile lengthened. It became real. His full, pink lips beamed with self-importance and his sharp, shovel-shaped teeth were laced with scorn. Pity and ridicule glazed the tip of each oversized canine like venom on the end of a Paiute arrow.

The wind, as though afraid of an approaching storm, had shrunk away to nothing and disappeared. László's hair, an obedient crimson veil, fell to his chest, serene and shining with his phoney supremacy. His beautiful face was rosy, peachy and forever young.

Underneath it all, in the glaring white light of the moon, was an unnatural greenish hue. Teddy had seen it before, a long time ago. The Devil was inside László. The sudden realisation hit him: the Devil had always been inside László. He wasn't hiding anymore.

'And whose fault is that?' László said.

Teddy's core began a shivering more deplorable, more ferocious than he'd ever seen in the soon-to-be-dead eyes of his prey.

'You knew what you were doing all those years ago,' László went on.

The shivers solidified into spasms at the top of Teddy's thighs, up around his ribs, through his limbs to his fingers where they took on an identity of their own. They probed and nagged Teddy to goad László until the Devil showed himself. He tried again to shove László. Again, László just stared at him.

'Are you saying that this was all my fault?'

'Yes, Schatzi, I am.'

Chapter Six

Teddy's anger was riled now. It wasn't the sadistic, sociopathic wrath that he'd inherited when he'd turned. This rage was all his own. It flowed through him, flourishing in the face of László's convictions. There was no way in tarnation that what the old vampire was saying was true.

'You seriously wanna try and convince me that becoming this murderous creature is what I wanted?'

He shoved László again. This time, László got his feet caught up in dead deer and briefly lost his balance.

'You were a slave,' László said.

No, that couldn't be true. Teddy advanced on him. It felt unnervingly true. He waited for him to regain balance and then shoved him off it again. László planted his booted feet and stood his ground.

'You lived in a basic bunk house with twenty-five other cowboys. You worked all day on your uncle's ranch and most of the night in his stables. You were only kept because you were free labour. Most nights, they beat you senseless for fun, see how much you could, how you say, "stand the gaff".'

Teddy was shaking both outside and inside now. He balled his fists and curled his lips.

'And did I? Stand the gaff, I mean.'

He didn't want to believe László, but it was impossible to come up with an alternative. His memory was patchy to say the least.

'You must have been staking me out. You seem to know all about me, more than I know right now?'

'I saved you from all that. If I hadn't, you would have soon been dead.'

László's concern was a whole heap excessive. His face creased up and he reached out to Teddy in a sort of quaking slow motion.

'They would have killed you,' he said, looking and sounding like he was about to cry.

They couldn't cry. Could they? Teddy didn't know what to believe.

'Teddy,' László cooed.

Something clicked inside Teddy's head. He was consumed by an inexplicable compulsion to silence himself, lower his hands, eyes, shoulders and anything else that might be seen as resistance.

'Come, Teddy.'

There it was again: "Teddy". László had used it last night. But "Teddy" was his name, wasn't it?

László stretched out the other hand to him. Teddy clapped his hands over his ears in an effort to shut László out. In the distant haze of his mind he heard voices, heavily accented Americans, the odd Spanish or English, all shouting short, familiar words. Whistles and hollers joined the melee in his mind, dust seemed to plug his nostrils. Had he breathed, he would have snuffed it out like a horse might've done. Trigger words. He knew all about using trigger words, in the Old West, they'd used them all the time to train the horses, the dogs, the animals. He jumped back, flailing his arms in an attempt to swat László's touch.

'Quit it, I ain't no animal,' he said quietly, 'and I don't know what you're talking about. I had a father, a mother, sisters and a home. I'm certain of it.'

Teddy stamped heavily on the gunk-covered ground as though that might get László out of his system.

'They were fine people, László. Good people.'

He shook his head: that's where memories were supposed to be stored, wasn't it? Scraping his scalp, he thumbed his temples trying to graunch his rusty memories to life.

'My sisters played the pianoforte,' he said. 'They mended my clothes for me and practised foreign languages on me.'

He scrunched his eyes shut, grasped his hair and pulled again.

'I helped them learn to dance, speak Spanish. Darn it, László, I used to speak a whole other language. And I taught them to ride. They trusted me. Sakes alive, I knew stuff. I was needed. Loved, even. I made my ma smile, I know I did and my pa was proud of me.'

'Is how you like to put it, Teddy, "corral dust"!' László took a step forward. 'Girls didn't ride. Teddy.'

Now his mind was split in two inside his head, if that was possible, and the two sides were at a stand-off. The trouble was he didn't know what to do to take charge. László took another step towards him.

'Don't touch me, László,' was all he could think of to say.

'They can't have loved you. Teddy,' László said.

'I said, "Quit it".'

'They made you do all those dangerous stunts in the rodeo.'

László was ignoring him.

'That's where I found you, Teddy. You were almost dead.'

'What? What happened to the slave? You're wrong. László. My pa...'

'You were the reason his rodeo was popular, Teddy. You were the reason for its success. Audiences flocked to see you. Your so-called 'family' took what you earned and kept you like a slave.'

'No, no that ain't right.'

Stop talking, László, he thought, you're bamboozling me.

'Your father handed you over to your uncle after every rodeo.'

László was in his head now.

'Get out of my head, László. I had a loving home. There is love in my memories.'

Something wasn't sitting right with it, though. There seemed to be a niggle of truth in what László was saying. Something wasn't fitting.

'Pa, I miss you!' he screamed. 'I wanna remember you, Pa.'

Aches that he'd believed he couldn't have throbbed in his head. Darn it, he needed to cry.

'Forget about it, Schatzi, it will only hurt you.'

The hole inside his chest, the one where his heart had been ballooned, seemed to expand. If he didn't do something to stop it, it would consume him, digesting him slowly from the inside out, wringing out indescribable pain. A pain that he deserved. He turned away from László.

'I cain't. I spent all ding day remembering it.'

Then he whirled back and launched himself at László.

'I tried to kill him!' Teddy wailed.

László merely moved his weight to his back foot and leaned away. Teddy, propelled by his anger but stalled by the disappearance of his target, lumbered onto the lawn.

'He was a good man, László. A good man.' He started back toward where László calmly stood. 'He loved me. I was his son and he had to shoot at me to get me to stall my mug, light a shuck...'

'Run away?'

Teddy paid him no mind. Great cramping pains, wave after wave, were swelling in his throat. He stopped. What was left of the decaying windpipes closed down and he bared his teeth, gagging and making a dry choking sound.

'What happened to my pa, László?' he growled. 'He would've gone insane wondering what happened to me.'

Teddy dove for László again. László grabbed his forearms and twisted them upwards. Teddy's feet skittered under him. He was immobilised.

'Stop this now, Teddy,' László said, glaring into his eyes. 'I've had enough.'

As though choreographed, László spun him around and from behind held him firmly in his arms. His long hands clinched Teddy's wrists like shackles, trussing his arms crossed over his chest, reining in any thoughts he might have of striking out.

'I only did what you told me to do,' László said, 'Teddy.'

His lips were so close to Teddy's ear. Teddy struggled: he wrenched his head to the side, he fought the submission that plagued his mind and the desire to give in again.

'Quit beatin' about the stump. I never told you to do nothing and you never do what I ask.'

He struggled again.

'László,' he added, using the same authoritative tone László had used.

It was stupid, ludicrous, downright horse feathers to think that he would've given up everything he'd had, for anything, least of all László. His memory may have been a tumultuous mix of steaming belly-wash right now, but one thing he knew for sure was that his family had been precious to him.

'There is no way. No way in tarnation would I have wanted you to turn me into this thing.'

He wriggled and stamped, trying to drive his Cuban heels into László's feet.

'This sick, brainwashed, cold-blooded murderer, constantly and completely manipulated by you.'

His goried, ripped T-shirt flapped and his blood-encrusted jeans creaked and snapped as he bucked against his captor's body.

'Let go of me,' he cried, 'I cain't abide your closeness.'

'Is like I said, Teddy,' László told him, his voice melodious again, the vowels rounded and the consonants soft, 'they made you perform in the rodeo. If you had not, they would have thrown you out of your home. I suppose it was only to be a matter of time until you had an accident which was fatal, ya? You remember?'

Teddy stopped moving. He hung his head, his chin almost touching his chest, and frowned deeply. Would László never stop?

'No,' he said.

'There, see, is better that way, ya?'

'But I will remember.'

He scrunched up his eyes. Rodeo. What had the rodeo looked like? Horses. He could remember horses alright. Far away in his mind, he heard the high-pitched screams of a horse in distress.

'Do not remember, Teddy. Is not advisable.'

Teddy squeezed his eyes. The horse, his horse, still screamed. He winced and tugged on his arms.

'Dang,' he said, 'I will remember.'

He tried to calm himself. Amidst the noise of the horse, there was something else: voices and lots of them. He couldn't make out what they were saying. He could tell, though, that they were exclaiming, gasping, shouting out. He saw his hands: they were gloved and grasping the reins. Beyond them, he saw the sky. It was blue, cloudless, and the sun scorched his eyes. Smudges of brown dust, insipid dry seeds and dismembered bits of grass tarnished that perfect sky. It was the rodeo in Kansas. And he was falling, backward. His horse had grassed him good.

'There was an accident,' he said dismally.

'You see, Schatzi,' László said, 'I am right. I am always right.'

László's lips were so close to his neck that he could feel them. They tickled his skin as László spoke. It made him twitch. It wasn't a pleasant twitch. And that made László grin, tighten his hold around Teddy and jolt him upwards and into him. Teddy's ribs twanged and he threw his head back as he stamped down again. His sense of touch had chosen now to return?

'You can feel that?' László said.

He squeezed Teddy harder until they both heard a rib crack. Teddy glowered, trying to keep still.

'I put the tie cord in my teeth,' he said, teasing forth the memory of his time at the rodeo, 'Just like I always did.'

His ribs throbbed: he needed to use his mind to blot out the pain, but he could not risk using it for anything other than dissecting the memory of the accident. If he allowed himself to be distracted now, he'd lose it again.

'What about when I do this?' László mused, nuzzling into his neck. 'Can you feel this?'

'No,' Teddy lied.

The revolting feel of László's opening mouth brushed against his neck.

'I gathered up my rope,' he said, 'just like always.'

He was talking faster. László's teeth grazed his neck. His sense of touch was growing stronger. As was the memory. It was as though the two were linked.

'I spurred my horse into top speed. Then I nodded for the calf to be released.'

No. No, he hadn't. He hadn't got that far. There was a second, although it seemed longer, when he did not feel László at his neck. A warm, innocent breeze kissed his skin and ruffled his hair. Then pain. Tearing, bursting, searing pain.

He screamed, crowbarred his hips into László's body and bent double so quick, it took László off guard. With all the might of one with a cracked rib and pierced neck, he hurled László over his shoulders. László spun gracefully through the night air. His boots glinted in the moonlight, the frock of his coat fanned about his thighs. Clearly much, much more wily than ever Teddy had given him credit for, he landed lightly on his feet.

'You will not remember, Teddy!' he shouted.

'Why in the dickens not?!' Teddy shouted back, 'Me and that horse were tight. She'd never have grassed me.'

He ran a hand through his hair. His hat. Where was his hat? He'd rested it brim-up on the ground. He scoured the area for it.

László bowled into him. Hooking him under the chin, he seized a clump of his hair and dragged him towards the house.

'I don't care about that ludicrous horse. If you remember, you will be defunct, you will not have worked, I will have to get rid of you. And I don't want to have to do that.'

Dumbfounded by László's latest revelation, Teddy's mind cleared like an emptied ash hopper. The glorious Technicolor images of his memory faded to sepia and then black and white and finally nothing. Nothing. His sense of touch shinned out, too, it seemed.

'No,' he moaned, 'gone. Cain't lose them again.'

'All my hard work,' László was saying, even now he wasn't listening to Teddy, 'rubbished because you have to have memories. And feelings. And love.'

He stopped, twisted the knot in Teddy's hair, hollered "love" in Teddy's ear and started trudging towards the house again. Teddy stumbled along behind him.

'All that persuading and cajoling you to forget everything, all that rationalising with you not to remember anything new. And the pathetic, gooey, sentimental hocus-pocus about feelings. And family. And belonging. All the time.'

Family. As though booted hard, Teddy's mind began to work again. His scalp stung and his ear rang. He saw his pa's face. It was so clearly defined in his memory, it could have been just hours since he'd last seen him. His thick, silver hair, cultured and refined by the near-black lowlights of its original colour, was being harassed by Kansas prairie wind. His rational, reasonable rancher's eyes, dark and friendly like night-time cocoa were weeping, full of fear and regret and his face was stricken with grief. He held Teddy's hand, gloveless now, its middle finger missing, the others twitching, and he raised it to his lips, kissed it and pressed it to his cheek. Teddy sensed no recollection of the sensation of his father's kiss, his lips on his skin, the tears on his cheek or even just his hand's movement.

'Please, don't die, son,' his pa said, his Midwestern accent broken and wretched. 'I love you.'

Love. Family. Belonging. It wasn't hocus-pocus at all.

'I gave you so much of my precious time and attention,' László was droning on, 'and you wasted it.'

For the past one hundred years or so, since that afternoon in Kansas, all he'd known was anger. So much anger, and to acknowledge the corn, Teddy had never quite known what to do with it. Well, now he did.

Teddy stood up straight, wedging László's arm in his throat. László, brought up short behind him, tightened his fist in Teddy's hair. The ripping sensation was acutely painful again. Teddy balled his fists. Thunderation, he was taller than László. How come he'd never noticed that before?

'Yup.' Teddy grasped László's arm and bent at the knee enduring the pulling of his hair. 'Wasted.'

Springing straight upwards, he made sure he took László with him. László relinquished Teddy's hair. Teddy whirled around and, clutching László by the frock-coat lapel, he held him close and slogged him a few times in his perfect, young face.

'You gave me anger!' he shouted.

He thrust László brutally to the uneven ground miles below.

'Nothing else.'

Darn it. He was falling, too. He hadn't thought about how he'd get back down. Without the momentum he'd just given László, and with a lack of body mass, he wafted to the ground like a dead hackberry leaf.

As soon as he landed, László met him with an effortless blow that sent him reeling back across the lawn. He registered that pain, too, but only slightly: his senses once again were fading. Handy, really, because a wallop like that would have taken any normal person's head clean off. Teddy flipped swiftly to his feet. But the older vampire stood over him and slapped him back to the floor.

'Is that why you never let me remember anything?' Teddy said. 'I might remember the wrong thing.'

'No,' László said, 'is not.'

Subduing László was like trying to catch a weasel asleep: never gonna happen. Teddy, however, found a deep-rooted recklessness and it kept him from accepting this and his own fate. He flipped up again. Again, he was slapped back down. This time, he fell a little further away.

'C'mon, László,' he said, 'clear it up for me, how did it happen?'

His individuality, the optimism that he'd been keeping hidden, ran unchecked and he provoked László for answers.

'How did you turn me?'

He twisted and, jumping to his feet, tried to run.

'Is not important. Especially now.'

Behind him, László pushed him back down. He landed on his face.

'You allers say that,' Teddy said through a mouthful of grass. 'Why, dang you, "especially now"?'

'Blaznit, Teddy.' László placed one booted foot on Teddy's back between the shoulder blades where his hands couldn't reach. 'Is unfortunate for us both. I am going to have to take you to pieces. Is that how you say it?'

He laughed in a self-congratulatory way.

'I mean really take you to pieces. Is me that will rip off your limbs and tear off your head. Unlike the sappy humans, I will leave you with your tongue. So that we can talk while I do it. You can tell me how it feels. But then, I will have to burn all the pieces.'

The foot was heavy and it pressed down on Teddy's back like a wayward anvil.

'Including your head.'

'It's more than I deserve,' Teddy said.

His body bucked involuntarily against the vice-like boot, his hands pushed at the ground, and his knees tried to curl under him. But László's foot had him hobbled to the floor.

'I'd rather die than be your servant,' he said.

Something stirred then inside him. The thing trembled as though fearsomely crying. His insides, although he'd never before considered that he had any, crumpled, immediately stretching out again. Somewhere around his middle something was spiralling around. It wound around his spine and he opened his mouth wide, letting out a howl of anguish.

'There is one thing about playing in the woods with a vampire who knows infinitely more about vampirism than you do,' László said. 'I managed to pick up a broken branch. Is an ancient oak. Older than you, I think. Unlike you, it smells divine.'

Teddy glared at the house. From where he lay it was beautifully appliquéd with blades of grass. It was his house, László had told him, but it was the last place that he wanted to be.

'Can't have you wriggling away while I dispose of you now, can I?'

László, the blatherskite, he never stopped enjoying the sound of his own voice. You'd think that over hundreds of years, he'd have gotten used to it. Teddy dropped his head, smoothing his cheek in the grass where he'd whiled away so many hours, blissfully oblivious to the wealth of life he'd left behind. Somewhere a blackbird sang him a lullaby. The thing inside Teddy set about struggling again.

'Killing you now, is the, how you soppy vampires like to put it, the humane thing to do. You have memories now. You are in misery. So ...'

'Shoot, László,' Teddy said, 'or give up the gun.'

His words were almost lost and came out garbled in amongst the involuntary howling. Had he been a God-fearing man? Had he believed in Hell? If, indeed there was such a place, then that was where he was headed. He closed his eyes. He didn't care.

We must survive.

A voice that sounded like his own spoke to him. It was in his head and it had a weird kind of independence.

'My hat,' Teddy groaned. 'If I'm gonna die, at least let me do it with my hat on.'

László might have had more than five hundred years' head start on him. But he was missing one vital ingredient: humility.

'My hat,' Teddy wailed, 'where is my hat?'

Teddy, on the other hand, might not be the best in a fight, but he was one of the best cowpunchers. He knew the land, and the sky and the way it worked. He knew critters, the way they talked, the way they thought and the way they hunted. Tracking and spotting the almost imperceptible lack of concentration in any predator was in his nature.

'Give me my hat.'

'Your hat?' László laughed.

Vanity. Now László had a whole heap of that.

'Is funny, ya?'

And overplaying it.

'Your hat is finally mine.'

And that made him complacent. Teddy folded his elbows upwards, flattened his hands on the grass and kicked out. Pushing off his hands at the same time, he propelled himself forward like a man-sized mudskipper. László's self-satisfied narcissism knocked him to the ground and he sat there, clutching his oak stake.

Promptly, Teddy kicked out again, uprighted himself and swiped the stake away from László. It whirled rustically back into the woods, knocking against more than one tree trunk as it fell.

'László, you predictable old slang-whanger, you never could resist a show of smugness.'

Uncertainty replaced the arrogance in László now.

'You're pathetic,' Teddy said, grasping László's clothes, pulling at his hair, batting away his flailing hands as he hauled him to his feet and up.

'You feeling me now?' he snarled. 'Well, I'm gonna take this Devil's head clean off.'

There was something else in László's eyes. It wasn't the Devil anymore. What was it? Fear?

'You were going to murder me,' Teddy's voice said.

He couldn't be sure just who or what was in control of his body. If László was afraid of him, then it couldn't be him he was looking at. Could it? He was confusing himself now. He wasn't scary, though, he knew that. At least he didn't want to be.

'László,' he said slowly, as though testing out his own voice, 'you ain't never gettin' your hands on my hat.'

'Schatzibar,' László squeaked, his voice slick with relief, 'Fledermaus, is just a hat, ya?'

Teddy screamed. Now he was angry. László grimaced.

'You jest don't get it, do you? My hat was never "just a hat".'

Just how special it was, he wasn't too sure. The stub of his lost finger tingled, as though to remind him of the memories that were striving to resurface.

'Teddy'…

'Shut it, László.'

He clutched László's neck in one hand, pinching with his thumb, squeezing with his forefingers. László stared at him: that fear was there again. Teddy grasped a handful of hair and yanked László's head back. He pulled him close and hissed into his ear.

'So now it's my turn and I'm gonna return the favour. Except I am gonna wrench out your tongue becase it's the most annoying thing about you. And when I'm done and you're cashed in, I'm gonna throw the whole lot in through that front door over yonder, set flames to it all and watch it burn to the ground.'

Still a nub of pity stabbed at the inside of his chest. It threatened to overthrow his newfound empowerment. He clenched his fists and his toes in an effort to ward it off. It niggled. A squirming little intensity somewhere inside.

'Do it, then,' László said, holding his gaze. 'I murdered you. Of course you want to take your revenge.'

'You what? You did what?'

'Kill me, Schatzi.'

Teddy howled.

'Isn't that what you want to do?'

No. It wasn't what Teddy wanted at all. He didn't want to be a killer, he never had wanted to be a killer. He stared down at himself. Everything about himself was frayed from the wear and tear of living from one hour to the next. Even László in all his finery looked shabby. The air felt dense. The sky having clouded over again was now a murky brown colour. The clock in town, or was it the city, or even out to sea, struck midnight and the blast of the last train blew through the dark. Teddy looked back at László.

'Is what you want, isn't it, Schatzi?'

The glimmer of emotion Teddy had seen in László's eyes had disappeared, swallowed back down, sucked into the bag of horror that was his existence. He stared at Teddy and his lips stretched over his teeth. Teddy saw no more than a healthy corpse with a self-congratulatory smile.

'Go to blazes!' he hollered, throwing László at the house. 'You even control my anger and my hate.'

Teddy ran. Leaping over the slaughtered deer, he had to get some distance between them. He couldn't outrun László. If it came down to a fight then he'd lose. Humility. Thanks to László, humility was something that Teddy had heaps of. It would always be there, on his side, reminding him that murder was wrong. But against László, that was not a good thing.

'Never,' he said, 'ever will I kill again.'

Putting a spring in his stride, he headed for the trees, pumping his arms, stomping his feet. He hoped he knew these woods better than László.

'You will not persuade me to,' he said over and over again, chanting like it would gee him up, 'ever again.'

'Go, then!' László shouted.

Teddy ran on. He had to get away.

'It's not like you haven't done this before,' László continued to shout. 'You'll come back when you lose track of time. You always do.'

Teddy didn't know if what László said was true. He hated to think it might be. He jabbed the toe of his boot into the soft, black peat of the forest floor and catapulted himself into the trees. Hand over hand he climbed, the luminescent lichen providing spongy friction while showing the way. He was lighter than the leaves, he swung his thighs, stretched his waist and hooked with his knees: his own momentum moved him forward fast. He dove between boughs then darted along the branches, slipping only once; cowboy boots were not made for tightrope running. He swapped to the next tree and the next until there were no more.

At the top, he stopped short.

'Now you listen to me, László,' he said, 'I'm gonna have my say now. I don't need you no more and sure as darn it, I don't want you. What I need is me, the cowpuncher. That boy didn't want to kill anyone. Nary one was he full of hate and I sure-fired don't think he ever got angry. But see, when he's around you, that's all he wants to do: kill and hate and be angry. So, you just stay away from me. You sabby?'

László didn't answer. Teddy surveyed the countryside below him. A prairie-like meadow sprawled over the rise and fall of the land. The dark streak of what could've been a fox, although it was quite large, pottered about, poking its nose into the undergrowth. Beyond that a long and crumbling drystone wall. The estate's border. He'd never ventured any further than the woods. At least he didn't think he had. Certainly, he'd never crossed that wall. Not by himself anyway. Not that he could remember.

A vagueness blanketed him. His escape was thwarted and he was immobilised there at the top of the trees, right on the edge of freedom. What now? Where to now? He'd always just done what László had told him, always come home when László called, fed when László said and slept when László told him to. Without László, he wouldn't even know what day it was, the time or anything. Where was his mother's voice now, warning him to think, telling him to take care? Where was the range Caporal reminding him to consider the code before he acted? He turned and looked back across the estate.

'Schatzibar,' László's silken, sing-song voice slunk across the treetops like an airborne serpent, 'come home now.'

László wasn't ordering him. He'd never actually ordered him to do anything. He was simply calling him home. Teddy flinched. He was reminded how the cowpokes had chirked their horses when they wanted them to get going. Had László done that to him?

But that house, this estate, wasn't home. As of now, he was homeless. He had an inkling that he'd been homeless before. Well, he must've survived it, then; he could do it again.

This was it, then. Perhaps this was the point in the past when he'd sloped back to László, eyes down, tail between his legs. His imagination, untethered now, started down the route of what might have followed; so he stopped it. He didn't have a tail. And he wasn't about to grow one.

Keep going, he reckoned, while the need to get away was still strong. Run far away from László, stop for the day somewhere sheltered and then, as soon as the sun goes down, start running again.

'Teddy. Come home now.'

Never, he thought, this is not my home. I ain't never coming back.

He jumped out of the tree. Launching himself as far as he could, stretching out his arms, his hands, stump and all, he strained, yearning to feel the tiny, fragile bones at the tips of his fingers pushing against his skin as he reached for freedom. Nope, nothing.

There was no stopping him now. However graceful it may have started out, his flight petered just before the wall. He waved his arms like a defunct churn-twister's windmill and made it over the old country road. With his feet above his head, he skidded face first and smacked into the hedgerow. Righting himself, he set off at a trot, rolling his eyes at the slight click of his Cuban heels on the broken-up asphalt.

Unsure of how his future mind would work, let alone his body, it made sense that the more difficult it would be to get back to László, the more likely, when the inevitable desire arose, that he wouldn't do it. Or he'd die trying.

With a smidgen of luck, in time he would stop hearing László's blatherskite voice in his head, too. Or he'd come up with a way to block it. He'd definitely never be under his control again. Never, ever again. Not for as long as he lived. Or something like that. Vampires were supposed to be immortal, weren't they? That was a whole heap of time.

'Fly at it, Hossy Stink!' he hollered, vaulted over the wall and sped into the countryside.

Chapter Seven

Teddy didn't have breath to lose or ligaments to stitch. With each stride, leap or footfall, adrenaline pounded around his limbs. He whooped and grinned, wantonly giving in to the mischievous abandonment filling his head. Open-armed, he embraced the ache to accelerate like it was an old accomplice, a soulmate, Blue Scrub. For a moment, he knew a sensational, seamless relation to the cowpoke on the range. It was a little like they were one in the same person. Hang fire: that is exactly what they were. He'd just never really known it is all. Until now.

A scrubby mound ripped the field in two. Teddy slowed and trudged up the hill. Ribbons of steel track, so smooth, so exquisite, ran along the top. The railroad. Teddy squinted, following their lead into the distance. He saw wondrous things, magical colours drifting on the waves of the countryside breeze: they danced with the squeaking of moths in the moonlight. Fantastic though his sight was, it couldn't see through objects or round bends, and his view was thwarted by a tree-lined lane.

Teddy crouched and reached a flat hand out to the rails. A scratch of a memory came to him. He fought the urge to linger there and indulge in it. He lost the fight. So clear it was almost real was the hustle and bustle of a railroad station. He was alone, either waiting for someone, or had just dropped someone off; his memory wasn't that clear. He savoured the busyness of others, the carpet bags and hatboxes. He was gripped by a restraint both anxious and excited that the train's whistle might go off at any second consuming him in scalding steam. When had he ever had the chance to be so childish?

The rails flashed like polished silver, strong, still and foreboding, but the ones under his hand buzzed, the air around them sizzling, which filled him with a weird sort of foreboding. He withdrew his hand and looked up to the stars as though the timetable was posted there. The stars told him nothing, although they were plentiful and they did look enchanting. He frowned. He should be able to tell the time by the stars and which way he was headed. As it was, he had no idea when the next train would come thundering through here. Or where it was headed.

He followed the train tracks, kicking up stray ballast as he went, cussing the dust that flew with it. It wasn't long before he grew bored of walking and picked up speed again. Gathering momentum, he launched himself into the air. His bloodied T-shirt slicked itself to the contours of his body, creasing and undulating as he flew. His belt buckle, the heaviest thing about him, tipped and strained against the forces of nature to keep his gore-stiffened jeans in place.

The railroad banked around a bend. Teddy flew straight across the line of trees and the lane that the tracks sought to miss. A typically old country hedge, recently laid, no doubt making the farmer proud, bordered the opposite side just where Teddy's flight died a natural end. Sturdy, oaky-looking stakes were braided together by some or other malleable and bountifully leaved tree. Teddy's flight arc tumbled towards them. The desire to avoid being impaled and subsequently discovered by daytime became a disembodied panic. It blinkered him. All he could think of was missing those stakes. He scrambled mid-air, looking like the cowboy-booted ghost of Johnny Reb fleeing the rifle-flooded battlefield.

He managed to grab the bough of one of the perimeter trees and swung himself out into the air again. He soared across the yellow planted field, rolling and twisting and smiling.

As though swallowed up by a mist that encroached on his space, bringing bitter reality to his quality pleasure time, Teddy forgot about his love of speed. He knew he was running away from somewhere, leaping and flying, but he couldn't think where or what from. And at such a speed, covering such a distance. Whatever it was, it didn't seem as important as it had at the start. And where was he going to?

His surroundings became no more than an annoyance. He wanted to stop. No, he had to stop, had to get his head back together. He just didn't know how to stop.

Elongating and flattening his shape had maximised his launch: surely shortening and balling himself up would minimise it. Following his own reasoning he curled his knees under his belly and hugged them.

He bowled into the earth, barrelling along for some considerable distance in a compendium of scrunched rolls, flailing twists and uncoordinated somersaults. The stems of whatever yellow-flowered crop this never-ending field was planted with were strong as corral poles, but they were not nearly sturdy enough to stop him. They curbed his progress, though, and eventually he came to a stop.

Holed up under the plants he sat, dishevelled, dilapidated and blobbed with yellowy-orange something or other.

'In all my born years,' he said, 'I haven't perfected an emergency stop?'

Gallingly, he couldn't remember ever having needed one. He shook his head. His memories, what few he had, were fading fast. He'd just crash-landed in what looked to be the pride of agriculture and he hadn't felt a thing.

Teddy resorted to his usual irrational action when faced with dilemma: he raised his hand to remove his hat and ran his fingers through his hair.

His hand was still caked in grime, too much to inflict on his hat, so he slapped it back to his knees.

He smiled, though the hat-shifting, the hand-running and the hair-raking was a habit László had allowed him to hang onto. László. Old, eccentric vampire who lived in his house, condescending old croaker who'd stolen his memories, sadistic liar who'd controlled him for over one hundred years. That was what he was running from.

Anger, the innate emotion of vampire kind, blazed throughout his body. He stood, intent on laying waste to the entire field. The flowers capered about daintily with his every move. The wind set them rolling like the No Man's Land Flint Hills, covered with big bluestems. Except these were yellow, and cultivated, and this wasn't Kansas. He grasped one of the plants, its stem woody in his fingers, ripped its heavy root ball from the ground and hurled it as far as he could. The scent of cabbage filled the air. He growled. He hated cabbage. Or any kind of vegetables for that matter. The flowers swayed again which, for some reason, frustrated him further; their uselessness was equal only to the witlessness of the farmer who chose to sow his entire field with gaudy, yellow flowers.

He made to stomp down on the plants, but he couldn't. He couldn't seem to get it together. His feet refused to go where his mind was messaging them to. He tried again. The energy of trying tired him out and he sank back to the ground. Sitting there, resting back on both hands, gazing at the sky, the bridge of his nose and the rims of his eyes smarted dully like they were out of date and therefore no longer able to support his flesh. A palpable, fatigued sort of toxin plodded along the inside of his limbs, his elbows gave way, and he crumpled flat on the ground where the leaves adorned the lower half of the stems like the skirts of the Cheyenne women. His belly weighed heavy as though to become his body's anchor while consciousness took leave.

Daytime!

The ground around him writhed and rippled, full of bugs and worms, and he was aware he was lying on the homes of a multitude of miniscule critters. He lay still. What the dickens difference would a few interloping grubs make to the state he was already in? His spot in amongst the flowers was homely now. He liked it there.

Just a moment longer, then he'd move. The soil was blocky and coffee-coloured. Teddy crumbled it between his grubby fingers and it smeared his skin, drying quickly and cracking when he creased his joints. He couldn't feel it. Darn it, his sense of touch had shinned out again. The bugs began beeping, foraging and chirruping loudly. So loud, in fact, he couldn't be sure if it was because of his deviant undead ears or simply the tranquillity of having sole occupation of the field.

'Quit yer bellerin',' he said. 'You're louder than a mauled charivari mumpin' for tonsil paint.'

He couldn't silence them.

'P'shaw, it ain't no great shakes.'

Nature, of which it seemed he was a freak, was a constant. It would continue to roll on through the years. It was like the cowpokes and the Longhorns. Unhurriedly, they moved with nature and nary one would they be halted. Perhaps he should do the same.

Perhaps, without László to remind him to hate everything, he'd learn to appreciate the hellabaloo of the bugs.

He lingered there for one moment more. Perhaps, after all, he'd been wrong to leave László. To acknowledge the corn, László had always been there for him. There was no denying that, for over a century, Teddy had relied on him.

László. There was something off about him, wasn't there? Something not quite right. Something an itty bit pokerish. What was it he'd said again?

'Darn it, Ted, cain't you remember?'

Was this going to be how it was every morning? He'd forget everything, all the new things that he'd learned, all that he'd struggled to remember. He didn't want to forget. Surely that meant that he shouldn't have to; not if he didn't want to. It was his memory after all. Wasn't it?

He liked that unstoppable smile that came with the spur-of-the-moment remembrance of someone, somewhere, something good. Something that he loved. Surely, he could nurture his memory, train it somehow. He had memories, he knew he did. He had the body of a twenty-year-old; he must've got to twenty somehow. He had the mind of a cowpoke and he talked funny, he said things others wouldn't understand. He had to have lived at some point.

Then there was his hat. Who would put so much stock in a hat? He reached up to take it off, comb back his hair with his defective hand and replace it. The hat wasn't there.

'Where is my hat?' he said.

He always wore his hat. Some momentous occasion must've been happening for him to have taken his hat off. He squirmed over, planted one hand on the ground and pushed himself to his feet. The birds, small enough to hop about in the hedgerows, started up a raucous, unharmonised racket.

'Darn it!' he hollered at them. 'Where's my hat?'

They didn't answer, of course. He couldn't talk to birds. He shook his head and closed his eyes trying to remember where he'd been the last time he'd had it. His memory had come over cloudy again.

'Sakes alive! Where the dickens is my hat?'

He was having trouble remembering anything at all.

'Think.'

He'd been running, leaping and doing his darndest to fly. If his hat had come off in flight, it should be nestling leisurely atop this crop. The hat was black, the flowers were yellow; it should be easy to see. He scoured the vibrant scene top to bottom, left to right, straining his eyes, overtaxing his sight. No hat. He searched along the path of destruction his tumbling had left behind. Still, he couldn't see his hat.

'This ain't right,' he said.

The hat should not have fallen off. It wouldn't do for a cowpoke's hat to go flying off as soon as his Quarter took off now, would it? He raked his hair, it was sticky. He felt that sickly, shameful drain on his insides again; he couldn't remember if he'd had stampede strings on his hat. He hobbled back the way he'd come through the middle of the plants. Perhaps he just couldn't see it.

He tried to run. The edge of the field with its vanquishing hedge came all too soon. There was no hat caught in the trees. He laid his hands on the top of the hedge. It wasn't very tall, waist height at most. His arms were weak but he was lighter than air, he should be able to vault over it. His fingers wouldn't curl around the heathering at the top.

He tried to push the hedge down. It wouldn't budge. It was as though he did no more than stroke it, except he couldn't feel anything. It was too late. His body was dying again. He dropped to his knees, his slurred cusses were drowned out by the tuneless squawking of crows or rooks or whatever large bird inhabited the trees lining the broken-down road on the other side of the hedge.

Oh, dear Schatzibar.

László's voice was in his head again. He huddled, hiding his face between the twiggy hedge and his defective hand. László didn't need to see his face, though, he'd know what he was going through. They'd spent so many years together and staying out late was something László had warned him not to do. He'd be only too aware and, very probably, pleased about Teddy's hopelessness, not to mention his clumsiness and just plain addleheadedness.

You stayed out too late.

He was so patronising. Teddy scrunched up as small as he could.

After everything that's happened to you tonight, you're left with nothing in your head.

László was right. As usual. Teddy's head was a blank space.

'László,' he whined.

He had to tell László something. It was something important. It was something about his own future. He grinned to himself, in his self-made den. He always had something to tell László. László was the only one he ever spoke to.

And nothing on your head.

A colourless vacuum manifested itself in Teddy's chest. It hurt.

Fledermaus, you aren't wearing your hat.

Teddy groaned.

'You have it.'

It was as though his heart had just disintegrated, just now; torn away while he was alive. He opened his eyes as high and deep as they would go, he stretched his mouth wide in a silent scream and grimaced in on himself.

I always knew I'd get it.

The void started to throb. He scrunched his face up. Did László know about this thing in his chest?

Didn't I always tell you I'd take your hat?

No, he couldn't. The overblown braggart would have claimed ownership of it by now. Whatever it was, it was more powerful than the daytime fatigue. The fatigue didn't hurt, it just drained.

Didn't I, Teddy?

Teddy lifted his head. He frowned. This yellow field wasn't familiar. He pushed himself back up to kneeling and looked around. Where was he?

You left it here, Teddy.

He hung his head and gazed at his grimy hands as they rested on his thighs.

With me.

The pain in his chest seemed to send out tendrils sparking and stabbing as they went. They coiled around his spine, escalating the hurting, filling him with soul-destroying sadness. Teddy flinched. This pain rang familiar. László had stolen something. Something that had belonged to him. What was it?

Teddy. László snapped.

Teddy raised his head wearily.

'Come get me, László,' he said.

I can't, Schatzibar, I don't know where you are.'

'I ran away,' Teddy said.

Just like a proper insubordinate twenty-year-old, he struggled with the suggested stupidity of what he'd just done and tried to justify it against the validity of his reason for doing so. He just couldn't remember what that reason was.

Come home and you can have your hat back.

'Home,' he said.

Above him a kestrel shrieked. They had those, kestrels, back in No Man's Land. And in Kansas. He smiled and began rocking gently. He gazed from under half-closed eyelids at the vibrant beauty of the pasture in front of him. He saw ten-foot golden-green corn stalks, swaying with the promise of freedom as far as the eye could see. From somewhere across the fields he heard the ornery lowing of cows. Longhorns? There was the banter of a cowpoke crew, their boots scraping on wooden corrals as they climbed to sit on the top.

Now that was home. He didn't need a stately home with a Blue Room and a swimming pool. A swimming pool, darn it, that was just plumb horse feathers. He hated lounging around. And he definitely did not need, what did László call it, Bear-rock? Or Roco-cock? Baroque, that was it. No. Hang fire. Baroque was a breed of horse. Whatever László called it, it was detailed, delicate, ornamental doohickeys. More like a load of high falutin', piddling, no-how indulgence. Darn it, sometimes he didn't even need a roof over his head. The stars were canopy enough.

'Hide,' the unfamiliar voice in his head urged; the voice with the twang of a Midwestern cowpoke. 'Cut sticks and hole up somewhere.'

Teddy fell to all fours. The stems here were patchy: their broken shoots scratched him and one or two tiny brown stones cut into his hands. Something had brought his senses to life again.

Your hat, Teddy, László said, louder now, more insistent, *you should have taken better care of it. Perhaps you will next time, ya? Come home and get it.*

Someone else had told him to take care. Someone he loved.

'I will,' Teddy said.

A woman was singing somewhere. "Git Along Little Doggies". She pounded bread dough in time with the "whoopie ti yi yos". Abruptly, the woman stopped singing as though she knew he was watching her. She smiled and switched to some or other Sunday morning hymn. Then absently, wistfully she told him to "Take care" and "Stamp your boots" and "Mind your hat."

'Ma?' he said slowly. 'Ma told me to take care.'

Teddy closed his eyes and for a moment basked in the wheaty scent of biscuits browning and cakes baking, all embroiled in the bitterness of caffeine brewing.

'Take care, Ma,' he slurred.

Home, László said, *come home.*

'Home,' Teddy said again.

A lone prairie wolf howled. The others wouldn't be far behind.

'Hide,' the creature inside Teddy urged.

'Ma, I …' Teddy wanted to tell her that he loved her.

While he was alive, he hadn't told her and he panicked at the thought that she might not know. But 'I love you' just wouldn't come out. He had a truly dreadful feeling that had happened to him before, too.

'I didn't take care, Ma,' he cried.

The kestrel screeched again. Breakfast time. Teddy heard the bird's wings swooping: the air whizzed with the power of its dive, and its prey screeched. The ground chirruped almost as one. It made him jump. Teddy glared at the garish yellow haze before him. Yellow, the colour revered by the Iowa tribe, the colour of day, of sunshine, hope and happiness. None of which he could have. Sunshine was something he reviled now. He never had before. He loved to be outside. His hat had always protected him from any stroke the sun strove to give him.

Home, László said.

'Hole up.'

Hat.

The hole in Teddy's chest returned, his body slumped, and he howled in pain. His mind meandered about and he thought he heard someone offering him a smoke.

'Quit it,' he murmured. 'Can't breathe.'

'Smoke!' the voice said again.

'I said, I quit it.'

The voice hadn't been in his head. Nary one had it called him or cooed to him or condescended like László did. It had no accent – no Midwestern twang and no Hungarian melody. He sat up on his haunches, momentarily alert. And then his mind slid back into a hotchpotch mire. He tried to still it, to listen out the way he knew, the way he'd been taught by some or other ranger on some or other ranch. There was that flare of self-worth, the same one that he'd felt in the stables on László's, no, his own estate. And there was the smile, too. He raised his face to look into the trees.

He couldn't see properly, it was like looking through a knothole, his peripheral sight had died. What he could see, he didn't know. He had no idea where he was, what was around him. Nary one could he keep it together long enough to piece the landscape into any useful kind of habitat.

He placed a hand flat on the ground: could he use the skills László had given him? No. He couldn't feel a thing. He was too tired and in this state, he had nothing. Except the unmistakeable sound of László laughing in his head.

You are dying, ya.

'Damn you to blazes, László,' he cried, 'damn you and all your blarney. You made me an outlaw. The worst that I ever did was pirooting a painted lady. And I only did that once.'

A snuffling and snorting disturbed the undergrowth not far from where he was sitting. It was followed by an excited panting. The wolf? No, the footsteps were small, and if it were a wolf, it would be howling by now. Instead, it barked. A dog, he didn't need any expertise to know that. The bark had been deep, it was a big dog. Teddy smiled. For a moment he considered barking back at it, but then he couldn't be bothered. He just wanted to sleep, here, under the sky.

'You cain't,' the Midwestern voice in his head ordered him.

'Addle-pot,' he retorted.

'Listen to me,' the voice urged.

There was something that Teddy had to do before he could sleep. Wasn't there always something for him to do, though? Some mucking or grooming, braiding, unpicking and rebraiding. His workload was never-ending. Couldn't he just ignore it? Do it tomorrow?

Someone whistled. The dog's owner. Perhaps it was a woman. Perhaps, if she found him, she might take pity on him, take him home and adopt him. Perhaps not. He wasn't the kind of creature that could be taken home. He'd been taken in and adopted before, though, hadn't he? A long, long time ago. The hardening of his joints became warm, gooey and comfortable. The dog barked again. László laughed.

'What is it, boy?' the human said.

It wasn't a woman. Teddy's memory showed him his uncle.

'Did you find a rabbit?'

The voice was soft and friendly, it had that rounded, happy quality. Teddy's uncle had never had that. The dog fussed, its paws ticking on the road.

'Was it eating my crops?'

It was the farmer. Teddy watched the flowers that bucked and bowed in the morning breeze, absently following the line of blackened, crushed crop where he'd made his unfortunate landing.

'Where…'

The human voice stopped short. Teddy couldn't make out how close it was. Or exactly where it had come from.

'Is there someone there?'

The farmer. It wouldn't take the farmer long to put two and two together, coming up with his being the culprit. He'd probably be branded a thief, which he couldn't deny. Unless he wanted to lie, which he didn't, ever again. One good look at his teeth, however, would be proof enough that he was worse than just a thief.

'I have a gun.' The farmer seemed to be hovering.

The gun wouldn't kill him. The daytime would, though. The dog barked, yipping and working itself into a frenzy. Dead or alive, he was about to be discovered. And if he was found, he'd be remembered only as a freak, a monster, a killer of men. Nary one, did he want that. László seemed to find this incredibly funny.

'In all my born days,' Teddy slurred, 'I never reckoned I'd be bellyin' through the bush.'

Flinging his cowpoke limbs pathetically, he flopped over onto his belly. He scrabbled forwards, slowly at first, his joints clicking with every movement. In his deformed clutch the arable land congealed into a million musket balls. Shoving it away, grasping at the rigid stems and ripping battered leaves, he grovelled past. With very little strength in his hands and a head that swam at even his own body height, he forced his crooked knees to bend up underneath him and, resting on his elbows, he crawled like a Cherokee scout, although he'd have been shot: he was ungainly with a disturbing lack of stealth.

As day began to break, no doubt beautiful over the bright flowers, Teddy slumped over the untamed boundary into the field next door. The land there must've belonged to someone less industrious than the dog-owning farmer. In fact, they appeared to have forgotten that they even owned it. The trees here seemed unwanted and uncared for; they sported the odd naked but not quite dead branch. For a moment Teddy thought they were cottonwoods. The one, directly in front of him with dark, broken bark and dry, bulbous leaves loomed familiar. Seconds later the recognition was gone. Thinner, wiry branches shot upwards or off at odd angles from their parent boughs. A variety of vine-like vegetation, some hairy, others with curling tendrils, some that appeared to be dead, strung everything together, the straggly ends just hanging there, greyly. Little to no grass grew here; there just wasn't room, only singular stars of flowers, luminous and lilacky blue, lay sporadically on vines of their own. It was too light here. The canopy just wasn't dense enough. Not here near the edge. If the sun that he longed to see did come out, it would filter through the trees and fry him.

With no one to nag him, Teddy had flouted the rules. He should be hidden deep under the covers by now.

A small, square, concrete structure stood nearby. For all its cute coronets and curved colonnaded windows, it was cracked, chipped, splattered with lichen and smudged a mouldy, swamp green to halfway up its walls. Hang fire, the smudging might've been his dying eyesight. He blinked slovenly. Nope. The green stuff was still there. Around the gap that formed the door, bracts of a darker green plant curled; one or two fronds were yet to unfurl and looked just like green fiddleheads with red keys. Other leaves, flat and with only three prongs, bubbled over the sills. Teddy's jaw dropped loose as he opened his mouth to holler, 'Haahlloa, stranger.' Instantly, he thought better of it, but couldn't close his mouth again. The building looked just like a sad, little summer house that no one wanted to sit in anymore, so it had been forgotten. He shuffled over to it, his belt buckle catching on the odd invasive vine, inhibiting his progress, but he reached it and peered inside.

Empty, thank the land! Although one of the ropey trees sprouted up through a corner of the floor. The building was actually hexagonal, its base a tangle of woodland. Under that, though, a scratchy pattern looped and repeated itself ornately. The roof looked to be sturdy, the foliage hadn't upended it, he could shelter here. Disturbing the mass of flora, he slunk inside.

As soon as Teddy moved the plants' runners and roots, the floor rocked and gave way. A hole appeared, jagged and just big enough for Teddy to slither through like a Sand Creek rattlesnake disappearing into its daytime den. He landed in the earthen, crypt-like pit below peculiarly, impossibly angled and very much dead. Again!

Chapter Eight

KANSAS 1887

Until tonight, the old caramel-coloured poke bonnet had never been used to camp under. During the rodeo season, it was stored away in the side trunks of Old Man Callington's platform wagon. Teddy stared at it. No how, was this camping.

He and his pa always drove home the morning after the rodeo's finale. The trails were safer then. Usually around this time, they'd be lying on bedrolls following fireballs that plummeted through the massive Kansas sky. Or they'd be mapping the stars and then commiserating over the pessimistic paths of the planets; the harbingers of winter. And before that? They'd have sat around a campfire with the other cowmen, kindred spirits, exhilarated to the point of childish chatter, reliving the rodeo. The poke bonnet was never needed. Usually.

Ordinarily, around Old Man Callington's rodeo, there'd be something to keep Teddy busy. Someone would have a point to raise, someone else would need assistance, and the remuda constantly needed wrangling. Nary one, did he or his pa harbour any desire to be left 'alone'. If they weren't dealing with something, then they'd be together. In fact, the only reason he was lying here now, like an old coffee boiler, was because he was dead. Or near as damn it dead.

Teddy's body was crushed and his neck broken. Along with it, pretty much all of his body's ties to his brain. Paralysed from what seemed like one half of his face down, he lay in the bed of the wagon. A slick and sinewy fluid trickled steadily from somewhere in his head to somewhere in his skull. It was as though his nose persisted in dripping the wrong way. Its pipes all boogered up and askew, it leaked into the ether that now engulfed the inside of Teddy's head. He could hear it. Most of the time it was all he could hear. It kept up a monotonous count.

His right eye was blinded. It was dead along with his ear and his voice. Still, he had one eye. He used it to scan the poke bonnet bows, following them numbly from the side to the centre. And back again. It was like he was there in body, but his consciousness had been left in the hallway and it eavesdropped through the open door.

Outside, the wind swayed and the summertime trees shimmied; dead and discarded twigs clattered onto Teddy's roof. The sun was done for the day and had set a while ago. There had been no clouds at all all day, and it looked to be a brilliant night for stargazing. But Teddy wouldn't be stargazing. He had only the twigs to look at. And they looked just like blackened, broken crucifixes.

There were some longer, wirier switches intermingled with the twigs. They reminded him of something. His good side twitched and there was an unexplained stab in his soul. It hurt like a wallop from a mallet, so he stopped trying to figure out what the switches reminded him of.

A fatal fatigue was encroaching slowly on his mind. And on his soul. At times, he couldn't remember where he was, his sight would blank out and he slipped into a white space. But then he'd realise that it wasn't a white space at all, what he saw was just the poke bonnet and he returned to following the wooden bows back and forth.

Tonight, unlike all others, the bows had been slotted into the wagon's shiplap sides bent over the top, the canopy had been tugged and hauled over them and judiciously secured along the edges. The end had been criss-crossed and zigzagged up until the whole thing resembled an off-colour Chinese lantern. A cast-off Chinese lantern. One that lay on its side, forgotten and left to rot in the mud. Only this one had a dead body inside, a gruesome artefact from the rodeo, a dire, demonstrative warning of the dangers of the competition. Or was it just a boy who wanted to go home to his ma?

Teddy's mind fazed in and out of compos mentis again. It was hopelessly lost. It took him into his dreams. And then his nightmares. And now he didn't know if he was alive or not; in purgatory or just held in semi-death, awaiting trial.

The wind-blown twigs skittering across the sturdy, yellow roof sounded like raindrops. Everyone would get soaked. Just like that once, when shelter under the insubordinate old poke bonnet had proven ineffective against the biting wind of a freaky Kansas storm. The driving rain that morning had been so loud that they could hardly hear each other's shouts. He seemed to remember their being soggier after they finished fighting with the difficult old bonnet, than the time they'd just stood under a tree, horses and all.

He looked downwards, along his inoperable body towards the driver's seat. The seat was empty, backed by half an arch of indigo sky, and black tree shapes were all he could see. There was no storm tonight. Kansas was being good to them. Sort of anyway.

Captain Clement Callington or, as he was more affectionately known, Old Man Callington, Teddy's father, had fought in the war alongside Lincoln and the Union. But that had been way before Teddy knew him. A cowman by trade, the only signs of his military background were arthritis, God-fearing ethics and a methodical, strategical approach to everything, the rodeo included. The rodeo itself had been a bid to alleviate the old cowpoke's festering envy over the freedom his ranch hands wielded. It soothed the restlessness that otherwise might have torn his successful settled life asunder. He'd harnessed the ranch hands' 'show-off my skills' sessions into a timed arena and started the rodeo. So Teddy's ma had told him. And she never lied to him. She never lied to anyone.

Still, the old man harboured a hankering for fast horses, risky riding and the rattling of travel over grassy, stubby prairie. Perhaps that's where Teddy got his hunger for speed from. Or had he always had it? It was of no great shakes, the old man just didn't do it anymore; too stiff. But he was more than happy for Teddy to give it a go. Darn it, he encouraged him. He'd nurtured his recklessness, trained his cautiousness. Or was it the other way around? Either way, he was always grinningly proud of him. Even when he made bad mistakes. A bit like today.

Respect. That was the faraway word he'd heard unanimously used when, thinking he was dead, they'd laid him there in the bottom of the wagon. Then they'd threaded up the top and hidden him away. Respect? More like solitary confinement. Teddy had never been paid respect before; he'd rather not be paid it now. No matter how much of a proud cowpoke he was supposed to be, deep down, if he was truly honest, he'd take living, however uncouth it may be, over dying any day.

He lay there, half-awake, and watched the poke bonnet prairie sky intensify, steadfastly and deliberately into night. Unfathomable was its beauty. Pristine and exquisite was its indigo, Union blue. Just like the Pacific. He'd never seen the Pacific. He imagined it to be majestically, mythically deep. At times, darker than even the Ozark outlaw caves.

Hold your hosses! How did he know about the Ozarks? The details were blurred like feverish delusions in his mind. True feverish delusions. He had a strong feeling of familiarity with the enormity of the caves. And their chilling blackness. And what was stashed there – silver, guns, powder and stuff; and of course, people.

Teddy stared, a bit like a Navajo warrior stares into the sky. Silently, he gave thanks to the Great Spirit. Or should it be the god of the land or the god of his father? It was too mighty a discussion to have with his worn-out self, right now. Pa would know the answer. But nary one had it ever seemed timely to have the discussion with his pa. A discussion on which name to use or, moreover, who got the biggest portion of his love: God or Teddy? It was both unimportant and plumb painful to even consider approaching. Sakes alive, he'd fight off anyone, god or otherwise who tried to take away the love of his family. Besides, the various powers had all just merged into one and, the jostling of religious groups had fallen insignificant at his entry to death. Somewhere he'd rather not be. So, he thanked his lucky stars for the gift of his family, however regretfully humiliatingly a state he'd been in when he received it. Or however deliciously surprising it had been. He loved them and that was that.

Debility pulled dully at the back of his jaw: he reckoned on his lips opening and his mouth slackening; he had no other sense of the rest of his skull. Death must come again soon. The best part of him had already gone, there was just this recurring consciousness to go. He tried to move, tried to draw attention to his lucidity. He blacked out. Again.

* * *

Teddy came around, again. Opening his eyes and staring at his hat. It sat on his chest. He could see its dark crown: a slight dent was forming there, where he gripped it to adjust it or, much, much more rarely, to take it off. Usually only at home. Inside. Or risk the wrath of his ma. The kindest, most caring woman in the world. The only woman ever to have seen him naked.

No. That wasn't right. There was one other. A curious wince spiked him behind his eye and in his heart. If he could have, he'd have cringed. He wasn't quite sure why, he couldn't remember, so he told himself again that his ma had been the only woman ever to bear witness to his nakedness.

Any injuries he'd ever sustained in the corral had been cleaned and dressed by her loving hands. 'You don't need any more scars,' she'd say, gently rubbing and then painfully pressing home the necessity of not doing again whatever it was that he'd done in the first place. Then, with that potency that only mothers seem to possess, she'd glared and smiled at the same time at his pa, demurely chastising him for damaging her son. This all much to the amusement of his sisters. Everyone knew that he and Old Man Callington would be back out in the corral the next day roping and branding.

No one would be able to fix him this time, though. Not even the Great Spirit or the god of anyone. He watched the sky through the grubby and apparently respectful poke bonnet.

He had no sensation of touch left at all now. Only internal emotions, and he really wasn't sure where they existed. He looked down to his hat again. It was more than just a hat. In that way indigenous only to cowpokes, his hat was his closest friend, it was his identity, his shelter and his home. Pa had given it to him. It gave him strength. So, when he felt sad or alone or just out of sorts, he could touch it, feel its stiffened fur felt or just think on it and he was reminded of the honest constant of his home and the love of his family. He so needed that strength now. But he couldn't move. So, he gazed at his hat.

He could never be without his hat. Never. It sat proudly on his chest. He'd much rather it sat on his head. He guessed its sitting on his chest was another mark of the respect that he'd rather not have. He gave thanks, although he still wasn't sure exactly who to, that they hadn't placed it over his face; then he wouldn't have been able to see anything at all.

There was a disc hovering above him now; some sort of puny, coffee-coloured smudge on the canopy. He glared at it. It was the moon. Tonight's moon of course. Milk Moon, Thunder Moon, Red, Harvest, Hunter: he couldn't remember the proper names right now. Once a month the moon put on a show that would rival Buffalo Bill. He'd never seen Buffalo Bill, though. It was supposed to be wild.

Another gust of wind wiped the poke bonnet clear. Momentarily the clattering of a fresh twig-load silenced the dripping inside his head. He glanced towards the driver's seat, desperate to catch sight of the waving treetops on his horizon. But he missed it. The wind was gone again. He traced the bows once more.

So, what was this, then? A second wind? A chance to do it all again? Die again. Just in case he'd missed it the first time around. It wasn't like he wanted to die all over again. It hadn't been nice the first time. But there'd be no living now. He couldn't move, couldn't speak, could hardly breathe or even think straight. All he could do was lie there and wait for death to come again. So, what was the point? What kind of a second chance was this?

Something bitter in his memory stabbed at him. It caused a sort of stutter in his already faltering heart. Something about his being a horse thief. Was that what this was all about? His penance. Hang fire, he was no horse thief! The bitter taste struck again. It was like an old, rusty peacemaker firing lead plumb laced with regret. A firing squad, tasked with burning a hole in his soul, lest he forget its significance. The significance, it seemed, was the only thing he could remember. The details were disappearing, lost in the swirl that was now his dying thoughts.

A gasp, abysmal and rasping, dragged his crushed chest inwards and somehow he saw fear. Fear all around him. The fear that he'd once seen in his father's eyes. It'd been there once when he'd looked at him. Just once.

But it was so deplorable that it had stuck clearly in his mind. Even in his death pit. And now his soul raked it up again. Why?

The feeling was fear alright. The unmistakeable fear of disappointment. No, of heartbreak. But it wasn't his. It was shards of horror in his father's heart and they showed in the memory of his eyes. They were the pains of misery that his golden son had wantonly conned him, the gasps of grief that his beloved heir was a liar.

Teddy's tired memory cried out that it wasn't true. He'd never stolen anything. His nightmares had somehow turned tangible. A lie, it must've been, had found its way to his pa. He'd panicked. His heart and soul had been torn apart by the terror that he was about to lose his treasured dream: his family and their love. Aches had wracked his whole body. Somehow it did the same now.

He'd fallen to his knees, pleaded and begged to be forgiven; he wasn't sure quite what for; the truth, it seemed, had been lost somewhere in the desolation of the Ozarks. But he didn't care, he just couldn't lose his family. Pa had taken him into his arms, professed his sorrow and promised that they'd move on together. So, like no cowpoke had the right to, he'd given in to his feelings and howled. If only he could howl now, too. But he couldn't. So, the power of that memory took a little more out of him. Gladly, he let his body sink into blackness.

* * *

The necessity for sleep was something that Teddy's body had forsaken long before tonight. If he slept, then he'd dream. And he didn't want to dream. Not tonight. Tonight, any dreams he had would hurt; he couldn't be too sure why or even how, he just knew that they would. So, he didn't want to go to sleep. He'd like to get up and go home now. Please.

In the makeshift arena his death had come on quite quickly. His body hadn't even had time to bruise before the blood had stopped pumping. His limbs, though, they'd appallingly, uncontrollably spasmed. His face had jerked and his lips curled. Hollering out had seemed to him to be the best way of managing the instantaneous yet monumental pain of his skeleton's splintering into an infinitesimal number of tiny pieces. But with everything inside him smashed, only an elongated screech had escaped his lips.

Everyone had seen Libby, his trained, trustworthy, unshakeable Quarter stall at top speed. Everyone's cheers had been halted. All around, even in the atmosphere itself, breath had been held. Teddy had tumbled heavily head over hind, smacking down on the dusty floor. For him, though, the scene had been everything that he imagined cinematic slow motion to be like. Just with a little too much colour added. He'd watched Libby's muscular weight, the strength that, until now, he'd proudly depended on as she seemed to hover above him for a second. And then she'd screamed and fallen, landing on him, her legs flailing, her hooves kicking skywards. His body was crushed instantly, his organs burst, he could feel each of them explode like faulty barrels of water. Gunk and blood and sickening sounds shed all over his spot in the arena.

Old Man Callington had been there then. Teddy had heard his prayers, seen the ropes of the corral where he'd been standing, swinging against the sunset as though nodding to the manhandling of the boss. Teddy couldn't see him, though; not properly. The only thing he could see was the crook of his arm. He guessed the Old Man had cradled his head as he'd died. He'd heard his sobs and tried with all the might left to him to ask him to move, tell him he couldn't see him. But he couldn't. So, to all and sundry he'd just lay there and leaked life.

To acknowledge the corn, though, it had been quick. Reassuringly so for those not actually taking part. He hadn't panicked. He didn't think he had. He hoped he hadn't. He couldn't tell, and he wondered miserably if he'd died bravely.

Outside, the rodeo was quiet. Uncharacteristically so. As usual, its arrival had called forth the skills of various businessmen to its captive audiences. This season, Missouri Murphy had rolled up with a portable saloon. He'd brought with him a piano, its player, more echoey than it was, and brightly dressed ladies, who made the place not only cacophonous, but profitable, too. Tonight, though, there was nothing. That could be due to his gammy ear. Most likely, there just wasn't any hilarity at all. Tonight was the contest's end; there should've been celebrating, singing and even trail-itching cowpokes' cussing contests.

Instead there was shock and sadness and now silence. The boss's son was dead. Beefed while roping calves. Would the rodeo's place in Old Man Callington's heart die, too? No one spoke. Especially no one sang.

Please sing, Teddy thought.

He wanted to hear them singing, needed to hear their raucous cowpoke doggerel, the playing of their Roots and Folk. It wasn't like he could join in; he couldn't. Even if he wasn't dead, or dying, or whatever this limbo was, he caterwauled. But if the cowpokes sang, then he just might not feel so plumb sewn up. He watched the corner of the driver's seat for a moment.

Where was his pa? If they got scooting, they might make it home before he passed on. Again. And then he'd get to see his ma and sisters one last time.

A finite spasm pulled at one side of his lips, his tear ducts emptied and water trickled out of the corner of his eye. Tears ran down the side of his face, amalgamating with the warmth of whatever was leaking out of his ear. He had consciousness enough to feel the cowpoke shame of crying, but no body to brush it off. He wished it'd stop. Still he stared at the empty driver's seat. There was no one around. So only the silhouetted treetops and the midnight blue sky bore witness to his tears.

Pa, he yearned to call out.

His voice sounded only in his head. He wanted so much to be with Pa. Just for one more minute.

I miss you, he thought, and he degenerated a little more.

It hurt. It hurt in the one place where he had any sensation left at all. His heart. Formidable hurt possessed him. It expanded his chest, pushing it upwards until he saw the brim of his Stetson. Then, at an achingly alarming rate, his body deflated. Now he could hardly see his hat at all. The pain-laden Death's trail he was on went back below ground. Until the next time he unwittingly released it. No one wants to die. It doesn't matter how much you fancy it up, no one, actually, really wants to die. Teddy pictured the town's Sunday morning Sin Buster sermonising his flock on the merits of death.

I should've listened.

He was sure to be cast out where there was wailing and, darn it, he couldn't even grind his teeth. The poke bonnet ropes unbunged. Teddy's one good ear pricked up. The grain bag-style closure whizzed open.

Pa! Frantically, his thoughts came jostling over one another: please don't leave me alone again. Unbridled joy bounded about his mind. His dead heart even quaked when the cotton poke bonnet rustled aside.

'Are you dying?' a foreign, complicated accent whispered in his ear.

CHAPTER NINE

A thick, oily liquid overflowed from Teddy's ear. It ran down his neck in a tepid slick. For just that second, his ear unbunged and the voice bellowed into his head. Then his ear began to slowly drip-fill once more. That voice that had whispered in his ear. He knew the conversation. It wasn't Pa.

'Look at you,' the voice said. 'What a mess you have made of yourself. Again, ya? Although the last time it wasn't so much your fault, now, was it?'

The voice was slow and deliberate. It was as though it spoke mid-yawn. It swayed and smooched and drew him in. And then it was clipped and faltered and dropped him. Teddy had spoken with it before. Somewhere.

'Teddy, my treasure,' the voice persisted, 'you remember me, ya? We met before. Twice. Was not so long ago. You can't have forgotten me.'

It hadn't been a good conversation; at least that's what he thought anyway. Tonight, his memory wasn't good. He just knew it was bad. He tried to call out.

Pa!

Nothing happened. He couldn't make a sound. Not even a moan. He forced the dregs of brainpower that were left to him, to focus on his limbs. He tried again to move. But it was useless. The effort tired him almost beyond consciousness.

'No. Don't go away again. Not just yet, anyway, ya.'

Outside the wind shook the trees. The black, twig-like daggers that had speckled the poke bonnet were blown away. None were replaced. The exquisite sky disappeared behind clouds, taking the smudged moon with it.

'Is me! Furisto Ladislaus Jagelovići,' Teddy's uninvited guest said. 'You know, Fürst? Archduke? I think Prince is the nearest you Americans will recognise to Furisto.'

A Prince? Teddy felt sure that he didn't know any Princes. There were no Princes in the West and he'd never been anywhere else. 'Sides which, he didn't even know what an Archduke was. So, such a person as this Laslad couldn't possibly exist.

'But is too lowly. In Old Royal Hungary, I was a King.'

Prince Ladislaus laughed. Teddy remembered that laugh. It was a hollow, mirthless sneer.

'You remember me, don't you? You thought I was the Devil. You complemented me wonderfully with that naughty little earthquake on the prairie. You remember? The night when you lost your finger, ya? You smelled so delicious that night. Or was that the night in your uncle's barn? What a mess you were in that night, but you smelled so good. You must remember that night.'

A million spikes suddenly prickled up and down Teddy's spine. His spine, though, had been the first place that'd lost sensation when Liberty had fallen on him. But still, something had got to him. Aphids and sawflies discharged from the wooden wagon, spurred on by the trickling of his juices, scraped away the skin of his back; they marched, rank and file through to his bones, gluttonously sucking out a liquid supper. He wanted, needed to scream. But he couldn't. He needed to writhe. But he couldn't.

He sensed the Prince was smiling. It was as though this sadistic Devil had let himself into Teddy's head. He'd taken control of his mind. He was using it as a means to poke about in his memory. When he found what he was looking for he made it into a prod to provoke the reckless side of Teddy's consciousness, persuading it to give him what he wanted. If only Teddy could be sure of what that was. His body seemed to know, though. As did his soul; it quaked sickeningly cold.

'You remember what I told you that night?' Ladislaus persisted. 'In the barn, ya?'

The endurance of excruciating pain was the only memory Teddy could muster about that night. He couldn't settle on how it'd come to be, though. It could be that the Prince had indeed done it to him. He certainly seemed depraved enough. The composure of his voice, the subtlety of the changes in its detail, even the condescension, suggested that he had not. Perhaps the physical mess that comes with the inflicting of pain on others was not something he actively involved himself in. Perhaps he always got someone else to do that bit for him. His lack of bodily presence and his disembodied smile laid corroboration to that fact; he wasn't above cashing in on the efforts of others.

Whatever had happened, it wasn't a memory Teddy wanted right now. Nary one, was it welcome; just like the Prince himself. He closed his eye and concentrated the tiny portion of mind still available to him on something more pleasant. He pushed the memory fragment and the Prince away. His spine, aphids and all disappeared again.

It, that memory of the barn, the Cross Truss barn, along with most of his old life, had purposely been forgotten. The past left in the past. And, as was the cowpoke way, never spoken of, by anyone.

In the light of the days that followed glorious warm and reassuring in the sunlight of the prairie, the nightmare of his having strayed, however unwittingly, into the sights of the Devil had seemed absurd. Setting amidst the apple-coloured comfort of his new home, surrounded by the glowing love of his new family, he'd risen above the ridiculousness of conversing with Satan. The insane possibility of his having won an audience with the Prince of Darkness, Laslas or otherwise, had become a joke. Not that he'd ever told it to anyone. The insidious visitation had been put down to some sort of hallucination, an appalling and foreboding embodiment of the abuse he'd been subjected to. Never in all his born days had he considered his visitor that night to actually have been a real man.

Teddy's subconsciousness had turned out most pragmatic and conscientious. To acknowledge the corn, it was way tougher than his heart. It had sifted through his memories and saved only the useful bits. Over a short space of time it had selected particular remembrances, cowpoke hardships, tack, stables, liveries and getting to know horses until he could talk with them. It had pared everything down and removed the pip where any pain or damage to emotions may have been suffered. Now only the lesson learned remained. Teddy could only remember what was relevant. He was more than happy with that. The Prince had been included in the clear-out. There had been no room for him.

Dirt and shame had been etched into his skin by the outcome of that night in the barn and time spent drifting in the Ozarks had followed it. The scarred, emaciated and almost feral waif that he had become was long since forgotten. All of it lost; mislaid in his memories, his mind or soul or somewhere.

When Teddy took control of his mind, he saw only the spark of promise that had been in Old Man Callington's eye as he'd loaded up the wagon the morning after the rodeo. The strange, stowaway wrangler had gone home with him cowering in the back, hidden in amongst the boxes of tack and assorted rodeo jumble. They'd all been happy to forget that day.

His decaying body warmed up now. Just a little. When they'd been introduced Mrs Callington's eyes had had that spark, too. With it, she'd combined hope. It was Captain and Mrs Callington's ambitious compassion that had drawn him free from the clutches of homelessness and despair.

Under his own control, his dead heart swelled and his cold skin tingled at the thought of her kind-hearted touch as she tended to his wretched body. His numb scalp had tugged with loving little pulls when she washed, combed and cut his hair. And so, he'd dared to let her care for him until he was strong again.

Ma, he thought, *I love you, Ma.*

He'd known then. His dreams had come true. He had a family of his own. It'd just taken time. That's all. The final tear dribbled out of his eye.

I'll never forget you. Never.

'What is this you are oozing out here? Is some kind of goo, ya?'

The Prince was still there. Teddy turned his eye as far upwards as he could. There was nothing to see. Yagivichi, or whatever he called himself, had no palpable presence, no humanly wholeness. Teddy had only half a nose: what he could smell wasn't pleasant. The stench could be Laslas. Or it could be the inside of his own head. His eye rolled uncontrollably backwards and all he saw was black nothing.

And then a ramuda. A golden-haired wrangler at its centre, surrounded by Pintos and Flaxeys, Mustangs and Cayuses. He was waving a dark-coloured, brand new Stetson, hollering and yelling, rope at his side, dust at his feet. And only three fingers on his right hand.

'Forgive me,' the Prince's inglorious voice interrupted Teddy's peaceful dying once again. 'I will move, ya? And then you can see me without losing control of your one and only eye.'

Teddy tried to ignore him. He was desperate to get back to the chocolate-coloured corral, the tall bluegrass, green hills and the sugar sprinkled mountains.

It didn't work. His mind was in too much of an unpredictable mire. The Prince, it seemed, had the upper hand and he asserted his influence. Those terrible memories were the ones he wanted to bring forth. The ones Teddy thought he had forgotten. They rose up wantonly. They staggered from their shredded and tattered existence in the dust-pebbled recesses of his half-dead mind. But they reconstructed themselves all slantindicular. They were familiar faces with unfamiliar eyes, loved ones morphed into shoddily sewn-together monsters, their broken limbs twisted and mismatched, their voices incomprehensible.

Now there were pains, too. Pains that went with the images in his head. His deadened body buzzed with a listless, desensitised sort of life. Internally, it juddered and then probed and stabbed back at itself. He couldn't move, though. He couldn't move at all. And those memories kept coming.

Sling your bunk, y'all, he screamed, *shin out.*

But he couldn't speak. He couldn't make a sound. No one would know. The effort of his attempt to outwit the invisible advances of Prince Laslas' malevolence sapped his energy. His life guttered a little more.

'Don't go,' the Prince cooed, 'is like I said before…'

Again with the "before". I cain't remember the ding "before".

'I can make all this go away. No more pain, no more oozing, no more slaving to these humans.'

On his good side, Teddy felt something. It was something palpable. Something soft like the fingertips of a doctor pressing their patient's skin before saying, "does that hurt?" Or the delicate fingertips of Ma as she investigated his corral-obtained bruises. Or the lover… that he'd never felt. But he'd often dreamed about. There was no one there, though, was there? Only the so-called prince.

Don't touch me, Teddy's sluggish subconsciousness cried, *don't you…*

'Touch you. You can feel me, ya?'

Sakes alive! He could hear him. Prince Yagevichi could hear him. Teddy began to think up all manner of insults. The cowpokes! He opened up his mind and let the undead memories rampage around as best they could.

His uncle's ranch. The Cross Truss. He'd lived in the doghouse on the Cross Truss for so long with so many cowpokes, he should know how to cuss when he needed to. The cowpokes came back to him, bantering, muttering, cussing and swearing. He hadn't completely forgotten them. "Don't do it," Dent had once told him. "You don't wanna wind up swearing at the boss now, do you? Or a purely purdy little lady."

The prince counted as neither of those. Right now, Teddy didn't care how foul he was being. In his mind he sounded coarse, vulgar, all the while hoping that he could insult the uninvited blatherskite, Lasislo.

'I can assure you, my mother was no such thing,' Ladislaus said. 'Yours, however? Your people? We don't know about. Your loyalty to those people you like to call "family" is very sweet. Is a little intrusive, but I can work with that, ya?'

Teddy swore. What he lacked in movement, he made up for in mind-bent screaming and howling. He'd sent the prince packing once. Apparently, twice. He could do it again. And then he remembered pain. Unbearable and mind-immobilising pain. Pain with incarceration. And hopelessness. And heartbreak. It was the pain, internal or otherwise that came with the Cross Truss. And he could no longer control it.

Exhaustion consumed him again and he fell quiet. All that effort, all the ranting and remembering poked his spirit a little further down its final trail. His mind would hardly work at all now. Too many thoughts! He blacked out.

* * *

'Let me help you remember?' the so-called prince said as he stroked Teddy's face. 'I won't go into the horrible details of how you and I got to talking before. It wasn't very nice for you. I twitch when I think about it. It must've hurt, ya?'

So, he was still here. And that line about "twitching", well, that was a stretcher for a start. Prince Unpronounceable couldn't twitch. He had no presence. It proved the lying tenderfoot to be no more than a figment of Teddy's own perishing, fragmented imagination. He half-closed his eye.

His hat moved. It lifted and flew out of his view. It seemed to him that he'd been able to feel it as it had sat there on his chest. Now it wasn't there, his chest was cold, empty and exposed. He missed it. He wanted it back.

A man climbed onto the wagon's fitted storage boxes beside him. His deeply laced boots creaked with newness. That was the only noise he made. The paint-peeled boards made no complaint of his arrival at all. It was as though he weighed nothing. Nothing at all.

He squatted there, punishing the air with the leathery odour released from the creases of the shiny, never-before-worn shoes. He can't have been much older than Teddy himself. His high cheeks were honey-coloured, his lips pink like those of a fashionable lady, and his black hair flowed long and loose about his shoulders. Streaks of crimson glittered as it flapped and folded over itself in the breeze. He looked real. He was tangible, pokeable and yet, he had no clout. Teddy watched him.

'Is me,' the man said, as though that explained everything, 'King Ladislaus Jagelovići.'

Make your mind up, Teddy thought.

Ladislaus seemed to study him for a moment. He seemed to be weighing up the worth of humouring him with an answer. He dangled Teddy's hat by its brim. He was holding it all wrong. He'd damage it. Desperation to get to it, snatch it back and slog Ladislaus for taking it in the first place spat from Teddy's temples. If Ladislaus could indeed hear him, he was ignoring him. He smirked, safe in the knowledge of Teddy's paralysis, and he fanned the hat as though hell-bent on antagonising him further.

Teddy tried to glare at Ladislaus' hands. Compared to his own they were much, much more cultured. And much less hard worked. He wore a ring of gold on the middle finger which made Teddy acutely ashamed that his own middle finger was missing. On his ring finger he wore a ruby that was almost as big as a man's heart. Teddy had never seen such wealth, not on such a young man, not even on Ma, and especially not at the rodeo.

Ladislaus waggled the Stetson back and forth. He knew how to gain Teddy's attention. The blue spectrum of night-time, kaleidoscoped purple and black with the large, expensive ruby. The off-white of the old poke bonnet flashed off the stone's huge facets. It smacked into Teddy's eye. He looked away.

'You see, Teddy,' Ladislaus said, 'you are just what I need. I have been, what do you say, toying? With an idea.'

He tossed his hands about as though the idea was of no great shakes. Teddy found that hard to believe, especially if, to work, it needed him to die.

'Is really just an inkling. But you can help me with an experiment to get it going. It will be fun, ya. I mean, just look at you.'

Teddy would rather not. He knew he was in a horrific mess and growing worse by the minute.

'Alright, perhaps not right at this moment, but I will fix that. And then, you will be a treasure. You will have the looks and we know you have the fight. You will charm and you will hustle.'

Fix him? He was as good as dead.

'And this?'

Ladislaus twirled the hat again. Again, the moonlight flickered off the huge ruby. Again, Teddy's anger flared.

'This is so proper, so refined, so gentlemanly. The women of Europe will find it intoxicating, ya?'

Europe? Teddy had no idea even where Europe was. He sure as tarnation didn't want to go there. He just wanted to go home.

'You will look like an angel in a....' Ladislaus turned the hat over and, observing Teddy over the top, read the name on the inside of the brim, 'J B Stetson.'

Teddy stared at his hat. He was no gentleman. He was definitely no angel. He was...he couldn't remember his proper name. The tag was just under the sweatband inside the hat's brim. He knew he was a proud cowpoke, celebrated rodeo roper, pretty much dead and futile heir to the Double C ranch. Ladislaus was talking complete balderdash.

Ladislaus smirked again and he scrunched up the brim. He peered inside and poked under the band.

'Ah-ha, is you?'

He tore out the tag that bore Teddy's name and stuffed it in the vest pocket of his fashionable three-piece suit. Teddy's frail heart thudded against the crushed, splintered wall of his chest. Something fizzed at the top of his nose and teased bruises around his eyes. He could do nothing, though. He couldn't even cry. All he could do was close his eye.

'Everyone will be so fooled by you,' Ladislaus went on. 'And by your accent and you are so young, you cannot fail.'

Teddy had no voice, never mind an accent, and he didn't even have a name anymore. The side of his head was plumb stoved in, his eye leaked gunk and so did his ear. His body was broken and misshapen.

'Everyone will love you, ya?'

Ladislaus sounded pleased.

'Forever!'

As though to revel in his sick and twisted desire to torment a dying boy, he put Teddy's hat on. Backwards. It didn't suit him. Stetsons suited pretty much anybody. But Teddy's didn't suit Ladislaus.

It especially didn't go with the business-type, thigh-length jacket. Or the sumptuous gold chain that looped from the second to top vest button and disappeared into the pocket, the way Teddy's name had gone. The suit was made of some hardy-looking wool stuff; it was clean-cut, brand new and black. Or perhaps it was green. Anyway, it was all the go in town right now. Teddy had seen a greenhorn belvedere wearing it about the rodeo. The Kansas sunlight had glimmered off the watch chain and the chap had stuck out like a clothes horse in a corral. He remembered how he'd thought that belvedere must be some high falutin' Anglomaniac; clearly thought he didn't need a hat.

And then the image was gone. Strange how his mind hadn't distorted that man, adding limbs that didn't belong on him. Ironic that it would remember the suited chap in such detail, and yet not something he needed to know right now. Odd how Ladislaus, an old Hungarian King of some description, had the same suit.

Ladislaus studied Teddy. He rested his arms on his knees and folded his hands. The massive ruby looked like a railroad signal.

'You like my suit?' he said.

And then he grinned. It was a purposefully slow stretching of his lips. His teeth were shovel-shaped, blocked, functional. But they shone bright white, they looked polished and special, like they defined him, they sure-fired were the teeth of a prince.

His canines were different. Ladislaus' canines looked to be an after-addition, which was just plumb horse feathers. By twenty years old a man would have all the teeth he was ever going to grow. If anything, he lost them. Yet Ladislaus' canines were longer, slighter and barbed like the vicious knots in farmers' wire fences. His canines were more like fangs. Fangs, the likes of which Teddy had never seen before; not even on the wolves of the prairie. Teddy was more than familiar with animal teeth. Life on the prairie had thrown up many an example of them. Many a run-in with the ranch dogs told Teddy that it was the animal's jaws that were just as powerful as their teeth. Ladislaus did not have powerful-looking jaws.

'Is good, ya?' Ladislaus said. 'My suit? Because I had to kill a, how you cowboys say, dude to get it?'

He dusted off the sleeves and flicked dirt from the knee of the dark woollen trousers. Teddy watched him, he hadn't quite got it right, but his meaning was clear. Dread prowled around in the back of Teddy's head. Suspicion froze the dribbling in Teddy's nose and twitched at the nerves under his eye.

The Prince had killed that dandy barber's clerk. For what? For his suit?

Ladislaus grinned again. He stared hard at Teddy. Teddy tried to shrink away. He wasn't yeller. Darn it, no cowpoke was. But those teeth were bad. And he was trapped.

Sakes alive! The truth, however slowly he'd latched onto it, however hampered by his lack of working mentality, was no way less explosive. It ruptured Teddy's already shattered mind, making him scream out inside. Ladislaus had killed the belvedere for his blood.

The memory of Ladislaus' words that night in the Cross Truss barn spewed forth from somewhere deep inside Teddy's soul. His chest rose, but his gasp could not escape. Instead it knifed him inside and stirred the pool of blood it'd made. His pitiful heart ached. What was left of his stomach churned in its disgusting organic juice. He wanted, no, he needed for his throat to gag and his paunch to air. But the muscles he needed to do that were dead to him.

Terror took charge then. Teddy lost control of his mind again. He stared wildly from Ladislaus' smile, to the driver's seat, to the trees, searching for help. To start with anyway, then he just couldn't stop it. The eye muscles spasmed. The lid would neither close nor open, stuttering somewhere in between like a wedged sash window, its owner trying desperately to slam it shut. And failing.

'Ah,' Ladislaus seemed pleased with this reaction, 'you remember me, correctly. At last.'

Yes, he remembered that devilish night now. Ladislaus had indeed introduced himself. Before that, Teddy had known precious little about vampires, only what had been told in the dime novels that the Cross Truss cowpokes had brought back from town. He'd thought vampires were just pokerish campfire taradiddles, ghost stories of twistical beings that hypnotised greenhorn humans, getting them to do their filthy bidding before biting their necks, drinking their blood and killing them. Was that what Ladislaus wanted to turn him into? Vile curiosity began to screw with his heart. Somewhere deep in his mind, he yearned to know.

Instantly, he hated himself for it. It was all so sick. There was no way he could be a vampire. No way on earth. But he couldn't be sure he was on earth. And with only Ladislaus for company, it felt more like hell.

Sling your bunk, Lazlawes, he moaned.

He made no noise.

'Don't say that, mein Schatzibar.'

Schatzibar! What in the tarnation was a schatzibar? Coming from the mouth of this blood-drinking murderer, a schatzibar was not likely to be anything good. Teddy did not want to become one.

Ladislaus grinned at Teddy: the wide brim of the Stetson hid his eyes, its dark felt picked out the red in his hair.

'Is Old High German and I can see that you are having trouble with it, so I will let you call me László.'

The self-proclaimed prince had a patronising, condescending way of reading Teddy's thoughts. Teddy hated it, hated him. Frustration fouled and festered inside him. He detested László with a fear so deep it courted infatuation.

Dear God, help me, he prayed.

'Schatzibar, stop.' Ladislaus laughed. 'Please, don't pray, ya. Is not going to help you.'

He squatted on his haunches, his hands clasped in contemplation. Anybody else would've gone stiff at the ankles. But then, László wasn't even a body.

'You will help me with my little experiment.'

László waved his hand again.

'Of course, it does mean that you will have to change a bit.'

He linked his long, youthful fingers through each other again and tipped his hands up and down. He grinned at Teddy's ineffectual effort to stop his eye following the glare of the ruby.

'I will help you with that when I turn you. We will use what you already have and that will do more than half of the job; is one more reason why I chose you to help me.'

He laughed again.

'You are really quite adorable. The rest, Schatzibar, is simple. All you have to do is forget everything. You see. Is easy because your past is something anybody would be only too pleased to forget.'

And then László seemed to speed up, as though he purposely wanted Teddy to miss what he was about to say.

'Also, you must forget everybody.'

No way, hombre. Teddy would never forget Pa. Or Ma. Or his sisters. Or his horses.

'Yes, you will,' Ladislaus went on. 'You will kill all the best people, ya? Every night, you will remember only how to behave like a beast, a hungry, wanton animal. And when you've finished, we will revel in your depravity, we will enjoy your remorse. No, wait, remorselessness, ya? We will feast ya? Every night. Forever, ya?'

Teddy couldn't do that. He just couldn't do it. He'd never lifted a finger, cussed or even muttered an under-breath oath of revenge on anybody. Not even throughout the physical and verbal abuse from his cousins, his uncle and aunt. Never throughout the labour-intensive neglect of the Cross Truss, the homelessness enforced by the slicking, the removal of the love of his sister.

I won't do it, Larzsly, his soul spat out, *you cain't come it over on me so, yer hear me? You are plumb takin' the rag off twistical. I ain't never, ever gonna slew it again.*

'I knew you'd say that.' László frowned so deep that the Stetson toppled forward, 'Or something of that sort.'

He grasped the brim on both sides and adjusted the hat.

'Schatzibar, I have grown tired of your resisting me. I have been patient. Have I not? I have waited, always in the background, for you to give up trying to make this pathetic human life worth your while. Mein Fledermaus, you are so much better than this. So, I have made you irresistible. Do you see?'

Irresistible? Unable to resist. Physically unable to resist you, Larszloh? Or just unable to do anything at all. The loco foreigner was confusing them both.

'You have always been irresistible, ya? I have only been sitting here talking to you because I like talking to you. You sound so funny. We will get on so well together.'

László smiled. He moved with a jaunty excitement. He picked up Teddy's hand and ran his fingers along his arm. Dust tumbled down, but Teddy couldn't see where it landed. Other than the swipe of his heavy canvas coat, he had no sensation of the movement at all.

'So, you will become my brother. Of sorts anyway. Nobody, you understand, is equal to me.'

Teddy watched László play with his hand. He pried the rigor-mortissing fingers apart. The insubordinate muck forks sardonically amused Teddy, although he couldn't smile. It was as though his body gleaned one last remnant of rebelliousness. He held on faster to his stubbornness than ever he had to the broncs in the corral.

'Ah, yes, I remember this.'

Ladislaus traced the stub of Teddy's missing middle finger, then he turned his hand over, pushed up his sleeve and stroked his wrist. He raised Teddy's arm and pressed his wrist to his cheek. Teddy might not have any sensation left in his limbs at all, but that didn't stop revulsion rising up through his stomach again.

'A teeny, tiny pulse,' László said, 'we must hurry.'

His smile disappeared. He turned his face to Teddy, his eyes still hidden, but Teddy knew they were staring hard at him.

'Schatzibar,' László said, 'I cannot be there when you wake up. Is too dangerous.'

He raised his chin high then and looked down his nose: his ebony black eyes penetrated right through Teddy's one good eye into his soul.

'Don't worry, I will find you before the sun comes up,' László said.

His gaze seemed hypnotising; Teddy couldn't look away, even though he craved it. In return, there was nothing to see in László's eyes. Nothing. Just his own reflection. What he saw was the image of himself before the gore of the accident. Looking at himself was the last thing he wanted to do. He closed his eye. He never wanted to see himself again: he wouldn't be able to stand it. He'd see only a messed-up, psychopathic murderer. His heart leapt painfully when he realised he, or rather the vampire, would be more than happy with that.

Teddy lay hopeless for what seemed like a long while. László had fallen silent, too. Still Teddy could sense nothing. Still he couldn't move. Still the inside of his head felt as though it were slowly being suffocated by a sliding, booming sand dune. Perhaps he was just too far gone. László may have decided against taking him. Perhaps he was saved. Sort of anyway.

He opened his eye. Inside, he swore. László was closer than before. Closer than ever Teddy would be comfortable with. He blinked. László's long, crimson-streaked hair snagged on Teddy's dust-encrusted eyelashes. It tumbled and settled on his now prominent cheekbones. The shock made Teddy's face twitch. The hair caught on his chapped, split lips. With one eye shut and the other blind, he hadn't noticed László's silent and weightless climb onto his chest. And he no longer wore the Stetson. Teddy couldn't see his hat.

Don't touch me! he screamed.

László nuzzled into his neck, sending a bolt of unpleasant surprise through the skin of Teddy's good side. The prince's face was cold, razor-sharp cold, and it pained him like the time he'd tried to grasp the ice on the water trough that frosty Kansas morning.

Thunderation, this was sick.

He tried to groan, he tried to wriggle, to tip László off, but nothing happened. A tacky, dry scrape of a lifeless tongue scoured the angle of his jaw orbing and bulging, thrusting and swelling, compressing and withdrawing. Sightlessly it searched, feeling for his faltering throb of a heartbeat. Teddy could do nothing. He stared straight up, straining his sight, trying to see far away from the head that bent over his throat.

'Don't be scared,' László said.

Teddy felt his lips then. He swore again. The only other lips he'd ever felt at his neck had been the immoral, wanton lips of the whore who'd taken his virginity. He'd sworn then, too. Those lips were hot, bloated, wet and he'd felt their intent bring his body to life in ways that couldn't be repeated. But László's lips, although they'd promised to do the same, were thin and callous and empty.

And his fingers! Fingers with no human warmth greedily caressed Teddy's cheek. They stopped suddenly and pushed. The poke bonnet and the bows whirled to one side. Teddy's head lolled. His good ear blocked up now as his other one emptied again. This time, though, it didn't start refilling. Dark and splintered boards like the inside of a pauper's coffin was all Teddy could see now. He wanted to die. Die now, right now, before this snorter could bite him.

A piercing, a pinprick, then a spear like a bradawl slid through the skin of his neck. It sliced, sharper than a Bowie knife through the muscles there. And it stung as it drove itself deeper, prising apart and partitioning his tendons. It pulsated, too. It pulsated stronger than ever he'd felt his heart had pumped.

Teddy's voice worked finally. It came out as a flimsy, strained whisper of a moan, as though the pain had oiled his larynx. He felt László move against him again. Then his voice was gone again, sucked out of him. But the throbbing continued. It pulled and ripped and wrenched at his insides. All his blood, the blood that was flooding his innards, slewed directly to his neck as though he was tipped upside down and shaken, so eager was it to be siphoned out of him by the calculating, murderous intent of László.

The fatigue that he'd felt returned in waves so strong they swamped even the white space of his decaying mind. And then that was gone, too. Just the mottled yellow of the wagon and the empty consciousness remained. Along with it, the tearing, the dragging and extraction of his life.

Then he heard it: László was drinking. Drinking from the gash he'd made in Teddy's neck. Teddy felt him licking, his rough tongue lapping like a cat at the wound in his neck. László gorged and gulped and then waited and nuzzled and drank again.

Somewhere inside Teddy's soul... deeper than that, though. Deeper than ever he'd even thought his nitty-gritty quintessence might go, something was awakened.

Do you taste good? he asked himself.

Then there was fear. He tried to scream, scream away the nightmare. He opened his mouth wide, but no sound came. His body began to enjoy the pulsing at his neck.

No, this is wrong. Teddy's head was crammed full of thoughts that, for his whole life, had been obscene to him: a *man, a vampire, the Devil is sitting on my chest, sparking and spooning on the pinky skin at my neck, kissing and supping at my pulse.*

Sickened by what he'd been subjected to, Teddy lay helpless. The biting was worse than ever his cousins had dealt out to him. It was more painful than the time his uncle had punched him, kicked him and thrown him by the hair out of his home. It was more appalling than the slicking. It was more shocking than losing Louisa. More sorrowful than the tears of his sisters at the news of his passing. More torturous than saying goodbye to Ma. And then, with the grief-ridden truth that he would live an eternity, never again knowing the evidence of Pa's love, his soul disintegrated.

He was nothing now. Even the weak recesses of his derelict mind had been ambushed by the indolence of László's death scheme. Exhaustion seized the shadowy pit that had been Teddy's heart.

'You must be happy, ya?' László said. 'You taste as good as you look.'

László grabbed and turned his face. Teddy stared, seeing only muddy, sandy-coloured light. And, of course the blurred outline of László which he didn't much care for.

'No, no, no, don't sleep yet,' László said. 'Perhaps I have overdone this. Sorry, is not something I do a lot of. So, you will take a little of my blood now. Not too much. I don't have much. And we don't want to make you feel sick. Not that you can be sick.'

He grinned. His perfect teeth a brilliant white smudge against his blurred, tanned shape. He bent his own arm and popped away the cufflink. Teddy watched it: a momentary distraction, a last golden reminder of the world he was leaving behind. It fell away like the instantaneous death of a star on the eerie brink of a sandstorm.

'You will find a victim,' László said. 'It is their blood you will want.'

Teddy's drained body just wanted to sleep.

'No, no, no, not yet.'

I don't want to murder people, Teddy thought.

To his own ears it sounded little more than wistful.

'Yes, you do, Schatzibar. This is the Wild West, isn't it? Murder is what people do to each other here. Is no, how you say, "great shakes". No one will notice.'

Twisting and rolling the dark, narrow jacket into the white shirtsleeve, László bit down hard onto his own wrist. Then he moved quickly, so quickly it made even Teddy's sleepiness ache. László shoved his bleeding arm at Teddy, pressing it onto his lips.

Teddy had no muscles, no life. All he could do was lie there with his jaw slack and his face leaking. He couldn't drink, he couldn't even move.

Saphead, he thought, *think of that in your master plan, did you?*

'You don't worry, ya? The blood will run down into you.'

Teddy watched the arm across his face. Still, he felt nothing. When László sat back, he raised his wrist to his lips and swiftly, with not much more than a kiss, cured the cut he'd made. With his last vestiges of consciousness, Teddy cried. The actions László had just made were like his own. Or any of the cowpokes. Thousands of times, with thousands of tiny grazes or cuts or splinters made by the razor-sharp grasses on the range or the rough timbers of the ranch, he'd licked or supped away bleeding that was no more than a messy annoyance. László smiled at Teddy: his new disciple.

'Is just time now,' he said. 'In the old days, dying took only a couple of minutes. I can't see how this would change. Dying is still dying. So, you can sleep now. And to help you, I will tell you a story. Remember, though, Fledermaus, don't be afraid when you wake up: I will find you, ya?'

László moved back to the boxes and placed Teddy's hat over his face. He adjusted it so that it sat reverently.

Teddy stared into the dark. He fought the urge to drift off to sleep. No matter how desperate his body was for it, sleep was the last thing he wanted to do. If he did, if he let himself sleep, the nightmare would start. The nightmare that he'd never wake up from. It was at its scariest now, before it had even got going. Once he was in it, he'd love it. That was the most hellish, the pokeriest thing. He plumb didn't want to be the randy monster in his own nightmares.

His fight was in vain, though. He could stay awake no longer. The sound of László's voice morphed into melodic. He was mesmerising as he told his macabre lullaby.

'A long time ago, in old Royal Hungary, as the world was on the brink of war with the Ottoman Empire, there was a young prince whose name was Ladislaus Jagelovići....'

Teddy fell asleep.

CHAPTER TEN

Teddy's stomach contracted. On and on it contorted. Finally, just when he thought it would never stop, it snagged on his core and hung heavily, as though waiting for instruction. Somehow something must've lodged in there. Some sort of tapeworm-type creature, humungous and serpent-like, had made the pit of his stomach its nest and it coiled there, relentlessly slithering, winding itself ever tighter.

The discomfort dragged him from his sleep. Trying to ignore it, he raised his eyelids. Just a crack, just enough to let his surroundings in. And to find out if anyone else was awake.

Nope. He couldn't see a thing. The cowpokes often rose before dawn. But not this morning, it seemed, and the bunk house was as dark as an overcast midnight. Everyone must still be fast asleep. The usual smells were missing, though. The sickly-sweet manly odour, ingrained in the wooden walls, wasn't there. Neither was the scent of nicotine or the early morning autumn, which came up through the earthen floor no matter what time of day or year it was.

Everything was so still, too. Sakes alive, it must still be dead of night. What in the Sam Hill was he doing waking up at this ungodly hour? As though in answer, the stomach cramps twisted into a solid stone blockage making him wince and clasp his middle. Then, their work done, they vanished.

Teddy closed his eyes again and cussed the cowpoke that had callously taken his bunk, leaving him to sleep on the floor. Then he cussed the stiffness of his clothes and the unease that the cramps had left behind. Stubbornly, he tried to drift back into sleep.

The cramps had other ideas. They started off fairly unassuming, so he shifted and snubbed them. As though to show their irritation at being spurned, they gnawed at his sides until he awoke again. He lay still. Then he began to count, as if that would help. He couldn't quite latch onto what it was that he was counting, though; time, he reckoned.

The cramps escalated quickly, graunching inside him as though his belly was disagreeably rusty and starved of oil. They pulled his muscles in on themselves and entwined them to a taut rope. This time it wouldn't cease. Further and further in his stomach went. He screwed up his eyes and his face and drew his knees up to his chest, scrunching his body, trying in vain to slacken the tension in his middle. He stretched his mouth open wide to howl, but the pain was beyond that, too. His scream wouldn't come.

'End soon,' he thought. 'End soon.'

Teddy had encountered hunger pangs before. Even hardened cowpokes need to eat. Most had a tapeworm. Usually they were so busy that they forgot mealtimes and their stomachs eventually becoming ravenous, reminded them. Or Coosie hollered from the kitchen. But never had he had them this bad. And not in the middle of the night.

He felt a little offish, too; like he hadn't simply gone to sleep. Whatever it was that he had done had been something deeper, something more severe; final, even.

Again, the cramps came to a head and, although they lingered menacingly, they faded. So, he took on a light rocking lest they get nasty again. His rocking was joined by the creaking of wooden boards in motion. He was moving forwards.

A wagon! Had he slept in the bottom of a wagon and not in the bunk house or on the prairie?

He frowned, trying to grasp some recollection of where he'd been when he'd fallen asleep. He remembered the rodeo, the sunshine, the arena, the wagons and the cowpokes. But that was all. It was all washed in hues of blue and no one was recognisable. Voices melded into one long, low hubbub, out of time with the images that portioned themselves off into lightning-coloured flashes. A little afraid, he shuddered and stopped trying to remember. Now there was nothing. Just the blurred black of the back of his eyelids. Darn it, to be this disorientated he must've been in one dickens of a comatose.

The pulsing in his stomach jolted painfully as the wagon tripped over stray stones in the rough trail. Teddy's cramps probed a little deeper and he stiffened, waiting for the pain to peak, longing for the ebbing on the other side. He balled his fists. His fingernails stabbed his palms. Darn it, they were getting too ding long. He needed to cut them. Or get Mort to do it. No, Mort was back in No Man's Land, wasn't he? Teddy lived in Kansas now.

When the pains softened, relinquishing just enough space for him to think straight, he noticed that the black blur of his eyelids was streaked with Union blue. He opened his eyes wider and looked straight into the crown of his hat. His hat! He'd know that dark felt anywhere. That's why it was so dark and he couldn't see anything. It must've been placed over his face when he went to sleep.

He raised himself up on his elbows. His hat toppled off. He sat up fully and picked it up. The sleek curve of the brim was a bit crooked. He usually took much better care of it than that: what was the matter with him? His hat was the most precious thing he owned. Aside from his family — if you could call them things. Precious though they were, he didn't own them. Too queasy to think it through any further, he realised that he had no idea how he knew that they were so precious, he just did. Perhaps his memory was a whole heap slower than normal this morning.

Infinitesimal grains of grit were embedded in the felt of his Stetson. He wafted it about: parched grass and a lone black fibre floated out. There was something gummy on the inside of the brim just where the little bow protruded. What had he been doing with it? Perhaps he was drunk when he went to sleep. That would answer the question as to why his memory was so fuzzy and go a small way to explain the stomach cramps. He must've been full as a tick. Dang, that meant he'd have been embarrassing. He'd have to start apologising. Annoyance niggled the pit of his stomach now, as well as emptiness.

The wagon swayed and lurched. It was dark there in the back. Teddy's sight, though, was as sharp as if it were the middle of the day. Better, even. He gazed about. The swinging of assorted tack and tools resonated with a sort of blue, speckled dust. Silver bits and disused spurs glinted debilitatingly brightly. He dropped his gaze and frowned at his beloved hat. He brushed the kinky brim.

Something wasn't right with his hand. He only had three fingers on it. Surely losing a finger would be a strong memory. He grinned. Possibly even a good memory.

No. Not good. It would've hurt.

Hurriedly, he raised the other hand and wiggled the fingers. Four fingers and one thumb; all according to Hoyle. He ran his imperfect hand through his hair, and clutching the crown in the time-honoured way, he put the Stetson on. The hat fit snuggly. He took it off again. Then he replaced it and left it on. The finger lapse obviously wasn't a problem.

What was a problem, though, was: he'd had absolutely no physical sense of touching anything at all. He knew the hat was on his head. He could see the edge of the brim. But he couldn't actually feel it on his head. It was the same with his clothes. He knew that they were wrapped around his body, but when he rolled his wrists around, he had no sensation of his coat cuff brushing his skin. His fingers were numb, too. Perhaps he'd gotten cold. He didn't feel cold, though. In fact, he didn't feel anything. He wiggled his fingers again. No. Nothing!

The horror of this latest discovery was interrupted by the sound of heavy breathing. Teddy was alone in the bottom of this wagon which by all accounts belonged to his father. He looked up to where the driver should be sitting. Hunched over the reins, the driver was recognisable. It was his father. Thank the land! Teddy would know that hat anywhere. It seemed that he hadn't seen his Old Man for a hundred years. His father would know what to do. And, to boot, he'd remembered who he was. Instantly, his optimism returned.

He opened his mouth to speak up. Before he'd managed to make a sound, though, his father exhaled a long, stressful breath. His shoulders juddered and the breath that he pulled back in was equally long and shaky. Something was wrong. Something was very wrong. To all intents and purposes, his father was crying.

'Pa?' he said, trying to get up and stumbling back down. 'Pa, what's wrong?'

The wagon lurched violently to the side and Teddy fell over again.

'Are you alright?' he said.

The wagon stopped. Teddy scrambled to all fours at his father's back. He froze, seized by the stomach cramps. He baulked. They were no longer confined to the pit of his stomach. They'd risen into his chest and formed a jagged wedge in his windpipe. His throat constricted and his jaws ground, just like the Longhorns, continuing to graze even when there wasn't any grass.

Salaciously, intensely, uncomfortably aware of his father's flesh, Teddy reckoned that his mind and body were behaving like two separate entities. His father's skin was warm, luxurious like the plump cushions of a parlour — you want to touch them, handle and stroke them, but you're forbidden. This was sickening. He was having thoughts that the Sunday preachers said no man should have about another. Especially his own father.

He looked away. But his eyes, led by his lips, were drawn back. He was craving the taste of his father's neck. That wasn't right.

'Help me, Pa,' he said, his voice measured and quiet, 'something ain't right with me.'

His father didn't answer. Teddy tried to clear his mind. The cramps were on the rise again. Teddy tried to ignore them. He'd done it before; ignore pain, he must've done. He just couldn't remember how. Or when. He climbed over the boards of their basic, box-style wagon and into the seat next to his father.

'Pa?' he said, meekly this time. 'Are you giving me the silent treatment?'

His father appeared to be refusing to look at him.

'Go back to sleep, Theodore,' he said.

Theodore!

'No,' Teddy argued, 'I cain't.'

The colours of his father's skin reflected the moonlight. Mystical tones of slate and midnight blue turning to ultramarine mapped out Old Man Callington's profile. The colours stole away any further notion Teddy might have had of speaking. He was mesmerised. Dang, his father was a handsome man. He'd never noticed how handsome before. Old Man Callington was a businessman and as far as Teddy knew, he'd always been wealthy. He was a good man, too, a respected man. But none of that mattered. He was quite beautiful; in an artist's portrait kind of way.

Teddy flinched. He wasn't thinking straight. His father was shaking, almost cringing. At the reins his hands were pale, they seemed to be holding on so tight the tension was making them tremble. Perhaps he was cold, too. Perhaps he was ailing after something. Perhaps there was something more sinister going on, something Pa and Ma were deliberately not telling him, and it was making him nervous. After all, Teddy wasn't supposed to have woken up, was he? Perhaps he'd stumbled upon his father in the midst of a momentary lack of parental responsibility. He reached out to take Pa's hands in his own, free them from the reins. His father snatched them away.

'I said, "go back to sleep".'

'Pa,' Teddy protested, 'talk to me. I wanna help. Let me take the reins, you're gonna put us in a ditch.'

His father turned to look at him then. He stared straight into his face. Teddy started. Pa's eyes were perfect spheres and they were white with fear. He was afraid? No, it was more than afraid. He was downright scared.

'You're not real,' he said.

As though his body had only just come back to him from vacation somewhere, it provided a distraction; the stomach cramps loomed.

'Hungry, Pa,' Teddy cried, 'I'm starving hungry.'

He spoke with a slight lisp. That was new. He'd never had a lisp before. Unable to hide the pangs, he clutched his belly. He stared at his father, pleading for his help. Then it all became too much and he doubled up and cried out.

'Oh my dear God,' his father whispered, 'this can't be happening.'

'Help me,' Teddy whimpered.

The desperation that Teddy had hoped to convey through his eyes turned sour. It wasn't help he needed. It was sustenance. His newfangled, mixed-up senses revealed to him the latticework of greeny blue and purply red veins under the cover of his father's skin. They glowed, they pulsed and rippled, swollen with the undulating of pumping through, fast-flowing torrents of peaks and troughs.

The rest of his father had turned pale, his face and neck the same ghostly white of his eyes. Even his lips had drained of colour. Teddy didn't care about that, though, it only served to further expose the bulbous pipes that threaded and netted his old man's life together in the flesh. Teddy's ears drummed with the frenetic beating of his father's heart. He couldn't hear his own heart, though: it was silent, motionless, dead.

His eyes darted from the rolling rungs of the windpipe at his father's throat, around to the hidden junction of his jaw just below his ears. How tender the skin was there, how bewitching the melodic throbbing of his pulse. A juddering in Old Man Callington's heartbeat caught Teddy's keen attention and he stared at the older man's chest, transfixed by the pounding under his clothes.

'I need to eat,' he said. 'Feed me, Pa.'

Then, as something dawned on him, he grinned. It was something small and insignificant. Something they'd both been happy to forget. Until now.

'Adopted Pa.'

Teddy thrust claw-shaped hands forwards. He grasped Old Man Callington's collar.

'Dear God,' his father gasped.

Teddy ignored him. He didn't have time for grace; he needed to feed. He pulled the man close and pushed one hand up under his chin. In a choking, pincer-like grip he held his father to him, slighting the hands that scraped for salvation, ignoring the stifled prayers and strangled cries. With his free hand, Teddy tore at his father's clothes. He was frantic with the need to get to his veins. That was where the blood was kept, wasn't it? He saw nothing but its dark crimson fatness. It was food. It meant survival.

Pierce the flesh, puncture the veins and draw out the blood, repeated over and over in his head. He could smell its wet, rusty aroma, sense its thick and slimy coating covering the inside of his father's throat. He saw its spellbinding iridescence and he was hypnotised by its beating, its pulsing, its rhythm. He was infatuated and, like a buckle bunny alone in the tack store with her hero, he had to get the man's heart. Instinct told him to use his teeth.

'Go!' his father shouted. 'Go. Now. Run. Gee up.'

Chain links locked and loosened. The horses whinnied and grunted and heaved. Bolsters groaned against the axle and the undercarriage clunked. The wagon was jolted violently forwards.

Teddy and his father tipped sideways over the back of the driver's seat. They toppled, awkwardly angled, into the wagon bed. The fitted storage boxes ruptured dangerously as the two bodies landed half on, half off them, rolled, and wedged in between.

The old man's skin, thinner than Teddy's, tore and splintered on the jagged edges. Blood beaded along hairline cuts. Teddy snarled impudently, like a frustrated drunk at the waste of a leaky barrel. Jammed under the weight of the older man, the scent of the blood, fine and just right at body temperature, sent him fantastically screeching and flailing, desperate to get to it before it cooled and hardened in the night air.

The trail through the Kansas farmland was little more than a rough track, and with a lack of guidance, the horses fell to unpredictability. They changed course. The poke bonnet bows rattled and swayed as the wagon teetered on two wheels. The horses veered off-road and the wagon jackknifed, bouncing the wedged bodies free. Teddy rolled over in the air, clutching his father to him and landing on top. He laughed, intent on draining the old man of his life. This was too easy.

One of the bows snapped free. It batted up and down, smacking against the planks of the wagon: its curved wooden end looked like a blunt arrow pointing to Hell. Yesterday, Teddy hadn't cared for what the bows were made of. They were just wood. Tonight, though, the bows' origin seemed of deathly importance. He stared, terrorised by the pointed end.

His hat was dislodged, and his head dragged downward by his hair. It didn't hurt of course. In fact, Teddy hardly noticed, except that a handful of hair is a surprisingly secure anchor and his father used it.

'You are not my son,' his father hissed into his face.

Teddy grasped the old man's arm, pushing back his sleeve and plunged his nails into the weak flesh. The man grimaced but wouldn't be thwarted. He continued to cling to Teddy, grabbed his free wrist and pulled. Teddy's body twisted and his father climbed over him. Pinning one arm under a tough shin, he sat on his chest.

'Suffer little children —' he began to quote the Bible.

He unpicked Teddy's fingernails and a stream of blood, tepid and sour and delicious, trickled forth. Teddy's lips twitched and his teeth ground into each other, further frustrating his need to be fed. Using both hands and all his might, his father brought his hand down and tucked his arm under his leg. He glared into Teddy's eyes.

'...forbid them not —'

'Quit jawin', old man.' Teddy strained against the hold and shouted, 'I ain't no child!'

He'd never shouted at his father before. His upbringing, eclectic though it may have been, had fitted snugly with the relationship offered to him by adoption. His dream of a loving family had fallen flush with his father's need for a son. Then he'd met his mother, and together, Callingtons' parental broodiness had nurtured his sensitivities into believing his dream to have come true. What had started as a friendship blossomed to a loving bond that cherished far more maturity than most parents had with their young adult sons. Teddy and his father had never rowed. Disagreements had taken the form of respectful forbearance: agree to disagree; put up and shut up. Their deep, enduring and mutual friendship led them, without fail, around to some sort of unspoken compromise. And until now, they had both loved that relationship. Until now, neither would have put it asunder.

'The light shines in the darkness —' his father continued reciting.

Teddy screamed.

'Sakes alive, you swallow that book?'

He bucked against his father's body. He folded his knees and used them as springs to catapult himself upright. It was as though he simply stood up. Without the use of his hands to push on? And with a fully-grown man sitting on his chest? Hang fire: if he remembered rightly wasn't he supposed to be dead?

His father was upended, shoved backwards through the air. Teddy grasped his ankle. Dang, he was quick as well. His father grunted on impact. Teddy lifted the leg high, bringing the body to him and with the other hand clawed at the chest. Like all older people, his father wore too many layers. All Teddy got was a fistful of clothes.

He dropped the ankle and shifted his grip from his father's chest to his throat. Brushing away the hands that swung in to clamp on, he held him just shy of the boards of the wagon bottom. His father wasn't a short man, but then, flat roper heels aside, neither was he and his own feet stood solid.

'Where's your heart, old man?' he said. 'I know you have one. I can hear it beating.'

He held the old cowman close and snarled into his face, mimicking the booming of a human heart, 'Boom boom, boom boom.' He tore away the man's garments.

An invisible force, like the initial blow of a No Man's Land storm, unforeseen and hard as tack, stopped him. Static, clutching his father and staring at his throat, he was stunned. His father was wearing a silver chain.

The only chain the Old Man ever wore was his functional gold watch chain. But this one was delightful, and it twirled and rolled around itself, coiling at each clumsy human breath. It twinkled with a delicacy not befitting an old rancher. Threaded along its charming, dainty line a tiny silver cross nestled in the bushy, greying chest hair.

'Ma's crucifix,' Teddy said. 'What are you doing with it? Why isn't Ma wearing it?'

The savagery generated by his starvation faded. Mama. She'd be nigh unto consolable by the loss of her son, her kitchen doorway confidant, her daughters' brother. It would be this man, this man that he held aloft in one hand, that they would look to for strength, this man who would bravely lead them in the hope of salvation of Teddy's soul, solace for his spirit and rest for his body. This man that he was about to kill and eat.

'She knew,' his father said, his voice cracking with fear and frustration. 'She said something wasn't quite right. She made me take her cross and chain before we left, thought it might help, said she had a bad feeling.'

'She knew?' Teddy was aghast. 'She knew this would happen to me and she still let me go?'

'Blind fool! How could she know that you would take the soul of our son and use his body against his own father? She does not now and never will believe in your kind. Get behind me, Satan, you leave her alone.'

'Satan?'

Teddy bared his teeth and grimaced at the name.

'Satan,' Teddy said. 'You think I'm Satan?'

Coming from his own father's lips the accusation sounded so utterly deplorable, sordid even. There was no enemy more heinous than Satan. Teddy let go. He was dumbfounded. Confusion swirled around his head now and it seemed to be trying in vain to meld with emotions that were unrecognisable to him. But they were strong and they lacerated the confines of his heart and ruined his soul.

'Help me,' he said. 'Who am I?'

And then the stomach cramps returned.

The horses whinnied and shook themselves, uncertain in their unordered standstill. The wagon juddered. Teddy's father stumbled, losing his footing in amongst the jumble of broken boxes and spilled rodeo gear. He sat heavily, his broken heart obvious in his pitifully stunted breathing.

Teddy looked from him to his own hands. He stared incredulous at the claw-like nails, the dirty, bloodied lines. He turned them over and was sickened further by the brown and red smears of his father's blood, sticking the golden hairs together. He turned them back almost convinced that they weren't his, but the missing middle finger on his right hand told him otherwise.

'I'll not consort with Satan,' his father said quietly.

'Pa, please don't call me that. I really am your son and I'm ...'

He couldn't say it. The words jammed somewhere between the sentiments, his craving to say them, and his lips. He wrapped his arms around himself, keeping his hands out of view, holding his own body. He needed to tell his father that he was sorry; sorry for forcing him to call his own son Satan, for forcing him to doubt his love for him. Sorry for dying. Sorry for waking as this monster and for the pain of having to say goodbye again. Just sorry for everything, anything he'd ever done to hurt him.

Jaded and silent, his father watched him. Underneath the suspicion in his stare, Teddy saw sadness. That, too, was his fault. He tried to say "sorry" again, but it just came out as a mutated, ugly hiss.

Teddy's skull was racked with the pain of pent-up misery, his face contorted, but he could not cry. The old cattleman sighed, his breath long and hard, his shoulders and chest seeming strained. He was fighting back tears of his own.

Teddy fell to his knees in front of him. The old rancher grunted and flinched.

'…'smee.'

Teddy reached out to his father. Old Man Callington balled his fists and slid his hands away. Pa didn't believe him. The cowpokes' dime novels had shown him images of undead, bloodsucking folklore creatures; vampires, if that was what he was now. He tried to purse his lips, lose the inane grin that had been plaguing him since he'd woken up, hide his teeth. He stretched his lips into as much of a line as he could manage. He tried to mollify his eyes. They'd always been the clear, innocent green of a reed filled summertime stream, now he just didn't know what colour they were. Red? Yellow?

He gazed into his father's eyes. He hoped he looked as wretched as his father did. More, even. He fumbled for his hat and holding it properly, the way his father had shown him, replaced it on his head. His father closed his eyes.

'Do not look at me,' he said. 'Do not touch me. I will never give myself up to you.'

Somewhere inside Teddy, heartless remorse pummelled invisibly at him. And then he felt a stab in his chest. It'd seemed tangible. He pressed a hand over where his chest had hurt. Nothing! No sensation at all. His stomach reminded him again that it took precedence. No, Teddy thought, there is something more important. More important than feeding.

Pa, I love you. Teddy screeched inside himself. Sakes alive, it was simple enough. He wanted to tell his father that he loved him. This, this awakening, reanimation, undeadness, whatever it was called, was a gift that many men had begged for, grown men had cried for it. He had been given the chance to tell his father how much he loved him, how much he'd yearned for a loving family, hankered after it to the point of make-believe and still even when those daydreams turned to nightmares, he'd longed for it.

'Pa, I...'

Opening his mouth wide and contorting his lips, he ached to tell his father how grateful he was, just for having been given the chance to be his son. He could let him know now how fantastic it'd been to share his home, his family. Ma. And his sisters; they had to know, too. His father was the only one who could tell them.

But the words wouldn't come. It was like he kept plumb forgetting just what it was that he wanted to say. The stomach pangs arched inside him again, reminding him that his survival depended on his feeding. No, this was more important. He tried putting it a different way.

'Tell Ma, I...'

'I said, "You leave her alone." You hear me? You stay away from her.'

Teddy reached out to his father. He tried again and again to tell him. He grabbed the man by the shoulders. Old Man Callington winced so Teddy let go.

'Look at me!' Teddy hollered.

'You will not tempt me, Satan.'

'I ain't Satan.'

'You are of your father,' the old man began to quote scripture again, 'and your father is the Devil. He has nothing to do with the truth because there is no truth in him, for he is a liar and the father of lies.'

'Darn it, I ain't lyin',' Teddy thought miserably.

'My son is dead,' his father said, opening his eyes. 'I saw him die, his body was crushed, his face trampled, his eyes leaked pus, and blood trickled from his nose and mouth. Do you hear me? His own blood drowned him from inside out. He was a good, loving boy and his soul is destined for Heaven. You cannot be my son.'

Eyes wide with effort, he thrust his hands forward.

'Leave me, Satan, you've failed.'

Jingle bobs clattered like the ominous rattling of a shaman's staff. The same way brawling b'hoys might clasp brass knuckles, the old man was grasping the hammered goosenecks of a battered pair of spurs. The chiselled rowels jutting out from between his middle and second finger, his father thrust them forward. He plunged them into the soft, fetid flesh of Teddy's chest between the strands of his braces.

Teddy screamed. It should've hurt like the blazes. But it didn't. The spurs had achieved no more than an interruption in the uniformity of the buttons in his plaid, wool shirt. Deep inside Teddy a knot of something like anger began unravelling. He grasped the goosenecks and yanked the rowels back out.

'You cain't kill me, Pa,' he said, 'I'm already dead.'

You will find a victim.

Someone was speaking to him. He'd abide by what they had said. He was starving and the only thing around to eat was his own father. Plumb dragged out with this fight, he pushed the old god-worshipper aside and climbed back onto the driver's seat. He'd dump the ranting old fool in the nearest town and go get something to eat.

A desperate last-ditch attempt by the Old Man knocked Teddy off-balance. Surprised by his father's bowling into him, he was thrown sideways. Arms and legs wheeling, he flew clean through the air. Vampires, he reckoned, despite all the supernatural enhancements, were obviously no weightier than the living. He may have landed all boogered up, but it didn't hurt a hooter.

CHAPTER ELEVEN

Teddy lay face-down in the dirt. His neck was cricked, and he was alone, miserable and, except for the excruciating emptiness of his stomach, he was numb all over. Silence and the stillness of night all around him all but suffocated him. Even the air seemed close, foggy, impassable, like a gluey summer quagmire.

'Yea, though I walk in the valley of the shadow of death....'

The old man shouted the shepherd's psalm. It sounded as though he was a long, long way away. Much further off than the distance a man could throw a body. He sounded angry, determined and scared.

Teddy had never paid proper attention to that psalm, until now. The words made him flinch.

'Darn it, Pa!' he hollered out. 'You shouldn't be alone. Not at this time of night in this country.'

Teddy had, after all, sworn to protect his father, hadn't he? He must've done. Well, if he hadn't, he should've done. He straightened out the inhuman form that he'd landed in. With clicking joints, he scrambled to his knees. He had to get back to the wagon and help his father.

An old, reliable, Civil War Winchester discharged deadly lead-plumbs in Teddy's direction. It clicked and locked and the hammer pounded again. His father was shooting at him. There was no one else around. Teddy slammed his body back down. It was himself, wasn't it? It was Teddy that Pa needed protection from. Himself and his hunger pangs.

Cartridges ricocheted. Teddy raised his eyes. He couldn't see anything. Nothing was moving and nothing was nearby. Nothing at all. The shiplap buildings of the Kansas farmland, the trees, the trail and even the wagon itself had disappeared. More shots rang out. They, though, were swallowed up, absorbed into the night as though the ground had banked up into a thick, protective poky-soddy all around him.

A feeble remnant of humanity, so fragile it was no more than a shimmer, clung on precariously somewhere inside Teddy.

'Don't shoot at me,' he cried.

He tried again to stand. Stomach pangs sliced through him, doubling him up. He stumbled backwards. The third time he tried, he managed it.

The rifle ruptured again. Noxious buckshot blasted into Teddy's chest. The metal pill exited the other side. He'd just been shot right through. With a rifle. A Winchester. He should be writhing in unimaginable pain. He should be gasping for breath, crying for his mother. But the bullet may as well have sizzled into its own pretty angel dust before it had even got to him. Dazed, smitten with hunger, but somehow still standing, he raised a trembling hand to where the shot had hit. There was nothing. His palm, though, was puckered up with dust pebbles that, over time, had hardened. That wasn't right. He studied his other hand. Rat droppings and what looked like spider's legs were squashed into it. He shook them both and watched the debris fall away, but he had no sensation of any of it. What in tarnation!

The rifle repeatedly rocketed bullets into him. His body blew backwards with the force of each strike. Prayers and verse garbled in double time echoed in his ears. The Winchester whirred, the explosive volley spun him sideways, he wailed his submission and stayed on the ground.

For a long time he lay there, eyes screwed closed. Hunger hounded him, spasming his body. Initially, he didn't care. When he did open his eyes, he saw only darkness. He closed them again. After a moment, he reckoned on fear of the dark being something he hadn't had the luxury of for a long, long time. As though testing out a bruise, he opened them halfway.

He moved his head this way and that, stroking his cheek against the floor. Dislodging dust swept and ruched in his ears. The rodeo arena in 1887 sounded like that. He so wanted it to be 1887. Somehow he knew that it wasn't, though.

'I'm scared,' he whimpered.

He sounded just like a tortured, delinquent cowboy.

'I don't know where I am.'

Ted.

There was that voice. He'd heard it before.

'Theodore?' his father called.

Darn it, who in the blazes is this Theodore?'

'I think I'm shot, Pa.' called Teddy

This time there was no answer.

'Pa, where are you?'

I'm here. You need to feed.

That voice wasn't his father, was it? Teddy considered calling out again, but his better judgement was telling him that he wouldn't get an answer, that calling out would be a waste of time, that there was no one there. He lay still. His father, his ma and sisters, his home and his life had been lost, forgotten in the dust storms and stampedes of the last one hundred years. He yearned to see them again. That hurt, too. It hurt raw like he'd lost them only yesterday.

This was no dream. He had never dreamed. And as far as he knew, the dead don't dream. So, this was his memory. But it hadn't shown him the death of his family. Maybe he had murdered them all. His own treasured family. Maybe he'd hunted them down. Or taken the wagon, driven home and then intentionally betraying their trust, wantonly murdered them. He had no idea if he had, or not. Perhaps his memory was toying with him, saving the horrific, incomprehensible, inconceivable truth of his family's death at his own hands for later. He turned onto his back, lay flat and tried to remember them again.

Nothing.

Teddy squinted. He pictured his father. He saw his mother and his sisters. But he could not find any remorse for the state of them at all. He thought hard, managing to trawl up the sadness of loss in his father's eyes when his only son had died. He even raked up the look of heartbreak he'd seen that time almost a year before when the old man had, for a terrifying split second, believed him to be a horse thief. He winced at that memory.

Nothing, it seemed, would trigger the memory of his killing his family. That couldn't be right. If he had murdered them, surely now he'd experience something: some remorse, some mind-bending hatred for himself, some gut-wrenching abhorrence for what he'd done. Sakes alive, he was trying to torture himself with it. But there was still nothing. As though a beading kind of fizz had covered him, Teddy's flesh smarted. It was an odd, impossible sensation because the dead don't sweat.

His wits seemed to sort of step away from his mind, distancing themselves from the rest of him. They kind of embodied themselves into one man. That man wore a knee-length coat, his trousers stretched, staunchly starched about lace-ups that were all the go for professional people. On his head, his well-worn black felt cowboy hat. That hat was adorned by a braided leather band so new it was still green.

He turned then and stared straight at Teddy. It was his father. His eyes held no fear. Nary one was there any love in them. In the darkness, Teddy pressed his hands to his temples. No senses. Patting about, he determined to find out just what he had done with his fingers. But that brought only the same result. Nothing.

'Darn it,' he muttered, 'what's happening to me?'

As though in answer, his stomach wrung itself around and his spine twisted.

Maybe, this chap ain't your pa.

It sure-fired looked like him. The man looked away.

'Look at me!' Teddy cried.

The man took off his hat. Holding it by the centre dent, he toyed with the band and said: 'What if you didn't kill them?'

'What if I didn't?' Teddy said, widening his eyes, releasing his temples.

The man disappeared. Teddy closed his eyes. He searched for the man. He was nowhere to be seen. There was just intense darkness. Teddy's stomach began to coil inwards. He'd always had faith in his father. Always. As far as he could remember, he'd had more faith in him than ever anyone could've had in any crucifix-brandishing preacher.

His own lack of memory unjustified total trust in this fellow, though. Once again, he was filled with a melancholy that made him ache in places that he didn't think he had. He had no idea what had happened to his family. He didn't truly know if he'd ever even been home.

The cramps that had come with the psychopathy peaked now. Teddy winced. Those cramps were going to be the burr in his boot, weren't they? No amount of wriggling would dislodge them. Whatever his memory was doing to him, whatever senses and emotions that denied to him for over one hundred years might now make a riotous comeback, the needs of his stomach would be constant. The little nubbin of annoyance turned to anger, traipsing and stomping over the desperation of missing his family. The shame of his trying to murder his own father was replaced by the irritation that he hadn't actually managed it. His muscles flexed, and his hands fisted. His lips smiled, and his body began to relax into its standard depravity. The smile widened, his teeth bared, and he grinned.

He needed to feed. Find the nearest town and feed. Town. Food. Survival.

Where the deuce was he? Surely, at some point over the last one hundred years, there would've been occasions when he'd not slept at home. He was a b'hoy of the worst kind, a bloodthirsty reveller, he'd be a gunslinger to rival the grisliest outlaw. If he had a gun. He relished the thought of a hunt, a bloodbath and a night spent in the dirt, wrapped in various limbs, drunk, dizzy and thoroughly indulged by torment, murder and screaming. Okay, an itty bit of the screaming may have come from himself, but hey, what was a vampire to do? Still, he never awoke like this. He always got home somehow. He was sure-fired sure he was inside somewhere, but this was not his room.

Then he frowned, he couldn't truly remember where home was. The grin disappeared. He didn't like this. He was never uncertain of anything. Perhaps that was what the memory was trying to tell him; he had no home, he never had had. Darn it, that wasn't right. Of course, he had a home. He lived in a stately home. Somewhere. He lived there with Ladislaus. Or was it László? It was Prince Ladislaus the ding Unpronounceable. Or was he a King? Teddy couldn't be sure. He had been told, hadn't he? He hadn't been listening again, had he? It seemed like such a long time ago.

'Perhaps I have overdone this.'

László's words resonated around Teddy's head. He shivered at the memory. That kinky, foreign shote! The lying, deadbeat murderer was his sire. But not just that, he was his mentor as well. Wasn't it László who'd taught him how to hunt, to track, to kill? Sakes alive, he needed him. Without László, he wouldn't survive till the end of the day. Or night.

'Mein schatzibar, is like I told you, I saved you. I could never hurt you.'

László spoke to him. He heard it quite clearly. It wasn't Pa's Midwestern drawl. Nary one was it that lazy, self-assured voice he kept hearing inside his head. What the dickens? Just how many people had access to his thoughts?

'Where are you? László, are you in here?'

László wouldn't answer.

'Answer me, László!' he hollered, scrambling to sitting and staring into the darkness.

Nothing.

'Stubborn old croaker,' Teddy muttered.

You need to feed.

Teddy had no idea just who it was that was talking to him now. He was so miserable that he didn't much care.

'I can set with that.' he groaned.

The middle of his body had begun to wind again, reminding him that he was empty. The cramps grew and expanded with wanton greed seizing him more tightly than before. He needed to feed. He didn't want to murder. Again.

'László,' he groaned, 'you stay away from me, you hear?'

Confounded completely, he closed his eyes. It seemed lighter with his eyes closed. A magical sense of freedom accompanied the realisation that knowing how to track and hunt had been an indigenous part of him. It seemed to be one of those things that he'd always known. He'd probably always known how to kill, too. His stomach continued to coil inwards. His wonderful sense of release settled back into the crowbar hotel that was his mind now. It was murder that László had taught him how to do.

He screwed up his eyes. The hunger pang did not stop. He opened his eyes as wide as he could. Just like he'd been taught; let in as much light as was possible. Which, in this place, wasn't much. But it was enough for him to be able to see.

Someone glared at him. Someone with a face that was as old as his own.

The jaw primed in a petrifying, voiceless scream.

Teddy scrambled back. He twisted around. Out of the darkness another corpse loomed. The lips long gone, the jaw distorted, the teeth jutting, it seemed acutely amused by this newcomer to its bedchamber. Its ribs protruding from the shreds of its shroud had yellowed worse than the wood of an overused lynch mob scaffold. This was death. This would've happened to him. It was gruesome pokerish. Yet, up until now, hadn't he been worse even than that?

Behind Teddy an arm dangled free of its shelf: it hooked onto him, its fleshless structure rattled as he tried to move away. The finger poked free of frayed gloves; over his shoulder, it pointed to the grinning skull.

Hastily, he brushed the arm away. It came apart and he was left holding the hand. There was that ruffling of his skin again. He froze. On his back, it rippled in uneven ridges, the crescents scraping on his T-shirt.

"Does it hurt?" László's voice burst from his memory. Instantly it faded again. The pale hairs on Teddy's thighs knotted against his jeans. Quakes sizzled across his skull, morphing the hair on his head into a million razor-sharp, piercing Bowies that scraped over his scalp.

A tremble, dominating and all-encompassing, ascended from his loins; it rolled around his middle, exciting the hunger pangs. He scrambled to his feet once more. But the tremors were such that he needed to grasp the corpse's shelf for support. Dry gags rocketed through him. But his convulsing body was coerced into awkwardly straightening itself, let the demon's scream up through his throat, out through his mouth.

Nothing came. Teddy bumbled away from the corpse, leaning dangerously into the first. Laughter. The empty, disjointed laugh of death echoed off the darkness. But death was all that he could see. The shivering and the scraping started again. He had to get out of there.

Door. Where was the door? There had to be one, all rooms had doors, even cells and dungeons. Teddy couldn't remember how he'd got in here, though. He stared about. A jagged half-square in the ceiling seemed to be the only outlet. Teddy leapt at it, catching the edges. He pulled himself through.

Boots scuffing on the dirt-strewn floor, he whirled around, racing against the growing unease inside him. Lichen suckered in blackened patches, ruining a smooth colonnaded door frame. Acting before thinking, Teddy hurled himself bodily through.

CHAPTER TWELVE

Belched from the building like an eggshell from a bullsnake, Teddy fell to his knees. He stumbled and crawled through the little gully that housed his mausoleum motel. Phosphorescent, lime-green ferns, thigh-high and vividly plentiful, bestowed a fleshy canvas over the black woodland floor. Teddy collapsed underneath them. He may as well have been waking up for the first time. Again. Maybe it'd been like this every night for the past one hundred or so years.

He stared at the wiry, green infrastructure above him. This was not Kansas. He couldn't be entirely sure just where he was. Darn it, he couldn't be entirely sure just who he was. Nary one, could he remember how he'd gotten here. He couldn't go back. Going back meant meeting with László. And László meant obliteration. Again.

Teddy dragged his body out of the little gully. An ancient tree with crinkly, Confederate grey bark and a trunk as hollow as the corpses he'd just run away from, made for a comfortable spot. Teddy slumped against it. Opposite him was the secret stone building he'd spent the day in.

On the surface, the mausoleum was more of an enchanted chapel, a peaceful pergola hung with luscious tresses. A picture of a blue room frayed at the edges, a handsome, crimson-haired young man playing its piano, flashed before him. He frowned and waved it away. Just like that thoughtful room, the mausoleum bore no sign at all of the nightmare lurking underneath it.

Teddy picked at the ground. He unearthed a squirming grub and hurled it at the mausoleum's angelic door frame. It made a dead weight thudding plap as it hit. Perhaps that was what his companionship did for peaceful places of remembrance – turned them into terrifying chasms for decaying ghouls. It was unbelievable that the little mausoleum even existed. A stroke of luck that no one remembered it. But then, no one would remember him. And that hadn't been luck at all.

'Sakes alive,' he said aloud, 'thems down there were jest corpses. Dead people.'

He gazed up at the brown and black dappled sky. Dead people. He was dead, wasn't he? Just not dead like that.

Is what happens to you if you don't feed.

'Git out of my head, László,' Teddy moaned.

The deplorable reminder of his origins began to once again ravage his insides. He clutched his middle, crumpled and then threw himself to the ground, scrunched up in pain amongst the lush nightlife.

László had shown him death one night. It was a grisly memory that he'd let Teddy keep. Nary one had he ever let him neglect it. It was, he'd told him, important; more important than love or family. It was tantamount to the survival of their kind. Funny because the only other one of their kind he knew was László himself. And László was a liar. As well as a murderer.

Nothing, dead, alive, liar or not, would ever stop the vice-like cramps, though. He stretched out.

'Quit it!' he hollered.

His body wasn't listening.

'I cain't feel pain,' Teddy tried to convince himself.

He writhed, gripped and released the wayward vines at the tree's base.

'I cain't feel anything.'

His voice withdrew to a whimper. However much he might try to ignore the calling of his kind, it was futile. The stomach cramps finally became too much to bear.

The unrelenting quest to survive that had been born with the vampire that night so long ago flooded through him like the Arkansas' currents sweep drown drovers. The demon teased him with visions of tasty morsels, warm young blood, hot older blood. His own paranoia of dying, sinful in its magnitude, nagged at him to move, to hunt and feed. It was all-encompassing, overseeing, he'd do anything to avoid death, to avoid winding up like the long-neglected corpses buried in that woodland hole. He unwound his arms from his stomach, stretched his face into a hideous grin and hissed in synchronicity with the interminable twisting within him.

The shrill squawk of a woman's laughter pierced the air. It was followed by the clink of glasses, the slamming of metallic doors and the chatter of voices. The town was close by.

Feed.

Rising like the spectre that he was, he turned his head slowly this way and that, picking up the sounds that reverberated away from every surface they encountered. Noises so small that they boomed unnoticed under the radar of men. But to Teddy's supernatural ears, those echoes danced between the plates of the bark and bounced up from the ground. In luminous shades of orange, yellow and red the sound waves pointed the way to his next meal in plain English.

Teddy was so long dead, he was lighter than air. No cracking of twigs underfoot or handhold, he made no sound of his own. Well, none that any human would hear. He followed the sounds, cautiously at first, rationally balancing his way. Then the monster inside him grew ravenous. Teddy became careless, crashing through the undergrowth: he ran maniacally, moronically towards the town.

A large house came into view, its lights glowed between the needles of fluffy-looking pines. Must be the owners of the mausoleum. László certainly had picked his spot well this time. This country, wherever it was, certainly suited him. Teddy glared at the house and then ignored it. It was an ignorance that incensed the wantonness of the internal monster. It went frantic with the fear that it wouldn't be fed.

'No,' Teddy said, 'not on my own. Not without László.'

He might be able to slip through the security without any problems: that was one thing being dead was good for. Dead bodies – well, those that have been dead as long as he had – have no heat to be detected. He had no weight to trip wires and no reflection to show up in the windows. Added to which, for some unfathomable, unexplainably saddening reason, dogs disliked him. Just doing nothing, simply by existing nearby, he had the power to make them cry uselessly before defecating on the spot and slinking away to hide.

Still, attacking the house was too risky. The demon thrashed and screamed.

Too risky? When did you start giving a tarnation about risky?

The demon hooked and etched like a silver miner's pick at Teddy's insides. The stomach cramps seized and paralysed him, skidding him along the ground, leaving a rill the length of the Chisholm Trail in the woodland floor. Bloodthirsty, salivating and snarling, he slunk back towards the house.

'Don't do this.'

Teddy tried to steel his limbs. He dug his fingers into the ground, clutching at strong roots.

'I cain't do this all by myself.'

The craving for survival told him otherwise. He stood.

'Do as I say,' he told himself. 'You will only make us do something that will lead to regret.'

Stretching out an arm and three fingers, he pressed his claw-like nails into the bark of the nearest tree. The stomach pangs struck again, but Teddy resisted. He winced and held his ground.

You need to feed.

Straightening, he released the tree.

'I know. Leave the humans to their safety in numbers,' he told himself. 'Find one on its own.'

In no way was Teddy in a good enough state for a food fight, especially as he couldn't be sure of his own strength. Rabble-rousing a whole roomful of meals was not a good idea.

He followed the house's pebble-dash perimeter wall. Low and fast, he shot across the manicured lawn. Silent and unseen, little more than a sharp gust of air, he ran the length of the driveway, pausing at the corner to get his bearings.

The house stood at the convergence of a fork in the crude country road. There was no traffic. The sounds which Teddy followed didn't falter on the promise of oncoming vehicles, although the hedgerows strove to muffle them. At this time of night and in this mood, Teddy did not falter on the promise of boundaries — he'd hightail it as the eagle flew. He gauged the height of the hedge opposite, the one that surrounding the fields lay between him and the town, backed up a couple of steps, ran and hurdled over it as though it were no more than a knee-high corral.

On the other side, corn plants and plenty of them stretched before him. Ten-foot-high, tough and tucked up with yellow cobs, they seemed suited to this country as well. Teddy was beginning to think that he was the only one who wasn't. In Kansas they made whisky from the plants. But this wasn't Kansas. Nary one was whisky the liquor that he desired. He ran at full speed straight through the middle of the field. He grinned and opened his arms wide, slapping down the plants as he went.

Another road, another corral and what looked like a playing field. White, tubular structures in the shape of huge aitches stood at either end. Teddy sped across the tightly mowed grass: he was unable to resist a somersault around one of the structure's legs. On one side, the field was surrounded by an eclectic collection of buildings. Teddy crept up to one. The doors were large, glass and closed. The space within cold, dark and quiet. Teddy squinted at the building. No matter how newfangled his eyesight was now, he couldn't see through walls.

Quit stalling. There ain't no one in there.

'You cain't know that.'

The demon was probably right, though. This must be a college. Or a university. Teddy had never actually been in one. Or at least he didn't think he had. Cowpokes, skilled and proud, weren't in general learned people. They were by no means stupid, but they didn't take kindly to book learning, academic types. The academic types tonight would not take kindly to him either.

He slowed and slid into the shadow formed by the corner of one of the buildings. Most of its windows were draped with identical material; some drawn, some closed. Fandangoing bugs and dust mites clotted the frames of every single one. Where there were dust mites, there were usually flaky people.

Thrills in the form of excruciating stomach cramps plagued at his mind's strictness for rational, logistical tactics. The booming throb of the pumping of other people's blood filled his ears. His teeth needed an airing and so he grinned. There sure were plenty of people here. Amazingly, though, there was no food ripe for the picking. The hunger pangs brought him to his knees. The monster wanted to stop enjoying the chase and get down to the business of hunting.

This building's entrance lay across the pavement from a formal road wide enough for two-way traffic. On the other side of that was a park cultivated and cared for by whom, Teddy didn't know. Nary one did he care. Beyond that was a row of what appeared to be shops of all types and sizes. None of them would be open and there would be no shoppers, but curiously, deliveries were being made.

The fastest route to the shops' rear entrances where they might find a vagrant or two, would have been straight across the park, especially at the type of speed Teddy travelled. Rowdy groups of youngsters populated the park benches, making it also the most conspicuous.

You need to feed.

'I don't want to die.'

Teddy stepped away from the wall. Instantly, as though he knew what he was doing, he swivelled and bounced back to it, planting a toe flat on the brickwork. He catapulted himself, flipping backwards to grab a corner windowsill with his fingertips. The window had the drapes drawn and it was dark, uninhabited. Never one for dawdling, silently and swiftly, Teddy hoisted himself up. He stood on the sill, reached up to the top, hooked his fingertips onto the mortar over the lintel, and swung over to the opposite windowsill. Thankfully, it had the drapes closed. He continued to climb the ten storeys, feet to hands each time until he reached the parapet, only exerting himself to make a longer leap when the inhabitants were home, or a window was undraped and orange light spewed forth.

Tap on the windows. Mesmerise them into letting you in.

'I cain't. I don't know any of that vampire stuff.'

From the roof he surveyed his hunting ground. And then, not knowing why, he looked to the stars. Brown, spongy clouds covered the sky. He blinked and returned his spying to the ground. A few people hovered awkwardly on the pavements: they were sucking at posh-looking cigarettes. None of them seemed to actually know each other, but even so, they clutched together, chatting like miniature committees. No one stood or walked alone.

Teddy turned in the direction of the road. As fast as he could, he ran diagonally across the roof. Not stopping at the edge, he leapt off, elongating his body as though to dive into a lake. Up there, the breeze had turned windy and, as Teddy was weightless, he flew a long way, planning to stop in the trees that lined the road. Then he remembered that stopping was something else he didn't know how to do. He began to panic, ridiculously waving his arms and legs.

Lumbering and swaying its way along the road was a tall, double-decked wagon made of metal and glass. It chugged monstrously, showing no intention of slowing, never mind stopping. Teddy slammed into the ground inches from the vehicle's flat front. Driven by an insatiable need to feed, he didn't much care for being run down: it wasn't as though it would kill him. Humans might know how to kill him, but none of those he'd seen actually looked prepared to do it. A slight sadness slipped into his angst, threatening to calm him as he stood up. No one believed in him.

'Idiot.' The driver slid aside his narrow window: contorting his body, he made it almost entirely through. 'You got a death wish?'

'Been there, done that,' Teddy snarled.

He thought about baring his fangs, posing and hissing, but he didn't have the time to play-act. Moths and flies intent on taking advantage of the vehicle's stability and the white light it was emitting crowded towards it. Teddy's stomach twisted. He took a step towards the vehicle and pounced. The insects were as light as he was, they used his methods of tracking food, too. En masse, they sprang when he sprang. Teddy found himself elevated in a spotlight with a face full of moths. Darn it, he needed that emergency stop. He balled himself up, willing himself to become heavy, and crashed to the ground. From that abysmally crouching start, he was instantly at top speed, darting into the shadow before the driver could lower his finger.

Teddy crossed his arms over his growling stomach and shook insect bits from his body. He staggered to the blackened space under a rose-adorned pergola. Gazing up at the pappery flowers that in the day would have been white, he marvelled at their beautiful blue hue. Gears graunched and the large vehicle rumbled away, the driver no doubt chuntering about the addleheaded kid covered in moths. Angry and weak, Teddy slumped. He lay, a decrepit corpse in the rose garden stiff with the blood of dead deer.

'I cain't do this,' he mumbled.

Get up. Hunt. Feed.

He crawled to the end of the arbour. Behind him, the park opened out to a flat area devoid of road or wagons. Bars that had clearly been restaurants spilled their occupants onto the patio. The townsfolk smoked and laughed. The men swore violently, the women didn't appear bothered. Then they used the same profanity. All of them, at one point or other, poked at flashing handheld boxes. Envy for their freedom and hate of their community seethed behind Teddy's eyes. It tumbled through his insides, balling into energy that fed the demon.

'Too many,' Teddy groaned, peering again.

His jaw loosened, his fangs glinted, and his eyes narrowed; he slunk low on all fours.

'Don't do this,' he begged. 'They'll have me staked and decapitated before the dawn comes up.'

Further down the street, Teddy saw a large building with banners outside labelling it an art gallery. A show was a different class of people. Perhaps they would make mistakes.

'Give me one last chance,' he pleaded.

Teddy stared at the sky again. Still no stars. The lattice pergola was easy to climb. From there it was a short jump to a tree laden with ineffectual spines and baby cones. He ran along the branch and leapt off the end, landing in a jumble on the roof. That roof attached to another flat one and then a pitched one, and so on, all divided by walls that were hardly worth the effort but, he reckoned, they gave each building individuality. Teddy staggered and stumbled over the rooftops until he reached the end of the terrace. There, he slipped down the wall in the shadows of the cornices and sills to the porch and then to the pavement.

He was swamped by lamplight as he crossed the road. Trying to appear ordinary, he looked more like a messed-up drunk, fraught with the danger of airing his paunch at any given minute. People avoided him.

Inwardly hysterical, outwardly jaded, he fell into the shadowy corner of the gallery's porticoed porch where a young trio lingered. Their distorted conversation came clearly into his ears. He shifted slightly, listening for the heartbeats, heartbeats that swelled louder than the words which were of no interest.

One young man hopped off the kerb and headed to the throng. The other two remained in the doorway. Darn it, still too risky. He really was barking at a knot tonight and he wondered if vampires could just 'go hungry' like people could. His stomach clenched painfully, his chest baulked as though he had a blocked windpipe and his mind whirled with images of the bucked teeth and threadbare flesh of that evening's corpses. His fingers twitched. His knees stiffened, and he had to seize the wall to stop himself from moving after the boy.

'Go,' the young woman said, 'I'll be along in a minute.'

She had a silky, cultured voice and there was a laugh in it, an underlying happy note. Teddy closed his eyes. The girl's voice was soothing.

Horse feathers! Don't be a saphead.

'If you're sure,' the young man said.

Teddy rolled his eyes. What did they used to say? He frowned.

Shoot Luke, boy, or give up the gun.

The two in the doorway fell silent. Their heartbeats quickened. Salaciously, as though he was in charge of his own imagination, Teddy envisioned the two. The girl giggled. The boy held her tightly, his arms crossed about her waist. He tried to gain access to her lips. She was coy. He groped her body. She submitted. Their blood ran fast. Teddy closed his eyes. Their heat was so close. They had so much blood. He pictured it coursing down his throat, saw it covering his hands, splattering over his forearms. A sinewy, slimy sensation wetted his thumb and forefinger and he realised he'd been holding them aloft, either side of his lips rubbing them together. He leaned back. The old building was harsh, its big cinder blocks coarse. Indulging in the imagination he hadn't known for years, Teddy smoothed his hands over his chest, slithering them across his unworldly powerful body, entwining his fingers in the wiry hair on his naval. The warm liquid blood he'd sensed seconds before left swathes the shape of his hands along his torso. He was in danger of becoming as intoxicated as the throng outside the bars and he hadn't even drunk the blood yet. Perhaps he could take both the lovers in the doorway. Wait until they become so distracted with each other. Then he could take one. And then the other. It wouldn't take long.

All too clearly, the boy tutted. Teddy heard his sharp intake of breath. He sensed his despondency. It ruined the illusions. But there was anger in the boy's soul, too, a blossoming, unvented wrath in his body. A demonic empathy with the vengeful boy arose in Teddy. It served only to give him the strength he needed. Intently, he watched from his darkened hiding place, hoping for the worst.

The gallery door banged shut. The woman was gone. The boy was still there. He stepped towards Teddy.

Teddy froze.

Do it. Do it now.

He waited for the boy to walk a few more steps past him. Then stepped up behind him, wound an arm around his throat and dragged him backwards into the shadows.

Chapter Thirteen

The boy that Teddy ensnared in the crook of his elbow had time only to grunt in surprise. Teddy tightened his grip. The boy stumbled and trod heavily on the flat, grubby nubuck of his boots. Teddy didn't feel a thing. Ankles twisting, the boy scraped stupidly at his attacker's dirty, denim-clad thighs, before falling onto him.

'Don't touch me Tender,' Teddy said, 'I don't got no feeling and I don't like to think of where your hands are going.'

He grabbed one of the boy's wrists. The boy was difficult, he steeled his arm. Applying some force, Teddy buckled the boy's elbow and folded the arm up behind him. He pinched it between their two bodies and tightened his hold around the boy's throat.

'You loco son of a gun,' he growled, 'I oughta strangle you where you stand.'

Don't be a lickspittle all your life, you need him alive.

The boy gagged and hissed and wriggled.

'Dang, if you ain't hell-fired afeared.'

Teddy laughed at him as he clawed at the one bicep he could reach. His fear was delicious, his clutches in vain, he managed only a grasping tug of Teddy's T-shirt sleeve. Teddy grinned as the boy slapped and gouged at the strap-like muscles of the strong cowpoke forearm across his throat.

'Lunkhead. You might as well throw up the sponge,' Teddy snarled. 'Like I said, I don't got no feeling.'

He yanked the boy's arm upwards again. The boy gasped, but other than that, took no notice of Teddy's command. He writhed and kicked. Then he bucked his body, in an effort to throw Teddy over his shoulder. Teddy was bigger, in better shape and fuelled by the scorn of the fact that the town's young people were so unfit. So...stodgy. There was no one here who'd give him a good fight.

'Thunderation, Mudsill, you blowin' out worse than a peeled alive cottonmouth at Coosie's shindy.'

The boy tried to speak but all he managed was a choking splutter. He went rigid, bracing his knees and planting his feet. Teddy squeezed him close and picked him up by his neck. He manoeuvred him into the gloomy recess made shadowy by the gallery's porch. Placing a toe in the crook of the boy's knee, he pushed. The boy's leg collapsed. Teddy stood his ground. The boy's spine strained and his shoulder sprained. His arm cranked up behind his back and he huffed and breathed hard on Teddy's arm. His heart beat in double time.

'Sweet deuce,' Teddy muttered, relishing the promise of blood.

He repeated the action with the other knee. The boy spluttered words Teddy had only ever heard in their literal sense. Hooked on by his chin, he hung, holding Teddy's arm for all he was worth. Which as far as Teddy was concerned, wasn't much. He released the boy's throat. Reckoning he was quicker than ever the boy could even think about reacting, he snatched up his wrist.

'Do I know you?' the boy gasped.

'I don't think so,' Teddy told him.

Jest get on with it, Ted. Stop playing with your food. Kill him. Eat him.

He stepped across the boy's legs and grasped the top of his scalp. The boy had thick hair. It crunched like straw and that made it all the more grabbable. Teddy twirled a good handful, pulling it through his fingers, forcing the boy's head back until he could see the terror in his eyes.

'Who are you?' the boy said, his throat muscles undulating alternatively as he spoke and swallowed.

Teddy couldn't answer him. Aside from plumb not knowing the answer, he couldn't speak; the boy's throat had captivated him. The muscles there were taut, smooth and moist, working constantly under the pure white skin. They were beautifully stretched one minute, malleable and luscious the next. Teddy squinted for a closer look.

Exposed by the askew dishevelment of his shirt, the curve and join of the boy's collarbone had become exquisitely vulnerable. The flesh there was thin, the bones smooth, military straight and ripe for the snapping. Teddy grinned. Somewhere in his hellish past, he must've enjoyed the gell and mucus within them.

Something sharp bit at his taste buds. They'd awakened. Cologne; it was like an apéritif and it had done its job, stimulated his appetite. Teddy stretched his mouth wide, letting in air, trying to get the spiking taste away.

'What are you?' the boy said.

Momentary scepticism halted the boy's heartbeat. It startled Teddy too. Then the demon began to preen inside him. It revelled in its own narcissism. It spoke in persuasive tones in Teddy's head.

'Yup, you are indeed, death-on unbelievable.'

'What do you think?' Teddy said.

The boy went into fresh spasms, convulsing against Teddy, scratching at him with shaking fingers. Teddy was forced to tighten his hold. When the thrashing and cursing didn't gain him his freedom, the boy sort of knocked at the top of Teddy's hand. It was quite sweet really.

'I have friends,' he panted, 'lots of friends.'

His dread was delectable. It buzzed on Teddy's tongue, deforming the rims like the distressed edges of overused saw blades, swelling and then butting against his teeth. He widened his smile. It was more of a forced grin. He cocked his head as though to endear gravity for help in volumising his face. He licked his teeth. The canines were pointed and long like newly whittled corral posts. They pricked his tongue. No saliva. No blood. Dang, it felt divine. Teddy couldn't settle on whether the fantastical phenomenon was to be had from the pure knowledge that his fangs still worked, or just the piercing of his tongue. Hang it all, it was right smart, Simon pure, ace-high.

'If you make me bleed,' the boy said, 'they make you bleed.'

His threat was pathetic. Teddy looked at him. Anxiety had made the boy's veins quite visible, they thwamped and slobbered, but still, it would take a fierce blow to drive the canines through the layers of flesh. Teddy's stomach lurched and his limbs flinched. His dreadful good mix of cowpoke stamina and supernatural bite should be all-fired strong enough.

'Don't think you can hide. They'll decorate this town with your blood.'

'Hesh up, you nippent saphead,' Teddy said, 'I don't know what they been book learnin' you 'bout my kind. I cashed in a long time ago. I bled out all my blood the first few times I got shot.'

The boy cried and blasphemed. His heartbeat skittered into a frenzy of fear. Teddy laughed. He saw its beating, followed its pulsing from just under the boy's ear, down to the base of his neck and back again. Its quickening made his own body react. He detected a weak, out-of-time tapping, and noticed that the boy was once again trying to pound at his hand.

Heat from the boy's scalp scorched gratuitously into his fingers. It weaved around the creases, scythed the calluses and prised its way between his skin and his nails. It was like his fingertips were defrosting. It hurt. It was amazing. He stroked the boy's palm with his forefinger, the boy was wet and slippery.

'Sakes alive,' Teddy said, loving his lisp, 'what're you doing to me?'

The boy's coarse, sticky hair flicked like the bristles of a livery's tough brush. Teddy watched, enthralled by the sensation when it groomed and tickled against his skin. He turned his hand over and over, tightening and releasing his fingers again and again. The hair looped, curled and tangled as it strapped itself ever tighter around Teddy's hand. The boy winced, squirmed and swore; which only made Teddy pull all the more.

'Stop!' the boy said, his sobs rasping, 'What are you doing?'

Teddy couldn't explain. He was mesmerised by the impression on his skin, left by his own food.

'You feel good, darn it.'

That was all he could offer. He taunted his prey. He couldn't help it; the more he teased it, the more he played on its pain, the more his own body rewarded him with physical sensations.

He wanted more. He craved more. He could touch things. Somehow he had nerve endings, senses. He flattened his hand over his chest, swiping away the gunk-covered T-shirt, eager to find the pummelling of a heartbeat there.

Immediately, the boy's head flopped forwards. There was, of course, no pummelling in Teddy's chest. The boy, free of the suffering inflicted on his scalp, planted a hand flat on the wall. He pushed back onto his incarcerated arm and began scrabbling about, trying to pivot and dislodge his attacker.

Now that Teddy no longer held the promise of fresh, human blood so near, the sensations in his fingertips faded. He moved swiftly, yanking the boy's arm upwards, seizing his free hand and folding that too, behind his back. He layered the two hands and held them in one of his. Cupping the boy's chin, he forced his head back until the base of his skull was chock to the top of his spine.

The maniac inside Teddy demanded survival, it terrorised him down to the very ancient myth of his kind. It also possessed him and it strummed along with the beating of the boy's heart. With each thump Teddy's yearning for that sense of touch grew more outrageous. His cruel desires sensationalised each jerk of the muscles that ran alongside. The boy swallowed hard and stared up at him; there was an urgency to it, like he was striving to accept his own demise. He rasped out oaths and he questioned Teddy's sexuality, his birthright, his ancestors.

The words caught in Teddy's ears. They jammed in his mind. They stunted his intentions. The boy had it all wrong; sure, he talked funny, he knew that. But it was just cowpoke talk and he didn't know any other way of talking. Even László, after over a century together, hadn't always understood him.

What he did understand though, was that this boy had insulted his parents. He had no right to do that. So, hang it all, perhaps he had turned out bad. Worse than bad. It wasn't as though that had been his intention. Nary one had it been theirs. He was all-fired sure of it. His parents were good people. He was all-to-pieces sure of that, too. Even now, after everything that he'd done, his ma would hug him to her breast, hold him tight and soothe away all his sorrowful, evil acts. If, of course, she could. His ma was long dead.

Teddy heard laughter then. Sakes alive, this wasn't funny. The laughter was hollow, more self-congratulatory than mirthful. It echoed right through his head. László. It had to be László. László was in his head. Again. But then he had been there for over one hundred years.

Someone else spoke to him. Another voice inside, although it wasn't the demon. He shook his head; in doing so he must've tightened his grip on the boy, because he cried out. In his own accent, the voice was strong, deep and partched with smoking, and it wasn't that much older than he was. It was knowledgeable, too, and when it spoke again, it didn't talk to him, it told him a promise. It was Dent. Caporal Dent. Dent had been a friend. This sure-fired wasn't the West, though. And Dent was dead, wasn't he? Dent had a saying, didn't he? What was it? It had been important. More than a saying, it was a code of conduct, higher and wider than the laws of this land, whatever they were. The code had been something to do with being decent to strangers, warning your enemy before shooting them. Darn it, he wasn't about to shoot anyone, and this boy wasn't his enemy. Neither one of them was being respectful, gracious or honest to the other. They were at a stalemate; one of them needed to be the bigger man here. Teddy got the notion that was something that he hadn't been for a long, long time.

'What in tarnation, shavetail?' he said.

His own words made him flinch, but he didn't know how to right his language.

'I plumb don't wanna bed you down.'

The boy wouldn't understand him. He let go of his jaw.

Then you'll die.

'Let me go,' the boy croaked. 'I don't have anything for you.'

Yup, you sure do: you have your blood.

The hungry demon inside him wound and slimed its way along Teddy's spine as though it were a tangible, gelatinous larva, leaving a phlegmy, toxic trail in its wake. Teddy's stomach wrenched and coiled. Under his ribs, the sensation solidified into a block. Then it excreted itself and moved on up again.

That's what I want. It's what I need. You will kill him, Ted.

Teddy grabbed the boy's scalp again. The boy whimpered. The entity lodged in Teddy's throat sought to work his jaws. It split again and set about infiltrating his whole face. It glared through his eyes, flared his nostrils and stretched his lips. The boy closed his eyes.

'Please,' he whispered, 'I'll make it worth your while.'

Teddy forced his sight down to his hands: one restrained his victim's wrists like a lawman's irons on a petty nibbler; the other was woven into his hair with meat hook fingertips.

'Quit bellyaching,' he said.

He hauled the boy to his feet, dragged him and slammed him face first into the wall. The boy cried out. His nose crunched. Thick, dark blood ran down the cleft in his upper lip. It spread over his mouth, etching the crevices black. It puddled over the rim and dribbled over his chin. Teddy smelled its rancid bitterness. He coveted its taste.

The boy screwed his eyes closed. He puffed and heaved in rapid succession through his blood-drenched, split lips. His face contorted awkwardly and water that reeked of salt leaked from out under his eyelids. He mumbled what sounded like a confession to some or other crime of passion.

'Varmint?' Teddy laughed, 'Do you think I can give you absolution?'

Addleheaded kid! He pressed on the boy's palm. The boy began to pray.

'And why do all you people pray? Sure as I am standing here now, it ain't never saved any of you.'

He took the boy's free hand and straightening his arm back, turned it vein side up. The boy wheezed out a muffled cry. His nose grazed the wall, rupturing its membrane and crashing the cartilage. Teddy's sinuses sensed it all.

'Darn it, if you don't smell good an' all.'

The boy fell silent. Teddy could no longer hear his heartbeat. He hadn't killed him; he couldn't have. In this heightened state though, he couldn't be sure of his own strength. Without László, he was out of control. Perhaps he'd scared the boy to death. Maybe he'd pushed a little too hard. His grin disappeared. Now he wouldn't get fed, nary one would the demon. He shook the body violently.

'Breathe,' he growled.

Quit cavorting around.

The boy's ribs rose. Teddy's grin returned. He used his teeth to rip open the boy's shirtsleeve. A cufflink popped from its mooring and clinked away down the gutter. Its glinting surface bemused Teddy. No more than a square of nickel, it lingered dangerously on the edge of the storm drain. An odd need to see the cosmos gripped Teddy. There may be a fireball burning its way through the vast, star-splattered sky. Oppressive, low cloud still covered this sky. In patches it was an orangey sludge colour as though bludgeoned by the town's street lamps. But there was not even one star to be charted tonight.

The boy's heart gave a sudden lurch. Teddy's throat constricted. A wave of throbs surged along his victim's naked forearm. His vein was crooked like the Little Colorado, bluer than horsemint and smelled just like a hot dinner should. Teddy needed no encouragement. He sank his fangs into the boy's wrist, biting hard, puncturing the vein and releasing the blood which burst into his mouth.

The warmth reawakened his tongue. He raised his head and massaged the wound before lasciviously laying his tongue over it. Ash. Dirty, acrimonious nicotine. The boy's blood teemed with it. In over a century, Teddy hadn't smoked anything. Now, his suppressed addiction to it took charge. Now, he didn't want to stop.

Satisfaction drew a moan from his throat. His senses might have been dulled by the daily death of his kind, but a shot of blood was all they'd needed. Now they were invigorated.

Teddy's victim kicked. He pounded his body into the wall, and his small, boring and functional belt buckle chinked on the concrete. Teddy lapped up the coppery pleasure of young, juicy blood. It was both tantalising and soothing at the same time. It soaked into his tongue and wetted the membrane that covered the sides of his mouth. The boy cried and screeched. Scratches beaded through holes in his jeans, on his face and his torso.

Blood fragranced with the decay that seeks to tarnish a body too long dead bubbled from the boy's wrist. It was perfectly warmed up, lightly spiced, although somewhat rare. It was just the way Teddy remembered it. He savoured it.

Leaning like a cowboy on a porch post, except the post was the boy, the shoulder blades closed in on the back of Teddy's hand. Minutes were all he had to enjoy his meal. He chugged and gulped. He opened his eyes wide, as wide as they'd go, stretching the lids upwards, pulling the rims down. The distant spark of life in them grew supernaturally strong. He gnawed at the boy's wrist and let the lids hang languid, nary one were they open nor closed.

The tissue in his skin flexed. He swallowed and felt the sinew that surrounded and infiltrated his muscles glisten. Internal electrodes began to flicker. Tendons up and down his body tautened, his muscles solidified, and his limbs strengthened. Then his spirit danced, freely, brightly and malevolently. He gargled and sucked.

Teddy was no longer weak. He ached to run faster than the Union Pacific Railroad, climb quickly up the forty-foot oaks, leap from the tops of buildings, and fly on the night breeze. He was no longer angry either. He was wayward, naughty. He wanted to cause mischief, deceive people, hurt them and then laugh at them.

Deeper than any of that, he had to get back to László. If he cowed down enough, licked the old slang-whanger's high falutin' boots, they could go back to the way things were. László would let him do this again tomorrow night, wouldn't he? And the night after that. After all, they were a couple of b'hoy deados together, weren't they?

He raised his face and waited for a moment, watching the cut he'd made on the wrist. He relished that last quivering, cooling buzz. Risk. Adrenaline. That was the sweet, secret ingredient. The boy's legs gave way and his body sagged. Teddy dove in for the final rush of life that would blow his senses sky-high.

'Hello?'

The voice of a girl. Angelic, innocent iridescence chimed in on Teddy's unsophisticated wavelength. He grunted like a foraging hog. Anger immediately balled inside him.

'Is everything okay?' she called out.

The voice wasn't in his head. Nary one was it the girl from the gallery. This girl's voice was deeper and yet younger. The boy squeaked something unintelligible. He tried to stomp and shuffle. More than anything, he just whimpered.

Teddy wrapped his hand tightly around the boy's wrist, consciously stemming the wound. He thought hard, his demonic need to survive focussing his mind. He closed his eyes. In his head he formed words, envisaging the letters of each one. His internal voice, Midwestern American by nature, boomed loud and clear, sounding out the commands like he was in the military. Then he pictured the boy, wincing with every strained breath, pressed into the rough cast wall by Teddy's own hand. He wormed his tragic demands through to the boy's head and saw them taking shape there.

Tell her to go away. Tell her everything is jest hell-fired screaming. You don't need anything. She has to go away.

'Help me!' the boy whimpered, his voice strangled, wretched, half-dead.

Jest tell her.

'Help,' the boy sobbed.

Teddy could send as many telepathic messages as he liked, but that didn't mean the recipient would obey them now, did it?

'I hear you,' the girl called out.

Laughter burst into Teddy's head again. Had he sent the message into the wrong ding mind? László had always said that he must be able to actually see where he was sending his communications. It occurred to him, once again, that he'd never questioned László. But László had sent him messages when he wasn't in the same room. Darn it, László nagged him when he wasn't even in the vicinity.

He growled and glared towards the girl. Wafts of air so delicate they were invisible to the human eye swirled around inanimate objects on the pavement, bumped off abrasions in the walls and chiselled into corners. Even the darkest recesses had light. White-hot or blue-cold particles and weird microscopic creatures revealed shapes and things thought to be secret. Their ebb and flow kept Teddy abreast of what was happening. He could not, however, see through walls and with no one moving, the air gave him no clues.

The boy was whimpering and rasping. Teddy's head was filled with László's laughter. Unable to think straight, frustration that his situation was getting the better of him interfered with his mind. He stamped and kicked out furiously, landing a high Cuban heel in the fragile ligaments of the boy's ankle. The boy screeched and his ankle snapped. The arms that Teddy held were wrenched into the air which only caused the boy to cry out again.

Quit yer bellyaching. Teddy tried telepathy one more time.

'I have a phone!' the girl yelled. 'I'll call someone.'

A phone? What in tarnation was that? Maybe she was scared. He could use that against her.

'...and I'm not alone,' the girl said.

The laughter in Teddy's head burst into a guffaw. It became raucous, hysterical, uncontrollable almost. Teddy lost all concentration. His senses ceased to feel, his sinuses ceased to smell and his tongue ceased to taste. It had all disintegrated. All that savouring, relishing, all that wonder at the orgasmic taste of blood was gone. Gone back down inside him, mingling with the dust that was all that was left of his innards, his grimy, slovenly, desensitised person.

The boy whined. Darn it, Teddy thought, he should've hauled this boy further away. He should've been more methodical, more rational. He'd had time. During all that struggling, chatting and feeling, he should've been dragging. He'd let the craving take control. The hunger had worked him like a puppet. Now he'd gone and done it again, hadn't he? The very thing he'd vowed never to do. He'd done it. Murdered.

Schatzibar.

László called in his head. He cooed like a boot-licking, randy whore.

You are, how you say, 'barkin' at a knot'. You cannot win. Finish him. Finish what you started.

''Elp,' the boy gasped, 'need am…am.'

He wasn't dead. Sakes alive! Teddy couldn't breathe a sigh, but he now knew relief. It was a Bowie in the conveyer that seemed destined to be his undoing. Thank the land, he thought, and he didn't care who was listening.

'Am…' the boy tried again. 'Get an am…'

He couldn't say it. His body didn't have enough blood left to work his voice properly. He was weak, nearly dead.

Finish him, Fledermaus, or you will die.

Teddy stared at the boy. Then he glanced away. The helpless, half-dead body of a twenty-year-old rodeo champ lay on the path not far off. That was pokerish; that boy, that broken-up body, hadn't been there a minute ago. László leered over the body, pressing his wrist to the mouth, watching, grinning. Teddy shifted his gaze. The image disappeared only to materialise again. Teddy blinked it away. As soon as his eyes reopened, he saw the wretched boy again. Wherever he looked, it was there, his memory seemed determined to form its gruesome reminder in the nearest available space. Teddy was that ruined boy. László, his sire, his master. The boy that Teddy held pinned to the wall mumbled incoherently again.

'Medic,' Teddy hissed.

He dropped the boy's arm, let go of his hand and watched him slump. The clicking of his mismatched bones should have been sweetly macabre. But it was just horrifying. The boy lay there, flopped at Teddy's feet, his arms useless at his sides, his wrists ridiculously bent, and his eyes stared. Teddy dropped to his knees and listened out for the faint pulse of the boy's heart. He was embarrassingly overjoyed when he heard it.

'Jest like I told you last night, László,' Teddy said, 'I ain't no killer.'

'Who?' the girl called. 'Who isn't?'

Teddy smiled. Then he started and purposely straightened out his lips. Something fanciful, enchanting, tripped around in his stomach now. It was small and ticklish, it made him twitch all over. Best of all, it outwitted the engorged serpent. The girl's naivety was ding endearing. It reminded him of himself out on the range. It amused him. Although he was all-to-pieces sure he'd never been endearing.

'Who's there?' she called again.

Her persistence seemed to have developed a persona and an agenda all of its own. An itty bit like his own demon. Unlike the demon, though, it was courageous, realistic and logical. Given half a chance, it was going to thwart his evil desires.

Come home, Teddy.

Chapter Fourteen

Teddy lingered there in the shadow of the gallery porch, the stricken boy at his feet. Mischievously defying László's orders was plumb pleasurable. László wanted him to do something, in this case kill the boy and come home. And, Teddy, was rebelling. Childishly, that thrilled him. He twitched again. He liked the twitching. He waited. He smiled, a genuine smile, he reckoned. No one spoke. Teddy waited some more. After what seemed like hours when neither the girl nor László had spoken. Teddy stopped smiling and yelled.

'You need a medic.'

'Right. I'm calling the police, right now.'

The laughter started up again. The police. Wasn't that what people in England called the marshals, the sheriffs and even the deputies? This was England, wasn't it? Teddy didn't think he'd ever been pursued by an English posse. Or, for that matter, a posse of any sort. Of course, he couldn't be sure. Nary one did he want to find out. He had no idea of the firepower, nor the hunting or the tracking capabilities of an up-to-the-minute, English posse.

He stared at the half-dead boy, momentarily appalled by the evidence of his poorly attempted murder. He glanced about himself unsure of his surroundings. A rattling clutched at his stomach. It was a sensation he'd had before. Recently. It was fear. If he didn't move now, it would seize his whole body.

He stood. His clothes creaked as though stiff. They were covered in dried blood and guts. He'd been licking at the wounded boy, hadn't he? He'd been supping and biting and savouring. If he was found here with this bleeding boy at his feet, holding no weapons to speak of, blood dripping from his teeth and hands…well, the conclusion arrived at would be right enough. He'd be judged and executed; gunned down where he stood. Hemped, at the very least. Then, when they figured out that the hemp party didn't kill him? Well, then what? The base of his spine began juddering. The pleasurable twitching fled. Only the evil remained, a heavy frozen lump. Instantaneously, it thawed. Then it froze again and started a feverish shuddering. His body and the evil within it didn't want to discover the "then what".

Laughter, hysterical and bloodthirsty, howled around in his mind. A bell, high-pitched and stagnant, fired off a round of three dull, monotonous pips. An alarm. A code. He knew code. The memory of it slammed to the forefront of his mind. Three of anything, smoke puffs, gunfire or just plain old whistling meant, 'Help!' He needed to leave.

He glanced about himself. The gallery building was old. Its windows, boarded on the inside and set low in the walls, were tall, taller than he was. In between, the blocks were of a light brown, rough cast. Excepting, of course, where the boy had been writhing and grazing his skin. There they were mottled, dark brown and red rough cast. The Capitol Building back home had been made of the same sort of stuff. Hang-fire; he hadn't killed anyone there. Had he?

Just like a cat gauging the height of its scale, Teddy studied the gallery roof. His eyesight was precise and coupled with his lack of weight, however much he'd just eaten, finding handholds and climbing up was easy. In seconds he was at the parapet and slunk over the carved cornice.

'The police are on their way.' The girl's voice drifted up to his ears.

As though hypnotised, Teddy stopped mid-escape. The girl's accent was divine. It was regal, smooth and polished in that way that only the English have. László's was melodic, his own drawled, but hers? Thunderation! He wanted to be read bedtime stories by her voice; she'd talk him into a sleep filled with beautiful, dulcet dreams. Darn it, a voice like that could even make his own memories delightful. What she actually said, or what time it was, wouldn't matter none.

In a way, a refreshing, homely way, the girl reminded him of his ma. Obviously, his ma wasn't English. But her voice had the same soft shape, an underlying kindness. It was of no consequence how she spoke; be it a hollering or a whispering, words of wisdom or words of scorn, she would never, ever sound hard.

'You poor boy,' the girl said.

Captivated, Teddy turned. She was humankind too. It wasn't that he could smell her. He couldn't. He heard her humanity, her pumping blood. But this, this extra sensation, wasn't her heart. There was something else deep within her. It was her soul, her very essence. It was warm and wholesome, and it glowed like the lustre of home lit up from the hog-wallows at the bottom of the range. He'd been human too, hadn't he? Once; a long time ago.

'Here,' she said, 'let me help you.'

Sakes alive, this girl was eager for this strange boy to survive. Compassion? Compassion was unmistakeably a human trait. László's slummy had a whole heap of compassion. It had irritated the Sam Hill out of Teddy. But now, without László watching him, reining him in if he showed even the slightest dalliance with curiosity about the world around him, he was fascinated. He wanted to know more about this "compassion" emotion. To acknowledge the corn, just lately he'd been having all kinds of unchecked emotions. Compassion was just one more. He must have had compassion.

'Oh no, no, no, no,' the girl said.

She sounded breathless, pained. Teddy loitered halfway between daring to indulge his curiosity, laying himself open to the wrong decision for the second time that night. Or making a clean getaway.

'Please don't bleed on me.'

He skidded back down the glass sky-light. At the gutter, he clambered back onto the parapet and, flattening his body along the top, lay on his stomach as though on a hard bunk, peering over the rim.

'What will Mum say?'

The crumpled body of the boy was right where he'd left it. It hadn't moved an inch, not even to unfold its uncomfortably twisted limbs. Crouching over it was the dark head of the young girl.

'Hi,' she said, 'it's okay. You're gonna be just fine, everything will be just fine.'

Teddy ducked back down and sat motionless in the gutter. He waited for the others that she'd spoken of to appear. Momentarily, he doubled himself up against the parapet.

'The ambulance is on its way,' she said. 'My name is …'

László's laughing crammed into Teddy's ears: *Teddy, you are all alone, come home.*

There were no "others". The girl had lied. Teddy thumped the old stone balusters behind him. They crumbled. Juggling with the loosened mortar, he fumbled it back into place. He folded his arms atop his knees, dug his chin into them and glared bitterly at the reflection of the sky in the glass roof. He was angry again now. He knew anger all too well. He hated it. Hate was worse. Although he was bewildered as to just who it was all aimed at: the girl for slighting him or himself for believing her.

Teddy, come home. If you don't, you are going to die.

Vampires, it seemed, weren't the only beings that lied. Well, now the boot was on the other foot. Humans lied as well. But then, surely that meant one thing. Had he, Teddy, been a liar all his life? He shifted as though uncomfortable and rested his forehead on his arms. He closed his eyes. Now he glared into nothing.

Teddy…

László, Teddy thought, I'll die if I come back to you. Then he added: and it ain't my home. Sling your bunk. I ain't listening to you.

He was surrounded by liars. Darn it, he was all-to-pieces just like a soft-horn tenderfoot; new to town, hazed and humiliated, and just plumb dumb.

'Hurry. Please,' the girl begged.

Teddy climbed back onto the parapet. He laid his cheek on the concrete and watched the sky. The girl's blood beat out the urgency of her plight. She didn't sound like a liar. He hung as far as he could over the cornice. Wedging a rigid arm between the ornately carved coving and his body, he propped it up soundly like a courthouse beam. The last thing he needed to do was topple over and waft down to the crime scene. From what he could see, she didn't look like a liar. But then, other than László, he didn't know what a liar should look like. Himself? He didn't know what that looked like either. It'd been over a century since he'd seen himself, looked into his own eyes, inspected his teeth or poked his nose.

No breath; he was statuesque. No heartbeat or pumping blood; he was as undetectable as stone. No longer with a sense of touch, he would not twitch. The odd night-time gnat or bug about the crevices annoyed him with its stomping, zooning and slurping. But, if a cowpoke is anything, it is strong-willed, so he cold-shouldered the rooftop fauna. As long as he didn't make a sound, no one would pay the roof a second glance. Darn it, people rarely ever look up. At worst, he could strike a pose and pretend to be a gargoyle. A gargoyle?

He gazed at the top of the girl's head, the tip of her nose and the sleek curve of her shoulders. It wasn't much to go on, so he let the breeze tell him what he wanted to know. The ether showed him how her hair skimmed her shoulders each time she moved her head. The atmosphere delicately fluctuated when she gathered it in swathes and smoothed it back behind her ear. A myriad of tiny tunnels inside her head brimmed with enchantment as the air there whirled, crashed and tantalised; it tempted him in, just like the sea that he yearned to leap into. He didn't think he could swim, though. 'Sides, there was that huge, debilitating self-loathing that he'd felt the last time he'd ventured too close to tumbling, moving water. Now that, was a memory that László had let him keep.

It didn't matter what he did, he couldn't not notice the girl's blood. It pumped intensely fast. He closed his eyes. Her heartbeat told of excitement and rebelliousness. Every time Teddy thought he had the measure of it, it swapped its rhythm, throwing him off-track as though in the know that he'd be compelled to concentrate on it again.

'Open your eyes. Look at me.'

Teddy did as the girl asked the boy to do.

'Please,' she said.

Teddy inched treacheroulsy close to the edge.

'Hello again. I'm not too sure what I'm doing. I don't think I'll move you too much. I'm just going to hold your wrist. Like this.'

The boy's wrists were large and manly. It took both of her hands to clamp around the wound. The miniscule red blood vessels there had gummed together, the destruction had stopped and the pumping had levelled off. But it was still deathly faint.

'Hurry up,' the girl whispered.

The unrecognisable fibres of her clothes rustled, rippled and ruched. Teddy was transfixed. Surely, in all his time, he'd seen a girl in jeans.

'What's your name?' the girl said.

Teddy opened his mouth to answer, although he wasn't sure what he was going to say.

'Don't answer that,' she said.

Teddy closed his mouth again. He'd been about to holler something out. Gol darn it, that was close. He smiled. Then he stopped that too. If she knew she'd just demanded the silence of the boy's attacker, aided him in his hiding from the law...what then?

Emotions were coming at him from all angles now. He should move. Lingering there was pandering to a whim, a naughty, wilful whim. Wickedly, he knew it. He liked it. Or he thought he did. Worse than that, he was having trouble adjusting to a mild, roguish curiosity without nearly getting himself killed.

"You will remember only how to behave like a beast, a hungry, wanton animal." his memory threw the voice of László at him.

He didn't know how to behave in this world. As far as he knew, he'd never been allowed out on his own. László or his slummy had plumb taken care of everything; any need he may ever have had and all the day-to-day, menial tasks that it took to actually behave like a human. He was a misfit, a saddle-bum, he didn't belong here.

A spiteful piercing, intensely stinging, scuffed over his back. It dug under and ruffled his skin from the inside out. It weakened and then burst through him again. Raising his flesh in lines, as though scars criss-crossed his skin, until it snagged and scratched on the thread of his T-shirt's weave. He winced and grimaced, showing his teeth. He hated those teeth now.

Perhaps this was what compassion felt like. Compassion was supposed to be kind, wasn't it? This was not kind. Perhaps this was fear. Again. Or remorse. Or regret. He sure as darn it had a lot of that.

In his endeavours to stay still, he balled his fists, tensed his thighs and stretched out his toes. He couldn't be found. He'd be reviled, caged, dissected. The lines in the skin of his back began to pulse: they beat out a reminder that he knew 'hate'. He'd been reviled, caged, scorned, and almost dissected before. Before László. Before his family. He just couldn't be sure why or how. He hid his face in the crook of his elbow. He didn't want to be hated. Not by anyone. Ever.

'I cain't feel you.' he told himself.

One of the scars roused itself even higher. Maliciously, it stabbed him, as though his body, seemingly more than comfortable in its newfound freedom, sought to agree with his mind which was in turn, agreeing with something in his memory. Something that had hurt. Overwhelmingly so. Something that he didn't want to think about. The scar ran him through. It sliced deeper than before, right through to the underside of his chest. So startled was he, that he fell into the gutter again.

'Dead.' he laboriously told himself. 'You are dead.'

Shrouded by the shadow of the cornice, he gritted his teeth and tried to lie still. To all intents and purposes, he was no more than a stiff in the gutter. A blood-splattered stiff with oversized canines. Below him, oblivious to him, the girl chattered on, a little like a drunk gunslinger - nobody actually listens to what he's got to say, but nary one does anybody move away.

Desperate to be rid of the pains he knew he shouldn't be feeling, Teddy hung on every word. The kindness, the tenderness of her soft reassurances, soothed his skeersome mood swings. She made him feel safe, which was odd because he shouldn't need anybody to make him feel safe. He was the monster around these parts. Though, to acknowledge the corn, he wasn't the only one. László scared him — a little. There was the demon inside him... that scared him an itty bit, too.

Yeller, it seemed to say, *you're yeller.*

Sakes alive! No ding way! In any outfit, cowards were not tolerated. Dent had said that as well.

Ignorance. That was what this was. Cowpoke or not, being faced with your own ignorance was never likely to be a carefree ride. It was confusion an' all. And a whole heap of not liking both.

He listened to the girl's heart. His internal turmoil began to mellow and he found that he was more than content to just lie there languidly feeling balmy and, much as he hated to admit it, satisfied.

'...sexy...' she said.

Nope. His eyes stared, his jaw slackened and his ears almost exploded. Hell-fired bent on antagonising him, his memory replayed her voice: '...sexy...'.

It threatened to play it again: '...*sexy*...'.

It made good on the threat.

'...*sexy*...'

Now it was plumb enjoying it. The curiosity of a cosseted teenager ensnared Teddy's mind. Only whores spoke like that. Hang it all! Hadn't he only ever seen a real-life whore once? Desperate to get a good look at the girl, he threw himself over and grasping the concrete, squashed his face to the tubby stone balusters.

The gaps were too tight. It was impossible to get even a fragment of a line of sight, whatever way he twisted. He was barking at a knot here; getting a proper look at the girl was futile. Momentarily disconsolate at missing out on a bit of decriminalised voyeurism, he dropped his hands to his knees and rested his forehead against the stone.

He was smiling though. The pent-up lump of fear in his stomach had been flattened. The painful scars from his past had been smoothed over.

He liked that smile. Once again, he sure-fired floundered at what he had to smile about. Surely, you had to have a reason to smile. It seemed like he'd been smiling for a while, too.

Whether or not, he'd meant to smile, something pleasant had happened. A memory had appeared. A good one, a vibrant one; it was animated and happy. It made the smile stretch, expand until it was well-nigh impossible to keep his lips from exposing his teeth. He sank back into the gutter and gazed up at the gaudy brown sky.

'Bring it on,' he muttered.

In bright daylight, in a building somewhere, his family, his virtuous, wholesome family, stood side-by-side. His pa, attentive to whatever he was facing, stood proud at one end of the line, while he stood at the other. He and Pa were both hatless. They must've been in someone's house. Someone that Pa knew and liked.

Pa! Teddy thought, his urgency threatening to shatter the memory, look at me. Please, Pa.

László began laughing again, disturbing him. Teddy closed his eyes, he clasped his ears. Stronger and much more significant, the memory was held prominent in his mind. He dismissed the laughter, mentally trampling over it as though it no longer mattered.

Pa remained stalwart, a little detached; whatever it was that held his interest was obviously worth listening to. That was okay, though. It was good, even a might pious. Perhaps not all memories held messages, thank the land. Perhaps this one was just a blissful, walking, talking picture. The details were sparse, but thus far, that seemed normal.

The family were kept from spilling out of their spot by the long, high back of the seat in front. They were in a pew. They were in a church pew. Pa always took the family to church on Sunday.

Dust speckled and spun in the sunshine from an old west window. Next to Pa stood his ma. Teddy knew the height of her chin, the sincere set of her jaw and the flowers of her dress and bonnet. He tried to look into her face, see again the sweet devotion to her family in her eyes, and the white flecks in her dark hair. Flecks that they all loved, because they all knew it was them, that had put them there. To do that, though, he would have had to break the line — and he had a hunch that wasn't the thing to do.

Ma had her arm around his youngest sister. Ellen. Her name was Ellen. Teddy could just see the peak of her bonnet along with the edge of a small book that she held. She cuddled childishly into the gathers of Ma's skirt. Then came Mattie, his other sister. How could he ever have forgotten Mattie? Mattie was quite a bit older than Ellen. Same age as he was. Or had been. Roughly, anyway. He couldn't rightly remember.

Intensified by the glass of the window panes, the sun was hot on his face; it was as though he was there in person. He listened for the chomping and regurgitating of woodworm in the walls. He couldn't hear them.

He looked down at Mattie. Her waist-length hair, the same colour as Ma's, had shed some of its fastening, looping and curling about her chin in matted tendrils. No doubt a consequence of her tardiness, it would've been bundled together and stuffed under her bonnet as she'd bolted through the ranch house door. So now it interfered with the blousy bow. Her neck was highly blushed: she held a kerchief to the end of her perfect nose as though to catch a run and her shoulders shook violently. Her cheeks were quite prominent, and, although he knew them to be the purely purdy pink of sugar pigs at Christmas time, right now they were a mix of scarlet and magenta blotched with stark white.

Perhaps Mattie had gotten sick. Perhaps the sunshine was beguiling, and they stood in the brightness of a Kansan winter. All three ladies wore summer Sunday dresses and none of the party, save the men of course, wore a jacket. So, nope; cain't be winter-time.

Mattie squeaked. As she bent her head low, the flower pattern on her dress wavered reminiscent of the Bluestem Hills in springtime. Her shoulders, devoid of all rhythm, jerked maniacally and her hands juddered and trembled. Overwhelmed with happiness, Teddy remembered the Sunday well. Mattie was having a fit alright, she was having a fit of giggles.

Teddy's body began to quiver. He had to look away. If he didn't, he'd explode noisily, stickily. Either that or his chest would collapse painfully, and he'd drop dead where he stood.

He tried to look around. The church was basic but amiable. It looked a little like the inside of a small, white-painted barn. The floor was blotted with the tread of the townsfolks' boots, the splinter-prone rafters were high, and the plank roof loftily pitched.

Someone's stare bored into the side of his head. Like a true saphead, he turned to it. Mattie. That was the flint strike to his firesteel. His body spasmed, his chest smarted and his jaw jarred. His eyes were wonderfully wet.

The mischievous deed done, Mattie looked away. Seconds later, her own shaking returned. Teddy indulged in a smidgen of sibling smugness.

The giggling was forbidden. The unpredictable disgusting snorts and the fluid-expelling guffaws were grievously disruptive. Teddy didn't want to stop laughing, or rather stifle it, however much it grated on his ribs. It felt too ding good. He hadn't laughed so properly jovially in such a long time. And the adrenaline of cracking up in church was something else entirely.

Perhaps the memory did have a point. He'd wanted so badly to feel good. Well, it was working. Grinning foolishly, he stole a look at Pa. Pa had gone stiff. So stiff that it was apparent in his very aura. The back of his scalp under his razor-short hair seemed to glow angrily.

Foreboding in her silence, Ma let go of her youngest and grasped the forearm of her eldest. She leaned close to Mattie's ear and said something so low and so pointed that Teddy didn't hear it.

Mattie stopped laughing. Teddy tried to stop, too. He pulled the corners of his lips in, pursing them until they pouted. Now he just looked like a beefhead in the bone orchard on All Souls' Eve.

Yet there was worse to come. He caught Mattie's eye. He hadn't meant to. He swore; he hadn't meant to. They were doomed.

Pa pincered his book firmly between his thumb and forefinger. He closed it over his hand and, holding it tightly, folded the free one over the end. It looked as though he were harnessing the necessity of keeping his hands occupied. He turned his Sunday bested body towards his embarrassingly quivering son. Teddy tried to gulp back his giggles. He bit his lip. It didn't work and the chucklehead face just got more addled.

Pa looked into his eyes, he seemed able to look past the whatever-it-was that Teddy and Mattie found so death-defyingly funny that they would wantonly disturb the Sunday service. His gaze froze the one tiny titbit of sense that remained in Teddy's soul. The distorted, upside-down reflection of an orangey-yellow-haired boy with a sappy smile, wider than a claim-stricken prospector's did nothing for his resolve to stop snickering. Pa opened his mouth to speak. Teddy was numbed into powerlessness. He did little more than look on. In sinister slow motion, Pa's lips formed the damning word:

'You…'

CHAPTER FIFTEEN

'… inbred, pig-headed, little-balled bastard.'

The sunshiny scene in Teddy's head vanished. Sakes alive – he'd forgotten where he was. So, was the girl talking to him now? But, she was still down there with the wretched boy.

He truly had no idea who his real parents were. That being the case he thought gloomily, he had no choice but to set for plumb not knowing about the first one. Pig-headed though — he hell-fired didn't like to think so. 'Sides, how in tarnation did she know? She didn't know him, did she? To acknowledge the corn, neither did he. Now there was definitely no way in blazes she could have seen him that close up, 'specially not that bit. So, "little balled"? No how.

'How am I going to cope with him all day at college?' she sighed.

Phew: the girl still didn't know about him in his hiding place, up here on the roof. Most probably, she didn't even believe he existed. He wasn't too sure he liked that. Darn it, Teddy thought, as an annoying nubbin of a niggle jabbed at him. College, though. The girl must be educated. She must have rich parents. So, probably not a whore.

'He stood me up.'

Bastard.

'And after I sneaked out.'

Fat's in the fire.

'Look at me.'

Teddy's smile stretched again. The girl's voice had taken on a soft assertiveness. The niggle morphed into a tickle, set to make him twitch. You twisting me again? he said to himself, blaming the demon for the twitch and attempting a futile chastisement, Quit it.

A grey, stubby-beaked, barrel-chested bird alighted on the parapet. It deliberated about, ducking and diving all the while.

'Darn bird!' Teddy muttered, 'Don't you dare dump on me now.'

It wasn't like he'd feel it. He didn't need to though, just knowing it was there and where it had been would repulse him. The bird sidestepped and warbled its way past him. An intermittent, yet insistent batting of feathers against rough cast signalled the arrival of another bird. The two pushed their plump bodies into the balusters' gaps and started up a sort of cooing, burbling banter. Teddy's aggravation was enflamed: his fear of being faecefied chipped away at his nerves.

'Sakes alive. Quit yer yammering, will ya?' he snarled.

In less time than it took for him to snip 'Git', the birds had started up such a hellabaloo that they were joined by another. Teddy snapped his body around; he grasped the tail of the middle bird and yanked it out of its spot. Immediately, the other two scarpered. Teddy sank his fangs into the bird's breast. Wayward smears of its blood on his teeth and lips brought his senses to life. The feathers were dry, tough and grimy. The bird stopped its prattling. He pitched it over the rooftops.

The rounded, dead thud of the body as it landed far away made him miserable. He flopped back and sat in the gutter. For no real reason, other than it had annoyed him, he'd just killed that bird; snatched it up and using his teeth, stabbed it. He didn't need to feed, he'd had no thoughts for his actions, no hesitation, no compulsion to let alone an innocent being.

Thunderation, Addle-pot, it was only a pigeon.

Teddy pulled his knees in close and hugged them. The monster in him had risen again. If he kept on letting the monster take him, he'd be plumb back where he peskily started. A murderer, a hungry, wanton beast of a murderer. He didn't want to be a monster anymore. He sure as darn it didn't want to murder.

'I'm just going to have to zone him out.' The girl said, her voice drifting up to him once more.

"Zone him out?" What in tarnation! Zoning out, all-fired sounded just like what he needed to do with his own inbred, pig-headed abomination – he scratched the "little balled." The girl was his saviour once again. If only he knew her name.

Teddy laughed. It was a strange little laugh, more a harrumph. It wasn't his usual overdone, debauched snigger. Nary one was it the full, riotous, belly laugh from his memory. It was unannounced, involuntary and not at all naughty. It left him feeling just a touch light-headed. The last time he'd felt light-headed was when he'd been privileged with a mug of Moon's Neck Oil. He'd soon learned the perils of such a privilege.

Suddenly deafening, high-pitched and fantastically gyrating, an inhuman wailing whitewashed the night. He plastered his palms over his ears and twisted, intrigued as the sky behind him lit up blue, like it had been flayed nights ago and only now dashed with cobalt shards. Instantly the colour swapped to the red of fresh watermelon flesh. Mid-crescendo and too close for comfort, the screaming was silenced. Teddy dropped his hands. A mechanical monotonous voice crackled in the siren's wake.

He squeezed and craned to view the scene below. Everything had been dowsed in a light so white, nothing, not even the bittiest critter in the crannies of the roughcast, could hide. Teddy hunkered down, flattening his dirty middle, scraping his ancient belt buckle into the gutter. Clamping closed his eyes and lips, he began to wish that his supernatural prowess extended so far as to switch his hair, from luminescent yellowy-orange to dull, dark but stealthy sable.

A serious shindig seemed to be taking place below him. Scurrying feet, tearing papers and the metallic rattle of little trolley wheels filled his head. The piercing of skin and the sucking of tubes, sounds that were clinical, skilful and in complete contrast to his own stabbing and squelching.

There were questions, too; friendly but shouted and then soft and reassuring. So many, so busy, such perplexity. Something was muttered about the boy's wound, the loss of blood, the possibility of suicide. Thank the land — medics. Teddy tried to make out the girl's voice, but the constant din muddied her dulcet, innocent tones.

More vehicles arrived, cutting their man-made scream as the first had done. There were more lights flashing so gaudily that Teddy saw red and blue blobs on the back of his eyelids. More questions, routine cooperation and then an air of acquiescence. The rustling of functional threads, more little wheels rattling, and the stomping of sensible shoes interfered in his eavesdropping. He covered his closed eyes with his palms, a vain effort to further thwart that sense - heighten the others perhaps — please?

His ears had once been so keen. Ace-high hearing was the cowpoke tracker's super-power. Toned and trained to hear not only the daily grind, but also the things that others missed: a change in nature, a ruffle of flora, the trials of prairie fauna. He'd known and could differentiate between the calls of all manner of prairie life: birds big and small, mammals, reptiles, insects even. He'd worked and whittled his hearing until he was able to tell the future from it. Well, more like make an educated guess. Most of the time, though, the guess turned out to be right smart correct.

Of course, that'd been before he'd been murdered. He really had very little idea what it had been like since. Tonight's performance being all he had to go on, it was peskily pathetic.

Surely all that hadn't been lost. It all had to be in the addled archive of his head somewhere. Add to that a little blood and all that came with it, the senses that he had now, the strength and the speed — he must've been invincible. Well, kinda anyway. Ary why, he would've have made the perfect hunter. And killer? He hadn't been a killer before. Not before László. He laughed that ironic harrumph again, thinking: László, I reckon I might know what you saw in me now.

Of course, I saw only the good in you, Schatzibar. Come home now.

'Darn it.'

László was still there. Teddy pummelled the roughcast in exasperation again. A grey tile cracked and slipped away, landing under his toe. Teddy stared at it. Somewhere in the back of his memory, a big, accented voice drawled: "Addleheaded kid." Teddy emptied his mind.

The boy's heartbeat was gone. Perhaps it'd stopped. Perhaps the boy was dead. No. No, no, no. If the boy died, that would make Teddy a murderer once more. He hadn't changed a bit.

Now, he really didn't want the girl to see him. Not solely, although mostly because she very probably would raise a ruckus, and he really wasn't of a mind to face a posse of townsfolk brandishing gardening tools, but because she was honourable, fearless. No woman that he could remember would have approached a scuffle. No woman that he could remember would have been outside wandering alone after dark. Spontaneously, and he was getting a little wary of his own mind's spontaneity, he thought of Mattie. Mattie might have snuck out.

Mattie didn't swear, though. He was treated to a recollection of the one time that Ma had reminded her that 'a lady didn't talk so straight'. But then, his image of Ma herself simpering and doing little more than sitting pretty was askew, slantindicular. The one of her and Pa discussing tracks, trails and wagons, destinations, business deals and finance was clear as day.

Teddy grinned. Of course, Double C; it wasn't just a brand or a ranch name. It meant Two Callingtons. Ma was Pa's partner; in more ways than one. Women hadn't changed; the world had.

Twitching dangerously, Teddy wondered what the women of this time were like to talk to. Worse was the urgent desire to find out. It was almost unthinkably skeersome. Almost.

The girl's heartbeat had slowed. He tried to picture her. But he couldn't be too sure what she looked like. He hadn't actually seen her face, just the tip of her nose. He raised his head and looked hard into the night air. He could make out only pigeons orange and warm as they dipped and flapped, bumbling blue amoebas and the weather, all directly in front of him. Hiding himself had meant hiding her, too.

'I see no reason why she can't go home.'

'C'mon, we'll take you.'

Go home? This was a new voice, older, this country and not in Teddy's head. The other one the same, was taking the girl home. Teddy's mind went blank. Everyone was leaving. He was still here. There was no reason for him to be here. He was surplus to requirements. He was destitute, undeniably so. Wheels crunched away until he could no longer hear them. Without all the hellabaloo below him, the night would be dolefully quiet. He'd be lonely.

He turned onto his back and stared at the sky, thoughtful that at least he'd have the stars for company. The brown clouds were exclusive in their persistence. He could leave, too, but he had no home to go to. He raised a hand and studied it, as though it could give him some clue as to where a creature such as himself could find company. His hand showed him only his own bloody, three-fingered, nightmare image.

He was a mess. Physically, his shirt was more like a dirty old vest, open and slack, patterned with dried blood and embellished with sinew. The engraving on his heavy belt buckle was chock-full of the same grime. His jeans were stiff and blackened by the indiscernible evidence of last night's killing spree.

Mentally, he was plagued by the painfully carnal emotions of a one-hundred-year-old psychotic murderer. Under that, he was a proud, protective cowpoke horse whisperer, and underneath yet all that, he was only twenty years old and still daydreaming of love. Washington Irving couldn't have come up with a character more mixed-up than that. Washington Iving?

Teddy thought of the girl, beautiful in her simplicity. Although he got the notion that she wouldn't think so. Nary one would his telling her so be appreciated. Still there were people, the girl for one, who were stronger. There were humans who still believed in the greater good. That was what he wanted to do. That was what he wanted to be. Darn it, he was all-to-pieces sure that's what he had been. Before he'd been murdered.

And now? If he was the one who came across a fellow being in distress, would he risk his own self to help them? He'd always been a bit of a risk-taker. Would he take that risk now? Perhaps it was his demon self who was shocked; he couldn't be too sure, but he was definitely rendered a little incredulous when the answer came back, only a 'maybe'.

He flopped his hand back to the gutter. The demon would try to take control again. He was all-fired sure of it. With its psychopathic need to hunt and kill, the stomach-churning yearn for the taste of human blood, blended with a desire to survive that could only be described as seedy, it wouldn't ever stop trying. It would wind itself up, until in its endeavours to throttle his own free will, it had peskily mashed up his insides. Just like it had done tonight.

This was it, then; he was nothing more than a victim of his own role model. László; the only model that he had.

Could he ever control it? Figure out what made the demon tick. Do a László on it, him, whatever. That might just mean getting to know it. He baulked at the thought. What he needed was to be himself, his own person, know his own mind and soul.

Somewhere under his jeans, deep inside the fleshy part of his belly, something bit him. Jest like a sandfly had gotten in there, it made him jump. There wouldn't be sandflies up on this roof. P'shaw, it was no great shakes; the fly had gone. He relaxed.

Almost straight-away something stabbed him in the same place, perhaps just a little higher. He wriggled and tried to ignore it. He was supposed to be good at ignoring any sensations he might have, and the nip was such a puny little thing. As though to prove a point, the little nip wound around its location like a bradawl might widen a hole. Teddy's top lip jerked and curled as the nip induced a nervous tick. He squirmed. Strangely instinctively, he sent his fingers to probe the area.

'Dang no-see-ums!' he grumbled.

As though having waged and won its war with his willpower, the nip vanished. Or rather, it moved to dig at a new spot, nearer his hips. This, whatever-it-was, seemed to be able to evade all efforts to dislodge it. Simply ignoring it wasn't working. It was becoming annoying. He needed something bigger, something more compelling. The something that had kept him from such attacks for the past one hundred years. Whatever that was, he needed it now, before this parasite tweak drove him insane. He rose and then faltered, rubbing the spot where the nip had so sadistically tormented him. For one hundred years, that "something" had been the demon. He needed the demon? No ding way.

Fatigue deep inside his bones, he slunk away over the rooftops. It seemed that the demon had, if nothing else, given him a whole heap of adolescent insubordinate insolence.

Stumbling back into to the woods, he could've made it to the tomb and died in comfort, but not wanting to join the dead just yet, he stopped at the top of the gully that enclosed the neglected mausoleum. Legs unsteady, he stabilised himself as best he could and gazed around indulging in the colours of the trees, the predawn sky, the ground and the plants. They made up a remedy that calmed him most pleasantly. He squinted, labelling them and adding them to his extensive spectrum. Closing his eyes, he collected the sounds of the forest, picked out specifics, layered them and mixed them into a sort of love song. He smiled again.

Then his knees caved in. He tumbled, sliding through the sloping undergrowth. Ferns slapped at his face, so he screwed it up — no sense of touch at all now.

Landing upside down just shy of the mausoleum entrance, one foot was tangled in the plant life and the other wavered about in the air. The weight of his boot making it top-heavy, it tipped forward like a rotten corner post in the rain. The only thing that stopped it toppling over altogether, was the rigidity of his jeans. Ain't such a good idea to rely on them for too long.

'Help me out here, demon,' he said, 'we are gonna have to do this together.'

Nothing. Teddy struggled to free himself. His joints didn't work too good. His limbs had grown stiff.

'C'mon,' he said, 'you're good to me; I'll keep you fed. You savvy?'

The demon stayed hidden.

'Darn it,' he muttered. 'Ding shavetail.'

His chin shoved into his chest, one arm dead, he tugged at the nearest root. Brown pine needles avalanched into his face, but his foot dislodged, followed the first, and his whole body fell over itself. He shifted and jerked until he righted himself.

'Sakes alive, demon!' he exclaimed. 'You're yellower and slower than beef tea surprise in the wintertime.'

Anger ignited within him and he bared his teeth and growled.

'I ain't yeller.'

His all but dead body leapt to its feet, its claw-like hands clicking as it flexed them. With a gaze that was now feral, it cast about in need of a target for its fury.

'László,' it called out. 'Help me, László.'

Come back to me.

László's eerie, old Hungarian voice filled Teddy's head.

'You're too ding late,' Teddy thought.

'László,' his body called out again, 'wait for me. I wanna come home.'

'No,' Teddy cried, 'don't move.'

Come home, Schatzibar. I'll look after you.

'No,' Teddy said again, 'László's a liar. You know he is.'

Lies. The demon liked lies. It liked to tell them. Be taken in by them — knowingly. Perhaps then, in the end, he'd known László to be a liar. Perhaps that was what had started it, the memories, the dual personality. But, by then, the demon had control. He, Teddy, had been hell-fired submissive to it. Well, not anymore. He adopted a supercilious, sing-song sort of voice.

'László's just trying to murder you again,' he said.

Save you, Teddy. I saved you before, didn't I?

The creature screamed in frustration; the noise was like a Winchester going off half-cocked in Teddy's head.

'There's not enough time,' he moaned. 'In less than two whoops and a holler, you'll die. If you try to get back to László now, you'll die in the open. And then you'll be found.'

The demon hesitated.

Teddy, mein Schatzi, don't listen to him...

'You don't want to be found, do you?' Teddy cooed, interrupting László. This was kinda fun.

'Stay here,' he went on. 'I'll feed you. Just like I did tonight.'

Okay, so that was a lie. Teddy had no intention of killing anyone ever again. He just hoped that the demon wouldn't realise it until it was too late. He hoped it had very little knowledge of him. Vampires, he decided, were basically immature, pokerish, b'hoys. So, he played on its basic need to survive.

'Only I can give you what you want,' he said.

The creature didn't move. Teddy hurled himself to the ground. He pushed his fingers into the soil, breaking up its mossy black covering, clinging on. Insects, negligent of each other's existence, teemed over his skin, their hard, black bodies scurrying and climbing over each other. Teddy grinned. The demon needed blood.

'Sling your bunk, László,' he said. 'You ain't never gonna take control of me again. You hear?'

He forced his fingers into tweezers and picked up little pinches of the bugs.

'And neither are you!' he hollered to the creature.

This might be horse feathers, but it was worth a go: he had to keep the demon subdued. Kneeling back and shaking the excess earth from his fingers, he said:

'Here's how!'

Tipping back his head, he stuffed two loads of mini-beasts into his mouth. Then he picked up more and, too short of time to shake off the dirt, rammed them into his mouth as well. Escapees dashed across his face.

Clenching his jaw and stretching his throat, he tried to swallow the bugs whole, the way he'd done the first time Coosie had given him prairie oysters. Teddy's innards were most probably not much different to the bugs' woody home. They'd just be fussing about in their invertebrate way in there.

'Goddam son of a …' his demon retorted.

He was actually going to have to eat them, wasn't he?

This life is ghastly. László interrupted, *Let me save you.*

'Darn it, don't listen to László,' Teddy said, errant beetles racing over his chin, 'he ain't never saved anyone in his whole, blamin' life.'

He reached out again and this time he grimaced as he pawed the ground and pinched up another helping of insects.

Don't do this, Teddy, come home. You're nothing without me.

'Jest out of practice is all. I don't need you. I won't need you.'

All manner of insects scooted over his arms now, bouldering over the hairs on the back of his hand, rounding his palm and pausing, confused by the lines there, then doubling back on themselves. Slowly, as though he could buy himself time, wait for the saviour that would never come, he fed the dreaded menu onto his tongue. Immediately, they ran amok. He closed his mouth, trapping his meal. A tickling a thousand times squallier than he'd felt earlier bristled on his tongue.

He closed his eyes and bit down. The sides of his mouth rippled like it was holding a ground squirrel's bee, his tongue was engorged, and his gums tingled. Pshaw: was eating a mouthful of bugs so disgusting an action that it caused his body to react? Perhaps this was how to control what he could and couldn't, did and didn't, sense. Do something, think of something, picture something so intense that it would kick-fire the subliminal animation controlled only by his mind. Dinging mind over matter. It was that easy. Lasciviously, he used his tongue to herd what was left of the repulsively panicky mouthful to his back teeth and chomped. Yup! There it was. The bugs tasted vile. Jest out of practice, he told himself, keep on it.

Come home, I miss you.

'That's corral dust.'

I love you.

'You're contemptible, you know that?'

Teddy ate another small helping. This time as he crunched, he didn't think about it, or the bugs. He emptied his mind. His tongue stayed flat, so did his mouth and there was no tingling. Nothing. Except the very thing he needed. The blood. Even that, he sensed rather than tasted. Just like tonsil paint, Kansas sheep dip, tarantula Juice, whisky, it brought his insides to life with such force that they burned. For some reason that reminded him of Moon and of Cleve and Dent and Virgil. He smiled.

'Saddle bums cain't be choosers,' he told himself.

The bugs were a meal.

'And László,' he said, 'I am just gonna have to "zone" you out.'

Perhaps, he could 'zone out' the taste of bugs' blood, too. Simply replace it for something good. He just needed to come up with what that was to be. As yet, he had very few options. It wouldn't be long before he needed a change from Moon. Or the others. He needed Ma's home cooking.

At the very least, his senses had been sharpened. He could taste the saccharine smell of sap as it condensed on the spines of the woodland grasses. He caressed a wayward ivy vine: its millions of ligaments stuck to his fingers. They were ticklish and he smiled again. He flattened his hand against the nearest tree trunk. Ensnared in the moment, he twisted fully around and hugged the tree.

'Haulloa, stranger,' he said.

The tree buzzed with life. He squeezed it. It was strong, stoic and wise. Closing his eyes to the moment, he nuzzled his cheek into its bark and curled his fingers into the galleys between the grey plates. They were warm.

Teddy opened his eyes wide. He stared at the bark with supernatural sight. The tree was swathed in loops of zany oranges, gaudy yellows and shrieking pinks. It was shedding heat. Dawn. His eyes closed again, this time without his consent. Death. He'd forgotten about death. Again.

He forced his eyes open. His sight was a sepia tunnel vision and holes began to appear on the peripherals. His jaw slackened, his mouth opened and out dropped dislocated bug shells. Dang shells. His dead body would not digest them. Nary one could he spit them out.

Teddy's limbs and digits would no longer do as he knew he was asking; he fell backwards, sitting in the very patch he'd harvested his supper from. His senses were gone now, he had no notion of the earth he sat in. The ground could scratch at him for all its worth.

'Move,' he lowed. 'Out of the open. Shelter.'

He couldn't think why he needed shelter - he didn't mind sleeping under the stars. In fact, he loved to sleep under the stars. Couldn't he just sleep here?

Something pulled at him, some sort of out-of-body being. It swivelled him over and knocked his arms and legs into crawling. He fell on his belly. Clawing the ground, his legs stiff and forked, his ankles rusted at odd angles, he shunted himself along. At the hole in the mausoleum floor, he fell through head first.

Unable to properly operate his own mouth, he slurred what he hoped was 'thank you'. After all, a cowpoke is always pleasant, even when out of sorts and, like it or not, the demon had helped him out. Unable to see the corpses he'd so panickily fled from the previous evening, he would've smiled. If he hadn't died.

CHAPTER SIXTEEN

There was a frost. A frost as plumb severe as it was powerful beautiful. In No Man's Land a frost was just as common an occurrence in late spring as it was in early autumn. In Kansas, as soon as the sun went down, the temperature would drop like a naked gunslinger beefed on a Dodge Street.

Teddy stood in a deserted yard. He looked at the sky. It was a pale and pure blue. It was daytime, although the sun was nowhere to be seen. Obviously his nightmare existence was yet to start.

Those skeersome memories were in here, too — somewhere. He wasn't sure how he was going to deal with them. So, he let his mind wander. He was perilously curious to find out where it was going.

The moon was still in the sky, too. The blueness milky as it reflected through its patchy, round whiteness. Teddy wasn't used to such brightness. He looked away. He missed his hat.

Ranch outbuildings, roofs and even the tops of the split rail corral bristled fluffily. The demon in him wanted to crush its snowy charm. Nowhere, it seemed, was sacred enough to hide. Even deep inside his own memories?

'Sling your bunk,' he said, shifting and shaking himself, determined to resist any wicked tendencies.

Nothing moved. Except for the glistening of refracted light on the ice. As far as the eye could see, everything was white, before it turned to twinkling translucent blue. Darn it, if the prairie wasn't the pink of prettiness.

Teddy turned to the doghouse just in time for the sun to slink from its spot behind the ranch house. Way too far away to be hot, it succeeded only in crystallising the earth even further. Feathered patterns, fronds and fans like those of the dance hall girls that he'd heard about, opaqued the grubby glass of the windows. Teddy scored a jagged-edged line from top to bottom. Still, he couldn't see inside; too dark. He turned to survey his territory.

A fair-sized herd of horses milled about where a fresh feed of hay had been hiked over the perimeter fence. It must be cold, Teddy surmised. Usually, horses thrived on the natural pastures, the freedom to graze and socialise provided by a ranch's range. If they could get to it, that is.

Horses! Horses were the business of the Double C. This was his father's ranch. This was Captain Clement Callington's ranch.

A horse snuffed at his shoulder. Then it bit into him. It wouldn't have harmed him, sense of touch or not. He was protected by the heavy bearskin coat of a savvy cowpoke.

'You wanna keep your tombstones to yourself,' he said.

The horse didn't seem to care a continental. It seized his coat again and tugged him.

'Light a shuck, will you?' he said.

As he brushed the horse's muzzle away, he stumbled back into the yard. The horse snorted in defiance. Then it bowed and bade him to follow it. The yard had been pock-marked muddy-brown by the Cuban heels of ranch hand boots. Rain filled and solidified: these left the landscape both uneven and unforgiving. Teddy pulled his bandana up over his nose; a habitual reaction of any cowpoke to cold weather. Or dusty weather. Or any weather, for that matter. He smiled. Under its cover and without the identity of his hat, he looked just like an outlaw. Well, didn't that plumb describe him dreadfully? He sure-fired hadn't set out to be an outlaw… but wasn't he just the worst kind? In front of him, the horse began performing what could only be described as a Bill Show act.

'Quit it, Puddin' Foot,' he mumbled. 'I'm coming, aren't I?'

They passed a nurly old crab apple tree. He remembered that old tree well. One too many of its bitter, musket ball fruits gave the horses the back door trots.

'Darn it, that was a peskily useless tree,' he told the horse.

It was a favourite of his ma's, so it remained, eternally safe. She could see it from the kitchen, she'd said. Her excuse for not going out there? "The corral is no place for a lady."

Mattie snuck out plenty, though. That was how she'd persuaded him to teach her to ride. If he didn't, she'd tell Ma and Pa he was accomplice to her sneaking around. Of course, he'd conceded. She hadn't needed all that Barnum. He'd have done anything for her. She was his sister, his ma's daughter. And then, hang it all, she'd still gone everywhere in the wagon. So, what good learning to ride had done her, he never knew.

The crab apple tree was bare aside from the ice that encased its branches and twigs. The tree was sure-fired beautiful — for once. In a frost, it was exquisite. Twistical. Teddy could see now why Ma loved it so much. It even wore several blobs of mistletoe with pride. It must be wintertime.

The horse stopped at the barn. Teddy stared at it. Then he stared at the horse. The barn doors were closed. The bar was across. He pressed an ear to the middle where the doors met. There was no one inside. He turned to the horse and shrugged. The horse flattened its ears and flared its nostrils, it stamped the ground.

'Whoa!' Teddy said, hoping to soothe the ornery horse.

He adjusted his bandana, revealing his face once more.

'Which one are you? Let's see if I can recall.'

It was a 'she', and she looked to be a Pinto. Her rich, chestnut base was splashed by crisp, white patches. When she shook her head, wafting her coal-coloured fringe, a faint, white star showed itself. Her eyes were blue, wide and rebellious. Presently they held a glowering glint.

Teddy reached out with one open hand. He smiled. Immediately, he pulled his lips back in. The horse hadn't flinched, though. She'd pricked up an ear, questioning him. Perhaps the horse didn't know. Perhaps his teeth looked normal. Normal for a twenty-year-old cowpoke, that was.

'How about you give me a smile?' he said.

No lisp.

'Come on, let's have a whopping three-by-niner?'

Still the horse's lips remained closed. But it loosened its other ear. Then the horse nuzzled its muzzle into his palm and sniffed him. He wondered what he smelled like. The horse didn't skitter away. Its nose felt softly luxurious on his palm. Its whiskers were wiry on his fingertips.

He could feel it. He could feel it?

The world in which he walked, the ranch, the yard, even the horse, immobilised itself. It became again a vibrant tableau locked, in time. Just like it must've been for over a hundred years.

Save only for the two resident skeletons, Teddy sat alone in the tomb below the mausoleum. His mind dared him to touch something else. Scoop up a handful of dust pebbles, swipe a cobweb, prod his own leg.

'No, for once, finish what you started,' he commanded himself. 'Get back to the yard. Find out which of the horses you're talking to.'

A sudden irrationality took hold of him then. He flinched, as though someone were poking fun at him. Giggling, he acted like he saw the joke. Only he had no idea just what the joke was, and there was no one around. Still his skin rose up in hot bumps. So he apologised to the horse. He hadn't meant to be such a saphead; the horse hadn't been ditched and he definitely hadn't meant to ignore it. Then he winced again, wanting nothing more than to hide his face. But from who? He searched for and sequestered that old cowpoke bravado, but nary one was he happy with that either. Scowling at the tomb's steadfast darkness, he pointedly ignored the skeletons' grinning faces, and closed his eyes.

Back in the yard, he walked around the horse; he stroked a hand along her back. The horse's coat was soft and smooth. The heat of her body underneath warmed his hand. She felt real, alive, free from the control of all humans; along with anything else for that matter, especially vampires.

Teddy rested his hand on her shoulder for a moment. Her strong heartbeat pounded his open palm. He could sense her resilience in every cell that pumped and bustled along her body. Her spirit was infectious, sending invigorating sparks into him. He gained a century of self-esteem. The horse pricked up both ears and reached around to nuzzle him.

'It's ding good to see you,' he said.

Running his hand along the horse's spine and then her barrel, he noticed that there were no spur scores. Teddy didn't hold with the use of 'can-openers' on his horses. The plains' Indians did well without them, so could everyone else. 'Sides the cowpokes had their voices… and a cowpoke's voice was ace-high!

This horse must be one of his. He patted her shoulder and then her croup and thighs. Good, strong muscles. The horse stomped again. Good knees, too. She whinnied and shifted, shook her head and wafted her mane.

'Quit capering about, will you?' he said.

Teddy moved back to look at her face.

'Caper?' he smiled.

Caper snorted and shoved him.

'Darn it, Cape. It's been over a hundred years. I have all-fired missed you.'

Teddy clasped Caper's face and rubbed beneath her eyes. She blew plumes of hot air into his face.

'Sakes alive, we gonna go for a ride?'

Teddy didn't care if the cold nearly scalped him, slapped him in the face and skewered his eyes. Caper was fast. She didn't prance about for nothing, she was itching to run and was wilder than a Cheyenne soldier's bangtail. She was his horse. Caper snorted and backed away.

'Whoa, Cape, that's not like you.'

Caper stomped again and scraped at the ground. She looked down to her feet. Teddy looked, too. There was nothing wrong with Caper's feet. But there was a mark in the frosted earth. Mottled and crusted with mud and frost, it looked like the discarded wings of a colossal and very dead prairie moth. Two quarter-circles had been grooved into the ground at the base of the barn door. So, the doors had recently been opened. Teddy thought about repeating the action and further investigating the barn's inside. This was, after all, his memory.

Something stopped him, though. Letting himself in seemed intrusive. The barn and in fact the entire ranch and range had never actually been his. He'd never actually inherited any of it, had he?

Teddy pressed his body to the doors and squinted through the gap. The opposite doors were closed, too. The wagon sat there, neatly parked in the middle, awaiting its next trip into town, the railroad station or just next door. Teddy stood straight. A sound caught his ear: voices, in hearty, happy, but much muffled conversation. The echoey tartness of a pianoforte, sweet, childlike singing and small, cultured applause formed an undertone to that.

'Ted?'

Pa? No mistaking it now. The sound of his pa hollering to him from the direction of the ranch house knocked him almost clear of the few cosseted senses that he had. Just like the scenery around him, he froze.

'Ted, are you done yet?'

Teddy's insides trembled. A trembling that grew so strong it clashed with his nerves, raisin' Cain along his spine and setting the base of his skull juddering.

'Theodore?'

Theodore? Theodore was Teddy's full name; after some liberal, lobbying, important lunch-providing chap, and calling him by it had been a 'thing' of the Old Man's.

Momentarily, he remembered driving Old Man Callington into town once, where he'd ended up hearing other parents doing the same thing. It had seemed to him like those others had an exclusive type of family pride, one that must come with the naming of a child, one that enforces a sort of sanction over their using the child's shortened name. At the time it'd been a mean reminder of his own lack of family.

Something wasn't right. Something wasn't sorted right. Whatever it was gave him the notion that the name wasn't quite his.

Old Man Callington had switched, hadn't he? From Ted to Theodore. He'd known Teddy's full name for a good while before he'd settled on using it permanently. But, the details weren't clear. The lines on Teddy's back itched and one jabbed deeper into his flesh. He shuddered. Something ominous, something that made his skin crawl, preceded that memory, so he shied away from it.

'Gol darn it,' Teddy hissed. 'Recall this day, will ya?'

He stood alone in his mausoleum. With such a sparkling secrecy that harboured some sort of specialness, this, he reckoned should have been the most important day of his life. Yet it was an incomprehensible blur. His memories were still there. He knew it. They were there in the inexplicable smile he caught on his face each time he heard or saw something that must've meant a lot to him. They were the seed of the impulses that he kept experiencing, the jitters, the tickles and even the pains.

'Theodore, come on inside, will you?'

'Go,' Teddy told himself. 'Go into the house.'

Right now, he wasn't feeling particularly brave. Nary one was he totally sure of what he was doing. All the while he lingered, though, both he and the memory iced over.

Still, he never could resist a risk. He gritted his teeth against the cold and turned towards the house. Raising his face, he saw the frock-coated figure of his pa framed in the kitchen doorway. Pa wasn't wearing his hat. Of course he wasn't; this was his home. Teddy slapped his hand flat to the top of his own head. His hair felt downy, plentiful, like it'd been scrubbed in an icy trough, dedicated to the pursuit of its looking clean. But his hat was not there.

Pa laughed, raising his hand. He was holding something, a glass. Something thick and fluid, the colour of heartwood and copper, flickered in the intricate facets. Pa's bourbon? This must be a special time.

Teddy waved. Pa turned, disappearing back into the house. Teddy took one step towards him and then halted. He looked back at Caper. Caper snorted, scuffed the ground and shoved him away. Teddy shook his head, straightened up and strode towards the kitchen door.

Scents of mulling raisins, apricots and apples warmed over his numbed sinuses. The closer he got, the stronger the smells. Molasses, dark, gloopy and sweet baked in a pie, steaming citrussy cake and cooling buttery cookies. It seemed that the Callington women had been cooking all morning.

The pointed toes of his boots came over cosy and his feet began to crave the warmth within the house. He stopped in the doorway, though. It was so long since he'd seen his family; even in his own head. Laughter erupted from further inside the house, and the pianoforte started up again. They all seemed so happy, perhaps he should stay away.

'There you are.'

Ma. Ma was beautiful — in a handsome sort of way. He reckoned on his being a bootlicker, but he was beyond caring. She was charming and spirited as though her life was beginning all over again every day, yet when the situation called for it, she was rational and proper. A band of glassy green and red beads braced a severe parting in her long, dark hair; although severe was something she'd never be. Just like Mattie's, Ma's hair was waist-length. Today, however, it'd been braided, looped and piled on the top of her head. Her cheeks were a little rosier than he recalled. That gratifying smile tugged at Teddy's lips. Full of movement, Ma was enjoying the apparent hustle of the day. Teddy's cheeks began to smart and tingle. If only he could blush.

'Stamp your feet and come on in.'

Teddy's cheeks might not blush, but they jo-fired puffed up with his grinning. Pride. This was pride. Under all the high falutin' newfangled trimmings was his functional foreman, Ma: Mrs C Callington.

'Close the door behind you, Ted…Theodore. You're letting all the heat out.'

Turning to look him over, she seemed as perplexed by his appearance as he was pleased to see her. His smile vanished and for a moment they stood wordlessly watching each other.

As though suddenly reminded of where they were standing, she spun away, her dress rustling and scrunching; the kitchen was no place for its ruffles, folds, beads and embellishments. She loaded an empty cup with a creamy, sugary substance from one of the enormous stove's simmering pans. Obviously satisfied with what she'd seen, she offered the cup to him.

'Ellen's eggnog,' she said. 'should warm you up.'

He stared at the nog-filled mug.

'You may as well finish it off.'

Teddy took the mug from her and slurped a gulp. Ma turned back to the stove and set about ladling something else.

Nutmeg stuck to his teeth, coating them grittily. The rest plummeted to the pit of his stomach. It proceeded to sit there, a slovenly mass too gelatinous to do anything else.

'Mr and Mrs Hamilton have arrived for dinner. They've brought Father Egan and he looks to be starving.'

Teddy gagged. No way would Father Egan ever starve. The man could live off his wobbling, inexhaustible supply of reserves from his overexertions at the meal tables of his whim-pandering flock. And the Hamiltons? They lived in town where Mr Enoch Hamilton was a lawyer. He was the real thing, mind, not just an apprentice; letters after his name and everything. Ma hurried out of the room carrying a steaming full gravy boat on a saucer. Gravy and fine tableware? This must be a special day.

'Ma, let me help?' Teddy called after her.

Ma stopped. Dead in her tracks, she hovered in the doorway, her colours suddenly gaudy, as though she'd been lynched and bludgeoned.

A blackness, bitter and cold, inched over Teddy's back. He turned - he had closed the back door like Ma had asked. The backyard, minutes ago enchanted by the pastel palette of the sunny frost, was turning, sort of fading, moulding, dying. He frowned, pressing his nose onto the small, square pane closest to him.

A horizontal vortex, just like the lightning-filled ones that they'd seen on the prairie, seemed to be accumulating on the horizon. It rolled grey and silent, neither growing in size nor deepening in density, but sucking up everything in its path. There was nothing in its wake. Nothing at all.

'Ma,' he said, 'what's with the weather?'

Ma was silent, too. As was the whole house. The joviality, the pianoforte, the clunks and bubbling from the stove had all ceased. Teddy listened. Even the pulsing of his own person had no sound. He turned back to his reborn world.

A line no bigger than a hairline crack worked its way along the back of Ma's mildew-stained neck.

'This cain't be happening,' Teddy gasped. 'I only just found you. I cain't lose you now.'

He reached out; a featherlike touch was all he managed before Ma split open. The horror of such a bisection was all the more harrowing because it was happening to his ma. He jumped back, crying out in miserable self-reproach that he could ever abandon her to face her fate alone. Inside, though, she was no more than a grey chasm. There was no spilling of her beloved guts, flesh and sinew. Her remains simply disintegrated before his eyes.

It was inconceivable that his own mind could do this to him: surely, he held only loving thoughts of his family. He stared about himself, only to realise that it was happening again and again. The colours around him swirled, unable to stay within their lines; they clashed, contrasting viciously, and then smeared and turned insipid. He cried out again, swearing incredulously. The more he did, the more the image collapsed. The yard, the horses and the ranch buildings were now non-existent.

Teddy balled his hands and set his jaw. He stood still; only his eyes darted about his decaying surroundings, searching for a way out. All movement stopped. He stared at the void that had been his ma.

'Ma?' he squeaked.

As though connected to the heart-rending pain of losing his ma for a second time, the churning, the breaching and the withering of all that he loved began again.

'What?' he yelled. 'I didn't do anything.'

The very ground that he stood on began to fall away. One foot wavered in mid-air; he snatched it in, balancing it on top of the stable one.

'Ma'am,' he whined, forgetting just who he was talking to, 'I just wanted to help.'

The sun warmed his back weakly. In the distance, Caper nickered, and ahead of him, the pianoforte started its jingling again. It was as though he'd blinked all that destruction away. Everything returned to the way it was.

'Ma'am, let me help,' he said, relief and disbelief at the same time broadening the smile he found himself wearing.

He moved around his ma to take the gravy boat from her. Shyly, he looked into her face. She smiled back at him, her eyes alive with the same pride that he had for her.

'No Ted…Theodore,' Mattie said, ducking between them, 'not today.'

Mattie as well? Mattie rarely called him Theodore. Don't interfere, Teddy told himself and he let Mattie take the china from her mother. She immediately passed it to her sister.

'Two hands, Ellen,' she said.

Teddy wasn't used to this. Never, as far as he knew anyway, had he been treated with such deference. It seemed that today there was very little ranch work to be done. What there was, had been surreptitiously overlooked.

Beside him, Mattie giggled. She flounced about as though she knew an especially pleasing secret and was enjoying keeping it from him. He was fast becoming familiar with the fact that Mattie always had something up her sleeve. Not that she was wearing any right at that moment.

'Ma, Pa,' she announced, 'you just take a seat. Everybody, come into the dining room.'

The ranch house dining room was somewhere that, until now, Teddy remembered only as a glimpse through the window in passing. Swags of spruce branches, some with their cones still on, had been swathed over the door frames, the mantelpiece and from the picture rails. Wide, red ribbons, bundles of cinnamon sticks and glossy, prickly holly dotted with berries had been set in the swags.

Folded paper pictures of a white-haired, overweight, unsuitably dressed man stood about. Teddy didn't recognise him. His baggy, bright, fur-lined clothes and equally unsuitable black boots were too plumb clean to suggest that he did anything other than pose for his painting. His fat face looked to be all too hearty for the weight of the massive sack he was hefting about. Each picture bore a whimsical scrawl. But the writing was illegible; more like the hieroglyphics used by the plains Indians.

The table was laid out for company. As were the sideboards. So laden with game, sauces, herbs and vegetables that he'd never seen before, not to mention sweet treats, it was difficult to imagine this room was ever used for anything less. Somehow, though, he knew that not to be true. His family were not at all pretentious. Nary one were they particularly privileged.

'Ted?' Mattie called. 'I mean Theodore, you're next to Father Egan.'

Teddy was right smart sure that he'd have taken his meals with the ranch hands in the cook shack. That, or wherever was favourable at the time. The thing was, he seemed to remember Old Man Callington being there, too. Perhaps this was just another outcome of the carnage that his memories had been left in. Still, he'd seen just what it would do if he tried to influence it. So, he kept his place and did as he was told.

The girls were bubbling over with excitement; they fumbled with the Callington silverware. No expense had been spared. Lean, thick slices of richly red venison were served up. Dark purple, pickled beet, and sharp yellow lemons were layered over the top. Mashed-up vermillion music roots, oniony turnips and white, cloudlike cauliflower were dolloped on the side. Teddy felt the tickling in his belly again. He blamed it on the fine china making him nervous, and let Mrs Hamilton take control of his gravy pouring.

He stole a look at Ellen. She caught his eye and smiled. Her dress was not nearly as lacy as Ma's or Mattie's; her cheeks, her nose, her entire face was still pinkly translucent. Her eyes held an innocence; a luxury that came with the naivety of the ways of the world. That was what kept her from taking anything, mostly herself, too seriously. An attachment to her gnawed at Teddy; memory or not, there was no way it could have been anything to do with that innocence. A spike of mischievousness niggled at his core and prickled the back of his eyes. So, he stared at her, eyeballing an imaginative hole in her temple until she looked at him again. She glared at him and poked out her tongue.

'Stop,' he told himself and he straightened up. 'No deviltry.'

The smile that now tickled his lips suggested that the hazing of Ellen had been nothing to do with the demon. It'd been a deeper desire of his own to annoy her. Instantly, the tips of his hair bristled, and he stifled a grimace at the thought that he might have something in common with the vampire. The demon was a shallow being, driven by a hankering to madden others. Teddy wasn't shallow, was he? Darn it, hadn't daydreaming been the thing that had got him kangaroo-courted the other day?

He dared to look again. Ellen was smiling and there was a mysterious sparkle in her eyes. He was warmed by a memory within a memory of her batting his hands away when he meddled in the fitting of her ribbony, bibbony hairband to his head. He'd threatened to invade her bedroom, leaving cowpoke footprints all over it or wring her favourite chicken's neck if she ever tried it again. He couldn't help smiling back at her, though. The need to annoy her may have been subdued for now, but it would be back. He knew it. And, well, maybe it was down to all this joviality around, but he had to acknowledge the corn; he liked it.

Teddy remembered just what it was like to be only twenty, faced with Ma's cooking and surrounded by his family.

CHAPTER SEVENTEEN

At the sight of all these sumptuous eats before him and the promise of some legal gluttony, Teddy's body began to react. The tender lining of his nose tingled with pleasure, right down to its tiny fibres. The gummy inside of his mouth bulged; he could've sworn his top lip did, too. His tongue may as well have lain on an undulating mattress of anticipation. He couldn't stop it. Nary one could he eat any of this. His body should know that. It was dead. It did not work — inside anyway.

'Merry Christmas,' Old Man Callington announced.

Teddy had no idea what Christmas was, but Old Man Callington may as well have chirked and said, 'Fly at it.' A sort of high falutin' charivari erupted with everyone delving into what seemed to be their own delight. Silverware chinked on china rather than steel on tin pots, pans or copper kettles. Balderdash and ballyhoo bantered up and down the table.

Teddy stared at the blue-rimmed, red-cameoed plate before him and was consumed by compassion. Or it might have been humiliation. It was a weird emotion. Neither good nor bad. Just melancholy; with a pinch of self-pity. There must've been any number of people who'd have been only too glad of this food. But he simply could not eat it.

'It ain't real,' he told himself. 'This is in your memory.'

The feeding of vampires, particularly himself and László, was something that he'd been coached in to the point of thoughtlessness. Dead blood was dangerous blood. Cooked food was worse. He tried to think of any snippet László may have given him that would prove beneficial right now. He drew a blank. In fact, he had a general lack of knowledge in the further workings of undead, vampire bodies. And that, darn it, seemed to stem from a total lack of interest in his ancestry — catawumptiously justified; just not helpful right now. Dang, had he ever actually listened to anything valuable?

There was, as there is with most things, a slim possibility that his body's reaction would be no different to anyone else's. Perhaps the backlash to Ellen's eggnog wasn't unique to him, perhaps none of the guests had fared well with it.

Greens, in the case of those that grow in the ground or on trees, curled his toes inside his boots — he didn't think that was anything to do with the vampire, though. And pie crust? He plumb had no idea what that might do to him. It wasn't something he wanted to find out.

'Theodore?' Ma said. 'You haven't touched a bite. Is everything alright?'

She spoke quietly, her voice full of that compassion. Was she sad, too? Perhaps he was making her sad. That was the last thing Teddy wanted. He picked up his fork, twirling it like a silver pistol.

'I just don't know where to start,' he said.

He kept his face away from hers, even though it seemed to be that all she saw was the boy of the memories.

'This all looks to be delicious.'

'Well, don't let it cool,' she said, putting down her own cutlery and squeezing his hand in hers.

Stunned and mesmerised, Teddy ached to close his fingers around hers, to grasp her hand and not let go. Her squeeze had been no heavier than the fragile feet of a butterfly that had once landed on his skin. Briefly, he saw himself lying still and apathetic in the balminess of the prairie summer.

He'd been bucked off by a lazy Blue, and a butterfly had alighted on his ungloved hand, slowly releasing its beautiful wings. The cowpokes had found it hilarious. Ma hadn't been there then. His knee started a skittering twitching; he dropped his free hand to it and clutched that instead.

'And don't be nervous,' Ma whispered, leaning close. 'Everybody's gotta eat, now, haven't they? Just start on the outside and work your way in to the middle.'

Then, sitting upright again and releasing his hand: 'Ellen, don't bolt, its not a race now.'

He could not eat. He didn't want to leave the table. He needed help. What would the demon do?

Kill them all.

Well, that was horse feathers. Teddy tried to recall mealtimes in the cookhouse. Cowpoke cooking was something of an acquired taste, and on some days that taste had taken a lot more acquisition than any cookie puncher would care to mention. He must've cowboyed up to heaps of Coosie's chewsies, but still, there was no way in tarnation he'd have eaten some of those skeersome tranklements served up. What had he done then? Hidden the food? Ditched it somehow?

Covert operations, lying low, sneaking around even, was in his nature. Use your surroundings — that was something all cowpokes knew. Sure enough, it wasn't long before Mattie craved the centre of attention. As soon as she had it, he switched plates with Father Egan. The preacher hadn't quite finished. The miracle of his replenished plate clearly astonished him. Teddy shrugged away the good father's silent enquiries. Father Egan cupped his hands in the universal sign of thanks and tucked in again. Teddy sat back, relieved, hoping it passed for satisfaction.

Just when he thought it was over, when all had been cleared away, the table was graced with pumpkin pies, fancy cakes, nuts and raisins. Mattie had some ridiculous idea of setting fire to the fruit cake before serving it. That's what they do in England, apparently. Something inside Teddy quite liked the idea. *It might burn down the house, too, and then spread to the ranch buildings, the horses and the people.* No deviltry, he told himself again. He joined the general dismissal of the idea as old colonial claptrap and switched plates with the good Father.

Then there were little cups of coffee. Horned and barefoot; just the way Teddy liked it. Its thick, silky blackness may as well have been liquid tobacco. It had an aroma so pleasingly potent that a nose, functional, or otherwise, wasn't needed to smell it. It penetrated Teddy's very pores, and it didn't so much as pick him up, but all-to-pieces knock him galley-west. Caffeine. Cowpoke and gentry, and every American in between, loved it. Nothing, not the freshest, most adolescent, virginal blood, could beat it.

Teddy hadn't had a good bellyful in over one hundred years. László and death had hell-fired cured him of any addiction he may have had to caffeine; he had no functioning insides to drink anything, save for you-know-what. Same with nicotine, he didn't have breath to smoke. The sad fact was, compared to his addiction to blood, caffeine and nicotine were a whole heap safer.

The trouble was, Father Egan was firmly rooted in British belly-wash tea.

Teddy looked around. The table, its coverings, the beverages and on more than one occasion Mattie was very much the centre of attention. Perhaps elsewhere, he'd happen upon an opportunity to tip the coffee away. Covertly, of course.

He could get up, walk around claiming No Man's Land eccentricity. After all, he was considered a foreigner in these parts, then he could underhandedly ditch the drink in a plant pot. Apparently not. No house plants were present in this room. Usually, there were, he was sure of it; their pristine plumage was so prominent that they were visible from the back porch. So, nope, he couldn't deposit the coffee there.

Could he just ignore it? Not drink it. Not likely. He wasn't that good at ignorance. He, just like all other cowpokes, adored coffee, couldn't live without it, was addicted to it. Concerns would be raised and questions would be asked as to why he'd left it. He was enough of a liar as it was; he couldn't lie again. Liar: the word stabbed him like an Arkansas toothpick. He desperately hoped he hadn't flinched. The concerns and questions of his family as to why he wouldn't drink his coffee were unanswerable right now. So, nope, leaving the coffee untouched would not work.

Just drink it. What was the worst that could happen? His body might dissolve slowly from inside out, hissing and wheezing as it disintegrated. He might implode. Or the coffee might simply seep back out of him, dribbling over his lips, running down his nose and eventually, disgustingly, pour out of every available orifice while he sat, all-fired compos mentis, trying to pretend it was all perfectly normal.

It seemed that there was no way out this time. His mind began to addle. Acknowledge the corn, Ted, all options are exhausted. He nearly forgot himself and snorted. His sense of irony had been piqued — he was plumb sure he'd never sensed irony of any sort before László.

He'd overstayed his welcome. Pep up, return to the present, think of something else; the tomb, the mausoleum, blackness all around. The memory should freeze; just like it had done in the yard. He opened his eyes as wide as he could, shook his head violently and fidgeted around. He tried to make a burbling sound, but his mouth was dry. So, he stretched it open to over-ample, screwing his eyes closed, making a guttural, growling sort of scream.

Steeling himself, he listened for the sounds of the company at the table. There was nothing. He opened his eyes wide, letting in as much of the night as he could, and stared directly ahead.

Ellen had gone. Manifesting itself in her place was a grinning, skeletal and senseless face, the gruesome corpse that he'd met just yesterday. Teddy looked away, his sight catching the amoebas as they bumbled around on the air, extending and retracting false feet and fingerlike appendages. His ears picked up the distant, echoing popping and flicking of fish.

Raising his head, he looked around. Darkness, just like he'd asked for. A dull ache began to pulse in his neck. He was no longer sitting, but he lay on the earthy ground. His chest was bare and the floor was cold. He scratched the ground, this was not his tomb. Nary one was it his family ranch house.

He lowered his face to the ground. The flesh of his back was taut, debilitatingly so. It was exposed, too. As were his arms. He flexed his fingers. There was only three on his right hand, the stub of the middle one smarted. He tried to raise his head again; his neck cricked so he gave up and lay still listening to the echoes of the fish.

His jeans, thank the land, seemed to be firmly in place, although they were hard as a floorboard. He tried to shift his legs. There seemed to be a layer under his jeans, between them and the lower half of his body. It bore the scratch of wet wool and his toes squelched in his boots. He must've been splashing about in a river somewhere.

A blast of freezing, damp air hit him in the face at the same time as a rhythmical ticking clicked close by.

'Who the hell are you?'

The harsh muzzle of a rifle prodded the side of his head.

'And how is it that you come to be in Bloody Bill's cave?'

Bloody Bill was dead. A psychopathic partisan ranger back in the Civil War, he was killed in one of his irregular battles, shot dead by the Union a long time before Teddy had been murdered. Teddy had read about it. The cave was familiar, though. He'd definitely been here before.

'He sure is pretty,' the slovenly southern voice added as the rifle prodded him again. 'Can you fix him, Bill?'

'Get up,' another rolling, menacing voice grumbled.

Teddy flinched at the scraping of a sabre through its metal scabbard.

'On your knees.'

There was no way, no way in tarnation that he would ever have known Bloody Bill. Fear, enough to freeze the blood that pounded in his ears, seized his entire insides. This fear was what his countless victims would have known. This was truly ironic, and yet Teddy could not harrumph away the remorse that balled in his throat. Quivering shamelessly, he raised his eyes to face his rebel executioner.

There was nothing but blackness. Bloody Bill was not there. Teddy shifted. The prodding muzzle of the rifle had vanished, too, and he was no longer cold. He widened his eyes once again. Now he stared at the upright slats of a timber wall. He listened out for the fish and couldn't hear them. There was the cracking and spitting of fire, though. He was sitting alone and scrunched, his space confined, no more than a child's cubby hole. Placing his ear to the wall, he listened again. A good number of booted feet were heading his way. He flexed his hands. Finger still missing. But he saw the airwaves move. He stared at his hand and, reaching out, flattened it over the opposite wall. Nothing. He scrunched his nose, nuzzling it and his cheek into the wall behind him. No sense of touch.

'Marshal?' a No Man's Land drawl hollered from outside. 'Send the murdering son of a bitch out.'

Sakes alive! Teddy scrambled to his feet. He was the only one here. He whirled around. The blackness whirled with him, blue and green and, nearest the outside wall, yellow and red. There was no answer from the towns' Marshal.

A fire had been started: its large, unpredictable glow was smudged against the night by the grimy window. The demon screamed in Teddy's ears. He clasped his hands over them, but it was no good. Fear, desperation, hysteria crashed around in his skull, the smashing of those sensations into the canals of his sinuses sent his sight swirling. His face jerked away from the vision of the fate that had been constructed for him and he spun around. His calves collided with a makeshift, fold-down seat and he collapsed to the floor.

'Send him out, Marshal. This is a small town and we're all settled that what we do here tonight will go no further.'

Teddy grasped the bottom rung of the door to his cell; his hands fit comfortably through the gaps, and he pulled himself up. The Marshal, the lawman, was deliberating. That didn't seem right.

'Marshal, is that a hemp committee?' Teddy called. 'Are they here for me?'

He couldn't see anyone else in the jailhouse. Nary one was there any other cells.

'Marshal? Is it…I mean a lynch mob?'

'I am a man of the law,' the Marshal's voice grumbled. 'That means…' The man's voice got closer. '… like it or not, I gotta get you in front of a jury for a fair trial.'

Teddy hid his face.

'Don't look at me!' he cried.

'What you did to those girls, though…' the Marshal stopped moving.

He spoke quietly, little more than a mumble.

'…defiling their bodies like that before you killed them…'

He halted as though the rising of his own sick bile thwarted him.

'You better be scared, boy; I am seriously considering handing you over to those mobbers outside.'

'Defile?' Teddy said. 'I cain't defile. I cain't feel anything. Anything at all.'

The Marshal retreated, his boot steps clicking and scuffing a little too loudly.

'Listen to me,' Teddy called after him.

Trying to believe in his own hopes, he added: 'Maybe I didn't kill them.'

A figure had entered the jailhouse.

'You were found in the midst of the murder,' the Marshal hollered, a might too judgementally, 'with their blood on your hands and your face and your clothes.'

Teddy raised his hands. In the glow of the fire, he could see no blood on them. His hands were spotless, beautifully so, as though they'd been licked clean. Even with supernatural sight, all he could make out was dark grime under his nails. He sniffed them, but it was no use, he couldn't smell anything. The toes of his boots jutting under the bottom of the door were splattered with something, though. His brown jeans were the same. Frantically, he stretched out his shirt; it was caked in dried blood.

Sakes alive! Sakes alive, this was one of those times with László. Scared of what he knew he was capable of, he conceded that the mob, were right — he was the murderer.

'You come for the prisoner?' the Marshal said.

The demon screeched again. Teddy covered his ears. He stepped away from the glow of the fire. He'd be burned alive. That was if he made it that far. More than likely, they'd tear him to pieces as soon as they got their hands on him.

'Have to say, I'd hoped you'd come earlier.' the Marshal spoke again.

How had he been caught? He should never have been caught. And where was László?

It was you, you cultus saphead, you got us staked. The demon was blaming him.

'There are no vampires in the Old West,' Teddy hissed. 'How would they know about "stakes"? They think "stake" is something you eat.'

The demon took no notice.

You sappy, chuckleheaded greenhorn. You had to leave him, didn't you? You thought you could do it better on your own. Now you've got us killed.

'I was expecting a US Marshal,' the town Marshal went on. 'You sure don't look like any US Marshal.'

'Obviously that didn't happen.' Teddy muttered, 'We, I mean I, or rather you, weren't killed.'

The demon was quiet. Teddy had begun to tremble. Somehow he'd survived this.

'What's your name?' the Marshal asked the newcomer.

The fire outside still burned, its colour an intense heat, although the crowd had gone suspiciously quiet. Teddy grasped the bars again, craning his neck to see what was going on.

'Is Jagelovići.'

László. Caged and faced with László.

'Let me out!' Teddy screamed. 'Let me go. Now.'

He squeezed his eyes closed. The demon was laughing in his head.

'It's László!' Teddy cried 'László is the murderer.'

He sank back to the ground.

'He murdered me.'

He pulled his knees up to his chest.

'Pa, save me, Pa,' he said.

His eyes burned and so he rubbed them with the butts of his hands. Instantly, he stopped; those were the hands of a brutal, cold-blooded murderer. He tried to look into the space around him, find out exactly where he was, but he couldn't see a thing. He sniffed. He had breath. The smell of his own body, new, laced with copper and mixed with fustiness of a ranch's yard, filled his head. His throat was sore and his nose singed as though burned on the inside. Sobs welled up in his chest, they rasped through his throat. He coughed as tears flowed over the sore brims of his eyes, streaming down his cheeks, gathering like an oxbow in a river at his nose. How had this happened? He'd done nothing wrong. He'd been a normal, happy child, hadn't he? Until, for no apparent reason, his family had turned on him. Sadness brought on a fresh bout of tears. Fourteen again? But, darn it, it felt good to cry.

It wasn't long, though, until the heaving in his chest began to hurt. His ribs must've been bruised. Even that was good; he didn't think he had ribs. A dull throb began in his head and his face seemed scorched. He stopped trying to sob, and lay, curled up on the tomb's floor, picking at the earth and eating leeches.

A couple of nights ago, he hadn't even had memories. The image of his family had been amazing, wondrous, almost unbelievable. And senses. He'd had senses, too. He'd known the texture of the things he'd touched. He'd smelled things. And tasted them. Well, sort of. Then those senses had lingered on, all the while he'd held onto the memory.

He craned his neck and nuzzled the air, trying to sniff it, inhale its odour, sense it infuse on his tongue and extract bumps from the gummy inside of his mouth. Nope. It didn't work. He was, once again, to all intents and purposes, dead. He reckoned that was how he always would be.

Chapter Eighteen

Teddy opened his eyes. He saw only the tomb. The fantastic darkness shrouded the dead, grinning bodies. The Callington family dinner scene that he'd somehow conjured up, a whole heap of weeks, or was it months, ago was steadfastly fixed in his head. It was so intense, so vibrant that it would not be dismissed, remaining there like the beloved antiques in his, hang fire, the Butler's house or was it László's? He stuffed a handful of teeming fodder into his mouth and tried again to recall it.

Scraps of the Christmas dinner cluttered the dining table, and in the bright blue and red china cups the coffee was still steaming.

This was where he'd got to last time, before he'd panicked and sent himself reeling into a past that he'd rather not have recalled. Not so vividly anyway. His memory was his now, and his alone to control. That meant it was up for storing everything. Everything that he did, everything that he said, everything that he sensed. Since that first time, since the crying; which was something he all-to-pieces did not intend to do again, with his natural state being one of optimism tinged with just a smidgen of adrenaline junkie, he'd conjured up other memories. At first reliving only fleeting fancies. He'd found his memory to be an archive of skills, risks, triumphs sometimes wholesome, sometimes just plain old success. There were also thousands of pleasurable little human rituals, like yawns and stretches, itches and scratches, fits of sneezes and the ensuing giddiness.

He'd settled upon manipulating his own mind, calling up a particular memory, the prairie, more of the Double C perhaps, or the rodeo. He'd venture into enticing forth the sensations that went with whatever it was that he was recalling, No Man's Land rain on a sweltering afternoon, the fluffiness of spiked snakeroot on the prairie. Or the gambling of roping, the frustration of dancing, everybody else's amusement at his singing.

Only ever were they the memories that he wanted mind. Visiting the loss and subsequent cauterisation of his missing finger wouldn't be a good idea. Nor, for that matter, was whatever had caused the issue with his back. Now he came to think of it, there must be a hundred years' worth of those nightmares. And very real they'd be, too.

The demon, the part of Teddy where evil resided needed to be kept placated. It was a contrary being and it drew a fine line between its host's discomfort and its own depravity. So Teddy kept it fed. It was odd: the more hungry he allowed the demon to become, the stronger it became. The stronger, the more psychotic, controlling and possessive. Since Teddy was determined never to murder, he couldn't let it get to that stage. He fed as soon as he roused. Perhaps his diet would never be as plentiful as a whole human of blood, but it was enough; the demon would never starve.

There was no way, though, no way in hell, which by his reckoning was a mere matter of standards, that were he to go for taste, he'd opt for his current menu — balloon-backed spider and glutinous grubs. He regaled the demon with tales of Coosie's chuckwagon chicken, which funnily enough was actually bacon. And then there was chitterlings and mistries. He couldn't tell the demon what had been in Coosie's mistries, becase he just didn't know. And chitterlings? He plumb didn't like to think about them. There had been, of course, beans. Beans, beans and more beans. And then he bolted down the balloon-backed spider and glutinous grubs.

By tonight, his faith in the workings of his own mind was unshakable. He trusted in it to get him out of the near-death scrapes he knew he'd wound up in throughout his past.

The Callington Christmas had more to it. For one thing, it was still there, constantly in the back of his mind, interrupting whatever he tried to do. Not that he did much. Sometimes, though, even through the simple task of eating; although, to acknowledge the corn, eating would never be simple for a creature like himself, he would see the table festooned with festive fare, and hear the herald of his pa bidding them all to tuck in.

Clutching his knees, Teddy settled on the floor with his back against the wall. He closed his eyes and thought of the Double C. He pictured Ma in her new dress, Mattie and Ellen giggling over the fine china, and Mrs Hamilton taking his plate to swamp it with gravy.

The air chimed with the chatter of dinner guests, it smelled of boozy, fruity rye and, of course, caffeine. Teddy grasped the napkin from between himself and Father Egan. It was starched, although it flopped, and breadcrumbs fell out or wedged under his nails. The napkin's embroidered monogram was rough under his thumb.

'Is everything alright?' Mrs Hamilton said.

She wasn't looking his way. Teddy got the notion that the question wasn't for him at all. Mrs Hamilton was gazing at Ma who, at the head of the table, looked deservedly serene. Nobody else spoke. Teddy was bashfully conspicuous. He laid one hand over his heart; or where he knew it used to be and bowed slightly. Twisting his napkin, he addressed his ma.

'Thank you, Ma'am, for this fine meal. It truly was unbelievable.'

Ma looked at her own place setting. She was smiling and a little too pink.

'Theodore,' Old Man Callington said.

His voice was the formidable Midwestern rumble that Teddy knew and loved. It was like the first thunder of a distant storm, just like the times when he'd been out on the prairie. Teddy heeded the unspoken warning and stopped talking.

Old Man Callington, his arms rigid at his sides, the military way, stood. Teddy sensed the guest's stares turn expectant. Capt. Clement Callington was about to speak. Reverently laying the napkin down, Teddy gazed at him. He was all-fired keen to hear what the Old Man had to say. His pa always said things that were worth listening to.

The Old Man cleared his throat. He seemed to have forgotten whatever it was that he'd planned on saying. So he said nothing. His hands were shaking, though. He snatched up his tumbler, just the same way that Teddy had seized upon the napkin. Still he trembled; only now the glass jolted back and forth, clinking dangerously whenever it came into contact with the chunky watch chain draped across his vest. Thank the land that the glass was empty.

'Clem,' Ma said, encouraging him with a nod of her head, 'I think it's time, don't you?'

Old Man Callington mumbled an agreement and then cleared his throat as though to start his speech all over again.

'Father Egan, Enoch, some help?' he cried.

'What is it, sir?' Teddy said, hurriedly getting to his feet, 'Can I help?'

It seemed as though he was speaking without actually using the power of speech. The body spoke. The boy in the memory spoke at the same time, but Teddy in his tomb hadn't uttered a word. Yet, his senses, his emotions were so real; just like the kick he got from the affection in the smile on the Old Man's face, whenever he caught him looking at him.

'Unfortunately not Theodore. Not today.'

Teddy glanced at the faces of those around the table. All pink, healthy and very much alive-looking. If anything, they were a little blotchy red with warmth and merriment. Nothing was fading or greying or crumbling, like it had before.

'I suggest we give out the gifts,' Ma declared. 'In all my born days! A priest, a lawyer and a businessman and you're each as useless as the next.'

Ma's impromptu assertiveness had the men at the table initiate a crucial study of their individual place settings. Evidently, it wasn't the first time Ma had called the shots. Teddy looked down at his twisted napkin, musing over just who the Double C's real decision-maker was. He suspected Mrs Hamilton of doing the same. And, perhaps — God.

With the placidity, elegance and swish of a lady, Ma removed herself from the room. Scraping chairs and a whole heap of unladylikeness followed as Mattie and Ellen, overlooking their difference in age, scrambled after her. A flurry of folded paper pictures billowed about after them.

Not knowing what came next and unsure of just what to do, Teddy remained standing there. A fractious buzzing infected him all down one side. Pa was hovering next to him. Teddy smiled crookedly at him, hoping it was the right thing to do. Old Man Callington had always been the embodiment of Teddy's hopes and dreams, so when his shoulder was captured by the Old Man's commanding hand, he let it guide him into the parlour.

'This one's for you.'

Mattie, kneeling below what looked to be the lopped-off top of a spruce, offered Teddy a deep, sturdy, oval-shaped box wrapped in tartan and done up with a massive material bow.

Teddy stared at the treetop. Just like a child, his eyes widened at the sight. It was beyond belief. Amazingly, considering it was a tree wedged in the Callingtons' parlour and, from its broad lower boughs to its topmost branches it sported ribbons, candles, trinkets and candies, it still bore the majority of its grey-blue needles. And he thought he'd seen everything!

'Dunderhead,' Mattie said, wafting the box at him, 'take it. It's a Christmas present.'

He stared at his elder sister as she held the box up to him.

'You're giving me a present?'

Yup, it was definitely not him doing the speaking. Although it did sometimes seem like it was. Well, to acknowledge the corn, it was him, just not as he knew himself to be.

'We've all got one,' Ellen squealed.

'Well, what's in it?' Teddy said.

A Christmas present. So, this is what Christmas is: gifts and gaudiness. He wasn't too sure about it. Then he remembered all the sumptuous eats — he could get used to it.

'Ted,' Mattie snapped.

The narrowing of her eyes displayed her exasperation. Quickly, Teddy took the box from her. He was a little afraid. What if this was one of her tricks?

'Thank you,' his voice said, it echoed in his mind, 'But I ain't too sure about this. I mean, it don't seem right. See, this ain't my Christmas. It's yourn. My Christmas is hard tack, settin' in the dice house, ridin' the line…'

'Open it, open it,' Ellen interrupted.

Teddy tingled inside. He had a strong impression that she'd have shouted that regardless of what was in the box or who was to be doing the opening. He looked to his parents for approval. Ma, skirts fanned out about her feet, was sitting on the very edge of her seat. Pa was stock-still and whiter than the ice on the corral. The eyes of both sparkled with an ardent wish for him to more than appreciate whatever was inside the box. If it hadn't been for that, he'd have handed it over to Ellen and bid her to open it.

He nestled the present in the crook of his arm, relishing for a moment its rigidity against his cowpoke body. He pulled the tail-end of the red and gold ribbon and the wrapping tumbled to the floor. Underneath was the real box. Its lid fitted neatly and there was writing on it. Meanly, Teddy's mind mangled up the letters until they were incomprehensible. The shape and mechanics of the box could mean only one thing. A hat. Could this be his hat?

His hat. He missed that hat so much. He loved that hat.

Teddy's skin rose up in bumps so high that, all over his body, they grazed the hot, gauzy cowpoke clothes this body was wearing. It was by no means just a hat. Something else had come with it that day. Something so important it could never be forgotten. If only he could recall what that special thing was!

The parlour was quiet. In fact, if it weren't for Ellen's incessant fidgeting and squeaking, they'd have heard the pace of Teddy's non-existent heartbeat. The Callington Christmas party were watching him with what seemed like a concentrated, hanging expectation. Their chins bobbed in encouragement and their mouths opened and closed, but no sound came out. Teddy removed the box's lid.

A brand new, Simon Pure, ace-high cowboy hat sat inside. Its high, dark felt crown and brim were yet to be dented or bowed. The hat was dignified, belvedere and cowpoke proud.

'It's made of nutria,' his pa said. 'Should last a lifetime.'

Or two, Teddy thought. He reckoned that he must've steamed it on the forge, perhaps shaped it in the livery. But, nope, he'd had patience; it was the one time in his life that he had. He'd bidden his time; and in that time, his hat had started to mould to the shape of his grip. Instinctively, his sight settled on his gappy right hand. Yup, the hat had a ding unique crease.

'It has no band on it,' Pa said.

Odd. Teddy was sure that his hat had borne a band around the base of the crown. It'd had dangly doohickeys on it, too.

'I was thinking that you might want to braid one for it,' Pa went on. 'And the thing is, my hat doesn't have one either.'

Yes, it does, Teddy thought.

'So, I was wondering if you might do two. Two the same — one for me and one for you.'

Teddy gazed at the bandless hat in his hand. The hat had been his identity. The band wasn't just any old size adjustment device. It'd been of his own custom-making. His fingers bristled, seeming to recognise the countless times he'd rubbed them over the band's intricate braiding. Minute sensors in the tips zoomed and vibrated, recalling the feel of the funny little buckle and the small metal motifs that had dangled from each end.

For so many years they'd been no more than two randomly connected crescents. For too long, they'd meant no more to him than mysterious little ditties. But now he knew better. The Double C. They meant home, family, belonging. They and he himself were the Callington brand. His pa had worn one just the same. Hadn't he seen it? Just the other night.

'Don't just stand there, Addle-pot,' Mattie moaned. 'Put it on.'

Precariously bewitched, as though the precious object belonged to someone else, Teddy judiciously pinched the plush, pliable crown. The hat was lifted clear of its box. He held it at arm's length and admired its wide brim.

'If you want, we can get some stampede strings,' his pa said.

'Well, I'll braid some,' he said.

'Of course. Just basic ones.'

'Nothing fancy.'

Pa frowned. It was a little too dismissive. He looked like a shouty, Shakespearean actor when, with wide gestures in the air, he began measuring out invisible lengths of leather strips.

'I can get you some leather,' he said.

'Quit beating the devil around the stump, you two,' Mattie said.

'Mattie!' Ma reprimanded.

Teddy folded his elbow and brought the hat back into his chest as if he were practising respect for whatever was in front of him. He sensed the amusement in his sister's eyes and looked away. Or at least he hoped he did. That inner foolishness he'd had that first time when he was with Caper had returned.

'Just put it on, will you?' Ellen nagged.

Teddy glanced at Old Man Callington. Old Man Callington nodded. Even if he hadn't, Teddy couldn't have stopped himself. Even if he'd wanted to, he couldn't, he was catawamptiously, blissfully, helplessly absorbed in his memory. He lifted the hat high, twisted his wrist and turned it over.

It was fully lined. At the back was a sweet, crisp bow. It and the silky lining were white. Teddy harrumphed. He'd always just thought that bow was a balled-up lump, fawn-coloured and frayed along with the rest of the ripped-up lining.

The Teddy in the memory vowed to never take the hat off. That was hugely irresponsible of him; but only Teddy alone in his tomb knew it. The boy lowered the hat, ran his free hand through his hair and then fitted it onto his head. Now Ellen's befuddled hairband exercise made perfect sense. The hat was a snug fit. It crushed his hair and with its smooth leather sweatband, caressed his temples. For one divine moment, it was all he could feel.

Old Man Callington cleared his throat again. Ma made a sort of squeaking sound. Teddy adjusted the hat; pulling it low, the brim shadowed his eyes.

'Wow,' Ellen said, 'you actually look quite handsome.'

He'd take her word for it. He touched the brim and, hoping his smile was a little anti-goglin', tipped his hat to her. Sakes alive, that felt good.

'You definitely look taller,' Father Egan said.

Teddy pushed the hat back. Now he could see better.

'Gallant,' Mrs Hamilton added.

Gallant? Now that sounded all-to-pieces good.

'Specially, now that you can't see your hair,' Mattie finished.

Darn it, Mattie. You always get one-up-on me.

'Is it all according to Hoyle?' Ma said.

Never, and he wasn't doing too badly at the memory thing now, had Ma ever spoken cowpoke. He was all-fired sure he'd heard an accent as well. Ma, Pa, Mattie, in fact all the sunflower Kansans he'd ever met, swore most passionately that they didn't have an accent. Having an accent was one of the reasons that he was considered a foreigner. Even if No Man's Land was just next door.

Poor Ma looked frail. Old Man Callington hurried to her side and took her hand in his. Teddy squinted at the floor: surely he didn't look so good as to make a lady swoon, now, did he?

Shamefully shifting, he was aware of his brown leather boots trampling over the green flowers of Ma's carpet. The Indians saw anything green as enduring — the carpet would survive. Darkness closed around him. The tomb, his tomb, was damp and cold on his skin and lonely in his soul. Darn it, he'd taken his mind off the memory. Now he craved the warmth of the Callingtons' parlour.

Almost panicky, he patted his head. His hair was still springy and plentiful. He'd lost his hat. Suddenly conscious of the deep hole inside where his heart should have been, he clutched a hand to his chest. He'd lost his heart, too. But not to some beautiful romance as Ma would have wanted; to something rotten, dark, dead and empty. Still, the void ached. It hurt like he'd never had any sense of it before.

'Ma'am,' he whined, 'it's the most perfect hat ever. I love it.'

He sensed pride in Old Man Callington's eyes, love radiating from Ma and his sisters.

He laughed. A happy, wholesome, heartfelt laugh. He couldn't help it.

'I ain't never gonna take it off,' he said, unable to stop himself.

But he had taken it off, hadn't he? So many times, and every time he'd simply shrugged, mussed up his hair and replaced the hat without any further thought. He turned his lying face away from them. So many times — just the once he hadn't replaced it.

'Some bottled courage perhaps, Clem?' Mr Hamilton said.

'No!' Old Man Callington snapped.

Teddy stared at him.

'Sorry, Enoch. I mean "No". Thank you. I'm just fine. You go ahead, though.'

That was more like him.

'Theodore, the label,' Ma said, her eyes darting from her husband to Teddy.

She shook her head to the lawyer.

'Check the label. You must read the label.'

Ma's voice had taken on a tremble, too.

'Cowmen,' she sighed, 'more interested in the hat than what is underneath it.'

Teddy bent and placed the hatbox on the carpet. Calculating his movements, he took the hat off and investigated the inside. It seemed to him that at that moment, there was only him and his family on the earth. All other humanity had simply disappeared, washed away by the importance of this moment. No one could have known the sensations he'd known back in 1886.

Halfway around the hat's interior, his fiddling found the uniformity of the manufacturer's stamp. It didn't matter that his memory couldn't or wouldn't show him words; he knew instantly the sensitivity of that stamp. The top swag and the stripes of the badge, the surrounding belt, the buckle and the knot. Perhaps it was the atmosphere, the people around him or even the preposterously dressed tree, but he remembered only too well what it said.

'J. B. Stetson,' he said.

Perhaps that stamp had been the reason for the many times that he'd taken the hat off. The desire to stroke it, the same way he'd done that day so long ago, had struck him so often, that he'd put it down to nothing other than an addleheaded habit. The void in his chest quivered painfully. He'd never been able to actually know its pattern, never known why it was that he'd had that hankering.

'Sure is,' Pa said.

Pa sounded pleased with his investment. Teddy was pleased as well. Ma did not seem to feel it, though. So, he continued his exploration of the sweatband. The other side held a stamp, too.

'The hat shop in town?' he said.

'Put it back on,' Ellen squealed.

Teddy caught her stare and held it for a moment. She got coy and settled down. He grinned. She stuck out her tongue.

'Check the other label, dear,' Mrs Hamilton said.

A functional nubbin of a label jutted out from the sweatband.

'The size?' he said.

From around the room, disagreeable sighs and stares coupled with a tense sort of impatience spurred him to probe about under the sweatband again. An oblong-shaped embroidered label had been sewn into the base just under the band.

Something, perhaps the quaking of his hands or just his insides in general, or the unbelievable brilliance that this moment had weathered the vastness of time itself, slowed him down.

He cradled the hat as reverently as he could and carefully curled back the band.

'"Theodore Callington",' he said.

Just like light leaving sound in its wake, the meaning of that moment smacked into him. He was now one step ahead of the boy in his memory. His body didn't have time to react properly. Instantly, time seemed to speed up. Teddy had to anchor his hands to the tomb's floor, lest he be swept three ways from Sunday. The pulse of this body was so stunning, so loud, it was as though he could feel his heart beating extraordinarily fast and hard. Just the way he'd done that Christmas all those years ago. He wanted, no, ached, to believe what was happening to him, but he didn't dare to admit it was true.

He raised the hat closer to his face. That small, embroidered label. That was the real reason for the habitual, monotonous hat removal exercise. For over one hundred years, he must've been searching for that label. Subconsciously hoping it would be there. It never was. Of course, he'd never have found it; it was here. In his memory.

'It says, "Theodore Callington",' he said.

The name ricocheted around his repressed mind, releasing everything it touched. He didn't need to read it. He knew just what it said.

'Callington,' he mused, and the word etched itself lovingly onto his soul.

His own anxiety confused him then.

'This ain't my hat,' he said, 'Callington ain't my name. I jo-fired don't know my last name.'

Pa knew that. It was something that, until now, had dumbfounded him. Involuntarily the ligaments and tubes in the flesh below Teddy's ears hardened and clogged. In harrowing, rapid succession, his nose seemed to tweak in and out. His lips swelled, his eyes singed, and he strained to toughen up his trembling jaw.

'Well, now…' Old Man Callington said, 'Callington could be.'

'If you'd like it to be,' Ma said.

His background fuzzed into focus again. Ma was smiling tenderly, he could sense its kindness go to work, soothing out the spasms in his muscles.

'If I'd like it to be?'

Mattie and Ellen giggled at his all too apparent sappiness.

'But…' He tried hard to correctly process just what it was that he was hearing, not to mention orchestrating just what it was that he wanted to say. 'Callington is your name.'

He stared down at the Stetson in his hands and massaged the label. Darn it, it felt good. When he looked up again, he looked Old Man Callington straight in the face.

'Let me get this straight?' he said. 'This "Christmas present" that you're giving me, it ain't only a hat, a daisy fine hat, mind, it's also a name? Your name?'

He stopped short again, and again toyed with the tag inside the brim. His entire life, or rather his entire existence, everything that he'd seen, everything he knew – and he must've seen and known a whole heap of incredible things, was worth no more than a hill of beans, if he couldn't have this moment in his memory forever. Whatever fantastical, twistical things had happened to him since this time didn't matter a jot. Because this was real. Real in the mortal eyes of this world. And that was what mattered, wasn't it?

'Theodore?' Pa said, 'the fact remains that I have no son. The good Lord, not to mention the fabulous Mrs C here, graced me with two beautiful daughters. I love them more than life itself.'

Teddy knew that. Everybody knew that. Ellen jumped up and in the innocently demonstrative way of a child, ran to her father. She threw her arms around his waist and squeezed. Not content with just squeezing Old Man Callington such that he staggered backward, she shut her eyes tight, scrunching up her reddening face. He indulged in her show of affection, laughed and kissed the top of her head.

'This one…' he said.

He stopped again and held out his hand to Mattie. For a moment, it looked as though Mattie was content to disregard her unrelenting quest for rebelliousness; more than likely, though, she simply waylaid it in favour of inclusion in the wholesome family scene. She rocked back on her feet, pushed off the floor and, smiling ruefully, tiptoed over to her pa.

'These two rather need a brother to keep them in line.'

'Pa!' Mattie's squeal came at the same time as Old Man Callington hugged her to him, so it sort of popped out of her.

'We, that is Mrs C and I, would like to have a son. But, forgive me, Father, the good Lord doesn't seem to agree…'

'Clem, the Lord moves…' Father Egan started.

'I know, in mysterious ways. But, well, see, the thing is that, we're not getting any younger…'

Both girls squeaked this time. He held up a silencing hand.

'Be rational, girls. We've talked about it and well, Theodore, we'd like you to give it a try.'

Sakes alive! A family. The Callingtons were giving him a family. Their family. Somewhere to belong to. Someone to spend time with. Someone who'd remember his birthday, who'd think of him next Christmas. Someone who'd miss him when he was away on the range, hold him tight when he returned home. Someone who cared if he ate or didn't eat, was too cold or too hot, happy or sad. He was speechless. As speechless as he should've been back then. Back then, though, he'd have had a throat to clear, breath to sigh and a heart to swell.

He sensed that the air around him had changed. It hovered heavy, fetid and acrid as though he stood not in a tomb, but in the undead embers of a long-abandoned blacksmith's livery. He was hot; his clothes and hair were closer than a massive Midwestern storm. The sun no longer shone through the parlour windows. The memory had gone.

For a moment, his fingers felt strangely wet and, listening hard, he could hear a faint scratching of a quill pen on paper along with the clink of glasses. Only until, studying his fingers, rubbing them together, there was nothing. He raised his hands up in front of his face. They were clawed in shape, but they were empty. He stretched them out as wide and far as he could, waiting for his skin to strain. Then he wiped them down the root-clotted wall. He may as well have touched nothing. Nothing at all. He cursed and stamped and slapped himself hard in the face, thighs, stomach. Nothing. Inside, his stomach tremored and the base of his spine twitched, reminding him of exactly what he was. He pawed the wall again and ate the creatures he found there.

He shook his head. "According to Hoyle?" his ma's accented voice abstractedly echoed about. He closed his eyes and saw the hatbox in all its wrapping. They, his family, his horses and the Double C remained wispily in his memory, stored there like fine traps in an untidy ice house. There was something else, too. It was stronger, much, much stronger than the hate that, up until now, had simmered inside him. This was a pleasant glow and it shone brighter as he remembered his family. He hadn't murdered them — he'd loved them too much and he knew, he'd always known, that, in return, they treasured him.

'No one,' he said, wondering, half-hoping that the demon and perhaps László were listening, 'nothing, not even time itself, can put that love asunder.'

He must have Callington kinfolk, ancestors of his own. Most probably they'd be in Kansas. He could go looking for them. Except he had no real idea where Kansas was. Then as a spider dropped onto his arm, he recalled miserably just exactly what he was. Even if he could devise a way to get to Kansas, no one wants a psychopathic murderer with unsightly teeth turning up on their doorstep, do they? Especially not in the middle of the night claiming to be undead — and not only that, but a long-lost relative.

Chapter Nineteen

Teddy relived that memory over and over again. The demon's hunger and hazing were the only things that kept him from regressing completely into history. On each side of him, lay the more appropriate incumbents of the lair; two impoverished skeletons, with only one or two wisps of white hair between them. Suddenly suffering an acute attack of sentimentality, Teddy came over sympathetic, reckoning that they, or rather the persons that they had been, had probably worn hats, too.

Dismissing the truculence of the occasional root protruding from the tomb's end wall, Teddy scrunched down, awkwardly stretching out his long legs. With his toe, he shyly chipped away at one of the concrete beds. It crumbled a little too much. Dust dropped loudly onto the gore that dirtied his jeans, so he let the concrete alone. From the corner of his eye he spied the empty-headed skull grinning at him. He smiled back, knowing only too well that his outsized canines would win, hands down, over the skeleton's crooked teeth.

'Howdy,' he said.

Safe in the knowledge that any reprisals for his patheticness were so far out of earshot they were in another time, he laboured on in his Midwestern drawl.

'My name's Teddy.'

A thrill twitched at the corners of his mouth and, if truly possible, his smile widened. He had a full name. He sure-fired intended to use it.

'I'm sorry,' he said, sticking his thumbs upwards, and pointing a greeting at the skeleton. 'I reckon I mean, my name's Theodore Callington. And you can call me Theodore Callington.'

Dang! That sounded good.

'Theodore Callington. That's my name, a whole name. Not just Ted, oh no. Or even Teddy Nobody-Knows-Anything-About-You.'

The skeleton of course, didn't acknowledge him. Which was a blessing; because if it had, he would've hightailed it out of that pokerish place. It seemed to Teddy that there was dead; and then there was right-smart proper dead.

'Who are you?' Teddy said, his ruminating echoing in the dark, forgotten hole.

For the first time in his life, he was the one with the name when those around him had none. At long last, he had a uniqueness, an importance, an honour to be upheld. His fellow camp-man did not.

Sakes alive, saphead; this is your chance to be the big sugar, the bulldozer in the bunk house.

Darn demon, Teddy ignored it. Actually facing for the first time, a legitimate shot at wearing the shoes of the 'lord and master', he couldn't see where the pleasure was.

C'mon, Ted, wear it large.

The demon. He shouldn't listen to it. Its only want would be to rule over him, control him, just like it had done before. Definitely, he all-to-pieces shouldn't engage it.

'I ain't never gonna be no braggert,' he murmured.

Darn Dent's code, jest for one itty-bitty hooter, wouldn't it jest feel ding good?

'Nary, would it,' Teddy said. 'Why don't you jest amputate your timber?'

The demon had been fed. Teddy had no stomach cramps. He'd sensed no hunger. As soon as he'd woken up at sunset, he'd fed it, just like he always did. It was like feeding the tapeworm of the old days and he'd been snatching snacks ever since. The demon was ignoring him.

Go on, holler at him, cuss him out, he's just nurly old buzzard food. It ain't like he's gonna fight back now, is it?

'No how,' Teddy said. 'I ain't never gonna be no braggert.'

Just to be sure, he followed that up with all the words he could think of that meant "No". Out came Spanish, Gaelic, Dutch and German and some African tribal concoction. Who said he knew nothing? Inside him an insurgence began to uncoil itself. It writhed upwards around his spine.

'Oh no, you don't,' he said, but his frustration did little more than fuel the growing insubordination.

Outwardly he grimaced. Inwardly he was angry. Spontaneously he glowered at the ceiling, searching wildly for the broken square that let in the night-time light. It would let out the malevolent bloodsucker, too. Against his will, his ears listened out for voices, laughter, heartbeats; the telltale signs of human life for the taking.

He gripped the roots that protruded from the wall at his sides. The demon had been pacified. Or at least he thought it had.

'What in tarnation do you want?'

Stiffening his grip on the roots, he scraped his heels through the earth, setting his shape and bracing himself as firmly as he could. The demon pulled at his middle, it bit at his thighs and punched at his feet

Hog-killin'. You've hoosegowed me for too long.

'You mean you want out to murder.'

Once again, the demon ignored him.

Now, I know you, Teddy, I know you better than you know yourself: you jest

love to hunt.

The demon had a point. It'd spent more time inside his head than ever he had.

'Huntin' ain't fun,' Teddy moaned.

You'll come around. Bime-by, you'll come around.

Teddy wrenched his eyes away from the ceiling. The demon sought the outside again.

'You cain't come it over me like this. I hate hunting. I hate violence. I don't know quite why, but I do.'

You come from a violent time, violence is all you know.

'No, no it ain't.'

Closing his eyes and staring hard into the darkness, he pressed his back into the wall, squashing the roots until they yielded.

C'mon, Teddy...

'Theodore,' Teddy whined. 'My name's Theodore.'

Let's go outside. It must be candlelight out there, you haven't seen the stars for a long time, you love to watch the stars. Remember?

Darn it, he needed a distraction.

'Hey, girl,' he said, his voice shaking.

He conjured up a memory.

Don't you shin out on me, Sycher.

'What's going on with you today?'

Teddy's feet skidded out from under him.

Teddy, you yack, come back to me.

He saw a horse, right in front of him. It was a beautiful chestnut pinto. He brushed loose bracts of dirt from his sleeves and stood, yellowey dust fell from his body

'You're just playing with me, ain't ya?'

They were friends, he and the horse, although she trained one sceptical eye on him. She skittered about, whinnying all the while, but she didn't back away from him. Showing the horse that he hid no advantages, Teddy stretched out flat hands. They were empty: he could, and just might, be submissive.

'You sure those mecate-type reins are secure?' Old Man Callington called from his perch on the top rail of the corral.

The horse flicked her mane as though she and the Old Man had an invisible affiliation, and she sure-fired meant to illustrate the argument. The reins clicked on the ground, sending out whirling little wind devils and puffs of Kansas corrall.

'Yup!' Teddy called out, not looking at him. 'C'mon, girl, I know you wanna go for a ride.'

The horse whinnied again and tossed her head. The reins flicked straight out towards him and he caught them. The horse shifted, bouncing and kicking at the ground. Cautiously, Teddy approached her. He talked to her, cleaning up his cowpoke voice and softening his heavy accent as though he were addressing a lady.

'She sure does caper about,' Old Man Callington interjected from the corral. 'You could try the snubbing post for …'

'Sir,' Teddy interrupted him, a quiet yet knowledgeable "You're not helping" tone to his voice.

Once again, he held a hand out to the horse, keeping it steady just below her nose. She snorted and stared at him. Then she made a rueful sort of growling sound, snorted again and dropped her muzzle into his palm, blowing out hot air and nuzzling him. He smiled.

'I know you,' he said, 'c'mon, let's do this together. I all-to-pieces wanna get out on that prairie.'

In one movement, he flipped the reins over her head and leapt onto her back.

'Slick as a whistle.' Old Man Callington whistled and called, 'Beautiful.'

The horse skipped sideways, twisted a fandango, reared and pranced up on her toes like a kitten playing with a frog.

'You don't like being called beautiful?' Teddy panted, holding on. 'Well, don't get your dander up, I'm ding sure he meant me.'

He wasn't at all convinced the Old Man had, though. The horse wasn't buying it either. She kicked her feet out into the air behind her, immediately bringing them back in and sitting on them. Then she rose up high, folding and flailing her front legs. She whinnied as if to say, 'Get off me.' Teddy knew how that felt. The horse had had enough. He loosened his hold and when she landed, he slid off. Sitting dejectedly in the dust, he hung his head and sighed.

'Come on up to the house now,' Old Man Callington said. 'Mrs C's gonna wanna take a look at you.'

The scraping of his boots on the corral rails ended with his walking away.

'Darn it, Caper,' Teddy muttered, 'the last thing we need is for the Old Man to get into trouble with Mrs C now, isn't it? You may as well jest acknowledge the corn; you need this as much as I do.'

Hot, hard breaths dislodged his hat and dampened his ear. A velvety muzzle nuzzled into his hair. Strong, square teeth nabbed a few strands and gave it a tug.

'Quit it,' he said retrieving his hat and dusting it off, 'I got bruises on my Sunday face and Bible bumps on my muck forks from the number of times you've grassed me today.'

Caper nosed him again.

'You breakin' my heart, you know that. I cain't get up no more.'

Rubbery lips curled over and brushed the top of his ear. Teddy dismissed her. Replacing his hat, he told her, he didn't want to know her. They'd played that game for a while: she'd pushed at him and chewed on his hair for attention, and he'd shooed her away. The more she hazed him to get up, the more he laughed and refused.

With the sun on the wane, he'd yielded. Caper had conceded, she'd stood still and elegant while he'd climbed back on. They'd ridden the circumference of the corral a good few times. She'd skipped about a little – mostly when he'd stopped talking to her. So, he'd promised her all the green, grassy paradises of the prairie, the best places to let fly and the challenge of the unexpected canyons that jaggedly spliced up the landscape like they'd been made with a badly blunted Bowie.

Footfall. Scurrying, compact and confident footsteps courted the fringes of Teddy's imagination. He stared about. The footsteps weren't in the corral, they were in the tomb. Someone else was in here.

Teddy squinted and then opened his eyes wider and looked again. Darn, he wouldn't have noticed anyone enter his corpse-encrusted lair until it was too late, he'd so absorbed himself in the playing with and "breaking" of Caper. Perhaps the tomb had another entrance. Somewhere over there in the dark earth, although the place was so small there wasn't much of an "over there".

The empty stalls resonated with tiny treads. Teddy tensed. The feet, seemingly sensing his presence, stopped moving. Teddy detected a heartbeat. It wasn't very big, but it was strong and whatever the critter was, it pumped its own blood.

An ominous, annoying grumble coiled about Teddy's spine. The demon was still there. It might be keeping quiet, but Teddy could sense it.

'Go away,' Teddy growled.

The scampering feet were joined by another set. Then another. They made little snorts and twitches and there was the dragging of a fat, fleshy tail. Teddy pictured all manner of small, hovel-dwelling critters. It wasn't hard to do; the bunk house had been infested with them. He grinned. Much to the amusement of the cowpokes late one night, Cleve had let them rile him so much he'd set about mousing in the cluttered space. The tomb critters continued their stop-start progression.

'Leave me alone,' Teddy thought.

Telepathy and how to use it may well be in his head somewhere. To get it out, he just had to remember his time with László. He sagged. That was something he had no intention of doing. Even if he did, the art of telepathy was most probably another one of those things that László had simply neglected to tell him.

Melodic clinking just like those of Comanche wind chimes, remenicent of some he'd heard on the clean, clear night air of the range, warned him of the critters' intention to desecrate the order of the skeletons' bones. Something tousled his hair. Sakes alive! The darn things climb?

'Varmint!' he hollered, slapping his hand to the top of his head, flinching at the spiteful reminder that he wasn't wearing his hat.

There was a sharp pain on the upper shell of his ear. Caper? Caper's teeth had never hurt him. Come to think of it, Caper would never, ever harm him. They were buddies, weren't they?

Spinning with the acute response of the reflexes that he reckoned he'd always had and, coupled with the bizarre night vision that he had now, he caught the critter first jab. Snatching it away from its perch, he swivelled it so that he could look into its face. It was indeed a rat. This long forgotten tomb was obviously its stomping ground. Teddy curled one lip and beared one fang. The rat stared back at him, rudeness and defiance burning in the beadiness of its eyes.

'Did you just bite me?' he said.

The rat didn't disagree. It didn't even blink. It seemed to be sneering at him, smirking at him for stating the obvious. It whipped its long and worm-like tail around in arcs, that once or twice licked Teddy's wrist.

'Am I not skeersome to you?'

Again the rat didn't disagree. It was big and black and pliable like a newly filled old leather canteen. It squeaked and stared and ran in mid-air.

'See demon?' Teddy said, 'Even the resident varmints ain't afeared of you.'

Reaching up, he stroked the rat's short hair the wrong way, disturbing its natural, shiny nap with a stripe of matt. He turned it in his gaze and stroked it right again.

'Nutria,' he said, 'varmint pardner, you're made of nutria. Ain't ya?'

He held the rat to his cheek and snuggled into it.

'You and me, bub, we gotta live together, we gotta...'

The animal's eyes glimmered. It took advantage of Teddy's lack of concentration, buckled up its middle, and sank its sabre-like teeth into his hand.

Teddy didn't even waste time on a cuss - it wasn't only his inner varmint that took an unbridled offence to the bite. He sank his own sharp canines into the rat's meaty plumpness and drained it.

'Darn it,' he said, with another ironic guffaw, skimming his fingertips across the dead rat's back, 'I just ate my hat.'

The rat was bigger and much less fuss than balloon-backed spider or glutinous grub. Other than that, it was sort of like comparing Coosie's chewsies with Ma's cooking or the meatballs and spaghetti served up in the Wichita restaurants.

'Darn it.' he muttered again.

Never, ever would he ever again murder another human being, and he'd forever stand by that — he'd just have to "cowboy up". He hurled the limp body away, lamented the missing of ice cream and soda and dismally added Underground Tomb Rat to his A La Muerto menu. Fur, however napped, was not a nice feeling on your tongue.

A bent for menace, very little to do with folklore, seemed to have surfaced in him. But the demon had finally been bested. Now Teddy had full control over his own utilities, it was he that had a hankering to do some hazing. The demon hazed him enough, he reckoned. Daringly, rebelliously, Teddy moved his eyes to study the nearest, could be the oldest, skeleton and grinned.

'You gotta have a name, too,' he told the skeleton.

The demon remained quiet.

'Then I won't be so alone.'

Ichabod. The word thudded through Teddy's ears, making him think of ghost stories and dead people.

'You can be Ichabod,' he said.

It suited the skeleton. Teddy tripped around to face the other corpse. Almost identical to Ichabod, its splintering yellow bones were covered by opaque cobwebs and swatches of threads. Its nose appeared to have gone to Texas long ago and the crown of its head resembled an old missionary cross-stitch cap.

The skeleton had no lips, no cheeks, and even less hair than Ichabod. Closer inspection was not needed to know that it didn't have a heart. But its smile was just as big — and as eerily infectious. Teddy grinned back.

'I reckon that we must be legends together, you and me,' he told it. 'Pardner, you can be Duncan. Or Dunc.'

For some sentimental reason he wondered what Dunc had looked like when he was alive. He shook the thought away. Now the only one without a name was the demon; and it sure-fired wasn't having his.

'I am Theodore Callington,' he said. 'I have a family. And a home. I belong somewhere.'

He sat down again, his back resting on Ichabod's stall. Shifting and fidgeting, trying to get comfortable was not easy with numbing limbs. Hang fire, there was an empty bunk, wasn't there? Badly manhandling his own body, he struggled up into it and lay back.

Closing his eyes, he smiled. Theodore Callington, ready to die. Again. At least today, he'd be a dead boy who wasn't staring. Sakes alive, he wished he had a hat to cover his face with.

CHAPTER TWENTY

It was pre-dawntime and already, the summer Kansan wind gambolled about, cheerfully balmy in the golden hairs of Teddy's fore-arms.

'Cape?' he stretched and drawled, 'This ain't such a good idea, riding in my unmentionables.'

Damp, fetid air like that of an overcast, late autum night in the woods settled across the dry skin of his shoulders. It irritated the lines over his back. He wasn't wearing unmentionables.

'Cape?' he said.

Caper was no longer bothering him. The grey shadowy streaks of the Double C corral posts and the unblemished Union blue sky vanished. All around was darkness. Teddy was lying, half-naked on his scratchingly rough concrete tomb stall. For some reason his enlivened sensors had reacted to the tomb's musty air on his skin. Perhaps he'd used this memory one too many times. The memory was one of his favourites and whether he'd needed it or not, its uplifting emotions were just darn irresistible.

Teddy turned over on his stall; he hung over the edge and scanned the floor for red smudges of tuck. He was halted by a stench. Hadn't the memory of Caper had ended, however abruptly, a good few minutes ago? Stubbornly he'd continued to lie there for a while, a habit he'd got into trouble for on more than one occasion. Any leftover senses from the memory should have fizzled out by now. The stench was a rancid, old smell that festered and swirled about him. There was no getting away from it. A tomb, any tomb sure should reek, although he reckoned, all the decaying that was to be done here had happened so long ago, the evidence was now more of a ghoulish sight than a gross smell.

Silkily, Teddy slipped out of his stall. Spying a rat, red against the blue of the ground and tracking its scratchings as they got closer, he stooped silently. The stench hit him in the nose. His snack escaped. Surprise thwarted all attempts of trapping it and he stumbled backwards ending up sitting between Ichabod and Dunc. They grinned at him.

'Y'all cain't smell that?' he said. 'Nary one should I be smelling it, mind.'

It must be strong. He stood and was rocked by it again. Every time he moved he was ambushed by the smell. Teddy pulled a couple of cave drawing-type shapes to test out the theory. His own poses reminded him a little too much of the Ozarks, somewhere he didn't want to go, so he stopped, stood straight and tried to think of something else. The stench ranked high amongst the most pungent smells of the bunk house on hot chilli night, but it brought a bitter, sour note that retched at the back of his nose. Worse than that, the stench seemed to be radiating from his own person.

'My sincere apologies,' he said, following that up with a mumbled, 'I wish I had a hat to tip at y'all.'

Something akin to a rustic, unravelling rope coiled inside him. He needed to feed. The trouble was that from what he now knew of survival instincts in the wild, in general, a sense of smell was vital in detecting the threat of becoming someone else's dinner. Perhaps a while ago he could've sat so still that the ignorance of the rats would have brought them to him. But not now. Not with this odour hanging on him. If he wanted to feed, then he needed something either too slow or stupid to move away from him. Underground tomb rat was off the menu.

'I ain't gonna catch me any chow in here,' he admitted aloud to himself. 'Hasta muerte.'

Armed with his memories of home, he reached above his head and hopped, anchoring his hands on the edges of the hole in the roof. Pulling himself up, he crawled through to the mausoleum floor.

The vines and brambles that wound and tumbled over the hexagonal floor were extra-vibrant. With a stab of loneliness, Teddy realised it'd been a long time since he'd been up here. He jiggled the sadness away. The spindly tree in the corner was still there, its limbs mottled luminously with lichen as its leaves glistened. They looked wet. There must've been rain during the day. Rain meant an infestation of bugs in anything dead or dying. Teddy shuddered. Thus far, such a plague hadn't been something he'd suffered with. It would be rife here, though; best not to stand still for too long. He clambered across the undergrowth and, once under the woodland canopy, found a suitably rotting, fallen tree. He sat by it and picked a hole in it. Inside was a cornucopia of insects to chow down on.

Outside in the open air, his horrific whiff should, to some extent, disburse. He grimaced at the mirage of cutting-out one of the herd at round-up. Nope. When a smell turned to a reek it lingered. The stench might disappear from his nose, but it wouldn't from his prey's.

A change of threads was needed, wasn't it? New or fresh threads weren't something he'd ever wanted for before. Up until now, such a thing must've been dealt with by László. László had had a sense of smell, hadn't he? László, the dandified, would-be prince, given to posing like the subject of a painting, much tossing of his hair and complaining if the outside should do so much as dare infringe upon his precious, polished boots. A molly like that wasn't likely to go gadding about with a tattered, foul-smelling bum. The only problem was: where had the clothes come from? Teddy had a pretty decent idea. There was no way, no way in tarnation, that he was going to repeat it.

Laying his hand inside the damp log, he watched the interrupted lines of ants and busying grey-backs climb subliminally on. They scurried and stopped and scurried again, apparently trying to make something out of this new, dry landscape. He shook them off. He wasn't in the mood for them. Something about the coming night was making him miserable. He was going to have to steal some clothes; pinch perhaps was more like it — pinching didn't sound quite as bad. "nibbling" sounded even better. But nary one did that really help.

As a cowpoke, he'd set himself high standards, they all had; stealing, pinching even taking was a formidable offence. Then László had happened and those standards had evaporated. He slumped like a sullen teenager on the soggy woodland floor. Leaves, up-ended little lime water towers, tipped their contents onto him; it ran over his exposed skin in fine, clear rills. He watched it and was depressed even worse. Sakes alive, he needed new threads.

Get up. Feed. You need blood, human blood.

The demon wanted feeding.

'No, I don't,' Teddy argued. 'It don't matter what blood I drink now, does it?'

The base of his spine cricked and his chest gagged.

'As long as it's blood, who cares? It's you who's hankering after human blood.'

He reached into the log for handfuls of bugs. Woefully, he raised his hands to his mouth. The woodland critters, unable to resist a dark place, jostled inside. Teddy bit down. Exoskeletons and antennae stuck in his teeth and cold, forest floor-encrusted, jellified bodies plagued the sides of his tongue.

'What I would like,' he mused, 'is meatballs and spaghetti, just like they get in town.'

Wichita is dead.

'Then we make a purely purdy pair, don't we?'

His home town would never be dead. The demon was lying.

'Shut your cock-holster, demon.'

Hands devoid of bugs, he needed another helping so he stood and rummaged deeper in the tree trunk. What he needed was family and home. The leaves around him were empty now and softly swaythed against skin. The rills of water had run dry. Teddy dug and picked at the log's inhabitants until he was satisfied the demon was fed. Then he stared about himself, seeking and finding his bearings.

Just as before, he used the noises of the town to direct himself. Having followed them through the woods, he shot across the driveway of the large house. The hedgerow was a little higher, but no problem; Teddy leapt over it. He ran the circumference of the field of aggregate.

The town was a miasma of sounds assaulting his tender ears. Mostly, they were strange and unrecognisable. He reckoned that the time before, being governed by the demon, he can't have been paying a whole heap of attention; the demon had a one-track mind. Tonight, he had more time and he sensed the inclination to do some sightseeing.

The first thing to hit him, almost literally, was the whirring and thudding; just like Kiowa drums, it was constantly beating. Then there was a sloshing of thick liquid in a tank. That was intercut with a soft, almost tantalising hissing and sucking. Once or twice he heard a muffled juddering sort of buzz and a screeching accompanied by a horn and hollered profanities that made him jump. It all went dull, though, and returned to the drums. Motor cars? Their sleek, glossy lines all the shinier for the illumination of the street lamps.

Close to him, a young woman started up a yowling, repeating it with inhuman rapidity. Sakes alive, was she in pain? She sure-fired sounded like she was in pain — loud, unabashed, screaming pain. Her artificial pitch was joined by a whooshing and pulsating of violins played like he'd never heard. Dang! He realised his mistake. The young woman was singing. Nope, he sure-fired did not want to sing along, but he knew he'd never get the sound off his mind. He gazed towards it. He could see its waves loud and clear. He couldn't see the singer, though.

The town, it seemed, or at least this area, consisted of incredibly poky, corralled lots of land. No vehicles were allowed, but the lots were by no means vacant. Men and women gathered there in equal numbers and many of them smoking. Teddy hung in the shadows watching them. Darn it, he hadn't smoked a quirley in years.

Bars opened their entire frontage, like their wall just folded away. Squat tables and chairs, light and metallic in appearance, spilled out onto each portioned-off plot. People squawked and jeered, lungs tightened and slackened, and blood pumped fast. No one else was walking around shirtless though. Nary one had it been the thing to do back in Kansas or even in No Man's Land, where in summer the Indians did it all the time.

A very familiar yet kind of dislocated foreboding dogged him, nothing that he saw tonight should be new to him. It may not have been this town that he and László had frequented, not that he could rightly say, but they definitely would've enjoyed the pleasures of one very much like it. Certainly, he had seen all these newfangled things before. They resided in those memories which were a part of his life that he did not want to admit association with; a part that he had yet to venture into.

There were new and glorious colours, too, waves of sound and heat flashing and gyrating around each other so fast that he had to look away. Scrunching up his eyes, looking only through orangey, spidery lashes, he headed for a quieter place.

A lowing, like a weary Longhorn, boomed loud and eerie. None of the townsfolk seemed bothered. The lowing was answered by what could be its calf and Teddy wondered where these two animals were. Their calling was so vast and yet nobody cared. The first came again. And then the answer. Teddy looked to the stars; the hour was growing late, all but a few of the buildings were deserted. Following the massive cattle drones, he climbed up to the roof of the nearest building, peered over the parapet and backed up. Then he sprinted towards the edge. He launched himself into the air, stretching his body into a dive to reach the rooftop opposite.

'Thunderation!' he exclaimed when he descended the other side.

Main street design, it seemed, had not progressed much in the last one hundred or so years. From his elevated, although rapidly decreasing position, it was glaringly obvious that the targeted landing site did not exist. The roof opposite was no more than one of those slumguzzling frontages, like the ones that lined Main and Market back in Wichita. The actual building began much lower down and was somewhat narrower than the one he'd just left.

Whatever kind of being he was, Teddy could not fly; he was falling. He was falling fast. Darn it, he needed to work on his landing. He reached out prostrate fashion, and took a punt on the air, aiming for a leaf on the breeze-type tumble. No pretty autumnal leaf, he was an angular cowpoke with Cuban-heeled boots. Velocity toppled him over and the wind knocked him sideways. He tried to save himself, but for all his fluidity, he was wrapped around a removeable bollard. He looked just like a groom the night before his wedding: half-naked, hugging a bollard and more than likely in a whole heap of trouble.

Pigeons, startled by this thing larger than a leaf on the breeze that had fallen out of the sky, burbled and flapped angrily away. Pigeons! He didn't get those in the woods. Flipping himself over faster than the bumptious birds could escape, he caught one by the tail and sank his fangs into its feathery chest. Staring dumbly at the clock tower across from where he stood, he downed the bird's blood. Ellen had been teaching him to tell the time using a clock face. Then he'd been murdered.

Murder! He recognised the place. It was here that on his first night away from László, and in sure-fired submission to the demon, he'd ambushed and drunk from a human boy. Repulsed by himself, he flinched. He'd have killed that boy. Then he'd have raced back to László. László would have killed him. Not just that, though; somehow he'd have made darn sure it'd hurt.

He lopped along the road, keeping to the shadows. This way, he was his own person; sort of. He dumped the dead bird. He was no longer a murderer of people. He lived in a tomb, on a diet of vermin and insects, accompanied almost unwaveringly by a bloodthirsty demon that would never forgive him for forcing it to live this life. Never, into eternity, ever.

He needed desperately to change the subject. Lucky for him; the giant mooing sounded again. The road that Teddy was on widened out, incorporating others, towers of coloured lights and people.

Teddy veered off into an alley. Tall brick buildings, bins and boxes lined the sides. He skirted large, round iron circles set into the ground. An old wall with an even older door in it closed off the alley's end. Teddy sprang to the top.

The wall formed part of a courtyard perimeter. The courtyard itself was tiny with a tall, cupboard-shaped structure in one corner. Using it as a stepping stone, Teddy leapt to the other side and ran the length of the back wall; the seam between a long row of similar courtyards and a narrow road that led the same way he'd been going a moment or two earlier. The yards were quiet, people were absent here, some of the houses were in darkness and in some, bluey-yellow lights flashed through the windows. In one of the yards, the owner had been remiss enough to leave the washing strung between the courtyard walls. The washing reminded Teddy of his reason for being here. There were only sheets, patterned and faded. Teddy drew the line at wearing a makeshift dress and continued along the wall.

At intervals, the wall stepped lower which added to the fun of his run. The houses, though, did not look at all happy. The further down the hill he travelled, the dirtier they became.

The terrace ended at a darkened service road. The other side of this road was lined with buildings that looked to be much older. They were stained the colour of soot and formed part of what appeared to be stone fortress walls. The town had seemed large and nowhere else had he come across such walls, although this was his first proper visit. It seemed odd that the entire town should be enclosed within these walls. Merry chatter, some singing, and the timekeeping of drums echoed with a deep, twanging baseline. Every now and then the accompaniment of a less than rhythmical, elongated strum of a guitar was amplified by the wind. Moon would not have been pleased. But, thank the land, the perpetrators of the noise were nowhere seeable.

The road was by no means wide and the wind was stronger than the breeze earlier. Teddy dropped down from the wall and lopped along the road to where a bastion with an archway underneath marked a bend in the perimeter. A weather-worn plaque set into the wall named the bastion after some or other saint that he'd never heard of. Next to that on the path stood a rustic-style signpost and just atop of it was the crumbling and cordoned-off walkway of the wall. Teddy jumped, used the post to swing his body to the walkway, and climbed the short way to the bastion's flat roof.

Now, he could see what the wall was defending the town from. The sea. He'd never seen the sea. Not sentiently, anyway. This town, near where he now lived, was a bustling port. The quayside was lit almost as bright as day with strings of stark, glaring white bulbs and huge, bucket-type lights of the same white, topping tall poles. Death-defyingly high, formal piles of rusty green or red steel boxes, freight big enough to pack-in the Wichita Stage and Team four or five times over, stretched either way as far as the human eye could see. Obviously, there were boats or what he assumed to be boats; they were most un-boatlike. Rather they were oceanic liners the size of at least twelve adobe white Double Cs heaped on top of one another. Teddy made a semi-involuntary whimpering noise; he couldn't imagine the sea to be deep enough to hold such ships.

The mooing sounds erupted again. They were infinitely more phenomenal than the first time he'd heard them. At the same time, black smoke billowed from the foremost boat's funnel. Overcome with a weighty sense of his own unimportance, Teddy stared at the departing freighter. At any minute his legs might give way, so he sat on the ample parapet. He looked to the stars; it was late, but dawn was still a while away. Of all the things in his life, the people who'd passed through it, the towns he must have been in, the stars were constant. Lying on bedrolls after the rodeo, he and his pa used to watch the stars. They'd look out for fireballs, meteors and planets. He missed his pa. Despondent and blue, he lay on his back and stared at the stars.

The sound of footsteps slapping on the road below reverberated off the roof tiles that he lay on. They echoed annoyingly around the peripherals of his melancholy. Someone was running up the road. Teddy tried to ignore them.

The closer they got, the more frantic the runner's pulse grew. The shoes squeaked, and their owner panted, the heart pumping faster than an overbaked hoss. Mildly intrigued, Teddy listened with one ear. The runner skittered and stumbled about, missed the archway and kept going. Probably not thinking straight, Teddy mused and went back to his hopelessness.

Six more footsteps, self-assured and burly, bounded after the first. When they'd rounded the bend at the bottom of Teddy's bastion, they shouted out.

'You know what happens to disgusting little pricks like you.'

Teddy twitched; blowhards, bullies. They had the running kid outnumbered three to one. Teddy was willing to gamble that the kid was smaller, probably a little on the passive side.

The wind ruffled his hair. On a normal day-to-day or rather, night-to-night basis, it wasn't something that he noticed. But then there wasn't any wind in his tomb. Those blowhards and the doomed kid must've roused something inside him. Something stronger than the depression that had engulfed him when he'd seen the colossal liners at the quayside gripped him. He swivelled onto his belly, the parapet's unyielding and unforgiving stone blocks were angled most rigidly, they were dully painful. He pushed himself up.

'Guys, it really isn't worth all this,' the kid wheezed.

The blowhards must've cornered him. Goose bumps rose over Teddy's chest. A shudder scuttled along his shoulders, stiffening his neck.

'You want me to tell that to my sister,' a bigger voice said.

A little further up, the road branched off into a small, semi-vacant lot. The hellraisers must be in there. Teddy craned his neck to see what was going on. Nope, still couldn't see through walls. He listened out for them again. There was nowhere else that they could be.

'You're dead meat,' a gruff voice said.

'You're so gonna be one fucked-up son of a bitch when we're done with you, you'll be licking your own sore arse.' A psychotic one made up the three.

Cowards, yeller sapheads who lacked the sand to pick a scrap with anyone who had a chance of fighting back. Teddy stared; he focussed on the road ahead towards the voices. Swirling waves of sound mingled with sparkling tones of atmosphere. These twirled and whirled like ribbons in the wind around the stone walls and the road. At the entrance to the lot, they turned fractious, serrated and lurid. The bullies were there alright. There was another aura, fear, and it clashed, sparking off the others. The kid was there, too. His heart was pounding so loud, Teddy suspected that he himself would be able to hear it.

Teddy sauntered to the corner and dropped lightly to the off-limits walkway. Alighting on his toes, he teetered dangerously but made no sound. So he ran along the top until he could see inside the lot.

'Come on, guys,' the kid tried again, 'it was her idea.'

The kid had flattened himself onto the far wall; his eyes were screwed shut and his chest rose high and fell low fast. Teddy had been right, he was the smallest out of them all. His exact age was difficult to tell, his blood was clean, bright and it flowed freely through taut veins: Teddy reckoned he and the kid were about the same age, give or take one hundred years. The kid's jeans, though, were stunning. They were skintight and they left very little to the imagination. It pained Teddy to even look at them. In fact, had the kid's shirt not been so modestly curved at the bottom, Teddy would have been able to age him by his virility.

'Bullshit,' one of the blowhards said.

'On your knees,' another said.

The kid's fear turned to outright horror. It clogged up the course of his blood flow, and his nerve ends began suffocating like the weeds of a dying ravine. He whimpered, keeping his eyes tightly closed. Teddy cocked his head: perhaps shutting eyes helped, although he couldn't think how.

'No. Turn around. Against the wall,' the sadistic one ordered.

The kid didn't move. Probably couldn't. Teddy sensed a run of sweat on the kid's spine. He flinched as though he knew that feeling. The three bullies stood in a crescent, facing the kid. Their bodies were defined by a manual labour that sculpted dusty, twistical shapes into their hair and illustrated their clothes with daubes of dull, dirty paint. Their hands were fisted, their muscles flexed and their eyes glinted with a lust for gratuitous violence. Dreadful pokerish to a kid in the dark. Teddy sensed an unbecoming bravado bellerin' through him.

'Wait,' the one whose sister should, perhaps, be defending the kid said. 'You two pin him down, it's only fair that I should get first go.'

Quietly laying one hand flat on the surface of the walkway, Teddy crouched, intrigued. Back in No Man's Land, at chuck time, the cowpokes had told stories of frontier justice fatalities and the evidence of vigilante lynchings. He got the notion he'd very nearly been the subject of one. But, as far as he cared to remember, he'd never actually witnessed a lynching.

Watch! It looks like they really are going to beef the kid?

Darn it, the demon. He should've known that something like this would attract the demon. He shook his head as though to dislodge it, make it disappear.

You need new threads. Let the b'hoys do the beefing. Then while the dead kid's waiting for the cold meats wagon, you'll steal his clothes.

Those jeans? Teddy looked down at his legs and tried to weigh up the difference between the current stiff-as-a-corral-post jeans and the kid's painfully tight ones. There wasn't much in it. He did desperately need a shirt, though.

Or you could feed.

The bully in the middle of the crescent started forward. Immediately he stopped. It'd been a con, but it had done the trick and given the other two a heads-up. The kid had darted sideways. Straight into the arms of the most unhinged of his assailants. The blowhard grinned, grappled him into a chokehold in one arm and a distorted sort of joint lock with the other. The kid clawed his abductor's arm as he was shunted back to the others.

'You should have seen your face.' The main one laughed.

Effortlessly, Teddy jumped down to the road.

What are you doing?

To acknowledge the corn, Teddy truly didn't know what he was doing. He couldn't watch these three thugs beef this kid to buzzard bait, even if the kid was guilty of whatever trumped-up charge they were accusing him of. The problem wasn't just the kid's being hurt, it was the vigilante, anarchic way the whole thing was being done.

Dismissing the demon with a crisp hand signal, Teddy walked to stand between two of the bullies. Their attention fully on their prize, they didn't appear to notice him. The kid did, though. He redoubled his efforts to free himself, he gurgled and glared, the whites of his eyes clear and clean. The kid's captor brutally shoved him towards his accomplice standing next to Teddy. Swerving to escape, the kid stumbled and fell to the floor, right at Teddy's feet.

Now the others had to notice him.

'Who the fuck are you?' the bully to Teddy's left exclaimed.

'Defence,' Teddy said.

'Stay out of this, Foreigner,' the crazy one threatened.

'This kid needs some representation,' Teddy said.

'This your boyfriend?' The one to Teddy's right laughed. 'Nice lisp, Cowboy.'

He moved nonchalantly and kicked the kid. The kid yelped. The blowhard glared at Teddy.

'You like that?' he spat. 'Stay and I'll do it again.'

Teddy didn't answer. It wasn't that he didn't have the energy, he didn't have the time. As the bully bounced back to kick out again, Teddy stooped and seized his rear ankle. Swiftly standing straight, he brought the leg up high. The bully was tripped upside down. He swore. Teddy grasped his flailing wrist and flung him sideways. The bully spiralled and collided with his accomplice on Teddy's other side. Both were winded as they toppled to the floor.

'I ain't nobody's friend,' Teddy said.

It was true. He had no friends. Something that hadn't bothered him, until now. Still, this was not the time to dwell on it, let alone get lonely. A frenzied profanity-roaring maniac launched itself, arms outstretched at him now. Teddy let him come. He clasped one of the wrists and twisted. Anchoring his other hand on the maniac's collarbone, he pushed. Tendons strained, one or two even snapped: it was music to Teddy's ears. The maniac hammered Teddy's arm, making him hiss. So he tugged briskly on the wrist again. The arm clicked out of its socket. The maniac roared, in pain this time. Teddy closed his hand around the collarbone, pulled the lunkhead towards him, and treated him to a flash of his teeth.

Give us a bite, the demon said.

Teddy opened his jaws wide; his fangs were long and luminous. He brought the boy close to his lips.

'Run,' he murmured into the boy's ear, almost losing himself in the feel of the lobe's velvet delicacy, 'Hightail it out of here. I only have to give in to this demon and we're all dead.'

The boy sobbed and nodded feverishly. Teddy threw him away. He flew backwards, crashing into one of the closed garage doors. Leaving a long, trough-like dent, he slid to the floor, sat dazed for a moment and then tried to crawl away. Collapsing on his dislocated arm, he swore again and, dragging it behind him, vanished into the shadows.

'Chris, you bastard,' the first boy cried.

He and his pal were back on their feet. Teddy stared at them as though he only just remembered them. They glared back. Seconds later they ran towards him. Their intentions were obvious – take an arm each. Teddy turned to them, steadied himself on sturdy feet and, allowing them their arm each, caught them. He swung his arms together, taking the two off their feet and slamming them spine first into each other. They were winded once more. Teddy grinned as he felt their ribs fracturing. It was so delicious, he didn't bother to differentiate which one it was.

Their heads whiplashed together. Skull walloping skull cracked and ricocheted around the road. Instantaneously, they both released Teddy's arms. He hauled the two bodies to the ground like he was slopping manure from his hands. He toed them and booted them, rolling them further away until they untangled themselves. Their apologies and excuses tumbled embarrassingly from their mouths. This irked Teddy and so he bared his fangs and tensed his muscles, taking on what he reckoned to be a menacing, vampire pose. For effect he added a snarl. The two took to blaspheming; pitifully they raised crossed fingers in front of him.

'I live in a tomb, under a mausoleum,' he said. 'do you truly believe your crosses will stop me?'

'Please,' one of them whimpered, 'don't kill me.'

Teddy didn't want to kill them. But they wouldn't know that, would they?

'Every man for himself; blowhards never change,' Teddy muttered. 'Sling your hook, varmints.'

The whimpering boy scrambled away. The other just gaped at Teddy.

What are you doing? Feed!

'Go!' Teddy hollered.

To the demon, human blood would be like caffeine to a cowpoke and Teddy really didn't want to kill anyone. The boy just stared, though. 'Mush-head,' Teddy thought. He howled and began writhing. He clasped his head as though to harness the depravity of his thoughts and glared at nothing.

What are you doing now?

Sakes alive, his hair felt amazing. It was silky and thick and luxurious. It would forever be stuck in Stetson-wearing shape. He tousled it and threaded his fingers further into it. The blowhard boy's heartbeat slowed. His blood pumped slower, too, so much so that Teddy got the acute impression that he was suddenly pacified.

Perhaps his act of a blood-sick demon was lost on the boy. To acknowledge the corn, he was behaving more like a half-naked, loco tenderfoot, sparking off on the feel of his own hair.

'I cain't hold it for much longer,' he cried, letting go of his hair, bending and wrapping his arms around his belly.

Dang, he felt good; his skin was still so supple, his muscles still so hard. The boy seemed more curious than scared.

'I gotta feed,' Teddy said.

Then he whined and clasped his knees. Finally, the boy upped and ran after the first. The demon said nothing, but Teddy could sense its anger.

'Better get used to it,' he said.

Still smiling, he turned to the kid lying, scared witless on the floor. The flicker of his fear-filled eyes as they disappeared into the crook of his elbow brought a damning reminder to Teddy. The kid had seen it all.

CHAPTER TWENTY-ONE

'I ain't gonna touch yer.'

Teddy said hoping he sounded truthful and considerate of the kid's situation.

The kid hid deeper in his arm, shaking his head, the rest of his body uncontrollably trembling.

'You can get up,' Teddy said. 'Like I said, I ain't gonna touch yer.'

Apparently strongly averse to taking his face from his arms or his arms from the ground, the kid curled his knees beneath him.

'Darn it, kid,' Teddy said, 'get up quicker than that. And don't be afeared of me. I never wanted anyone to be afeared of me.'

'I saw your fangs,' the kid said, his voice shaky. 'I saw what you did to the guys. You're a vampire. I mean, really?'

'Wasn't my idea.'

'I don't want to die.' The kid raised one eye. 'Not like you've got in mind anyway.'

'I don't got anything in mind. Like I said, I never wanted any of this. And I ain't gonna touch yer.'

Now that he'd said it, voiced his own recognition of his condition, his body reacted; returning to the desensitised, undead creature that he was. He shuddered, not so much because of the wind chill, but more in sorrow of losing all sensation.

'You feel the cold, too?' the kid said.

'I need new threads is all,' Teddy said. 'An' I'm all-fired sure, I jest skeered them off.'

'Have mine. If that's all you want. Have these.'

Teddy hesitated. Those jeans really weren't what he wanted to wear.

'It's the least I can do,' the kid said.

'I cain't jest take your threads,' Teddy said. 'What will you wear?

Sitting up the kid frowned with his whole face. He looked offended, somehow Teddy had hurt his feelings. It was as though he'd seen right inside Teddy's mind and, reading his thoughts, had been snubbed by what he found. Teddy was dumbfounded; he frowned, too. Wasn't he supposed to be the supernatural one? The kid scrambled to his feet.

'Well, thanks anyway,' he said.

Alarming snips of remorse began to tweak inside Teddy. It'd never occurred to him that when not pretending to be something that he wasn't, he might be wearing his sentiments blatantly in the expressions on his face.

'Tell you what,' he said, shifting awkwardly, 'We'll trade.'

Having emotions, it seemed, was one thing; having them and being around people was something else entirely. '

Now the kid looked doubtful, but he complied, removing his shirt and handing it over. On Teddy the fit was tight, but it was better than the nothing that Teddy was presently wearing. Appreciation now emanated from the kid. On his mental yardstick, Teddy notched up one success.

Without his shirt on, it was plain to see that the kid's jeans hung dangerously low. In fact, a whole heap more than the strangely non-existent drawstring of his unmentionables was on display. Teddy's innards, or what was left of them, froze in a new kind of terror: his own dire lack of underwear. He couldn't, of course, be sure exactly when it had happened, but it was split-fair to say that his flannel Union suit had long since perished. Must've been roughly around the time that his sense of touch had gone, too. From then on, he reckoned, he hadn't needed undergarments. Or, for that matter, layers of any sort. Clothes had plumb been for the benefit of others. Until now.

The kid was peeling away his jeans. Teddy feigned interest in the fastening of the shirt until the kid was done. He offered up the jeans. Snatching them, Teddy darted into the shadows.

'Are you shy?' the kid said. 'I mean, vampires aren't supposed to be shy.'

'No, I ain't shy,' Teddy replied, stepping out of his own jeans which didn't even crumple. 'I jest cain't be cuttin' a swell with my Sunday-face for strangers on the street.'

'It's cool,' the kid called back. 'I mean, you don't know me…'

His voice went strangely quiet.

'…I might be deranged or something…'

And detached.

'…it's cool to be afraid.'

'Cool,' Teddy said.

Too busy lamenting the loss of the feel of the night air on his naked thighs, Teddy lost track of just what the kid had said.

'Hang fire, I ain't yeller.'

Sakes alive, the differences in the way that they used the same language were worse than a mantrap in the tall grass. The kid spoke today's language. Most probably just like all the folks in this town. Teddy was stagnating in the 1800s.

'I mean, I ain't yeller, like, my skin ain't yeller. You sabby?'

He unthreaded his belt and tossed the jeans to where he thought that the semi-naked kid stood.

'P'shaw, what I'm tryin' to say is that to acknowledge the corn, I reckon,

I need to apologise for clippin' like that.'

The kid didn't answer.

'Darn it, you'll only get sweet on my ass.'

Squeezing into the kid's jeans, which were not only skintight, but also excruciatingly small, Teddy called out: 'Hey, kid.'

Listening intently for any sign of life, Teddy peered out from his protective shadow. The kid had gone.

'Thunderation,' Teddy mumbled.

Shirtless had been preferable to pants-less. Particularly when your underwear is missing. Fair play to the kid, though. Faced with a vampire, shy or yeller or otherwise, anyone with any sense would have done the same. Teddy wriggled and hopped and yanked the jeans into some sort of a semblance of wearability. He re-threaded his belt but, no matter how much he cajoled or even pleaded, the fastening would not conjoin with itself. Applying too much strength would merely render it even more useless than it currently was. Tugging at the shirt hem to cover the open fly, Teddy waddled away from the parking lot. Being 'all the go', it seemed, was something else that had gone the night he'd gained his freedom from László. This night also was not going well.

Laughter, frivolity, the skipping and jumping of heartbeats wafted to him from the crest of the hill. Keeping to the service roads and alleyways, Teddy hobbled towards the hub of activity. Ambling seemed to make walking easier. He disturbed a cat from its mousing. Scarpering at impossible angles, it leapt to the top of the wall and poured itself down the other side.

'Slick as a whistle,' he muttered, envious to the point of bitter.

A mouse eyeballed Teddy suspiciously; still it did not desist in scurrying about its business. Close by, another one twitched. Teddy ducked down to swipe them up. Already overstretched, the stitching of the jeans gave up the gaff. The back seam ripped open. The mouse stopped scurrying and stared at him. It sat there, whiskers twitching condescendingly. An increase in bantering chatter ensnared Teddy's attention and squatting there, comfortably as only a cowpoke can, he turned his head. The mice took advantage of the distraction and fled. Pigeons and blackbirds did the same.

'Yeah, you best jest amputate your mahogany now,' Teddy said.

Spilling out of the bar nearest to him were people, each holding the door for the next to pass through. He watched them. Strangely, sensing tranquillity, he was the calmest that he had been in a long, long time. More than that, he was sure-fired serene.

Then everything stopped moving. It wasn't that his heart stopped or skipped a beat. It couldn't. He didn't have one. It was more like his whole world stopped spinning and the vivacity of his phantasmagorical vision mellowed into soft, summer-edged watercolours. At the sound of an enchanting voice amidst the throng, his ears twitched and tingled deep in their canals. He knew that sound. He smiled and fancifully regressed way back to the likes of a feckless teenager. He liked that sound. He turned towards it. It made him feel like he could, and maybe would, do better, like he could achieve the unachievable, like he was still a good person. He stopped smiling and stared.

He'd seen something. Something wonderfully unfathomable, something mesmerising. He was sure of it and yet he could not pin it down, he could not own it. The last of the line of people passed through the door. The soulful, delightful, inspirational tones that he'd heard so clearly vanished, once again absorbed by the unbridled end-of-day ambience of this town's main street.

Testing the jeans' durability, Teddy stood slowly. The door to the bar was wrenched open, tiny September seeds, invisible to the human eye, were sucked up and showered down. Through their veil, he saw her. She was the embodiment of his fantasies.

The girl was beautiful. No, not beautiful. Beautiful was a picture, a painting, a masterpiece. She was more than that. She had a prettiness, a purity that he had never seen before. No, hang fire, that wasn't right. He had seen it before. And in this lifetime — since László.

He was confused, but it was good. He was afraid, but he felt strong. He was half-naked, but he didn't feel vulnerable. He was plumb unsure just exactly what he was thinking. Perhaps, just like in the beginning, his memory had snuck up on him and was showing him someone from his past. He just didn't recognise them. Yet.

He folded his arms across his chest, flattening his hands against his torso and pinching them there under his arms. It was all he could do to combat his body's urge to fly across the bunches of smokers and touch her, make sure that she was real.

Transfixed, he drifted out from the shadows screwing up his entire face and blinking hard a couple of times. When he looked again, she hadn't disappeared. He tried it again and thought of someone else, replacing her in his mind's eye with Moon and then Mort. But that just made him grimace. He tried everything he knew, even shifting about, to manipulate his memory. The girl hadn't faded.

A small cluster of the people had broken away from the main throng and arranged themselves ready to cross the road. The girl called out to them. Teddy's memory thumped him hard. She was the girl from outside the gallery. His saviour when he'd teetered at the top of the trail to his old murderous ways. Her nose was still purley purdy. Her hair, shorter now, was still dark. Having the chance to look properly at it, he saw it was black and richly shiny like the coat of a rare and graceful Friesian. She absently gathered a swaythe of it and smoothed it behind her ear. Teddy smiled like a mama would've done.

The girl caught up to the cluster. A concern for her protection gripped

Teddy, and as though right there with her, he surveyed the road, turning his head right and then left. Possessed by a formidable longing as soon as he looked away from her, he hastened his sight back to her.

The road clear, the group walked away. Teddy was filled with a pitiful loneliness; he got the notion that he was inadequate, as though the group were headed somewhere that he, for a very fundamental reason, wasn't allowed to go.

Well, ain't that the truth?

The demon was back and obviously sadistic. Teddy hadn't fed it in a while. Then a rush of excitement hit him. It had been so quick and so sudden that it left a sadomasochistic enjoyment in the misery that whirred inside him. He wanted more. Hang the demon.

Whatever was going on inside him was making him smile — dunderheadedly. He could have sworn that he was filled with happiness, bliss even. It was dizzying, so much so that it was difficult to stand still. Traditionally, happiness hadn't been the demon's way with him.

'Quit it,' he said.

He flattened his hands over his belly. Wasn't that where most of his sentiments seemed to start? But this one wasn't there. He probed and massaged but he couldn't find it. It was somewhere inside him, he knew it. It was fluttering in his nose. Now it was tingling down his spine. Now burning in his nether regions?

'Darn it, demon, that hadn't better be you.'

Without warning, he became possessed by a desire to see the girl again. A desire so strong it turned him dangerously desperate. He had to see her. Just lay eyes on her. One more time: that was all he'd need. Once more with the raptures of incredulity. Please. In fact, if he didn't see her again, he'd die. Hang fire, he was already dead. But this need, this simultaneous desire and distraction, it actually hurt. It was wonderful, intoxicating, infatuating even. It was turning him inside out.

He strained his eyes, glaring into the night. Nothing. She couldn't have disappeared now, could she? But his sight was a spaghetti-like tangle of manila hemp. Where had she gone? He searched again, beseeching the bricks and mortar with his stare, his mind frantically quizzing the ants and beetles that busied about in the cracks of slabs. The answer, of course, was zero. Still couldn't speak to bugs. Infuriated, forgetting where he was and unable to focus on anything except his goal, he started forward. He clattered into the pavement furniture.

'You okay, mate?' a young man asked him.

Teddy righted himself and attempted to straighten the chair. The night tickled his hips under the shirt tails. Physical feelings again?

'No,' he said absently, staring somewhat stunned at the owner of the voice.

An uneasiness nagged him to avoid drawing any attention to himself. Too much entanglement with these people would bring forth the demon; then there'd be consequences to pay for. Consequences that he didn't want to pay for. He needed to opt out of society, but that didn't mean he wasn't going to be lonely.

'What's the problem?' the young man said.

'Nothing.'

Teddy stumbled, trying to gain cover from the shadows.

'You just a bit bladdered?'

'No,' Teddy said.

Bladdered? His jeans were ripped, that was all. There wasn't anything wrong with him. Nothing that a good exorcism wouldn't sort out. It was just that this latest acquaintance did not look equipped to perform such a task. 'Just pacify him,' Teddy told himself, 'and be on your way.'

'Well, you just spilled my missus's drink. You going to buy her another?'

The boy seemed to be sizing Teddy up. There was something tyrannical in his eyes. It occurred to Teddy then that the people of this town weren't so far removed from those on the frontier. 'Sides, even if he wasn't a monster of mythical proportions, he couldn't possibly do as the boy asked — he had no money. The boy, apparently, was waiting for an answer.

Keep on it. Stare him down.

Teddy's hands clenched, his biceps flexed and his shoulders set.

'No,' he said through gritted teeth.

The demon was, as ever, spoiling for a fight. Teddy wasn't. He was anxious to keep the demon hidden. There were just too many people about.

'What's going on with you?' the boy said.

His chair scraped ominously along the ground as he stood. The boy was one big bulldozer. He motioned to his girlfriend.

'Apologise to her!'

Teddy glanced at her. She looked as skeersome as the boy did. The demon sniggered in Teddy's ears. Inside his body, it jabbed and bit and coiled. Teddy pressed his palms to his belly again.

Let me have this, Teddy. Please.

'No,' Teddy said, 'go boil your shirt, will ya? Lickspittle.'

He turned away from the boy. The demon grabbed his spine. Grimacing, he doubled over, clasping his knees for support. The too tight shirt flipped up on itself. The jeans strained, popped and came apart. The boy and his girlfriend were treated to a ringside view of Teddy's young and somewhat toned backside.

'Put it away, you shameless son of a bitch,' the boy exclaimed.

'Little wanker,' the girl sniggered through an immoral little giggle.

'Don't look, Gorgeous,' the boy responded.

Teddy straightened.

'Hang fire,' he said, turning back, 'I didn't mean...'

The demon laughed. Teddy sensed his own jaws straining to open. He clenched them shut. The demon tugged at his belly again. Teddy winced.

'Quit it, you varmint freeloader,' he hissed. 'I don't want no scrap. I'll only wind up killin' and I all-fired don't want that.'

'What did you say?' the boy roared, 'Couldn't your mama be arsed to teach you any manners?'

The boy pulled himself up to his full, thumping height and narrowed his eyes at Teddy.

'Too busy fucking around on your pissed-up, crap-headed dad.'

This had nothing to do with Ma or Pa. None of this was their fault: they were good people, they always had been.

'Apologise to her, now.'

More than likely to get the towelling of his time here on earth, Teddy's family's honour was worth it. Reminding himself that pain was all in the mind, he contorted his body to the side, taking a clear, good gander at the girlfriend. She glared hard at him. Then she smirked and winked.

'She don't look gorgeous,' Teddy said.

As he stared directly ahead, Teddy could see only the expansive chest of what was about to become a badly picked opponent. Nevertheless, he stepped up close and, looking up into the boy's face, said: 'In fact, she's so ugly, just one smile from her would poker up the meanest gunslinger and have him cuttin' dirt to church, crying for his mama.'

Snatching up the nearest chair, Teddy instantly slammed it back down, one metal foot aligned perfectly with the boy's. Hoping the demon would take notice, he snarled aloud: 'Stay out of this, Leech. I all-fired don't need none of your help.'

With all his might, he jammed and wrangled the chair as though screwing it to the floor. The boy howled. Teddy listened for the splintering of bones, waiting for the boy to react. As soon as he bent, Teddy rammed the metal, corrugated backrest up into the boy's nose. Blood, deep, rich and coppery, smeared the top of the chair; he could almost feel the numbness set in. The boy's hands flew to his nose. His girlfriend swore again. The demon screamed with laughter inside Teddy, who butted the whole chair into the boy's stomach and shoved him backwards.

Stepping away, he swiped at the girlfriend's table, flinging the glass, what was left of her drink and all its trimmings into her lap. Ice tinkled as the glass smashed to the floor. Shocked and wet, she shrieked and swore for a third time.

'Darn it, darlin,' Teddy called, twirling around and walking backwards towards the service road, 'you sure-fired are the hitch in my giddy-up.'

The boy, clearly accustomed to pain, flicked blood from his fingers and kicked the chair away. With little more than a cringe, he ran at Teddy, hurling himself forwards.

'Dang,' Teddy muttered.

He was seized about the waist and half-carried, half-dragged the width of the road.

'Help!' he managed.

The demon was silent. Teddy stumbled and fell. The boy hauled him back up by the shoulders of the shirt. The seams ripped.

'I apologise,' Teddy said quickly. 'Sakes alive, I apologise.'

'It's too late for apologies,' the boy replied, mercilessly slugging him.

On their side of the road was an entrance to the park where Teddy had climbed the university buildings. More of a ragged gap in the park's perimeter hedging and Teddy was sent crashing through it. He landed on his face mid-crescent of a rose garden. Thankfully, his sense of touch hadn't kicked in. But, regardless of whether he'd notice it or not, without the demon's help, this bulldozer of a boy would finish him off.

'Varmint?' he mumbled, not too sure of what exactly he should call the demon.

The boy had followed him. He crunched the thorny plants under booted feet that found their way to Teddy's middle. Grabbing Teddy by the collar and belt, he lugged him back up, and propelled him further ahead.

'You a fairy? Are you?' the boy snarled. 'You weigh nothing at all.'

Teddy skittered and scrambled towards a wrecked, lightning-struck tree that once must've been beautiful in the middle of a flower garden. Now, though, its limbs were awkward and pointed. He smacked into it, swivelled around and was punched to the floor.

'I'm gonna tear you a new arsehole and it won't be as pretty as the one you've got now.'

'Please demon, you were right,' Teddy cried, turning and crawling away. 'Without you, I'll get us both ripped to ribbons.'

Teddy anxiously stared about, hoping to find some sort of escape route, weapon, anything to hinder the fast-approaching boy. A thin, cylindrical bandstand, its fretwork ghostly white against the dark of the park, stood directly behind his assailant. Teddy pushed himself up onto his elbows. Too late: the boy gripped his shirt front and pulled him to his feet.

'Nope,' Teddy said into his face, 'I do the tearing around here.'

Swifter than a kestrel plunging to its prey, he swiftly slapped away the boy's tattooed forearms. Faster than his opponent could even register surprise, Teddy added a cheeky blow to his face. He ducked then, avoiding the comeback. His opponent's swing lumbered him forward, so Teddy dived around and booted him roughly in the backside. His jeans ripped again. The boy's spine buckled, sending him face first into the tree. He pivoted, swore and ran at Teddy, arms raised to grasp him about the ears. Slimmer than his opponent, Teddy slid between the boy's hands and anchored his own on the oncoming shoulders. Using them as a springboard, he catapulted himself high, arching his body into a somersault. Knees bent, feet angled, he alighted lightly in the roses behind. Booting the boy harder this time, the boy bolted into the concrete base of the bandstand. His face connected with the intricate ironwork; immediately, his head bounded backwards, cricking his neck.

'No one insults my family,' Teddy said.

'Fuck you,' the boy spat.

In seconds, Teddy was on him, sandwiching him between his body and the bandstand. He clutched a fistful of the boy's hair and crushed his face further into the ironwork.

'Enough…' he barked.

Snatching one of the boy's flailing hands, Teddy jammed the palm first onto the protruding end of a metal frond. Gunk, trailed by a line of fiery blood, poked out of the other side. Amidst the gurgling of the boy's scream, the demon cussed in Teddy's mind.

Taste it. Lick it. Drink it.

'I will not kill this boy,' Teddy said.

The boy began hissing, snorting and swearing; he puffed and panted, his body went rigid, and the other hand scraped and batted at any part of Teddy it could reach.

'That is enough!' Teddy hollered. 'You cain't use me to kill this boy.'

Teddy tightened his clasp on the boy's head and bared his teeth. He grimaced and lurched and squeaked as his stomach flipped and the demon quaked.

Take him. Feed me.

By now it was more than likely that the demon needed only the slightest sip of human blood to give it the power it needed to take full control. Teddy shook his head hard. With his free hand, he held onto the bandstandrailing like it was a lifeline. The boy stopped struggling. Teddy let go of his head. Now it was time to run.

Under his own ribcage, the boy's expanded, lifting Teddy to his toes.

The wheezing of the huge breath that'd just been drawn in rattled in Teddy's chest. Darn it, the boy was about to shout out. A brawl was the last thing Teddy wanted. With one hand he ripped the shirt that the kid had given him away from his body Just in time for the boy to lean back and open his mouth, Teddy stuffed the shirt in.

Defeated, the boy slumped. Head resting on his own biceps, he hung on with the other hand. His chest rose and fell rapidly with short, repeated breaths, and his parched lips around the check-shirt gag cracked every time. He gazed through exhausted, bloodshot eyes at Teddy.

Teddy got the notion that he knew only too well what it was to be both defiant and submissive in the presence of mind-bending pain. Shame sliced through him. Humiliation sluiced up those creeks it left behind. Somewhere in the back of his head a half-broken, Midwestern voice commanded him to: "Say it!" He flinched. He didn't know what "it" was. 'Sides, his body had begun to burn all over, as though his skin had split open in a thousand places and any muscle tissue he had left had frozen in what seemed to be involuntary anticipation of another stinging attack. Those lines, the ones that he'd felt so long ago, on his back rose up again. The too-long nails of his fingers punctured the palms.

The boy mumbled and gagged something, probably profanities. Teddy stared down at him, the pitiful sight bringing on a sudden guilt. His frown deepened and there was genuine sorrow in his eyes.

'I'm sorry,' he said.

The boy's heartbeat sped up. The scrunched-up ball of shirt in his mouth pulsed hastily as his breaths came at an alarming rate. His body began to convulse and his fingers trembled. His wide eyes, filled with contempt, rolled over in his head.

Is he dead? You killed him. Don't eat him.

'He cain't be dead,' Teddy said.

That would mean that he'd killed again. This time the emotions he was wearing had been read wrongly. He placed his fingertips gingerly on the tender spot just below the boy's ears. Nothing. He tried the boy's wrists. It was useless, his fingers were dead.

The boy sagged against him. Teddy hooked him under his armpits, closed his eyes trying to shut out all movement, and listened for his heart. It hadn't stopped. The boy must've suffered a faint from all the panting. Teddy's fingers tingled and a jab shot through his chest. He was momentarily stunted by a longing for freedom, for love and for friends. He listened again, lest the beating of the boy's heart had been in his imagination. It was stronger.

A sort of release swamped Teddy, he gave himself a shake and smiled. The demon had collaborated, it'd actually listened to him.

Never a braggert be. Braggerts ain't tolerated.

It quoted his own code. It was still there. It would always be there.

Teddy rolled his eyes.

He didn't have time for games; the boy would recuperate quickly. Gently, he lowered the body so that it would be kneeling on the ground.

'Dang.'

The boy wasn't long enough. So Teddy jostled him upwards, the exposed naval hairline crushing into his face as he hoisted the big, burly body, stuffing it under the metalwork. It lay on its side with one arm aloft unwittingly grasping the frond. 'Just like wrestling an ornery steer onto a wagon,' Teddy told himself. He glanced at the boy's jeans and his T-shirt. He hadn't ever considered himself steer-sized, but this boy looked to be about his height. Jumping and clutching the bandstand railings, he vaulted over the top and darted to the boy's shoes, unthreading the laces and removing them.

'I am hell-fired sorry about this,' he said.

Frantically unhitching his old leather belt, he peeled off the now tattered skintight jeans. Cutting a caper to get his feet freed, he fell over. He cussed himself out for not taking off his boots before starting this feverish endeavour.

'Truly I am,' Teddy said.

Levering and wiggling the semi-conscious boy out of his own jeans, he pulled them on and relooped his belt.

'Thanks, Pardner,' he said.

He checked the boy's heartbeat again. It was indeed growing stronger. Carefully, softly cooing apologies, he threaded the boy's good arm through the sleeve of his T-shirt. Thanking the land for the genius of the material's stretchiness, he pulled it over the boy's head. The boy mumbled something incomprehensible and his eyelids inhumanely flipped up and down.

'Darn it.'

Take him. Beef him now. Feed me before it's too late.

'Light a shuck, varmint.'

Teddy bent low so that he could look into the eyes. When the lids flickered again, revealing the watery green of his pupils, Teddy grinned. He deliberately displayed his teeth, suddenly transforming his expression to deathly, menacingly serious.

'Bo!' he barked.

The boy fell back into his faint. Lesson learned; Teddy moved quicker. He gathered up the T-shirt and, hopefully without bumping the boy about too much, manoeuvred it over biceps and around triceps. Sakes alive, this boy was a bulldozer. When the material dangled from the boy's forearm and there was just his fretwork-stabbed hand to go, Teddy halted. With the strengthening pulse, the hand would start bleeding again, as soon as it was released. The demon would, once again, start hazing Teddy for food.

He steeled himself, closed his eyes and pictured the corral, Caper and the Double C remuda. He indulged in the memory of bangtail horses rollin' high, weaving low and spinning in the prairie sunshine, of buttoning down his pride, honing his bravado, ignoring the impatience of the cowpokes and bustin' the broncos. Opening his eyes again, he couldn't properly focus, but he managed to slide the boy's hand free and the T-shirt loose.

Holding the T-shirt between his own teeth, he remembered his mother, Mattie, Ellen and even Enoch Hamilton and Father Egan seated at the dining table, the sumptuous eats, fruit cake and caffeine. The rich, red scent of venison gravy filled the air and his tongue curled with the bourbony promise of oaky caramel. As the boy's blood began to bubble, he bit down hard.

Finally, he let his mind rip with the sounds of cowpokes at work in the corral, shouts of 'hot iron!' as woodsmoke festered in his nose and the strength of braided rawhide rope grazing his fingers. Moments later, the boy was hog-tied with the skintight jeans.

Feed me. Now.

The demon screamed and bucked inside Teddy. He knelt at the boy's head, feeling not the concrete bandstand, but the stubby, dust-ridden grass of the corral. Tugging the shirt from the boy's mouth, he shredded it, jumped up and used one half to bandage the boy's hand, wrapping it tightly around; once, twice and back through the loop to secure the end. He fashioned the remaining half into a pad, hoping for some semblance of comfort when he placed it under the boy's face. At least it might protect him from the harsh, cold floor. Teddy reached out and laid his hand gently on the boy's back between his shoulder blades; it rose high. He stood, faced back towards the seating area, and in his best impersonation of the boy called out.

'Oi, 'elp me out, will ya?' He sounded terrible and decided never to do that again.

Chapter Twenty-Two

Teddy didn't want to hang around to see if his request for help was granted, so he slipped into the shadows of the night-time park. Shrouded by darkness, he slowed to a saunter. Marvelling at the ease of the garment, he stretched the T-shirt over his head, poked his arms through and smoothed it over his abdomen. It wasn't a bad fit. Perhaps he was bigger than he'd given himself credit for.

'Two scraps in one night?' he muttered. 'Either I have bad luck or perhaps I should just stay out of town.'

He started back towards the university buildings.

'Cleve would be so proud, though.'

Now that he had the appearance of normality, he didn't need to hide.

Just so long as he didn't smile or speak to anyone no one would know he was any different from the next man in the street. His muscles strained, contorting and twisting his stomach in on itself. He faltered and doubled up, wrapping his arms around himself.

The desire to feed coiled and graunched and tore at his insides. It would make him weak. The hunger pangs would not cease, they'd continue to attack, growing stronger until he was forced to hunt and to feed just to subdue them.

Aches clawed at Teddy's sides. They pulsed up and down, stopping only to hurl themselves inwards. They dragged his insides with them into an abyss of pain, and he fell to his knees.

'Quit it,' he moaned.

Do not ignore me. I will survive.

Survival: it was the demon's only goal. For over one hundred years, it had survived, and if there was one thing Teddy knew for definite, it would continue to do so. By hook or by crook, it would continue to survive. Only now, it needed to co-survive with Teddy, the sunshine-coloured owner of its bodily dwelling place. The relationship was a whole heap more hate than love, and right now, it was more Teddy adhering to it.

As though to ram its need home, the pains wracking Teddy's stomach spread to his spine. They worked their way upwards, spiralling over themselves like overzealous snakes in a breeder's pit, each desperate not to be left at the bottom in the scavenge for food.

'Wait,' Teddy whimpered. 'Please.'

His lips were twitching, his jaw locking, his eyes blazing. He crawled, one arm grasping his stomach as though he could harness the pangs. The nails of his other hand scratched frenetically at the dry earth. The park around the college buildings was more spacious than planted: there were no trees, no flower beds or rose gardens here. The summer must've been good, too; the grass was short, dry and brown.

Eat, chow, chuck, and very soon — or become the monster. There was no way, no way in tarnation he'd give in to its murderous bent. He tried to cajole this determination to commandeer his entire consciousness.

The sense of disgust that came with his munching insects, squishing out the gloop from the emaciated grubs that he exposed with his scratching, before swallowing it, was of little botherayshun. He no longer cared for their foul bitterness, something that was usually unbearably distasteful; but fudging it over was not something he had the luxury of right now. Taste, touch, smell, all senses he could control, surged and floundered and then hurled him into disarray.

In the wrong hands, that "disarray" would become lustful, sinful. Teddy could not let that happen. He crawled and chomped down on any morsel he scraped up.

The grassland came to an end. The stomach pangs peaked and ebbed, but they lingered with a threatening hold over his insides. Teddy still needed to feed. He lay on the edge of the park, half on and half off the smooth, black walkway. His resolve to stay harmless faded to terrifyingly low. Time was getting late, the chatter of human voices was now only sporadic, as was the busying about of small mammals.

Teddy's gaze was jerked towards the sounds of people. He turned, balefully and glowered towards the town. The demon's resolve to murder had strengthened.

'I will not feed on humans,' Teddy murmured.

He sounded puny. Infatuated with the promise of body-temperature blood, the demon didn't even humour him with an answer. It had the upper hand and they both knew it. Teddy's stomach stiffened again. He screeched and writhed at the searing, stabbing evil tendrils that climbed up his spine. His jaw opened wide and his teeth were laid bare. He baulked and railed against the horrific roar that the demon sought to draw from him.

A large, coarsely winged insect, its body ribbed, furry and fat, stumbled inside Teddy's open mouth. A moth. It wouldn't be long until it started craving light. For the sake of its addiction, it would suffocate itself, exhaust itself, extinguish itself trying to get to it. It would become no more than a negligible addition to the decay that already festered inside Teddy.

Life on the range had introduced Teddy to the company of many a moth. As soon as the sun went down, and the campfire lit up, they'd been plagued by them; crawling, flitting critters carrying more dust per body than Arizona in a heatwave.

A campfire, that was what he needed. A campfire would bring his supper straight to him. Tinderbox. Where was his tinderbox? It was vital to the survival of cowpoke life, on the range or otherwise; its contents were so simple, so small. But it was something that Teddy didn't have. He struggled to his feet. The demon made its presence known once more and knocked him back down. He gazed about himself. There was nothing here that would help him.

Feed me.

The pains woven around Teddy's body were almost at insufferable point. Every inch of him throbbed. The smarting of his spine had become a continuous, glaring agony from the base of his neck to the top of his head. His eyes narrowed, he snarled and stumbled like a hungered, savage beast towards the town.

The pathway was lined with waist-height, white-lit bollards and one collided with his legs. Spindly, thin-legged flies alighted in Teddy's hair. Something stripy with eyes that all but covered its head landed on his face. He tried to swipe it, brush it into his mouth, but the winding of the demon was all-encompassing and he swiped it away. Instead he lost all balance and fell. On the way down, though, he hooked one booted foot around the bollard.

'I will not murder again,' he said, frantically pushing himself backwards and curling his whole body around the post, clutching it and cuddling it.

Beetles and flies barrelled into the post halfway up; they tumbled back down, only to buzz back up again in what seemed a fatal craving to reach the white light at the top. The light itself was pock-marked black, purple and blue. In places it was opaqued where wings had stuck to it, the bodies long since disintegrated.

Pulling himself as close to the post as he could, Teddy hauled himself up it. He rested his head on it. With the light shining through his hair and skin, he should attract a multitude of insects. All he had to do was eat them.

Teddy closed his eyes and let his mouth hang slack as the stomach cramps twisted once more. Insects began to blunder into him. He whined, gurgling, when his insides wrenched, mangled and wrung themselves out, but he would not let go. He ate, crunching down when he had a mouthful.

Drops of blood, varying in their size, began to collect inside him. The demon pulled, but Teddy held on. The raging of the stomach cramps slowly lessened. Teddy frowned and grimaced and ate again. His consciousness grew stronger and, startlingly, he recognised the repugnance of his actions. There could be no stopping, though. The demon needed to be fed. He should have done it before now.

Teddy thought of Ellen's unwavering efforts to wow him with sorghum cake. The cake was truly terrific, his response was typically, brotherly mediocre. As much as she loved to try him, though, he just loved to haze her. He thought of obliging Ma when she needed tough, strong arms to pull difficult, cooling taffy. The cramps subsided to a strain. He smiled when he remembered Mattie laboriously beating cookie batter over and over and back on itself.

So carried away on his memories was he, so enjoying the scents of the kitchen, the sherberty tang of the taffy, the laughter and Mattie's scowling, that he ate more than he needed to. It was only when something particularly harsh spiked his mouth that he stopped, although he couldn't resist loitering with the bollard for a moment. Flies crept through his hair: their tickling was heightened by his fantasising. He flinched and jumped to his feet, madly shaking them out.

'Darn gnats,' he mumbled.

A stray greyback ruffled the hairs on his forearms, raising goose bumps across his skin. Savouring the sensation, he smiled at it and then flicked it away. It seemed as though with that thoughtless action, he flicked away what was left of his senses. The bustle of town was almost gone, too.

Teddy listened for the town hall clock. Spinning around, he searched for its ticking. He found it, but there was no chime and, nary one did the mechanism whir or click to suggest that there would be one anytime soon.

Stunted then, Teddy sensed an odd sort of failure. It wasn't as though he'd failed at anything – in fact, he'd achieved something; he'd helped the nobbish kid out of the jam with the bullies. He should be pleased, but he wasn't. He was lonely. He was gonna miss that kid. All his life, well that life that he chose to remember, he'd been surrounded by people; darn it he hadn't even slept alone. As he'd just learned, though, being around people was just too dangerous. Miserably, he resigned to getting back to the mausoleum.

He was gonna miss the entire town. The place reminded him of home. His memories had been so strong here. Wistfully, he wondered what had happened to his dust-ridden home town in Kansas. He edged forwards and stood, toes outcropping over the corner, gazing up and down the empty streets. White light from lines of lamps atop posts and bollards made the place look ghostly. He half-expected to see the stage, ornery horses and all, judder to a stop just up the street. If he ever did come back here, he'd have to keep his wits about him. For now, though, dawn couldn't be too far away. He turned to leave.

'Hello.'

Teddy froze. The beautiful girl, the girl of his dreams, was standing right in front of him.

'I saw you looking up and down the high street and I thought you might be lost.'

She spoke to him. He gazed addleheadedly at her.

'Can I help?' she said.

There was happiness in her voice and he saw freedom in the sparkle of her eyes. There was something else, too. Something that weakened his knees and blew him bodily into the ether, only to bring him back nanoseconds later, dumbfounded and goofy. It was acceptance.

She laughed then. A small, pretty laugh like an unspoken plea to be shown, in that instance, the goodness in his heart; he knew, that she was only too sure it was there. Dang, he didn't have a heart? Maybe it was that he amused her. He forgot all about the ridiculousness of any incompetence he might be possessed by. Any ineffectiveness he may have suffered, however momentary, was replaced by a fascination, as though all the questions of the universe had been answered in that one delightful laugh. He wanted, no ached to hear her laugh again. More than anything, he wanted to hear her laugh at something that he'd said, he didn't even care if it wasn't meant to be a joke; he just wanted to make her laugh. Then he'd be happy. Then they could come and sever his useless tongue and limbs, tear off his head and burn the rest of him. But then, if that happened, he wouldn't ever see her again. Ever. Immediately, he was unbelievably sad.

'Hello?' she said again.

Speak, he thought, say something. "Howdy, Ma'am." That didn't sound right, did it? Whatever he said, he sounded strange, foreign, ancient. Worse still, he had no hat to tip. Hang fire, nary one would that be right. There he went again, speaking his funny language. "Nary one": who said, "Nary one"? Teddy couldn't be entirely sure what it meant even.

Without warning, his body gave him a sense of his tongue. It was a dry slab, and it sat there thick and heavy, too big for his mouth. Flammable as tinder, the back of his throat began to smart. It was just like the time when he'd been faced with Christmas dinner at the Double C. He couldn't speak. Even if he wanted to…he couldn't. The girl looked at her feet.

'Well, if you're Okay…' she said.

The goose bumps came up again. The wind tousled the girl's hair. The bumps rippled over his entire body. His sense of touch had returned. Somehow this girl was reaching into his subconscious, ekeing out sensibilities that he didn't even know he had; affectations that were so new to him he couldn't identify them. Darn it, he'd thought he was the master of his emotions.

The girl turned away. Wait, Teddy hollered. At least he did in his head. I ain't "Okay". I ain't what you think I am. He plumb pined to be just exactly what she did think he was. He didn't care if that were a skeezick sodbuster, or even a scabby maggot herder. Anything. Anything that wasn't what he actually was.

I cain't speak, he thought desperately. If he so much as opened his mouth, if the telepathy should actually work this time even, he'd scare her away. More than anything else, he didn't want her to be scared of him.

'Elizabeth?'

A dull thud broke into Teddy's thoughts. For one sappy moment, he was all-to-pieces sure, he'd been shot through the heart. Now, that just wouldn't be possible, would it? A young man stepped up to the kerb. He stood next to the girl. In fact, he stood so close that he touched her. Then he raised a hand and laid it lightly on her arm. It might not have been, probably wasn't, but Teddy was sure it was done purposely slowly.

'Elizabeth,' he said, eyeballing Teddy, 'come on, it's late and you have work in the morning.'

The girl didn't move. For a smidgen of a second, she dallied; Teddy was certain of it. Then she looked up at the boy and smiled. Her smile was the welcoming, trusting smile of a friend. Perhaps even a close friend. Teddy knew real hate then. Just for a fragment, it was a pokerish seething. The demon stirred.

'Sakes alive,' Teddy cried inside, 'you're with that dude?'

He wanted her to look up at him like that. Don't be with that dude. The "dude" stared at him. One grin, Teddy thought, one grin and — he looked away. It wouldn't be right. It would be wrong of him to assert his hideous power over this dude. It was wrong to do it over anyone or anything, for that matter. He studied his boots, they were a little grimy still. Teddy saw Elizabeth's petite feet turn. Her feet were perfect. They pivoted and took her away.

Sharply, Teddy looked up. But it was too late; Elizabeth had gone. He was paralysed now. He remained there, watching the empty space at the kerb and then, silently craving to have Elizabeth back, he stared after her departing car.

Perhaps, if he hoped hard enough, some fanciful god in some serene realm would pity him and, miraculously, Elizabeth would return. She might smile at him again, ask him to speak to her again, laugh again. Just like the heroines in the penny dreadfuls, she'd fall into his arms and they'd kiss — he conveniently forgot about his past and his fangs.

Still, he lingered, not too sure why. Behind him, the sky turned from black to purple and then to two-tone indigo and blue. Elizabeth must've been tired. She'd face the alarm call in a few hours. But she'd stopped to check on a stranger, enquire if he was "Okay".

The oncoming death of Teddy's body seized his muscles. Or at least he thought that was what it was. Woefully, he acknowledged the corn: he'd ignored Elizabeth.

'Forget it, Ted…Theodore,' he said, his speech just a mite slurred. 'Face it – she'll have forgotten all about you by now.'

He was standing on the walkway, in full view. He had to move. If he didn't move, he'd drop down dead, he'd be this town's man for breakfast. Then, when, if he was unlucky enough, the sun came out, his unpainful and yet apparently agonising death might be witnessed. An investigation into the charred body found on the pavement would be held, his teeth would be found, and all hell would break loose. If, of course, he didn't move. He slouched back into the shadows of the park.

He raised a hand to run it through his hair; his elbow was stiff. The sky paled a little more. There was always something, it seemed, to keep him out late. The sunrise would be beautiful like those in paintings of the Nativity. He so wanted to stay and watch it.

Teddy's joints tightened as though he'd been dowsed with a pail of cold water dealt out by the cowpokes, only this was time to go to bed, not time to go to work. He set off at an unstable jog towards his mausoleum and to Ichabod and Dunc. Not two whoops and a holler later, he was running faster than the motorway traffic; minutes after that he'd reached his charming but lonely woodland.

There'd been no jumping or leaping or flying. Strangely, he had no appetite for indulging in his inhuman abilities. He sat on the mausoleum's lichen-stained roof, catching and eating rising gnats, thinking of Elizabeth and watching the stars flicker and fade.

Two fights in one night... Hang fire, hadn't he already said that? He really should go to bed. Cleve would be proud of him. He'd said that, too. A beautiful girl, he relished that thought; Ma would be pleased. He looked down, although he wasn't too sure he'd meant to. New threads; the less said about that, the better. Too late once again, he slithered back into his tomb and died.

Chapter Twenty-Three

'What?' Silas Truss spat.

Teddy's breath thudded out of him. He couldn't say anything.

'What was that you said?'

Salacious impatience gorging tangibly in the corners of his mouth, Uncle Silas slammed Teddy into the wall of a barn. With one startlingly strong arm across Teddy's collarbone, Silas held him there. His other hand twisted Teddy's hair, pulling his head back, jarring his spine. Teddy hissed at the stinging in his scalp. His feet in hand-me-down boots slipped on the barn floor. Uncle Silas pressed him upright with his body. Teddy clung onto his uncle's arm.

'I thought I heard you say you was sorry for ever thinking you'd leave us.'

Silas glowered into Teddy's eyes. Letting go of his hair, he slapped Teddy's face. It wasn't hard; more degrading, really. But still, a confused resentment began to rise inside. He closed his eyes and tried to quash the feeling. His uncle slapped the other cheek with the other side of his hand and snapped his fingers in front of Teddy's eyes.

'Look at me, Owl Hoot,' he sang, clicking all the while. 'The only reason you're still alive is because you, under my charge, have gotten so damned good at bustin' those horses.'

A repugnant giggle, despicable in its excitement, severed the charged air. Teddy shifted his gaze. Cousin Kenny leaned on the handle of a broom. A broom that, no doubt, he'd been struggling to work with. Teddy concentrated on his chucklehead cousin; a welcome distraction from the pressure of his uncle's hate. Kenny raised his chin and glared back at Teddy. The broom tipped away from him. Flailing, he fanned the air until he caught the all-important handle again.

'I told you to look at me,' Silas hollered.

Teddy grimaced and stared at his uncle.

'Now, if you go off on the trail, where does that leave me? Did you ever think about that?'

Silas jabbed a calloused index finger into the side of Teddy's head. Pain, dismally loud, shot through his temples. Kenny lost control of the broom again.

'I'll tell you where that leaves me!' Silas shouted into Teddy's ear. 'Without a Wrangler! And I sure as hell don't wanna pay one while you're gone off spreading your spoosy seeds in the squaws on the prairie.'

Kenny guffawed. His pent-up amusement splattered spittle into the night air. It glimmered in the kerosene lamplight like shards of shattered scruples; with nothing to set themselves to, they tumbled out of sight. Silas released Teddy.

'Now, you ever try and leave this ranch again, and I'll have 'Rastus here hunt you down and drag you back in gory pieces.'

Erastus leaned lazily against the knotted timber wall opposite; he bit his thumbnail, flicked out his pointed finger and sneered at Teddy. Uncle Silas leered close to his face, rancid, excessive saliva leaking opaquely from his tongue as he spat out the words: 'Never forget that.'

Teddy sagged.

'You jest keep your head down and get on with your horses,' Silas said.

Wary in case that wasn't all Uncle Silas had to say, Teddy made to leave; he shouldn't have come, darn it. Rumours, rife not only in the bunk house, if of course the cowpokes were to be believed, of Silas Truss' involvement in the Slicker Wars, seeped into Teddy's nerves. Just like the buyer's spike that contaminates a stubborn landowner's whisky, the thought made him weak.

Silas rammed him into the wall again. Teddy choked. Desperate for clear air, he craned his neck, straining his face away from his uncle's rank mouth.

'You remember that lesson on loyalties I promised you?' Silas said.

Teddy didn't, but he reckoned on it being an all-to-pieces waste of energy to say so.

'Let's start with manners,' his uncle sneered, then, grabbing Teddy's jaw, he said: 'Pray tell you're sorry.'

Blunt fingers squeezed until the ridged, gummy insides of Teddy's cheeks crowded his tongue and his mouth was forced open.

'Say you'll be here forever, yes? Till your dying day, yes?'

Teddy clawed at the hand, shaking it off. He glared into the bigoted eyes of his uncle. He was determined to keep quiet, stare the old slicker down, show him he didn't care for his bullying. Silas slapped him again. Harder this time, hard enough for the sound to reverberate off the walls. Teddy's gaze was driven away again.

'Say it, you balmy son of a bitch.' Silas grew more impatient, if that were possible. 'Give us that cowpoke word of honour. I know Dent. He'll have learned you that balderdash code he lives by. Well, tell you what, I'll teach you my code.'

Teddy tensed. Uncle Silas' code? His stomach constricted and his breath began to rasp. If Uncle Silas meant a slicking, that bloody and disgusting vigilante punishment, he'd end up delirious in his agony. He'd say anything and, if he survived, he'd be left hideously scarred. Four years earlier, obscene reports from the *Chronicle* of Missouri 'slickings' had regularly been read aloud as after-dinner entertainment when he'd lived in his uncle's house. The victims, those that didn't die, had left town as soon as they could. Any that didn't leave were just never heard of again. Erastus and Kenny loved those stories. They'd loved them so much; Aunt Laura had repeated them over and over until they scared Teddy witless and Louisa left the room. Missouri, Teddy thought grimly, was just one state along. It was horse feathers, though, by his own account, Silas didn't want him to leave.

'You hankering for a stay of execution!' Uncle Silas shouted into his face. 'Huh? Is that why you're so goddamn silent.'

'Tell the Judge here, you're never gonna go anywhere,' Erastus' half-broken voice chimed in. 'Say it, swear it.'

Silas kneed Teddy in the stomach. Teddy gasped and doubled over. Silas straightened him out, cuffing away his struggles. Teddy's cheeks twitched, his lips worked, but nothing came out. He couldn't speak. With all this abysmal breathlessness, his mouth had dried up.

'Tie him up, 'Rastus,' Uncle Silas snarled.

Erastus took hold of his hands, sniggered and grinned.

'Boy, are you gonna get it.' he grinned as he began to wind the end of a long rope around Teddy's wrists. Once, twice…

'What's this?' he said, flicking at the stump that was Teddy's middle finger. 'You been damaging yourself, Cuz?'

'Where? Let's see,' Kenny said, wanton bloodlust whetting his childish voice. 'Don't tell Ma.'

Teddy winced. The finger had healed well, but it would be a long while before it became hardened like the rest of his skin. He folded his mutilation inside his other hand and exhaled a long, shaky breath. He ached to cry out, cuss and swear, sing even, anything other than yield to their demands. But he just didn't trust himself to speak. He balled his hands into fists.

Erastus wrung the rope tight. It burned. He tied off the hooey knot and stepped away. Holding the other end of the rope, he thrashed it high. Teddy's hands jolted and he recoiled at the rope's cracking. It was a reaction that the three vigilantes found incredibly funny.

'Corn sarn it, guys,' he tried to reason, 'you're my family. You're supposed to want me here. If you don't, why don't you let me go?'

His heart faltered; he told himself it was triggered by fear.

'Not this again,' Erastus said, 'we've been through this before. Haven't we, Cuz? Which means that now you're just being a baby. We do want you.'

'No, we don't,' Kenny said.

Unable to keep the bile-ridden sniggers out of his voice, he clearly thought he was joining the 'How to ridicule your cousin's sentimentality' game.

'No one wants you,' he continued before anyone could stop him. 'What do you think you are doing here? Huh? Where's your mama and your papa?'

Erastus rolled his eyes. Kenny didn't know how Teddy had come to be there any more than he did. Darn it, Erastus had probably been too young to remember what had happened. Really, all any of them knew was what Uncle Silas told them. That they were family. Of sorts. Or at least supposed to be.

'Enough, boys,' Silas said. 'Half the county wants him.'

'Please, Uncle Silas,' Teddy said, hating the beg that had become apparent in his voice, 'I want to work for you, I really do. I just don't... I mean cain't... I shouldn't be treated like a slave no more. The days of slavery are plumb over.'

Uncle Silas backed away from Teddy. He studied him like he was wondering what to do with him. Teddy waited, his chest rising humiliatingly high and falling agonisingly low. His uncle took another step backwards. He looked Teddy over again and smirked.

'Well, they ain't on my ranch,' he growled. 'You just woke up the wrong passenger.'

He shucked off his coat, revealing his sagging gun belt; the ivory grips of a peacemaker protruded over the top of the holster.

'Kenny?' he said. 'Go fetch me a switch.'

Move, Teddy urged himself. Run. Do something. You're gonna die here.

Kenny's broom handle hit the floor, its clunk muffled by the muck and straw. A line of moonlight, white-hot as a newly sharpened knife, stretched across the floor when he opened the door. It slit Silas' sneer in two and glinted off his yellow teeth.

'Wait,' Silas ordered. 'There's an old hickory just outside, get one from that.'

'You cain't do this to me,' Teddy said. 'Slicking's against the law.'

They stood in stalemate for a good few moments. A torrent of sweat was unleashed from each and every one of Teddy's pores. It lingered like soup before running down his spine, soaking his union suit, pooling in the small of his back. He watched his uncle watching him. The callous glimmer in his eye, the narcissism in his grin, the oath to spilled blood that was etched into his fisted hands, all horrified Teddy through to his core.

'Do I look like I care!?' Silas thundered. 'Your days of thieving my horses are up. Just confess to thieving horses and we'll get it all over and done with, won't we?'

'What?' Teddy hadn't stolen a thing, ever.

'Horse thief,' Kenny snorted.

'Don't do this,' Teddy cried, 'I ain't no horse thief. You know I ain't. I cain't confess to anything.'

'Sure you ...' Kenny started.

'Kenny?' Uncle Silas hollered. 'You still here?'

The shard of light from the door guttered and Kenny squeaked. The boy wouldn't know a hickory from a cherry. A moment passed and nobody budged. Teddy was rooted to the spot. This is horse feathers. The bag of nails that was his mind and body slowly fused together with the foreboding need to move.

'Addleheaded sap,' Silas muttered.

He spat out a lump of saliva and barked out an order to Erastus to help Teddy shuck off his top half. Then he turned and walked to the door, kicking viciously at his son as he passed. The door swung closed behind him with such force that the latch slipped into place.

'C'mon, little doggie,' Erastus sang, 'whoop-ee tyin' you up.'

He leered and lashed the rope again. It was an old rope, it still had a hondo tied in the end. The end that Erastus held in his right hand. The rope was cracked down again, jolting Teddy's hands violently.

'Stop doing that,' Teddy said.

Trying to look brave although, to acknowledge the corn, he was more desperate for a respite from terror, he narrowed his eyes at Erastus.

'What's the matter, lil' shaver?' Erastus flicked the rope again: it bore a long rill out of the straw-festooned floor. 'Has the big boy got your rope? I'll do what I like.'

Erastus' brains were all in his brawn and most of that, thanks to the good living of a cow baron's son, was sloppy. He was an incompetent fool when in the corral and had proven on many occasions that he was just as bad when out, too. He was cack-handed. His strong hand was also his lazy hand.

'Well, you ain't working it right,' Teddy said and grasped the rope.

It didn't take much; he was, after all tied to one end. He pinched it between his thumb and forefinger, closed his fist around it and yanked. At the same time, he whipped it high. The whine of braided hemp blazing a trail through Erastus' skin was almost palpable. The boy cried out, dropped the rope and clasped his free hand to his palm. His face was a picture of hurt disbelief. He looked like he was about to pitch the fit of a two-year-old.

'Theodore,' he cried, 'you're gonna pay for that.'

With Erastus screaming like a baby, Silas would return in double time. Teddy spun around and sent high undulations zipping down the long rope. It coiled in the air with the rhythm of a hypnotic viper, long and lean and golden-brown, whirling gracefully fast, leading the hondo to its spot. The hondo bit out at Kenny by the barn door, toppling his hat off his head.

'My hat,' the air-headed boy wailed, gesticulating wildly before launching himself along the ground.

Teddy heaved in a breath to clear his head. Ambitiously, he sized up the distance to the door. He took a step back, anchored his weight and beat the rope a third time. Ridges like a mountain range hurled themselves at the barn door, the hondo caught and settled around the latch.

Erastus, having put nursing his hand on hold, sprang at Teddy. Teddy dropped to his haunches. He scrunched up tight and ducked into Erastus' paunch, levering with his shoulders. Erastus flew, his spurs high, the sharp rowels cutting through the night, the jingle bobs ringing like a child's Christmas. He yelped and crashed, a crumpled heap on the dirty floor.

Teddy twisted the rope and flicked it once more. He dashed to the open space opposite the door. Curved aftershocks propelled the catgut loop upwards, taking the door latch with it. The door swung open.

Kenny, hat on head, arms outstretched, rushed at the door with the shriek of a delusional sibling. Teddy flipped the hondo home and looped it into a loose overhand knot. All the while keeping a close eye on Kenny's progress, he threaded it back up through one of the newly formed rings. The old hondo formed the stopper for a new one; one that Teddy could work with. He opened up the new loop into a high-speed spin. Rolling it and his wrist over, he aimed at Kenny. Just as the clueless boy touched the open door, Teddy's hoolihan dropped over him. One yank and Kenny's arms were tied tight to his sides. He fell straight backwards like a toy soldier toppled by a marble.

Teddy looked down to his hands. Erastus' knot was a simple wrap and slap; they used it for branding. Teddy was no panicking calf, though, he'd be out of Erastus' knot in no time. Flattening his palms together in prayer, he bent so that they were in line with his knees and stamped hard on the free rope. It snagged under his boot and tautened as he pulled up sharply. On the other end Kenny cussed as he struggled, writhing like a Longhorn larva.

The two loops rolled over themselves, pinching and tugging at Teddy's skin. Raging scarlet engravings had burned into his wrists, but the rope gave way and he was free.

Erastus was back up now, though. He snarled and swore promises of barbarous retribution. Then he ran at Teddy. It was to be expected and Teddy turned as though he had all the time in the world. The grossly inflamed and contorted face of his cousin intent on bleeding as much pain out of him as he could brought back everything the cowpokes had taught him. He met Erastus' nose with a sturdy slug, immediately diving out of the way. Erastus, spurred on by his momentum, unable to see for cupping his hands over his haemorrhaging face, smacked into the wall.

Stumbling and scuffing in his ill-fitting boots, slipping on loose straw, Teddy ran for the door.

'What in the tarnation is going on in here?'

The Mohawk sight of a double-barrel rifle peered around the door before Teddy could make it through. Its miserable grey muzzle found his chest and Uncle Silas followed it. Anger bristling through his whole body, Silas took in the sight of Kenny squirming on the floor. Then he looked over Teddy's shoulder, observing slowly where Erastus sat whimpering. Finally, he glared at Teddy.

'Pa,' Erastus howled, hastily foisting the blame of his uselessness onto his younger cousin, 'Theodore broke my nose.'

'Damn fool,' Silas seethed.

Teddy couldn't be sure which one of the three cousins Uncle Silas was talking to, but he didn't dare to question him. Nary one did he dare to move. The rifle's brass receiver, etched in old war wounds, was patterned anew with well-placed fingerprints — it'd been broken and closed recently. The gun was loaded.

'You! owl hoot!' Silas shouldered the rifle. 'Get your hands where I can see them.'

The gun's sight was completely futile in its significance. At this range Silas' shot would've taken Teddy's head clean off his shoulders. It looked like the old slicker knew that, too. His yearning to try it out foamed around his tar-damaged teeth. The muzzle wavered under Silas' wrath. Teddy raised his hands. Deliberately, carefully, as though even the slightest scrape of his brown denim jeans would set the gun off, he stepped back into the barn.

"Rastus,' Silas drawled, 'can you please get this boy shucked off?'

Teddy took another step away. He couldn't shake his gaze from the gun's half-cocked hammer. He backed right into Erastus, who grunted and snivelled and thumped him hard in the kidneys. The slug reanimated Teddy. He cried out and collapsed to his knees.

Erastus leapt over him, dancing high from one foot to the other. Ruthlessly, he kicked Teddy in the face. Teddy was hurled to the floor. Mirroring his cousin, he cupped his nose in his palms. Erastus waved at him.

'A nose for a nose,' he said.

'I never meant to hurt you,' Teddy groaned.

Erastus had, though, and that added to the pain. Teddy's eyes smarted, they were beginning to swell.

'You loco as a coot?' Erastus howled, 'How'd you work that one out?'

Teddy blinked away excess mucus. Erastus yowled with laughter. Instantly he stopped and clasped his nose again, stamping noisily several times. Beside him, Kenny began to snort.

'Pa,' he said, 'are you sure that we're related?'

'You're gonna give me a slicking,' Teddy said. 'What did you think I was gonna do?'

'Never...' Erastus shouted, planting a pointed-toed boot in Teddy's middle.

'Fight...' He kicked again. 'Back...'

Teddy stomach wrenched as his breath burst from his lungs. He scrunched up and opened his mouth wide. Sore, dry retching scored his windpipe; his gasping for air was halted mid-heave.

'Ever.' Erastus didn't seem to care which bit of his cousin he kicked at now, 'Ever again.'

'You'll lose,' Kenny sang. 'You're outnumbered. You'll always be outnumbered.'

Silas' toe prodded Teddy, denting the rough sleeve of his coat, bruising further the long-forgotten biceps.

'Get up,' he commanded, his voice quiet.

Teddy stayed on the cool ground; he wasn't ready yet. He needed to hold onto his stomach a little more, wait for the ache in his eyes to clear away. The inside of his nose congealed and solidified and his ears popped. His uncle's voice bounced off the aches in his head, pulsing against the inside of his jaw, ricocheting through the shuddering in his stomach. Uncle Silas was muffled and far away. Finally able to breathe again, Teddy gulped loudly. Grit and straw sucked their way over his lips.

'I said, "Get up"!'

The rifle's hard, smooth muzzle pressed into his ear. It fitted neatly, like a plug. A plug that was primed and wanton to shatter his skull to sacrifice. Teddy let it guide him to his feet.

'Take your coat off.'

The muzzle prodded his nose. His nose cleared and ran with sour blood.

'Sakes alive! Ras, help him out.'

'If it's all the same to you, sir,' Teddy mumbled, 'I'd like to keep it on.'

Silas let the rifle rip. The bullet fired down the barrel and exploded from the muzzle. Black powder, dirt and straw clouded the air as the deafening shot impacted in the earthen floor. Instinctively, Teddy jumped away from it. He swore and lost his balance. Stumbling to the floor again, he stared at the smoking crater the bullet left behind. It stank of bitter sulphur which skinned his nose and brought on fresh bleeding. His uncle was shooting at him now?

The cowpokes would have heard it. Darn it, the barking squirrels deep under the prairie would've heard it. Teddy hoped, for their sake, that they all stayed away. Uncle Silas was thirsty for torture and humiliation; in this mood he was liable to start off another war.

'It ain't all the same to me,' he raged, levering the rifle. 'Nor to my poor boys here.'

The spent cartridge emptied and the next one was chambered.

'They want, and I think they deserve, to see you get what's rightfully yours.'

Teddy did as he was told, but he shouted: 'What in the tarnation! What's rightfully mine?'

His hands began to shake, his spine quaked and he wondered morosely what it looked like. Or if it would show itself.

'This ain't "what's rightfully mine".'

His shoulders bucked a little too violently as they shrugged the heavy coat away.

'You've taken everything that's mine. Even my sister. And now I don't got nothing.'

His fingers trembled. He couldn't grasp the buttons of his shirt. Erastus yanked at his braces.

'Darn it, I don't even got my freedom.'

'Well, obviously,' Silas said, 'and it seems I didn't do a good enough job with you now, did I? You still wantin' more from me. So, I'm gonna switch you till your insides fall out through your back. And you're gonna retch up your own shit. If you don't, then I switch you some more till you do. Sabby? Now, get gone with that there shirt.'

Chapter Twenty-Four

Teddy's family had left him there, hanging from the rafter by his arms. A wretched, hopeless figure slicked in blood; too tired to hate, too drained to do anything. His tendons, so valiantly holding his body together, stretched almost to their limit. Mercilessly, they clicked and graunched before solidifying in mind-numbing torture.

In an attempt to evade the pains from his overstrained chest muscles, Teddy stood flat on his feet. The attempt was in vain, exhaustion engulfed him, his legs gave way and, with a grunt, he fell to hanging on his arms again. It'd worked to start with. It must've. Until the pains had set in. Then they'd come more and more quickly and by the fourth or fifth repetition of standing to hanging, the whole pitiful routine bought him only moments of respite. In the end, the pains were continuous and the constant movement from feet to arms and back again kept him doggedly, agonisingly conscious.

He rested his head on his upper arm. His hair, sopping wet from sweating out the hard labour of pain management, lopped into his eyes. Droplets of salty water fell onto his sockets, slashing at him with their iciness. Isolated patches of unblemished skin on his shoulders bristled in the knowledge that the No Man's Land winter was fast approaching.

The rest just burned, bloody and sore, a nauseating reminder of his uncle's threat.

Too weak to shake the freezing salt water out of his eyes, he closed them. It hurt to even do that. His eyes, the lining all around, the very ligaments and even the lashes seemed to take on his body's aches. He raised the lids a little and looked at the straw-flecked blackness at his feet.

The sharp odour of his own body plucked at his sinuses. Like an angsty prisoner, it repelled itself off the walls of his throat. He tried to swallow it. But, for all the cold sweat, his mouth was dry and his throat scorched. The smell tumbled through his insides and rested heavily in the pit of his stomach. And there it cringed and coiled, as though desperate to keep itself segregated from the equally heinous and cloying metallic odour of drying blood. He moved again, trying to hold his head atop his spine where it naturally belonged.

Teddy's neck was in no better shape than his shoulders. He soon found he couldn't keep his head up. He returned it to his arm and resorted to shallow breaths. Anything deeper would bring on the nausea caused by his own disgusting scent.

His shattered heartbeat couldn't handle his breathing's haste. Seconds passed and then he desperately drew in a long, replenishing lungful of air. His torso expanded and the millions of cuts and abrasions that covered his back split open again. Unbound crevices in his flesh bubbled with fresh bleeding, and any untouched skin cracked under its plastering of spilled, congealed blood.

The effort of taking that one luxurious gasp had depleted the internal stock of serenity that he'd all too painstakingly scraped together. Teddy screamed in pain. He gurgled profanities. He opened his eyes fully and stared vacantly ahead. His back began its arduous task of knitting itself together, starting with the burst banks of the many gashes put there by the hickory switch of his own uncle.

Teddy's spirit was gone now. It'd left him a long time ago, when the slicking seemed to have been going on for hours. When each swipe took on an agony of its own, smarting for an eternity, not quite diminishing before the next one stung, in exactly the same excruciating vein. When the whoops and cheers for more from his cousins had melded into one continuous whine. And when the blood had gushed out of him, glooping and bleeding and never failing to entertain. That was when his spirit had submitted to their wants.

Like a bewildered, caged beast, it had cowered in a corner of his mind, separated from the need for hope from his soul and the yearning for strength from his heart. Only when he'd cried out that he'd never leave the Cross Truss, that he'd work extra hard, never asking for anything in return and never, ever again would he be tempted to fight back. When he'd apologised to Erastus, for what he couldn't remember, and to Kenny for something else. When he'd promised on the CrossT brand that he'd give them everything he had left — then they had stopped the barbaric corporal punishment.

So, now he hung there, stinking and blood-stained, thinking not of his outrageous behaviour as he'd been instructed or, as he most probably should do, how he was to get out of the barn before they returned; but of love and of family.

'What have they done to you this time?'

Teddy raised his eyes as much as he could without actually moving his head. He could see no one. The barn was in darkness. It was the middle of the night. He shut his eyes again.

'So, the rumours are true.'

Teddy could sense no presence. Nary one could he smell another person. Of course, it was entirely possible that the potency of his own odour blotted out all others. The barn was all-to-pieces empty.

'One of the Slicker posse. Who'd have thought you'd be related?'

There was definitely a voice; it had a note of awe in it. Teddy tried to move his head. Again, his skin split with the stretch of his movement. Again, his muscles graunched. He grimaced and then stopped moving.

'Who's there?' he murmured.

His voice was little more than a croak. He badly needed water.

'The old slicker has nearly killed you, ya? You don't think that next time he will, ya?'

Thunderation! The German – the one he'd heard in his head just a couple of weeks ago, when he lay stricken with the cauterisation of his finger. That German. He was here again? Now?

That German was the Devil. Teddy woke up suddenly. It wasn't as though he'd been dozing, he hadn't, he couldn't, but now; now he'd been spoken to by the Devil, it seemed as though he had been asleep. He stood on his feet: the shot of pain that had become standard each time he used them, seared up his calves, exploding into his thighs. He craned his neck which cracked sickeningly. He glared at the repeated whiplap that held his hands tightly together, connecting him to the rafter. Darn it, he'd tried to get out of it when the first switch had hit. He'd failed and then become distracted. He wrenched his arms to and fro, trying to gain some slack.

'You tried to kill Moon,' he muttered. 'You ripped up the prairie and threw the fire at Dent.'

'Stop,' the Devil said.

Behind Teddy the sound of laughter played at being hearty, healthy. But it was hollow, as though it had no real sense of mirth in it at all. The Devil had no heart. And as for healthy, Teddy reckoned the Devil had none of that either. Trying to get a grip on the rope between his hands, Teddy strained to galvanise his muscles, heave his body up and get his feet off the ground. He really wasn't sure how it would help, but he had to do something to get away.

'Stop, please,' the Devil said, 'I can't do any of that earth-moving stuff.

You flatter me…'

'No, I don't,' Teddy interrupted him. 'You're twisting my words.'

He tried again to tense his biceps, set his shoulders and yank hard on the rope, but the simple act of keeping himself upright had weakened his muscles. They refused to work. Wincing was all he could do.

'I can do a great many things,' the Devil said. 'Things you wouldn't believe.'

'I can believe anything. Quit patronising me with your whimsical blarney.'

The Devil's laughter halted like it had been all an act, and now there were more serious matters to attend to.

'Ya, you can, can't you?' he mused, 'I mean look at you. For a moment there, I think you really believed that those brutes were the Devil and his spawn, ya?'

Teddy couldn't answer. He hung his head. His hair dripped coldly. The truth was, he had considered it. When the hickory switch had shown no mercy to his anguished begs for a let-up, he'd considered it. When the three slickers had whooped and hollered at the bloodletting, he'd clung to the hope that his heart wouldn't let him be turned outlaw. When Silas, or perhaps Erastus, flicked the switch, once again opening up one of the singeing, searing, very first gashes, sending sparks of pain whizzing, like flames along lines of black powder, across his skin, he'd been almost sure of it. His parents were good people, he was sure of that too. So, how could Uncle Silas be the Devil? And, if Uncle Silas truly was the Devil, then who was this chap he was talking to now? He said nothing.

'But, believe me, my treasure, when I say I cannot move the earth or throw things about without using my hands. And I cannot control the weather.'

Teddy frowned. He'd always imagined the Devil to be made of nothing.

Well, perhaps not nothing as such, but a mass, an entity of some sort, reddish with black vacuums swirling in its murkiness. Frowning hurt, so he stopped doing it.

'There was an earthquake that night,' the voice said, its complicated accent nightmarishly soothing. 'It was over in Kansas. I suppose, out on the prairie, it may have been that, that you all felt. Ya?'

It was as if the voice had no body at all. No all-over, personable aura, no roundness, no breath. Then something touched him. He tensed. That hurt, too. He breathed hard, measuring inhalations before trying to stretch the rope again.

'Teddy, my treasure, please don't tire yourself any more than you already are. Not on my account. I don't want you to get any more hurt tonight.'

'Then why,' Teddy growled, 'are you here?'

Giving into the pains once more, he stopped struggling. He was conforming to the German's request. He hated himself for it, but the respite, however momentary, may as well have been a month spent in the healing spas of Eureka Springs.

'I want to help you, clean you up, stop the bleeding and the hurting, ya. It must hurt. Does it hurt?'

Teddy closed his eyes. Wasn't it obvious? He rested his head against his arm again. Foolishly, he flinched as the stench of his own body kicked the back of his throat. He puffed out pain through parched lips, the deep ridges in them breaking open, and then the crests chafing back in on themselves. His breaths were quick and sore.

'Yes, darn it,' he whispered, 'it hurts.'

Dainty fingers touched Teddy's lacerated back. The lust-filled stroke was subtle, so silky that any normal human being wouldn't have felt it, but Teddy's flesh was open, and his nerve ends raw to the touch. He bristled at what he reckoned could only be the touch of the Devil.

'Don't touch me,' he groaned.

'You feel that?' The voice sounded surprised. 'Oh my treasure, you must be right at death's door, ya?'

'I ain't dead yet,' Teddy said. 'Ya?'

He did want so badly to sleep, though. He wondered grimly if that were the same thing as dying. His next thought scared him; it didn't seem so bad.

'Good, I don't want you to be dead. If you were, then I would not be able to be here …'

Sakes alive, there was no end to this guy's blarney.

'So why are you here?' Teddy said. 'Why is it that you show up every time I get into some blood-soaked mess?'

'Teddy,' the voice patronised him again, 'blood-soaked messes seem to be your thing. Is what I like about you. Trouble is always finding you, and you make such a bloody job of it. And those three…'

The voice paused. Teddy frowned, the pressure on his eyes flashed like angry punches at the forehead of his skull. The freak was stuck for words. A menacing promise of more aches stopped Teddy's grin before it had formed. The Devil shouldn't be stuck for words. He was supposed to know everything, wasn't he? Just like the Christian god was supposed to know everything.

'I don't know the translation for "Neid". I am sorry, is remiss of me. Those three brutes, if they had killed you, there would be nothing left for me. Or you, for that matter. And they would have done nothing more than win themselves some silly human satisfaction.'

Teddy sighed.

'So, they left me for you,' he whispered. 'What am I? Some sort of sacrifice?'

'No, although you make a very suitable one, and I do want to drink your blood. But I don't have anything to do with them up at the house. And

I don't know what they plan to do with you. Except to kill you; in some inexplicably bloody way, I think, ya?'

An unbearably painful reminder that he could no longer hang on his arms scoured across Teddy's torso. He shifted to his feet enduring the hot, tearing fires, hot as glowing, branding irons peeling away his soles. Again. The German was probably right, much as he hated to admit it: his uncle and cousins did seem to like practising violence on him.

'Please, Teddy, my treasure,' the voice said.

The pounding that ravaged Teddy's feet wound its way through his calves, numbed his knees and throbbed in his thighs. As it began its powerful repetitions, he moved to standing on one foot only. Instantly, the pains stopped in the alleviated leg, but doubled in the remaining one.

'Let me help you out. Ya?'

Teddy swapped feet. The pain became unbearable. So he returned to hanging on his arms. The tendons pulsed as though they'd rip right out of his shoulders. He closed his eyes and tried to ignore the pain. That hurt, too. So he screamed out his frustration.

'Stop. Don't cry, Schatzibar.'

'I ain't cryin'. And I ain't shitsiboo.'

The man touched him again.

'Don't…' Teddy croaked.

'Ya, ya.' The touch disappeared. 'Come on, Teddy, say you'll let me drink your blood. You've already shed enough. A little more won't hurt. Is easy, ya? Help me, help you. Ya?'

Teddy kept still and silent and tried to exude resistance.

'If you say you will let me, then I will take away all the pain.'

So, this guy was no different to Silas. There was the same want for Teddy's consent to some or other bloodlusty gain, a gain which held nothing but misery for him. It just came in a different accent, was all.

'You will be mine, of course.'

And there was the clincher. Teddy thought of the code, of the promise he'd made. If he left the Cross Truss, with or without the Devil, he'd be branded a liar. A cowpoke with a broken bond. No better than a horse thief, outlaw in need of a lynching.

'But remember,' the German said, 'I can take all this pain away. Being mine is a small thing to pay for my dispensing of all this horror, ya'

What was Teddy's promise worth to a bunch of liars anyway? It was common knowledge that Silas Truss and his boys were bunko artist liars. Aunt Laura as well, most likely. They were rustlers, too, and murderers.

'Your uncle will think you are dead.'

And, hang fire, hadn't he just taken a lynching?

'Then you can come and bite back your revenge.'

Teddy didn't want revenge. He wanted love, someone to want him, to want him to want them in return.

'Come on, Schatzibar, we will share, ya?'

'No, leave me alone,' he said, miserably shivering, cold all over now, 'They'll come round. And I'd rather belong to them than you.'

'No, they won't "come round", as you say. They're pretty nasty.'

'Sling your bunk.'

'Schatzi —'

'Stop touching me. I ain't no shatsey.'

Teddy waited for the response. The German would try to persuade him again. He seemed to have taken a shine to him.

Teddy heaved in an agonising lungful of air. The lashes opened up again as his ribs expanded. He opened his mouth and screamed away the pain, but that just wasn't enough. So, he stretched his mouth wide again and hacked out a sort of barking, coughing noise. He stood on his feet and pain rushed up his legs, slicing into his loins. He hollered and swore and then coughed again. Tensing his muscles and cussing, he yanked and agitated the rope. He spat out death threats that he knew he wouldn't keep, and eventually hung there, his body flinching and jumping with pain as he sobbed into his arm.

When finally he fell silent, dreaming of a loving family again, the rope slackened. It uncoiled, whipping around the rafter until, totally loosened, it dropped. Teddy's legs, unable to support the unexpected weight, collapsed. He sank to the floor and lay there, alone in the straw-flecked darkness.

The dawn broke. No Man's Land would be beautiful under the autumn sunshine again. Teddy slunk away.

CHAPTER TWENTY-FIVE

Alone in the darkness Teddy lay, curled onto one side, his arms stretched in front of him, his hands clasped in each other. Rather than the pulsating of the scars that patterned his back, those scything slashes that were by now malevolently familiar, it was the nip in his belly that niggled him.

For one more minute, he resisted the pestering of his mind to open his eyes and the harassment of his stomach to get up. Instead, he attempted to open out his hands. He fully expected his fingers to be rusted into fists that held tight to a restraining rope. Nope. No problem at all.

The moment that he did open his eyes, Dunc grinned at him. Teddy gazed lazily around, heartened by his tomb. Impressive; he hadn't thought he was capable of such a thing; he didn't have a heart. Something was happening inside him, it was homely, secure, comfortable. He liked it.

He ran his hand dreamily along the curved edge of his stall; the concrete had worn down over time and now it shone colourfully like stained glass refusing to be outdone by the night. His fingers tripped and tumbled over it. No sensation in the tips.

He lay straight, staring at the cobwebs that, dangling just shy of his nose, swathed the ceiling in architectural swags. His stall was more like a comfy, cosy bunk and the tomb was more like a chiffon-swathed boudoir. He turned back onto his side and leaned over the edge, smiling at Ike below him. Ike looked serene this evening in hazy grey and mottled spidery earth.

'Ike,' he said, 'it sure-fired is good to see you this evening.'

Teddy's stomach twinged again. It began to coil inside him.

'It ain't good to see you,' he mumbled. 'Cain't deny it mind, after that memory, my day…I mean night, should be a whole heap worse.'

The scampering of critters, too obsessed with eating to evolve, came to his ears. It amused him. He smiled. That wasn't normally the case. Usually, they didn't bother him either way. The vermin were tuck, that was all.

Hanging further over the edge of his stall, he stretched an arm down and flattened his hand on the floor. Arching his back and scuffing his boots on the ceiling, he flipped free of his bunk. Between his feet, he trapped one of the many rats that so rudely and yet routinely scavenged this home of the deceased. He smiled at its squeaking, beeping noise jumped up and, folding his knees high, squirmed so that he could snatch the rat from his feet. The exercise reminded him of leaping through his own rope's loop.

Unwittingly, he wondered if he'd ever be able to revel in the curl of Elizabeth's smile at his roping skills. The rat was plump and he sucked out its blood. The sensation of nutria against his lips or even fur on his tongue wasn't there. Teddy landed messily, bouncing and hopping. Or, he wondered, what about the amused twinkle in Elizabeth's eyes, over the daft ironies that were Cleve, Moon and the others?

Another rat sidled along the base of Dunc's resting place. Darn those interloping varmints, they just didn't learn. Teddy stamped down hard, crushing the tail under his boot. The rat squeaked and mockingly, childishly, he squeaked back. Bending to it, he scooped it up and drained it, pumping the pudgy body absently as though he had better things to think about. Elizabeth.

Hunger pangs averted, he tossed the two lifeless vermin up through the hole in the ceiling. Then Teddy sat on the floor, closing his eyes and relishing a more than welcome, yet oddly misplaced, intense contentedness.

'Well, at least now I know what happened in the Cross Truss barn,' he said, lifting his eyelids a little and eyeing Ike through his lashes, 'it was just a slicking, is all and László saved me.'

Thunderation! Dread, plunged to the bottom of his being, vanquishing the optimism he'd got up with.

'In all my born days, Ike.' he whined, 'It looks as though László might have been right.'

Teddy winced. Ike grinned at him. His very own memory had proven László to be right. Apple pie right! Teddy had indeed been worked like a slave on his own uncle's ranch. Most of the time he'd been worked longer, harder even than his horses. Then, his chores finished or not, he was worked over. Catawamptiously chawed up, it seemed. László had been right about that, too.

'No.' Teddy frowned, 'No, no no. László cain't be right about everything.'

Teddy stretched out his legs, leaning back gingerly against the wall. The itching and smarting of the slicking scars didn't happen. Teddy realised with a little lament, that he'd been expecting it. Perhaps this would be the end of it. Now that he'd recalled the slicking, the scars would stop their aggravating.

'There's been worse times than that though.'

He straightened Ike's bones.

'There's the time that László murdered me for one.'

He tossed a dust pebble at the opposite wall.

'And the time he sired me, fathered me, bit me, whatever the correct term is for it.'

More vampire stuff László had conveniently forgotten to mention during that long, drawn-out brainwashing process.

'No how,' Teddy said, 'Ike, the slicking had happened before László vampirised me.'

Worse, had been the day that Pa had believed him to be a horse thief. That day jest didn't bear thinking about.

'There's a whole heap of things nastier than László.'

The scars had stung and pierced his flesh the time when he'd been hiding from Elizabeth. That very first time he'd seen her. Elizabeth: he smiled and then frowned at himself. Back then he hadn't known her name.

"Sexy."

Teddy's memory replayed him the pleasant sound of Elizabeth.

'Haulloa stranger.' he mused, laughing, contentedly forgetting the Cross Truss barn.

She grew more vibrant as he thought of her again. She gained an effervescence against the starkness of that night. She was his saviour, his heroine. She just didn't know it. Probably she wouldn't be very impressed if she did. Vampire saviour can't be something that too many people aspire to, can it?

As though to remind him of something, Teddy's neck stiffened. He mussed up his shoulders in response. His biceps twinged. He tipped his head right back and stared at the ceiling. The scars had hurt before that night, though, hadn't they? There'd been another time, hadn't there? It'd been when László had told him how he'd saved him.

'Sakes alive, Ike, that also was true.'

Teddy trembled. Panic set in, so did fear. László hadn't been lying. But it didn't make any sense. Not ten years later, László had found him and murdered him. Darn it, László had done a good job on him. Never quite lying. Always just fibbing.

Teddy hung his head. Resting his chin on his chest, he stared at his hands; they lay looking pathetic on his thighs. Thighs that now bore the blue denim of the stolen jeans. The ones he'd got just after he'd seen Elizabeth. Or was it just before? Ary way, she was beautiful, enchanting. Pain, as blistering as the lashing of Uncle Silas' hickory switch, ripped through the skin of his back.

'What in the blazes?' he snapped, darting away from the wall, rounding on it and glaring at it, as though it had done him some grave injustice.

There was nothing there. He contorted himself, patting his back.

'I cain't feel you.' Teddy said.

It seemed that his back would play up, reminding him of what it was like to be truly hated, whenever he was faced with the possibility of knowing shame. Or revulsion. Why would he need a reminder of his hate-ridden past when he thought of Elizabeth? To feel that from Elizabeth would be a whole heap worse than it had been back at the Cross Truss. He leaned back on the shadowed wall just below the hole at the other end of the tomb. The lines on his back twinged again.

'What in tarnation,' he yelped. 'I cain't feel you, I all-to-pieces, won't feel you.'

Then there'd been the time with László. That had been the first time he'd felt the scars. It'd been at the house, when… he faltered and ran a hand through his hair. The deer. The scars bit and piked again. He grasped his scalp, pulled his hair and stamped. The time when he'd remembered his murder. Back then, he'd had no clue as to what the scars really were. Now he knew. They were a keep-sake from confinement and control, a very real reminder to dread submission.

He wriggled back against the wall. Not so much as a whisper of a sense of touch. Surely, a memory as horrible as the night in the Cross Truss barn would have left him with a month of Sundays' worth of fingertip feelings, at least. But there was nothing.

'Never...' he tried again, gyrating and schmoozing his way up and down the wall, '...ever, again. Never will I ever be under anybody else's control.'

Sakes alive – he'd thought he'd got it licked. His doggedness to be free from László's control was so adamant it bordered on mutiny. The tethers that had held him were so intricately, cleanly cut, it was as though his seamstress had sought to make a tailor envious. The demon was under his control rather than he under it. In fact, the boot was so well fitted onto the other foot, it could be branded, patented by that very same tailor. Darn it, the demon was far from well behaved but, by its very nature, it would never be virtuous, pure, innocent. Like Elizabeth. Teddy stared vacantly into the space between Ichabod and Dunc.

What's the matter, lil' shaver? Erastus' voice taunted him.

He jumped away from the wall. Teddy's skin crawled; the scars scratched against his clothes.

Say it, you balmy...

Teddy shook himself free of the memory. Why tonight were his scars acting up as though they'd got hooked on a new musical?

'Addleheaded kid.'

Now Cleve was having a go at him. Still, Cleve had a point. Addleheaded described him perfectly, he was so, jo-fired at sixes and sevens. Thinking with his head had never been his strong point. And thinking with your head, rather than your heart, could keep a cowpoke and the rest of his crew out of trouble.

He smiled again. He so wanted to make Elizabeth laugh with the ingeniously ridiculous and surprisingly clean insults the cowpokes thought up and hurled at each other.

Teddy scowled. Carefully he wondered how Elizabeth would take the story of his losing his finger. The memory roused the fondness he'd had for that spring's Cross Truss crew. Now that he could recall it, he could tell her.

'No, hang fire,' he moaned 'I cain't tell her.'

She didn't know him. She probably didn't want to know him. He was a monster; pokerish folklore, a superstition that no one wanted to come to fruition. Perhaps also the reliving of the memory would hurt.

Teddy closed his eyes and tried to recall what he'd been doing just before he'd died that morning. It had to been a whole heap momentous to oust such a horrific reliving from his subconscious. Immediately, he saw Elizabeth's innocent face. He even heard her soulful voice and inhaled her captivating scent.

'Oh c'mon, darn-it,' he said. 'Elizabeth cain't be the cause.'

Focus, Ted…Theodore; concentrate, he told himself. There was the fight and the jeans. And of course, he'd seen Elizabeth.

'What in tarnation?'

That hadn't happened then.

'Sakes alive, concentrate.'

Saying it aloud might make it come true. He'd seen Elizabeth before the boy at the bandstand. Thunderation, his thoughts were a balled-up bag of nails. There had been the moths as well. And he'd seen Elizabeth again. He shut his eyes, screwing them up tight. He'd left it too late to feed, almost falling back under the hex of the demon. That had been right before Elizabeth had spoken to him. Darn it, she was so ding perfect.

'Ain't that the truth?' he said, smiling.

Then sensing the need that the statement needed fortifying, he gave it an ironic laugh.

'I sure-fired ain't perfect, though.' he said miserably,

In order to verify the truth, he raised his gappy hand in front of his eyes.

'Ain't seeing reckoned to be believing?'

He marvelled at his hand. It seemed to have taken on a milky, mesmerising appearance; even its missing finger was somehow fascinating.

'This ain't right,' he said.

He'd seen his hand before. Darn it, he'd been there when the finger had come off; it hadn't been a pretty sight then. He waved his hand around, doing the same with the other one. He looked like an illusionist at the carnival.

Slowing and turning his hands over, he waggled his fingers. Then he smiled, satisfied. Aside from the missing finger, his hands were those of a fit and healthy-looking young man. The long, straight bones danced up and down like the hammers on Ellen's piano. Was that what Elizabeth had seen? He hoped so. He shook his head.

'It ain't no shakes what she saw.'

His knees went weak. He let his legs fold under him and sagged to the floor. The ground seemed to come up a lot quicker than ever it had before. On the way down, his thigh connected with the edge of Ichabod's stall. Bumping off the concrete, his body jerked and thudded into Dunc's bunk on the other side of the narrow tomb. A little dishevelled and a whole heap disorientated, he finally settled on the floor. He laughed aloud; the ridiculous shindig had tickled him pink. Immediately, he clamped his lips closed.

'Lunkhead.'

He chastised himself for his own sappiness. Perhaps he should seek out the rest of those bad memories. Reiterate the need for keeping the demon corralled. He shuddered.

Nope, perhaps that wasn't such a great idea. Fearful that he wouldn't be able to cope with the emotions they'd raise and the effects that those emotions would wring from him, he'd buried the the memories deep. So deep they'd have too far to trail to be any more than an itty-bitty botherayshun to him. After all, in many of them, it was entirely possible that it would be he himself who was the one dealing out the debilitating pain. Now he knew only too well how it felt to be on the receiving end. Somehow the slicking had come back to him.

'Jest don't let them control you is all,' he told himself aloud.

He could do it. Especially, since he seemed to have been possessed by a euphoric notion that he could do just about anything. Nothing would control him again. Overcome by a delicious need to stretch up to his full height, he stood, puffed out his chest and flexed his muscles.

"*Hello,*" Elizabeth's voice said again.

Teddy was instantly ensnared in a calaboose of tree roots. The sound had been so bright, so seamless. It had been as though she'd been standing right next to him. He ducked down.

"*Hello.*"

The second time he heard it, her voice was softer, more cultured, if that were possible. Hang fire, it wasn't just that, was it? Both it and she, darn it everything about her, was smooth, exquisite. Like a precious stone that had been found in amongst the tack of the livery, she mystified him. He yearned to know where she'd come from. He hated the thought of having existed for so long without knowing her. He drooped. Squibob; he had a lot of hating to do.

'No. No hating. I am sure-fired done with hating.' He said.

Dirty, dust-ridden and tacky, cobwebs clumped in his hair. Darn it, he'd lived here for long enough, hadn't he? He should know the tomb's coordinates, the height of the ceiling and the width of the galley between the stalls better than the nose on his face. Which, of course, he hadn't seen for over a century! Ary, way; he could, if he needed to, get around in the pitch black. Closing his eyes, he decided to test out his theory. He pictured the tomb in his mind. He saw the floor and his nubuck boot toes as he stood on it, the ceiling, the hole in it that he'd made on his first morning there, Ichabod and Dunc's stalls, the empty one above Dunc and of course, his own. He turned and climbed back into it. And then climbed back out again. He adopted a sort of Ta-da pose and opened his eyes. In the millisecond it took for his eyes to focus, he saw Elizabeth's face and her kind smile. He smiled, too.

Darn it, he couldn't move without thinking of her, couldn't blink without seeing her or turn his head without hearing her say *hello*. And smiling. He seemed to be doing a lot of smiling this evening. A couple of times, it'd been a ripe old while before he'd even caught himself doing it.

Perhaps he was getting sweet on Elizabeth. He couldn't get sweet on her. Could he? He didn't have any of the components needed to get sweet on anyone.

'Seriously, Ike,' he said, 'the way she moved was just like a lullaby.'

Ichabod didn't say anything. Teddy dropped down to sit beside him. This time it was a clean movement.

'Pshaw, pardner, you ain't never, not by a jugful, seen nothing like her. She's a lady. She wore this light, little dress, it swayed and swished over her, rippling like a springtime mirage on a prairie morning. You better believe me, Ike, she was, I don't dare say, still is perfect, beautiful, silky, delicate. Darn it, I cain't find words wonderful enough to describe her to you.'

Teddy picked the stretchy, wool-like cobweb off his hair and ears and peeled it free his eyelashes. It was stubborn; no matter how much he tried to flick it away, it clung on. So, he watched it as it wafted on the tomb's infinitesimal breeze. The web's silvery, see-through threads sparkled in the night. It was pretty. Something else he hadn't noticed before meeting Elizabeth again. Twisting around, he wiped the web on his jeans. Scrunching up, he sat with his back resting on Dunc's stall, his ankles angled tightly and his feet squashed flat against Ichabod's. Ichabod grinned at him. He looked away, bashfully.

A rat scurried from its hideout somewhere in the darkness. Teddy smiled. Again. Those rats reminded him of purely purdy, red heifers scarpering from the shoot at the rodeo. The rat froze when it saw him. Steer didn't do that. The critter's shrewd eyes protruded and glinted like freshly washed berries on the frosting of a cake. The vampire, with its supernatural reflexes, pounced and won.

The rat, refusing to be taken quietly, whipped around and bit. It flipped its tail the other way and switched Teddy with it.

'Squibob!' Teddy shrugged.

The critter's coat looked to be velvety with a luxuriously charcoal sheen. Elizabeth's hair was just like that.

'Sakes alive, Ted.' he said, 'Elizabeth would not appreciate being likened to a rat.'

The rat squeaked and bit him again.

'Nope,' he told it, 'didn't feel a ding thing.'

He sank his teeth into its side, draining it in seconds. Nothing. No sense of touch. Yet his mind was chock-full of the smooth silkiness of soft, glossy hair, the depth of mysterious, dark eyes.

Perhaps, he was finally, in control of it all, finally, he could relish the moment without losing himself to it. He could transpose emotions, images, sensations onto those he needed to evade, without the pitfall of daydreaming. He'd be invincible again.

He stood and, stroking the rat's head, leaned on his stall. For most of his life, he'd been at the beck and call of his emotions, dreams and feelings. Well, this time around, he was the biggest toad in the puddle – this time around, they'd be at his beck and call. The only trouble was, he wasn't too sure how he was doing it. He slouched, one hand on his hip.

"*Dunderhead.*" Mattie's voice manifested in his head now.

Sakes alive, he couldn't keep his mind on anything. Hang fire, he was posing now? Teddy didn't normally pose. It didn't suit him. For some insane reason, that made him smile.

He straightened up and pitched the dead rat at the wall. It thudded. He smiled at that too. Without inviting it or receiving any warning, he recalled the first time he'd heard the pumping of Elizabeth's heart and was enchanted all over again.

He'd been lying in the gutter of a rooftop, he should have run away. But he hadn't. Elizabeth's voice, her heartbeat, her humanity, had enthralled him. Why hadn't it possessed him the way the blood of all other humans did? Perhaps she was stronger than the demon. He winced; perhaps not. But was she stronger than the demon's need to feed? Yes. Of course. The demon would always need to be fed, but Elizabeth's humanity was stronger. And so was Teddy's desire for Elizabeth to be safe.

His need for her love, was stronger. Elizabeth. Even said with his no-nonsense, half-the-time-proper, most of it lazy accent, the name was more melodic than Ellen's piano playing.

'Eelyezabuth. Ee-Lyza-Beth. Eelissabearth.' Teddy said

Now he tried to actively say it, it wouldn't come out right. So he just sat and thought of it, over and over again. Then he actually dared to wonder what it might sound like if she were to say his name... Theodore.

That was just too much. Elizabeth would never say his name, just like she could never see him, never know him, never love him. It was horse feathers to think that she might. They may as well have been on opposites sides of the world.

He let his shoulders slouch and stared at his boots. He may as well accept that he'd never see Elizabeth again. Melancholy swamped through him. Pokerishly strange, he seemed to warm to being that way. Incredulously, the miserableness seemed to soothe him.

A kind of rattling took possession of his middle. He knew that sensation, he'd had it more than a couple of times now. It was fear. Yet, he had nothing to be afraid of. This fear was dread at the onslaught of crestfallen sadness.

Teddy knew heartbreak, too. This couldn't be heartbreak, he didn't have a heart. It was more like hope-break.

His body was saying, 'Go get her,' his back was saying 'Don't do it,' and his mind wouldn't let him leave her alone. He leaned back on the wall and slid down it until he slumped, a crumpled collection of limbs on the dirty floor.

'It ain't never gonna work,' he told himself. 'Face it, you cain't have her.'

He closed his eyes, shifted about and settled on cross-legged. Clutching his ankles, he tried to focus on something else. Something from his past – his Cayuse, Spanish lessons with Ellen, being kangaroo-courted and dunked in a trough for sleeping in, driving Mattie into town, roping with Pa, caffeine and bear signs, Wichita, No Man's Land, the railroad. Anything! Elizabeth's affectionate laughter stopped him in his tracks.

'Lunkhead,' he said.

He was talking to himself. He'd been talking to himself all evening, hadn't he? Talking to Ichabod and Dunc, of course, didn't count.

'I'm jest gonna set here,' he told himself as sternly as his slovenly drawl would let him, 'and indulge myself in my memories of the Old West of America.'

He ran a hand through his hair and, looking himself over, straightened his belt. His boots had gotten grimy, so he scratched at the neatly stitched sole. He frowned as he chiselled out chinks of mud from the heel, flicking them away. The satisfaction at their whizzing through the air was a thrill in itself.

'What in tarnation are you doing?' he said. 'Anyone would think she can see you.'

He frowned and, once again, ran a hand through his hair. Elizabeth would chastise him fondly for not wearing gloves that day on the range. He'd argue that he didn't have any; she wouldn't let him get away with that for an excuse.

The hope-break vanished. Sakes alive, where was his willpower? He was all-to-pieces sure he'd had some. Immediately he resolved not to think about Elizabeth, there she was, in his thoughts again.

He'd forget her. Simply not remember ever seeing her in the first place. It wasn't like he hadn't forgotten people, places, times before. He could do it again. Acknowledge the corn... if László could do it, then so could he.

The way she'd stepped over the threshold of the bar, so carefree, so graceful. There was amiability in her every step. It was as though the very concrete became chivalrous to her delicate, sweet feet.

Nope, this dog ain't gonna hunt. He wouldn't be able to forget her.

'Theodore,' he whined, 'quit beating the devil around the stump.'

He was desperate to see her again. And again after that. It would be good. He could learn from her, he knew he could; things that only she could show him: places, people, feelings, writings, jokes and humour, songs and love.

And there he stopped short. Love. He could sense love within him. He knew love. He loved his family: his father, his mother, his sisters. He shook his head. This just wasn't the same. It was love alright, but it seemed other-worldly. It held something else, something unfathomable, some sort of bonus to the love he had for his family.

It was strange. It possessed him, but it didn't shackle him, and, he was more than content to be held in its hands. For a love so passionate, it didn't seem to care to be requited. He was happy just to love her. As long as she was safe. As long as she was happy. Nope, Elizabeth might never be able to love him, but, hang it all, he could, would and did love her.

As he sat there, smiling to himself, his insides began to burn. His fingertips tingled. He laid his hands on his belly, the place where he thought the burning was rooted. It moved. It swirled and swept around within him. He tried to follow it. Sparks spiked him wherever he touched. He wrapped his arms around his middle. His body was an inferno. Darn it, if only he had bodily fluids, he could so use breaking out in a sweat right now.

Twisting around, he stretched out. Yielding to the need for an anchor of some sort, he planted his heels on the wall. He was vaguely aware of Ichabod and Dunc watching him, grinning as though they were part of some very British society who knew the answer to this new sensation. Teddy flattened his hands against their stalls.

He stared hard at the ceiling, widening his eyes, letting in the darkness. He saw Elizabeth and his body began its sparking again. There seemed to be no hiding from it, this relentless probing up and down his whole form. Every inch of him was throbbing and he couldn't pinpoint where it started. Curiously, though, it did seem to have a destination. A common end where the pulsing and prodding met. Somewhere that he wasn't quite sure what to do with.

He tried to lie still. It took all his resolve. This sensation was divine, a little like the giddiness that came with whisky, except the disgrace of drunkenness hadn't come with it. This sensation had a wantonness, a mischievousness that was also rational and, somehow, he was in control of it. Or at least he should be.

'Sakes alive!' he squeaked, 'What is this?'

For the past one hundred years he'd been dead. It'd only been for the past one hundred or so nights he'd been exploring his emotions, his senses. And he'd never thought he'd ever have this one ever again. Cautiously, he lowered his hands, laying them flat on his hips, not quite sure if he should venture to that unmentionable area. He was a vampire, an undead, he couldn't see how or why he'd ever have a use for it. Now he had an overwhelming desire to find out about it.

Under his fingers and palms the denim of his stolen jeans was rough. Not only that, it was also taut. That discovery alone seemed to spark a fresh bout of the salacious fidgets. Teddy stretched his body out again, kicked at the wall and craned his neck to look at…he didn't know what.

He widened his eyes, desperately seeking satisfaction. And then he closed them in submission.

Elizabeth's face smiled at him again. He saw her bare legs as she strode from the bar, her hands as she waved to her friends.

Another ebb in the phenomenon relieved him and, gaining a little sentience, he inched his hands lower, inwards. He got the shock of his life. His body, it seemed, could respond and it certainly had, responded to the sensations fusing his nerves together. He didn't think he could do that. And what was to become of him now? He had no bodily fluids; that was something he knew for sure.

He snatched his hands back. Pulses throbbed throughout his body. He had to combat this. He didn't want to, though. It felt too good. So, he let it take him and do what it would with him, his body and his hands.

'Elizabeth,' he moaned, 'I do so love you.'

Finally, he lay still, quietly delighting in the sparks that were jabbing at him all over. All too soon they began to fade. Darn it, he was enjoying that.

'Come back,' he whimpered. 'Don't leave me. Do what you were doing.'

Slowly, starting in his feet, edging up his legs and through his thighs, careful now to avoid that region so new to him crept an essence of the sensation. Warm and in need of nurture, it settled in his middle, his chest and, even oddly, the top of his head. Teddy scrambled, his antique belt buckle clanking, to the far wall of the tomb.

'So, help me, Elizabeth,' he said, 'I sure-fired love you.'

Saying that felt good, too. He curled into the wall.

'I love you,' he said again, 'I love you.'

He scrunched up tighter. Sakes alive, this was what the boys in the dice house had talked about. He'd pretty much accepted that it would never happen to him. This was what Pa had told him about. He'd dared to imagine that it might just one day happen to him. This was what László had warned him to stay away from. He'd stupidly heeded that warning and given up on love. He refused to think about what had happened next.

Teddy smiled. Yup, he was under someone else's control again. *Elizabeth's.* This time, he knew it. He wanted to be there, and he would relish it. Darn it, he might even look forward to it.

Chapter Twenty-Six

For a long time, Teddy curled in his tomb savouring and murmuring his love for Elizabeth. He snacked on death-wish rats, indulging in the feel of Elizabeth's ebony hair,

After a while, when he'd run out of rats, he'd started to miss her. He had to see her again. He grew lovesick like the twenty-something that he was, and with twitches and an invisible tugging in his limbs, he began to pine. Just once, one more look at her. He needed that. Or he'd go insane. Then he'd leave, absquatulate, shin out, stall his mug from this place. He had no idea just where he was going to go, though. Back to the States somehow?

Hastily, he jumped at the hole in the tomb's roof. Hurriedly, he hoisted himself through. The woodland was in darkness, but by no means was it quiet. Kneeling amongst the vines that snaked over the mausoleum floor, Teddy smirked. Momentarily he was bewitched by the night-time ruckus.

'Thank the land; some things never change.'

Teddy gazed up into the woodland canopy. It changed constantly with the wind. The patch of sky beyond though, was a bland blat of unmoving brown. Leaves of all different shapes fell in Teddy's face. Anxious for a clear route to his love, he swiped them off. All clues of the town were blown away by the wind. Sound waves swooped about the trees, sparkling turquoise, teal and cobalt.

Standing straight and unable to stop the fidgeting and flexing of his fists, as still he could, he lowered his eyelids and listened. The entire woodland stomped and zoomed and busied about under thousands of tiny feet and wings. Some kind of fox barked and screamed, while something larger snuffled. A bird trilled out a long, guttural call. A bug-eater. He'd know that monotonous rasping anywhere or anytime. A chuck-will's-widow drilled out an answer.

The branches creaked; the sound waves transformed to bottle and lime-green. They curled, reared and bounced in the wind.

Nighthawks, bug-eaters, chuck-will's-widow: Teddy remembered their calls. They lived in pine trees. There were lines of pines near the house with the driveway, across the road from the field, on the way into the town. The wind blew again. The sounds peaked, and then troughed, red around objects too robust to move. They painted a map through the trees. Teddy set off toward the birds, the town and the love he'd thought he'd never have.

He vaulted over trees that had fallen long ago across his path and bounded and swung over bramble-tangled bushes that stood in his way. Obtruding branches snagged on his clothes and he wasted time unpicking himself. He stood flexing his hands, watching the woodland, plotting his path before running again.

Coming alongside the nastily fissured trunk of the first pine, he leapt straight up. Hooking his hands over a bendy, red-brown branch he began flapping and writhing his weightless body, oscillating in rhythm for the next gust of wind. Letting go, the wind carried him, flying feet first over the needles.

As usual, his landing was messy and he half-tumbled to the front lawn of the house. The same as the night before, he shot across, gauging and jumping the hedge opposite.

Low, bushy crops with fleshy leaves had taken the place of the arable.

Teddy smiled. He hadn't noticed them the night before. Remembering that a cowpoke is always considerate, Teddy skirted the crops, keeping to the edge of the farmer's field.

Hunger began to twinge distantly inside him. Darn demon, the only way to stop it nagging him would be to become it again, and there was no way in tarnation that he was ever, ever going to do that. Slowing to a trot, he scanned the field. Little, blood-red dots jumped and mingled in the plants and around the arable. Teddy squatted to take a closer look. They were bugs; some species of striped orange and black, ant-shaped cricket. There were heaps of them, too, and they were making a meal out of the plants' leaves. Just like topping the meadows on the range, he picked them off as he passed. The only difference was that, this time, he ate his pickings; he'd never eaten the "topped" dead heads. The seeds made the horses sick — dickens only knew what they'd do to a person.

At the last plant, his stomach might have settled, but his love for Elizabeth, his desire to see her again, had heightened to catastrophic proportions. He had to get to the town.

'Elizabeth,' he muttered, 'my love for you is so strong…'

Love is horse feathers, there ain't no such …'

'You can slide, mister… it is stronger than any hold over me that you might have.'

Just to be on the safe side, though, he stopped and picked up a hand-sized stone. Whacking it once on the hard road, it split in two. He pocketed both pieces. Now all he needed was the tinder for his spark and he'd have a campfire.

Arriving at his usual spot: the park beyond the university buildings, he ran to join a group of people milling about on the pavement. The colourful garb of the ladies was torn, yet sophisticated, floaty and perfectly asymmetrical. For others the material stretched so tight over their curves and figures, he thought they must've neglected to put their dresses on.

The heels and even the soles of their fantastically patterned shoes were impossibly high. If it wasn't for the informally dressed boys among them, he'd have thought he'd come across a travelling theatrical troupe. The red of human warmth escaped from ladies' skin like steam from a railroad boiler. Never before had he seen so many wonderful womanly shapes or skin. A lurid, red-lit, one-room crib skulked in the recesses of his memory. He blinked it away and shifted his gaze; "never had he seen so much womanly shape or skin", outside before. Occupying his mind with a wish that he had a coat to give, he moved among them, trying not to touch them.

He couldn't see Elizabeth amongst this crowd. Which, in a disconcerting way, he was glad about. He closed his eyes, concentrated and listened out for her. He couldn't hear her. An unbroken, high-pitched tone droned on in his head; squawking and cackling constantly dinged in his ears, the hubbub around him may well have swallowed up her voice. So he focussed on the kindness, the roundness of her intonation, the compassion he'd heard, not just the first time, but last night as well. Still he couldn't hear her. He was about to move on when his shoulder was bustled aside as a young man bumped into him.

'Sorry, mate,' the young man said.

His eyes were so wide, their dark pupils unnaturally massive and he swayed. He seemed to be trying too hard to focus. Teddy said nothing.

'You alright, mate?' the young man said.

Acutely aware that he'd been in this exact situation the night before, Teddy realised that he needed to leave — right now. The young man stumbled, his feet falling over Teddy's long-toed boots. Teddy reached out to steady him.

'I'm good. Take care now.'

It was the only thing he could think of to say. The only thing that might just be close enough to the language that these people spoke. The young man tried to right himself; the more he did, the worse his fall became. His feet wound themselves up in his legs. He bumbled and slurred. Teddy grasped his arms, stopping him from falling down completely.

'Jeez, your hands are cold.' the young man said, slapping his hand over Teddy's. 'You sure you're alright.'

The young man held on tight.

'Yes, I'm good,' Teddy said.

'Are those your teeth?' the man slurred, weaving low and peering up as though to look under Teddy's top lip.

Dang! This boy wanted to chat. Of all the people drifting about here, Teddy had found the one that wanted to get to know him. He didn't have time to chat.

'Smithy!'

Another one, much the same, perhaps a little older, slung his arm around the young man's shoulder and leaned on him.

'There you are. Where you been?'

Now Teddy was supporting the two of them. Over their heads, he watched a car come close to the kerb. It wasn't Elizabeth's. Wrong colour. Wrong driver. The door was opened and after some unladylike argying, four of the young women jumbled inside and the car pulled away again. It was replaced by another. The cluster of people at the kerbside would rapidly be depleted.

'Nowhere, man,' Smithy said. 'You disappeared with that guy.'

'Oh yeah. That was ages ago.'

The absent conversation was tiresome. Teddy wished the young man would let go. Perhaps he should say something.

'Here, Del,' Smithy said and after a frustratingly long delay, Del smiled. 'You're a dentist. Dr. Del; take a look at this guy's…'

Smithy tried to stand up straight and regain focus on Teddy. All he achieved was a clutch on Teddy's other arm with his other hand. Teddy gazed at Smithy's hold: it reminded him of a blacksmith's cast-iron tongs.

'...I'm sorry, mate,' Smithy said, 'what's your name, again? Teeth. Oh yeah!'

'Vet, man,' said Del, 'I'm a vet.'

'They're all the same, aren't they?' Smithy smirked.

Both began a grunting, shaking, uncontrollable giggling. Erastus and Kenny all over again. A newfound hate began to rise in Teddy. He really needed to leave this place now.

'Show us your teeth, mate,' Smithy said.

Teddy placed a hand over Smithy's and closing his fingers around its sides, he squeezed until he heard the crackling of splintering.

'Giss vart my nayme iss?' he said, overstating his grin and widening his eyes.

He sounded terrible, but given that these two were drunk, and as such their consciousness would be soft around the edges, their imaginations high as a bucking hoss's hind legs, he opted for pretending to be a vampire. As László was his only role model, he tried to imitate him.

'Give me yourrrr blud. I varnt to drrink your blud.'

Teddy laughed; he was no good at impersonating anybody, be they Hungarian, British or otherwise. Thank the land, though, Del and Smithy took it completely the wrong way. They each turned to hurry away; they bumped into each other. Del, a little larger and heavier, lost his footing, grasped Smithy around the middle and took him down in a cosy sort of tackle. The upshot was that Smithy let go of Teddy's arms.

'Jest yanking yer donkey.' Teddy smiled, regretting again that he didn't have a hat to tip.

Before anyone else there got the notion that he was worth a chat, he jostled away through the crowd not caring who he hassled. He headed for the main street. Reckoning that from now on his best gamble would be to avoid all contact with people, he climbed the side of a building. From the top he scrutinised the street. The town was pretty much empty. Elizabeth was nowhere to be seen. He ran along the rooftops, leaping dividing walls and diving over gaps. At the other end of the row, he scanned the town on the other side. Still nothing, other than the odd scrunched-up body in the odd doorway. Elizabeth had to be here. He'd seen her twice now, both times in this town. She had to be here somewhere.

The clock on the town hall tower chimed. Half past whatever the hour was. He looked to the sky. The stars would tell him what the time was. The sky remained an overcast smudge, although now with the street's lights, it was orangey-brown. Darn it, he'd have to rely on his body clock.

A far-off dull and disconnected screech filled his ears and for a moment he stopped to listen. The noise ended the same way that it had begun — suddenly. The low and elongated mooing from the harbour took its place. Teddy shook his head, straining for any sound of Elizabeth. A masculine voice somewhere was swearing. Another one was sobbing. Otherwise, the town was quiet.

A figure moved along the middle of the street. It hopped up the kurb and headed towards the quay. Teddy's stomach flipped. He dove off the roof. Falling head-first, he reckoned, would be the quickest and most direct route to the ground. Nary one was the building that high; three, maybe four storeys with a porch that ran its length. Using it to break his fall, Teddy caught hold of the threshold in a handstand. The weight of his boots tipped him backwards towards the ground. He landed flat on his feet.

The wind skittered crumpled leaves and empty paper cups over the complicated crossing, the road and path. Teddy let it carry him along the road, alighting on the opposite corner. A grease-smeared newspaper clung to his leg. He stomped and shook until it dislodged and bowled on its way.

The figure had disappeared. Teddy ran to look over the top of the hill. The railroad station at the bottom was dark and empty. Everywhere was closed up for the night.

'Dang!' he said, he should be better at this.

He turned away and kicked a drift of leaves: they swooshed into the air and then spun and dispersed in a wind-devil of fiery colours. A pigeon burbled its discontent at being disturbed and waddled nonsensically out from the safety of its roost. It'd almost completed an indignant about-turn, before Teddy pounced.

The ships mooed again and the clock struck. Still no sign of Elizabeth anywhere. Teddy pitched the drained pigeon onto the railroad track and headed back to the bar where he'd seen Elizabeth last night. Surely the bar would still be open. Elizabeth should be there.

The bar's doors were closed, the furniture stacked in front of them and, save for the white of a lamp atop a pole, darkness was the only light. There were no people around at all; anywhere. Bars closed a whole heap earlier here than ever they had back in the Old West. It wasn't even Sunday. Teddy frowned. Friday, that paper had said.

Slowly and just a little dejectedly, Teddy walked to the large plate window. A little afeared that his dirty hands would smudge it, he touched his nose to it and peered inside. The reflection of the flagstones, the lines and mortar in between, the canvas cordons around the patio area and even the colourless furniture were highly detailed in its surface. Teddy was not. He cupped his hands around his eyes, leaned in closer and stared harder. It didn't help. The darkness all around him had turned the smooth, polished window into a mirror. One which Teddy could not manipulate. Ary way, there was no sign of life. Teddy thudded his fists into the glass. A tiny crack, no bigger than a whisker, appeared.

'Darn it,' he said.

Hurdling the cordons, Teddy ran the length of the yard to the unkempt service road that ran the other side. He looked this way and that, up and down the road. There was no movement at all. Just the wind blowing the sounds of the park around.

Teddy ran back to the other end of the yard. The main road was empty, the crossings silent and still, buildings were dark, doors and windows were closed, there wasn't even any bunting or banners wafting around aimlessly. He closed his eyes and listened out. Insects chitter-chattered, cats prowled their beat and there were the calls of the wildlife, but there was no sign of Elizabeth.

It was no good: Elizabeth was gone. The nothing that was Teddy's insides balled up in a great knot of anguish. He was overbearingly unhappy, like he was experiencing the loss of his oldest, greatest friend. He sat on the kerb and gazed at the sky, wondering miserably what the time was.

The wind had blown the cloud cover threadbare and, for a minute, the moon put in an appearance. A star twinkled weakly. Then another.

'Okay,' Teddy told himself, 'look for the Big Major.'

No, that wasn't right. It was something to do with a bear. The Dipping Bear? The Big Bear? Teddy tipped his head back as far as it would go without causing himself to fall over. He stood up and turned around a couple of times, squinted and realised he hadn't got a clue what he was looking for.

'Focus, darn it,' he said.

The sky must've been polluted by moonlight: the stars were too few. He looked for the moon. It was a skinny crescent. It wasn't casting much light at all. It looked more like one of Mort's toenails had been flung up there and snagged at one end; it now dangled precariously. Nary one was it particularly high.

Teddy straightened his neck which had gotten stiff. One of the canvas barriers behind him rippled in the wind. An unprecedented gust tipped one of the metal stands over. It hung there supported by those either side of it. Teddy's eyesight blurred as he contemplated the slumped enclosures. There was a sort of popping in his ears and his hearing seemed clearer, he listened to the sounds of his surroundings as though for the first time. The screeching of some or other bird twanged so loud it made him start. He screwed up his eyes. But he didn't do it intentionally, it was as though they'd closed on their own, as though they'd reacted to some sort of shock. Printed clearly on the back of his eyelids, he saw Erastus. Or rather, he saw the sole of Erastus' boot.

A wretched, frenzied urgency arose in him. He balled his fists and braced his biceps. Anger, a bent to hit back, possessed him. Erastus wasn't there, though. Erastus was long dead; safe from the retaliations of his younger cousin, the parentless boy that he had so readily abused. After all that time, Teddy was finally prepared, not to mention equipped, to fight back.

"Rastus!' he hollered, 'I should kill you for what you did to me.'

He seized the nearest of the canvas border stands and hurled it into the wall, its supporters following like streamers in the night.

"Rastus, you better thank the land I cain't get to you.'

Grasping a stack of chairs by the leg, Teddy flung it into those belonging to the bar next door. Thin metal clattered across the road, a table wedged itself in the hedge. Brazenly, Teddy laid waste to the bar's pavement seating.

'Come on, demon,' he yelled, thumping the window once more, 'Come on, if you're good for anything, bring me 'Rastus.'

The demon slumbered on.

'Don't ignore me, I can beef you. And him.'

Still nothing. The demon should be there; it thrived on his anger. Teddy grasped a fistful of his hair and yanked. It did no good. The demon was nowhere to be heard.

Finally, filled with humiliation, Teddy leaned on the plate-glass window.

It shattered and he stumbled. Rarely, if ever, did he lose his temper. He massaged the sides of his nose, although he couldn't be too sure why, it just seemed to be the best option when you've been kicked in the face, whether you can feel it or not. His fingers rose and rotated in front of his eyes. He even saw the pink and white nail of his ring finger and knuckle of the smallest one. But there was no sensation there. Not of his pudgy, pliable skin under his fingers, nor of the pressure that he was putting on his face. With all that emotion inside him, he should sense something, shouldn't he?

He stared around himself, hunting for some item that might trigger the memory of Erastus' boot again. Or his fists. His forehead, even. Teddy wasn't bothered which it was.

He ran across the unkempt road into the park. There was the bandstand, its fretwork so well meant, yet so spine-chilling in the dark. Its metal might do for what he had in mind.

Standing apart from it was the lightning-struck tree. From top to bottom the ancient, majestic tree's trunk had been ripped open. The remnants of its once strong branches were now little more than protruding barbs. Teddy smirked with the irony of how they were alike; although he was not now, nor had he ever been, particularly honourable. The tree's insides, however, were as dull and blackened as his own. An oak: much better.

Scruffy barricades as orange as Teddy's hair circled the tree. "Danger" and "Keep Out" signs animated by the wind tapped petulantly against them. Well, danger hadn't stopped him before, and that had been before he was dead. Teddy sprinted towards it. Just before colliding with the tough, mesh barrier he leapt into the air, alighting on its crest and immediately springing to the top of the tree.

What the Sam Hill are you doing now?

'Howdy stranger,' Teddy said, 'I reckon I'm mighty pleased to hear from you.'

He grimaced with the annoyance that he actually meant it.

'You can help.'

Darn it, telling the truth would make it withdraw again. Perched on the top of the broken oak, Teddy placed the palm of his hand on the tip of one of the wrecked branches.

'This ain't gonna hurt a hooter,' he told himself.

Just in case he was wrong, he cradled his nose with the other hand. Closing his eyes, he pictured Erastus. Then, just to be sure, he thought of Kenny and Uncle Silas. When he saw them clearly, their leering grins, the lust for bloodshed in their eyes and the way that they'd pretty much salivated as they took turns in describing the lacing they were about to give him, he jammed his palm onto the spiked oak branch.

Holding the gruesome picture of his only blood kinfolk in his head and with the taunting of their laughter echoing in his ears, he cautiously opened his eyes, and stared at the injury he'd just given himself. The wooden, spear-like branch pierced right through his hand. It should've hurt. With the memory of his bloodthirsty relatives firmly in his mind, the mere sight of such an impalement should've been sending shocking, debilitating surges of pain right through him. But there was nothing.

Sakes alive, shaney, you're staking yourself. You're a darn cultus yack.

Teddy smiled. He'd intrigued the demon.

Quit it. You'll hurt yourself. You don't want to hurt yourself.

'Nah, you mean I'll hurt you.'

This is horse feathers…

'You cain't control me. Not no more. It don't matter what I do, so long as I have…'

Horse feathers… First love and now this.

Teddy ignored the demon. He scanned the park, the yards and the bars, even the university buildings. It was night-time, the place was asleep. He narrowed his eyes and looked closer. A family of foxes rough-and-tumbled in the grass. Their teeth needle-sharp, they nipped and launched springy ambushes on each other.

Keeping one eye on the foxes, his mind's eye on his uncle and the rest of his consciousness on the demon, Teddy eased his hand back along the branch. The deadened skewer emerged. The tattered, empty hole in Teddy's hand was exposed. He smiled crookedly; he even had one or two splinters, they reminded him of jerked beef. But there was no pain at all. He'd wanted, all too consciously to stake himself. What he hadn't wanted was any sensation of it.

Teddy shook out his hand. Still nothing. He stared at the hole in his palm and saw the night sky on the other side. Nothing – no sensation of the agony it should be causing him. He'd succeeded in switching off his senses. Now could he switch them back on?

'Now for the tricky bit,' he said.

Acutely aware of how much he didn't want to know the pain of the torture he was inflicting on himself, he clutched the awkward treetop as firmly as he could with his good hand. Bracing himself, he hunkered down, setting his knees like rivets, tensing his thighs and squaring his shoulders. If this didn't work and the excruciating torment of staking himself shot him down, the last thing he needed was to fall onto the oak pikes.

He ran what should now have been a worse than defective hand through his hair and listened carefully to the foxes. Their yelps, squeaks and baby snarls reminded him of the ranch dogs' puppies. Little, half-feral beasts with floppy ears, bushy tails and big paws, they'd bedded down, a fuzzy family in his stables. They'd shared a common interest, those dogs, the horses and Teddy, and that was running so fast your speed hungry spirit was the only thing beating you, cornering so tight your shoulder grazed the ground; vast, exquisite skies that mirror the wide open prairies below, blue in spring, red in summer; but most of all: freedom.

The wood beneath Teddy's fingers was humid, even a mite doughy. He skimmed his thumb along it. The tree was starting to decay. It paled where Teddy pressed it. The air, acrid with the bite of wet charcoal, plucked at the back of his throat.

'Thank the land,' he said, 'they're still there.'

Suddenly he knew what it was to be shot in the hand. As though the bullet had passed right through so quick it left only singeing flesh behind, pain seared through his palm, into his wrist and up his arm. His limbs were enlivened with the absurd brutality of an undead's nightmare. Finding no heart to stop, it slithered back down his arm, tormenting his palm and, when deprived of flesh to chew on and regurgitate, it lingered there, tearing out an ululating throb.

Teddy teetered in his spot. He closed his eyes and cleared his mind, concentrating on nothing. Then he indulged in his love for Elizabeth. The tickling of the cut of her hair bobbing under her jaw took the place of the pain. He relished the delightful whimsy of her laughter. The culture and the kindness in her "hello"; outshone the special memory of the fuzzy family in the stables.

'Elizabeth,' he said, 'as long as I have Elizabeth, you, demon, cain't get to me.'

All sensation he may have had, any lingering trace of scent and taste, disappeared: only the warm satisfaction of love remained. Teddy rammed his hand back over the pointed tree.

'And nary one,' he said, sliding it up and down, twisting it back and forth, 'can anyone else.'

Chapter Twenty-Seven

Jumping down, Teddy fully intended to creep as close to the foxes as he could. Perhaps they wouldn't notice him, and he could pet them. His legs gave way and he collapsed onto the tree's orange fortifications.

He fumbled his way back to his feet. There was that drain on his energy, dragging at his joints. Death. He looked to the sky. Of course there weren't many stars. The diluting of the night sky wasn't coming from the moon; the dawn was coming. He should be getting back. He turned away from the town toward the university buildings.

Darn it, he was doing something, wasn't he? Something important. He got the notion that he'd been looking for something.

Run, skedaddle home.

Love. That was it. He'd been searching for love. No, no he hadn't. He had the love inside him. Love for Ma. No: Pa, Ellen, Mattie. No. This was his own love, borne from his own...his own what? Heart? He had no heart. Soul, then, did he have a soul? What did it matter? It came from somewhere inside him. No one else would or could do this love the same way that he could, and it was all for...for what?

The wind tripped across the park. It whispered soulfully through the autumnal stems of the nearby plants. Humming through smaller spaces, it sounded just like the Cheyenne, Grass dancing on the plains, singing and praying as they worshipped mother earth. It was enchanting, joyful. It reminded him of Elizabeth.

Elizabeth. He'd forgotten her. How could he have forgotten her? To forget her was as bad as selling his soul to the Devil. Hang fire, hadn't he already done that?

'Sakes alive, I cain't die now,' he muttered.

He hadn't serached the quayside. The quayside was dangerous. For a split second he entertained the idea of avoiding the other side of the hill, the old town walls and the sea. A train chuntered and hissed in the fussed-dark air. The lowing of the ships called to him.

'I cain't leave her,' he said.

To leave this town was to leave Elizabeth behind. Teddy turned and ran. He didn't pause at the top of the hill; he didn't have time. Half-skidding, half-toppling, he made it to the bottom.

A flurry of large, white-breasted birds circled above the port. Every now and then, one would plummet from the group. They were as big as prairie chickens. But prairie chickens didn't fly and sounded nothing like these birds. The ships lowed again. The quayside answered. Now those, sounded more like the muted stirring boom of the prairie chickens.

Teddy lumbered along the line of houses, businesses and bars. Clinging desperately to the reason for his being there, he climbed to the top of the town's curtain walls, and surveyed the area. His fantastic vision more of a tunnel now, he saw only one or two warm bodies. They moved with what seemed to be a mission around the quay. None of them were Elizabeth. Too heavy, they disturbed the natural flow of the airwaves too much. Or at least that's what he thought they did.

Nearer to the sea the wind blew stronger and Teddy was blown backwards. He flew clean off the top of the wall. The wind dropped. He fell to the ground narrowly missing the arrowhead spears of a wrought-iron fence lying there, unable to move he didn't care about death.

It was hopeless. He hadn't found Elizabeth. Disappointment drained him further than death ever could, and sadness swelled within him. He eyed the fence. That evening, he'd been so positive. It'd seemed so easy: find Elizabeth, look on her one last time and then move on. Yet, to acknowledge the corn, the task that he'd set himself was almost impossible. He reached out and wrapped a hand tightly around one of the fence's black bars. The dull pike was cold to the touch and the paint that had run unchecked was hard and unpickable. The wound that he'd given himself smarted. He stared at it as though he had no idea how it had got there. Ary way, it would be gone by night-time.

He could have thwarted all those sensations, dispensed with them and amused himself by his own control of them but he just didn't have the wherewithal.

'So help me, Elizabeth, I do so love you,' he slurred.

The wind, trapped between the quayside buildings, gusted in more of a torrent. It rattled leaves against Teddy's virtually lifeless body. A gloopy sump landed atop the fence that he was holding. A dark, red-pigmented splat dripped onto his hand. One of the birds, must've been the one whose turn it was to dive, had missed its calling, been caught by the wind and impaled on the fence post. Eyes staring, its immaculate white chest rose and fell erratically. At close quarters, empty, useless beak was quite lethal.

Ace in the hole, Addle-pot. Hide.

'I cain't,' Teddy moaned.

I cain't control you. You'll die.

'I don't care.'

Ted…

'Theo…'

There ain't no such thing as love. If you die, I win.

Just how the demon had worked that one out, Teddy was too plumb tired to place. If he died, it died. He twisted a smirk away from his lips. It worked — in one corner.

'You'll be a daisy if you do,' he said.

Some guy, sometime in history somewhere, had said something about being a "daisy". Sakes alive, Teddy couldn't remember who that guy was. Perhaps it was the demon. Ary way, the demon was trying to wind him up again and just like a truculent teenager, he bit at the bait. He had to get up.

He hurled his pathetic body over. Summoning his rapidly ebbing strength, he scrunched his middle and pulled himself up the fence bars, just like he was climbing a rope. Creasing an elbow around the railheads at the top, freeing up both hands, he inched the bird from its impalement. It twitched and flapped in vain. Keeping his tunnelled vision on its beak, Teddy sank his fangs into its chest and downed its blood.

The meal would gain him time when he awoke that evening to find another, but death might still claim him; there was no avoiding it. He dropped the dead bird. Grabbing the nearest railhead with his right hand, he grasped the next with his left, and, dragging his feet, pulled himself to the corner where the road turned.

A small, square, non-descriptive building, no bigger than a store cupboard, stood apart from the rest. It had no windows in its old stone walls and seemed to house nothing but its own door. Teddy, his limbs going wayward as though they'd been assembled backwards, and his body broken, approached it. He looked for all the underworld like he didn't care. He didn't have a single thought in his head.

The door was fastened securely with a latch, shackled through that was a substantial padlock. Teddy reached out and grasped the lock. Enveloping it in his fingers, he gave it a useless tug. He dropped it again, rested his head on the door and gave up.

If you die, you'll never see her again.

The demon certainly was encouraging him. He couldn't believe for one hooter that it had his best interests at heart. It had less of a heart than he did. Ary way, he didn't want to miss seeing Elizabeth again. He gazed at the strong lock. Thinking of pulling Taffy in Ma's kitchen, he closed half-dead fingers around it. The metal groaned as it rubbed against itself. Picturing the new gate he and the ranch hands had built for Pa's corral, he jabbed the lock downwards. Dang, those gateposts, taller than he was, had been heavy. And then Pa had decided the gate looked so good, he wanted to replace each and every one of the corral posts. Teddy grinned; the job had taken a lot of muscle, sweat and cussing, but after all that, it was a death-on decent corral.

Teddy stared at the padlock in his hand. It'd split in two. The latch fell open and he let himself into the building. The door was old, but the hinges weren't, and it swung shut behind him, plunging him into darkness.

Teetering at the top of stone spiral steps, Teddy started down. He misjudged the first one and tumbled head over hind the rest of the way. He stopped at the bottom, lying in a heap of limbs so broken, no living being could ever impersonate it. Clinging to his ridiculous dream that his love might yet be returned, he died.

* * *

When the sun went down that night, Teddy became conscious only of absolute pitch blackness. Slowly, he unfolded his incredibly curled limbs and then, unsure of where he was, lay still, awaiting reprisal. Nothing happened, no-one spoke and not even the darkness moved. Boots scuffing flatly, he rose to his feet.

By way of figuring out what this hole he'd woken up in was made of, he executed a half-hearted, flamenco type stamping. His Cuban-heeled hoedown dying muffled, like undeserved applause, he determined, the floor was made of old and earthy bricks. He hollered: 'Haahlloa, stranger!' and his own voice answered him, its sound ricocheting off the walls and then that too, disappeared. The place was as still as his tomb. More still, in fact. There was no sign of life at all.

'Darn it.' he muttered, 'No breakfast.'

Deciphering the place would be a whole heap easier if he had a light. He raised his hand in front of his face and waved it around. The air fluctuated with the ripples that he'd made. He stopped, forever thunderstruck at his overnight restoration, his hand was of course, fit and young. He waved again. The room around him was then revealed. It was large and apparently empty. It could be a hideout for him, a new home, although he might miss Ichabod and Dunc.

Teddy repeated his gesticulating with both hands. Purple and green waves emblazoned additional parts of the room. They bounced off arches and architrave, showing him shadowy alcoves in the walls. The whole place was old; in fact, he'd go as far as to say, ancient. The waves faded as soon as he stopped flapping, leaving him, once again, impotent. He flattened his palms on the nearest wall.

'Dunderhead,' he said, 'No sense of touch, remember.'

The Cross Truss bunk house on overcast No Man's Land nights, had been this dark. The stables had been pitch, too, when finally too sleepy to continue, he'd dowsed the kerosene lamp. Both were as rank as each other and both were surprisingly noisy for the middle of the night. Now he came to think about it, differentiating between the two was all-to-pieces problematic. Cowpokes, perhaps, got up earlier. Horses didn't sing or cuss in their sleep; but then, they did mumble and grunt a lot. The stables were marginally less stifling: he'd gotten a better night's sleep in there. But that led him back to the first problem – one too many lie-ins had led to many a trough dunk, whatever the weather, sometimes without even the consolation of a kangaroo court.

Under Teddy's calloused, cowpoke hands, the wall was cold, rough stone. He followed it hand over hand, venturing a little way into the unfamiliar room. Then he halted and repeated the waving exercise. Right next to him was a small, wall-mounted box. He tapped it. Short, stark sound waves rose, fussed slightly and expired.

The hotels in Wichita had had lights. They were flamboyant, frilly, gas-fuelled things. He smoothed his fingers over the ancient stone room's box.

The saloon had lights, too. Hang fire, the saloon wasn't in Wichita. He hadn't ever been into any other town. No, perhaps he had. He frowned, his memory of the saloon was hazy.

The box was made of some sort of hard-wearing stuff. It wasn't wood or metal or even carpet bag. Whatever it was, it was secure, smooth - some sort of newfangled stuff. Darn it, if he was ever going to be able to recognise anything produced since 1887, he'd have to recall those László times. A thin rope threaded out of one side of the box, and on the top, front corner was a switch.

Never one to shy away from an unknown outcome, Teddy flicked the switch. The rope buzzed. Teddy jumped away and the buzzing leapt around the room. Seconds later, lights came on. Teddy grinned; standing with one finger on the switch, he was guilty as charged. All around the room, basic, boxy and boring lights were attached to the walls at regular intervals.

The herringbone brick floor had been swept and what looked to be a fireplace in one end showed no signs of soot. Teddy was the dustiest thing in there. He couldn't stay here. Swept floors, working lights and a distinct lack of cobwebs meant someone had been here. Recently. He was lucky he hadn't been discovered. He grinned and the demon whined; lucky was a strange thing for a vampire to be. Another day holed up in this stone vault was not a good idea.

Teddy turned away from the room. He darted back up the steps and into the night, searching as ever, for food and love and a home.

* * *

Never would he ever stop looking for Elizabeth. Never, ever. So, he hadn't found her tonight. Or last night. But he would find her. One night soon; he knew he would. Until then, he'd keep guarded, he'd never forget her. So, it stood to reason that he'd see her again. Didn't it?

The town, despite its ancient fortress walls, its vaults, outhouses and history hundreds of years older than himself, was nigh on impossible to hide out in. Everywhere, it seemed, was populated; every nook and every cranny, even the darkest hole was adorned with gaudy, quirky-shaped writing, boogered-up names that not even cowpokes would come up with, and symbols that he'd never known; never in all his lifetime of being surrounded by the plains Indians. Nowhere, anymore, was secret. Nowhere would be deserted the whole day through and nowhere was ghostly. On the outskirts of the town, he had come across a sprawling cemetery. It was neatly plotted, trimmed and cared for. He gave it a wide berth.

This morning the sky was overcast again, and he lumbered like an inattentive drunk through the countryside. He did, however, have the sight of a supernatural being and so had little trouble seeing what was in front of him. Or to the sides. Or even miles away. It was just tunnel-like was all. Ary way, there was no traffic now. All humans anywhere near would be safe in their homes. Not that he'd break in. Even if he could, he plumb didn't want to. After all, it wasn't like he didn't have the know-how or the abilities. Yup, the humans were quite safe. From Theodore Callington, vampire extraordinaire, anyway. He couldn't vouch for their safety from each other though.

He'd return every night to the spot where Elizabeth had said, "Hello". He'd wait there, or in one of the other places he remembered having seen her. In respite from the offensive feeding of his obscene demon, he'd study his memories, rifle through them, tweezer out fragments that would lead him to her.

The town hall clock had struck every quarter of an hour. Teddy had caught its midnight chime and counted the tolls. It'd been somewhere between three and four when, once again, he'd discontentedly accepted that Elizabeth had gone. If, indeed, she had been there at all. But he preferred not to think about that.

He'd wound up taking a different route out of town; the many, varied signposts hadn't offered much of a clue towards finding his way back home. Home. He couldn't think of anything else to call the tomb he shared with Ichabod and Dunc. If nothing else, it was somewhere he could hide out every day. Plus, it was a source of food. So, he moseyed down this road between pine trees and ditches, hoping he was on the right trail.

Now, it wasn't as though he was on a timetable, was it? He had time and if he searched his whole life through, only ever finding Elizabeth on his final day, it would be enough.

The sweet, supping trill of a woodcock raced overhead. Instinctively, Teddy ducked. Either side of him tall trees, bare till over halfway up, stood in uniform lines like they were roll calling for the building of a new fort. A pine forest. The tomb's scrubland sat adjacent to a pine forest, didn't it? Perhaps this was it. He closed his eyes, listening for the chirpy drill of the nighthawks. Yup, there they were; along with a large, snuffling mammal.

He stared into the trees. Following one of the needle-strewn rides between the pines he noticed that, over yonder, the trees' formation petered out, becoming ragged and giving over to a tumble of unidentifiable vegetation. Then his view was halted by thick, gnarled trunks. He squinted, waved his hands in front of his face and, leaning into them, quipped: 'Bo!' Throwing the swirling sound waves that he'd made into the air between the trees, he watched as the colourful rings decreased and coned into the eye of a tiny tornado, before smacking into the trunk that barred his sight. The tree's bark was rugged with deep clefts, its leaves waxy, small and ugly. Oaks, large mammals and unkempt woodland. It was worth a gander.

Teddy turned and teetered at the side of the ditch-bordered road. On both sides deep, narrow troughs brimmed with brambles. Fertile, fleshy and yet malevolently spiny, they nettled around the pink bowing spires of some or other wild flower, choking it. A furry-leaved, mint-coloured plant curled and spiked upwards, cunningly moving in on the flower's space. Supernatural or not, he did not want to end up in there. Momentarily he frowned, absent-mindedly blanking out the ditch's wicked intent with the more troubling reason for its name, Bar-ditch. He couldn't recall it, so he shrugged. The movement too much, he staggered about and eventually toppled in.

Ensnared by vines and pinned by thorns, his clothes were smeared green and dotted once again with yellow stuff. He cussed, loudly wasting an inordinate amount of time untangling himself, only to discover he'd clambered back out onto the road.

'Sakes alive,' he groaned, lying face-up on the gritty surface.

Getting to his feet seemed like too much effort. His voice slurred a little. Darn it: daytime! He turned himself over and pushed up to his knees. Shaking his head, his gaze locked onto something else that seemed to have come a cropper in the ditch.

A car, black, large and shiny in places had crashed the trench, three-quarters of it hidden in the depths.

A grin pulled at the corners of Teddy's mouth. He eased them back in. His nose began to tingle and the excitement behind his eyes became dangerously tangible. It could be the demon awakening. But, just like usual, he'd kept it fed; it shouldn't be wanting for blood. Perhaps it just wanted out again.

Or perhaps the sensation had very little, pretty much nothing at all to do with the demon. It was a teenage, "life on the frontier", morbid curiosity to investigate the demise of others. Leave the crashed car, he told himself, move on. It was way past time he was back at the tomb anyway.

'I'll go in the trolleybobs of a bedpost.' he said aloud.

All-fired undesirous of adhering to his own weighing up of risks, he crawled towards the wreck. Burn marks, darker than the night, streaked the road, mapping out the car's final trail. Teddy hadn't noticed them before; he did now, though, his gaze being closer to the ground an' all. Twisting around, he tracked them, calculating and plotting them back to a natural camber in the road. The wreck had made one death-on gash in the ditch, before finally succumbing to the restraint of the undergrowth.

Sticking up in the air such that Teddy could perch on his haunches underneath, half of the tail-end axle was visible. The wheel was hugely wide, the tyre, too. But little else was showing; the car's underside was either in the ditch or clamped under metal covers.

In order to get a good look at the wreck, Teddy shuffled out into the road. The car was silent and unmoving. The doors were closed and from this side there was little damage. The driver and any passengers should have walked away, stumbled perhaps, but other than bruises, they'd be okay.

Stepping up to the car and recalling Pa saying, "It's made of nutria", he stretched to touch the smooth-looking surface. The memory was a strong one and for a second, missing his hat threatened to steal the moment. More than one silvery metal pipe protruded slightly from under the car's tail end. Teddy poked inside. The pipe was cold and lined with velvety, wet soot.

Teddy ran his fingers along the car's metal rim. Whoever had left the it there had been gone some time. It was as cold and wet as the pipe. Thunderation, bog-ridden steers out on the range got better treatment than this vehicle had. Teddy's feet twitched with the recollection of his first springtime round-up; as the rookie waddy, wading into pungent bogs to dig indignant steers back out had become his job. His fingers spasmed; darn short-handled shovel. Just like the ungrateful steer, the car reacted violently. It sank, screechingly crunching further into the ditch. Teddy yelped and bounced back out of its way .At least now he could reach the door. The latch was strange, long and shiny. Teddy closed a hand around it and gave it a yank.

'Dang!' he muttered as the door flung away.

Teddy caught it and slouched, resigned to waiting for the car to counter the intrusion. As soon as it settled, he climbed in, gently replacing the door. This time, the car stayed perfectly still. Teddy smiled. Not quite fitting back in its frame, the door rocked nearly closed beside him.

The seat he sat in, although awkwardly angled, seemed to want to claim his body. He exclaimed as he grasped the hard-wearing frontage below the car's sloping front window, the other hand on the door.

Staring at his fingers, the material beneath his legs and the carpeted inside of the door, he wondered what it would be like to the touch. So he summoned the memory of bluestem grass — not as fluffy as it looked. The car's interior, although obviously man-made was just the same; it looked as though it should be malleable, and yet its surface, all-to-pieces plastered with infinitesimal dots was right-smart solid. The carpet lining the inside of the door was more like the nutria of his hat. He squirmed in his seat; against his bare arms the material was cool, slick and artificial. Above his sight was a sturdy flap made of the same hard stuff as the front. He flipped it down. There was nothing but a mirror on the other side and a little sliding door that, when closed, would conceal it. Amused, Teddy clicked the door closed and back a couple of times before scrutinising the reflection that, of course, only his disembodied clothes were a part of.

Behind him, the seats looked luxurious, more suited to a parlour than a car, and the rear window sloped similar to the front one. He gazed about himself in wonder. There was nothing to suggest how this vehicle should work. But it would travel faster than Blue and move with the fluidity of Caper.

A scent tripped his sinuses. It was delicate and pleasing. He tried to sniff it out again. But it was gone. He thought of Caper prancing about the corral. He recalled Blue's breakneck standing start. The scent was there again. There was someone sitting next to him.

The sight of a fresh dead body shouldn't be anything new. One time on a trip into town with Pa, they'd been accosted by such a sight in the mercantile window. On another occasion they'd been unfortunate enough to happen upon a posse posing for a picture with their gunned-down catch. The body slumped in the darkened seat next to him shouldn't be even an itty-bitty botherayshun. Except it smelled so enchanting.

Teddy stared. The body didn't look one hooter like any outlaw. Even in death, outlaws retained a certain defiance. This body did not. Both the obvious and the missing lumps and bumps told him it was not a boy. It's pretty head and its cultured neck were angled slightly away from him, its short, dark hair mussed about its ears.

Don't touch it, the demon squirmed inside Teddy.

Thorns that had broken in when the car had veered off the road pricked the perfect skin of the girl, spilling droplets of toxic blood. Teddy edged a little closer, fidgeting, unsure of what to do.

What are you doing? Why are you still here? Don't touch it.

The girl was quite petite, the jawline peaceful, the lips parted as though she slept.

It's dead. Keep away.

'Elizabeth?' Teddy croaked.

Elizabeth, gentle, flawless and forever beautiful, sat next to him. They were alone together. It was a thing that he'd set himself to only ever daydreaming about. But, right now, she was muted, cold and unmoving. That wasn't like her. It wasn't like her at all.

Teddy stared, completely at a loss as to what it was that he was seeing. Momentarily, he couldn't move. It was only two nights ago she'd been a vibrant, laughing and caring girl. This couldn't be right. He laid a hand on her arm.

'Elizabeth?' he said again.

Elizabeth didn't respond.

'Talk to me, Elizabeth,' he pleaded.

Teddy listened for her heart. Nothing. Darn it, Ted, concentrate, will ya? But he couldn't close his eyes; he didn't want to shut out the sight in front of him. He didn't want to lose Elizabeth again. Not even for a second.

'I cain't hear you.' he said.

Murmuring pleas that she talk to him, he let go off his hold on the car and took up her hand. Whimpering at the weightlessness of her arm, he pressed for a pulse.

I said, don't touch it.

All thoughts of anything that would help him regain his senses had vanished. Elizabeth's body did not respond to his touch. He needed to hold her close; he didn't know why; it wouldn't help, he just needed to. He reached out with both arms.

It was impossible. Wedged in between them like a chaperone was what must've been the brake. Alongside it was something else, a sort of metal stick with a hat. Teddy sat back in his seat and kicked a Cuban heel at the front window. It shattered, blew out into the road and he clambered out before the car could move. He reached back in and hauled Elizabeth into his arms.

Cradling her to him, he leapt off the car onto the verge the other side of the ditch. Carrying her to one of the rides between the pines, he fell to his knees, clasping her to his chest. Nuzzling into her hair, he whispered professions of his love for her, he told her all the things that he'd been aching to share with her. He fancied that he saw a flicker of her eyelids. It made him smile, the way he'd done when he'd first seen her, first heard her voice.

Inside himself, something prickled. It was only a little tickle, but it proved undeniable and it played on his ribs.

'No how,' Teddy muttered.

Elizabeth wasn't dead. She couldn't be dead. As soon as that terrible word had entered into his mind, he missed her. It was inconceivable to him how much he missed her. He wanted her back. He wanted her back more than he'd ever wanted anything. His chest hurt. The void where his heart should've been seemed to wring itself out, right through to his spine.

Leave her.

Teddy hid his eyes in Elizabeth's hair again. He wore his sensations, his emotions on his face, he knew he did. Not that Elizabeth was going to see. He looked up again. Not that anyone was ever going to see.

He stared about himself. He couldn't remember where he was. For a hideous moment, he looked at Elizabeth and was unable to remember who he was. Or why he was kneeling in the pines holding such a pretty girl.

Daytime. You are going to die.

The demon. It was reminding him of what he was. He hated himself. He laid Elizabeth's body on the ground in front of his knees, straightening the hem of her blouse, smoothing the creases in her jacket until they were neat. He adjusted her legs, crossed her arms and eased her hair from her face, marvelling at how gracefully it fell away from his fingers. Perhaps he could somehow alert people to her body lying there on the soft, pine forest floor. Perhaps find her family, somehow let them know she was there. Elizabeth's kin would want her back, too.

He had to leave. Just one kiss and then he'd go. He leaned closer to Elizabeth and then he stopped. He couldn't do it. Not without her say-so. Nary one could he leave her. Teddy's stomach tensed a little. It was heavy, as though his last meal was ripe to repeat on him. The demon.

The irony was too great. Why, when he was so chock-full of evil, did he get to live? As though annoyed that its needs had been ignored, the demon pitched Teddy's insides around.

In over a century…no longer than that, never, had Teddy known how good it was to be in love. Now he'd found it, he had to say goodbye to it and this time, goodbye would be all-to-pieces forever. Teddy's eyes closed out the pains that were now assaulting his abdomen, his chest, his limbs and his soul.

'Dear God,' he said, opening them and raising his gaze to the sky, 'help me.'

Then he gazed into the face of the girl he knelt beside: the girl he loved. 'Elizabeth…'

He couldn't do it. He couldn't leave her. He didn't care who found his body, or what became of him when the sun came up; he couldn't say goodbye.

'Elizabeth, I do so truly love you.'

Elizabeth's eyes opened.

ENDS